A Word to the Wise

A Word to the Wise

David Heinzmann

FIVE STAR
A part of Gale, Cengage Learning

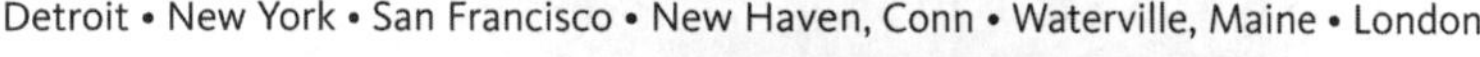

GALE
CENGAGE Learning™

Set in 11 pt. Plantin.
Printed on permanent paper.

LIBRARY OF CONGRESS CATALOGING-IN-PUBLICATION DATA

Heinzmann, David.
A word to the wise / David Heinzmann. — 1st ed.
p. cm.
ISBN-13: 978-1-59414-847-7 (alk. paper)
ISBN-10: 1-59414-847-3 (alk. paper)
1. Chicago (Ill.)—Fiction. I. Title.
PS3608.E383W67 2009
813′.6—dc22 2009032243

First Edition. First Printing: December 2009.
Published in 2009 in conjunction with Tekno Books and Ed Gorman.

Printed in the United States of America
1 2 3 4 5 6 7 13 12 11 10 09

To Alicia

Prologue

Marcy Westlake had seen this Cadillac before. It wasn't the plate she recognized—she wouldn't pay attention to that sort of detail—it was the color. It was a deep, dark violet, too elegant to be called purple, but that's really what it was. She had never seen a car quite like it. That said, she could not quite remember where she'd run across this one. She just knew she had. Marcy knew cars, and paid attention to them, because she had sold Lexuses for ten years. She knew the competition, and she knew that this shade of purple was not a normal Caddy option. Her mind was wandering through the spectrum of Cadillac paint selections instead of analyzing why the car that had just passed her was slowing down now and crowding her on this dark, desolate stretch of road through the forest preserve.

Her mind was loose and unfocused, as it always was after sex. She had gotten through the momentary anger over him coming and then almost immediately rolling out of bed and into the shower to clean himself of her. That cold, thoughtless act always scattered her confidence and crushed her resolve to put her foot down one way or another. It demeaned her, and in doing so strengthened his control over her emotions for a few more days. From the shower came the sound of him clearing his sinuses, like scraping ice from a windshield. The vulgarity of the sound removed any lingering warmth from the room. His timing was impeccable. She waited in bed, clutching the bleached motel linen around her naked body, accepting his dismissive good-bye kiss and then staring through the TV after he left, emerging slowly from the fog into a mild despair over the depth of the mess, and then letting the tears roll and turn Larry King's crazy owl head to foam.

After twenty minutes of feeling deserted in the way that an empty motel room by the expressway will make you ache with hopelessness, she had dressed and left. Her shoes squirmed faintly on the carpet as she strode down the long corridor, like someone writhing in pain but trying to keep quiet. When she pushed back the glass door at the bottom of the stairs, a curtain of freezing air hit her in the face. It felt good and Marcy breathed deeply as she crossed the white concrete edging the parking spaces. She clicked her key chain and the Lexus beeped and lighted itself. She slid into the cold leather, and the motor purred to life.

The purple Cadillac might have spooked her because it seemed familiar, but it had the opposite effect. Somehow, she accepted it as benign precisely because she did believe she'd seen it before, even if she could not say where. It was crawling along now, and she crawled along behind it.

She had wanted to drive a little, just to feel the car get warm while the jazz music on public radio wandered around in the dark intimacy of the leather and glass. The expressway was faster, but she had a road she liked through the forest preserve. After he once told her it was stupid to take this route because it was *further,* she never went any other way. She told him so, and he said women were idiots. Anyway, finding this kind of solitude and darkness in the overdeveloped suburbs was not easy. At this hour—just after nine in the evening—her forest preserve road was deserted. She drove in the blackness, surrounded by naked trees, free of the milky haze of road lights. These were her desires lately, to be alone, in the clear, to feel that there was room to breathe her own air.

The road skirted along the edge of the parkland now, with a narrow snow-covered meadow before a stand of timber on her left and a luxury housing subdivision being built across the road. It was still mostly open field, but the particle-board shells of 4,000-square-foot houses stood out against the darkness in the distance, their raw blond and white surfaces catching a little of the moonlight. They looked haunted even before they were lived in.

She drove, one slow car in front and a big vehicle behind her—some kind of truck—closing in from behind, through a series of S-curves. Barely paying attention to the road, her thoughts shifted again. She had not talked to her son in five days. She didn't dare consider what he must think of her. The thought of what he knew sickened her. And here she was, still answering the call to lie down on that motel bed. She shouldn't have gone down to Champaign. At least she should have taken care of her business before she went to see him. Hc was smart and saw through just enough of it to understand that his mother didn't know what the hell she was doing. She was going to have to deal with this. Give him the gist of what was going on because she could tolerate being on the outs with absolutely anyone except Brandon.

Marcy came to her senses suddenly. The car in front of her had nearly come to a stop. She finally put on her turn signal and started to ease into the left lane to pass the Cadillac, but immediately the car lurched left and blocked both lanes and Marcy had to bring her Lexus to a hard stop. Her breath caught in her throat as she realized the man was already out of the car and coming her way.

Her hands felt numb as her blood shifted and raced, pounding through her heart, suddenly. He walked right at her with his gloved hands at his sides, black leather coat buttoned tight. Her impulse was to hit the gas, but she was in drive. Her mind could not quite compute *reverse.* She was frozen for an instant, and suddenly it felt like the moment was gone and she was too late. He was walking right at her with his eyes on her, like he was already there. His eyes had hold of her, even if his feet and hands weren't quite there yet. He was coming. Her mind was racing crazy around the idea that she didn't recognize him, but, just like his car, she felt she should. There was something familiar in his walk and in the smile he was beaming. He raised his hands from his sides as if to say, don't worry, he just wanted a word.

On one side open land had narrowed and there was a dense black forest of bare, skinny elms, on the other side a deep ditch and then the white stubble of a snow-covered open field, those ghostly new houses now closer, the open rectangles of unfinished windows staring right through her like she was not even there. Black eyes watching something else unfold.

CHAPTER ONE

Augustine Flood was down to the last real sip of his martini. He drank proper martinis—gin with a healthy splash of vermouth—on the rocks, with a twist. It mattered because he constantly had to explain himself to bartenders who were too accustomed to people ordering martinis when they really meant chilled vodka with olives. One more tip of the glass and Flood would be sucking on withered ice cubes, which was fine because he meant to leave the bar after one, walk home, heat up dinner, drink a glass of red wine and read a book until the news at ten. It was bitterly cold outside, and the weather would probably lead the news, but there would surely be some kind of vague "I-Team *Exclusive*" about rumors swirling.

Such speculation had been needling Flood all week, and now it threatened his plans for the rest of the night. It was making him a magnet for gossip at Keefer's bar. People liked talking to him anyway—especially when they were drinking. He was like a post to steady oneself against. But at the moment, he was suspected of knowing the secrets behind those rumors. All the other lawyers standing around the bar this Wednesday evening tended to drift his way, sooner or later, to ask him whether the U.S. Attorney was ready to file charges in the casino investigation. The grand jury was supposed to be secret, but everybody knew it was hearing the prosecutors' evidence in the casino probe. The question was: Did they have a case? Flood said he didn't know, which gave everyone the impression that it was true charges were coming because it must be too sensitive for him to share what he'd heard. Certainly he had heard, and surely he'd dish the details if it were just a bunch of FBI scuttlebutt about how the U.S. Attorney was chicken-shit and not going to seek real charges. But Flood really did not know much more than anyone else. He had a friend at the paper who was digging, but he had not asked any of his former fellow agents at the FBI to tell him anything. If he had to ask, it just would have reminded him that he was no longer in a position to know. Flood had enough of those reminders.

"Augie, what the hell?" said the fat man in the bespoke suit who was now hoisting his wide bottom onto the next bar stool. "Let's eat. You wanna eat?"

"I'm good, Paulie," Flood said. "In fact, I was about to get out of here."

"Bullshit." Paulie belched into his hand before he said it, and then waved at the bartender, wagging two fingers downward at their empty glasses when he had the man's attention. He was actually called Paulie Junior. His father was a much better known lawyer than Paulie Junior would ever be. Paulie Senior was a big-time defense and divorce lawyer who tried everything in the media, won all sorts of criminal cases he should have lost and in the end became an actual Chicago legend by getting nailed at the peak of his career for defrauding his clients. He did his time in a Club Fed like the stand-up guy that he was, paid his fines and restitution and still had plenty squirreled away to retire to the Bahamas and live like a king. Paulie Senior never came back to Chicago for anything. He sat in his condo in Nassau, sipping good rum, speed-dialing his favorite prostitutes and watching the Chicago news on his dish. He emailed all sorts of unwanted advice to Paulie Junior who was trying to live down the old man while he made a good living representing drug dealers, murderers and elected officials.

"So, whattayou think, Augie?" Paulie Junior asked. "Is the G gonna hook up Nicky?"

Flood shrugged. "I really haven't asked anybody what's going on with it, Paulie."

Paulie Junior smirked, as if Flood was taking his turn at a little game they were playing.

"I say he skates in the end. Somewhere along the way, the G. is gonna shit the bed with this. I don't mean any disrespect to your boys at 219, I just think they're, you know, going to screw it up."

"Maybe they won't even indict him, Paulie. Who knows what they have and don't have on the guy."

Paulie Junior shook his head. "You know. Don't tell me you don't know."

Flood would think of Paulie Junior the next morning as he was standing at his living room windows, damp and chilly from a shower, sipping coffee and looking out from his twenty-fourth floor perch at another pink sunrise lifting the gray from the office towers across the steep canyon of buildings that flanked the river. The front page of the Tribune was on the dining table behind him reporting that federal charges would be announced later in the day against several people tied to the scandalous West Bank Casino Venture LLC. The boys at 219 S. Dearborn St., otherwise known as the Dirksen Federal Building, were finally going to do something. The story, by his friend Keith Reece, predicted that charges would be limited to just a few people, but that the investigation continued and more defendants would likely be added in the coming months. The feds typically went after the lowest-hanging fruit first in these public corruption cases; nail the dirty bureaucrats and minor players, and then squeeze them until they gave up the marquee names. Because no charges had been formally filed yet, Reece did not name names. But reading between the lines, Flood knew whom the list included, and he could tell that Bepps himself would not be charged in this first round. The boss of the Chicago Outfit was still on his feet, but, while he might be skating, as Paulie Junior suggested, he was skating toward open water on very thin ice.

Flood looked down at the khaki tea of the river three hundred feet below. Jagged plates of ice the size of trucks floated toward each other, gradually filling in the channel like a puzzle that could be solved only by a deeper descent into the coldest winter misery Chicago could offer.

The streets were no longer dressed in Christmas lights and greenery. The glitter and garlands had all been packed away by the Streets and Sanitation crews, and the city was stripped down to its hard, cold grayness, seasoned with a dusting of road salt, the air littered with clouds of exhaust and puffs of human breath, all of it freezing in ascent. Looking into the sunrise, the glare on Lake Michigan beyond the mouth of the river turned the water black and silver. Calming his eyes looking west, he could almost see the spot where they would have built the casino.

Flood did not really relish reading the story in the morning, and he had not wanted to talk about it with Paulie Junior at Keefer's the night before. It wasn't his problem. If gangsters wanted to bend City Hall's arm for a chunk of the casino business, that was fine—nothing new. If the government wanted to nail their asses to the wall for it: great. But it shouldn't be any of Flood's business. He did a different kind of work now.

He would have a new assignment, coming to him an hour later with a single ring on his office phone—an inside call.

"Flood," he answered quietly, sitting at his desk in his shirtsleeves.

"Hey, Augie, can you come in here a minute?" It was Cronin, on the speakerphone. Flood hated when lawyers popped the speakerphone button and then sat back in their swivel chairs, prattling away at full volume, with him on the other end wondering who else was in the room listening. Alan Cronin went on, "I want to introduce you to somebody."

Flood put his suit coat back on and walked down the hall, padding along the Persian runner, past Jamie clacking away on his computer, past Marty Drew's big office and down the corridor to Cronin's suite in the corner. Flood wore a plain navy suit, a stiffly starched white shirt with a straight collar. He straightened his gray tie.

Cronin's door was closed, so he knocked and opened it without waiting for a further invitation. The partner was sitting behind his desk, chair pushed back, one skinny knee draped over the other. He was in his shirtsleeves and suspenders, listing slightly to the left so his right shoulder pointed forward, dipping into all comers. It was Cronin's subconscious defensive posture. And it immediately put Flood on low alert as he crossed the threshold.

The stocky man slouched in the red leather chair to Flood's left had Cronin a little on edge. Somewhere in his mid-forties but looking older, thinning reddish blond hair, the color maybe touched up a bit, a beard covering for his fleshy face, and his egg-shaped torso encased in an ugly multicolor sweater. This sweater's yellow background held a test pattern of purples, blues and oranges. His sweater was matched with a pair of pressed, starched chinos that gave Flood the impression that he must live alone and send all of his laundry—socks and underwear included—to the cleaners. He had a gold Rolex dangling conspicuously from his wrist, a couple of pale gold rings on his fingers, one of them a braided wedding band.

Cronin didn't stand up. He just made a pistol of his thumb and forefinger and named Flood for the client. The man turned to size Flood up. He frowned and didn't make much eye contact, as if Flood's frame was what mattered. Or he was afraid to look him in the eye. Flood couldn't tell. The man finally leaned forward and extended his hand.

"Dan Westlake."

Flood shook his hand, but Westlake still hadn't really made eye contact. He quickly sank back and looked again to Cronin. Flood sat down, studying Westlake, and so far found nothing to grasp.

Cronin's office had recently been remodeled. He'd installed wainscoting up to chair rail level and had it stained a dark walnut. The upper part of the walls had been painted hunter green, with Cronin's collection of Irish landscapes in watercolor, framed in oversized mats, lining the walls. The pale watercolors looked bad with the dark green walls, and Flood figured he'd be fighting the urge to say something about it for a long time. Along the back wall, there was an oxblood leather sofa that matched the chairs. Nobody ever sat on it because it was piled high with golf equipment swag collected in several years of building a client base at one Democratic golf outing after another. A couple of extra golf bags, boxes upon boxes of balls—most of them embossed with the Irish names of candidates for Cook County office from fundraisers. *Friends of Edward "Pappy" O'Rourke, Democrat for Board of Review, Sept. 8, 1999, Silver Lake Country Club.* A dozen boxes of that kind of thing. Golf shirts in a rainbow of colors, each with the corporate logo of some company that made itself rich on government contracts. Cronin couldn't get enough of the stuff.

"Dan's come to us with a delicate sort of . . . situation," Cronin finally said. "He knew about your background and wondered if maybe you could help out on this thing."

"My year in the Merchant Marine?" Flood said. "Good. I'd love a nautical adventure."

"Funny," Cronin said.

Westlake frowned and Flood frowned right back. He didn't like conversations that began this way. Cronin turned back to Westlake but kept talking to Flood.

"Dan was asking how many years you were with the FBI, Augie."

"Eight," Flood said, annoyed, feeling like a trick pony being trotted out before some spoiled child.

He wasn't *with* the FBI anymore. He was a lawyer in private practice, and as far as he was concerned the former didn't have anything to do with the latter, especially when it came to the typical clientele of Cronin, Drew and Guzman.

"Dan's got sort of a delicate situation," Cronin went on.

"You already said that, Alan," Flood said. "Why don't you tell me about it."

"He needs some help locating somebody."

Flood looked at the floor.

"Would you like me to try to guess who it is?" Flood said, trying to uproot the bush that Cronin seemed intent on beating around.

Westlake shifted in his chair and grunted meekly. Cronin offered a single nervous chuckle. Flood waited. It was Cronin who worried him. He was sitting in his own office, with his own secretary outside and his own pile of toys on the couch, and something was pulling him out of his element.

"My wife," Westlake finally said. "She's been out of touch for a few weeks. It's unusual."

"Unusual?" Flood looked at Cronin and then back at Westlake. "Have you called the police?"

Cronin raised his hand, as if to slow things down.

"It's not like that," Westlake said.

Cronin chimed in: "She's fine. She's just sort of cut off contact."

"We're separated. Working things out, certainly, but separated at the moment," Westlake went on. "And I just need to reach her fairly soon."

"But she's cut off contact?" Flood asked slowly, making his point. That didn't sound like *working things out, certainly.*

Westlake fidgeted, and Flood could tell he was fighting the urge to say something; like that he wasn't here to pay for the privilege of having Al Cronin's lackey step out of line with a bunch of nosy questions. He threw a mildly accusatory look at Cronin.

"We have some money," Westlake finally said. "It's in an offshore account, which I need to access. But I can't take money out without her."

"It's in her name?"

"Right."

"Her name only?"

"Yes."

"But the money belongs to both of you?"

"That's right."

"Where do you mean by *offshore?*"

"A bank in the Caymans."

Flood wasn't saying anything more, but his smiling silence was asking, *why does a man keep his own money in an offshore account in his wife's name?* You want my FBI experience, Flood thought, here it is: this is how crooks behave.

Westlake was searching for words in a little micro-fit of frustration.

"She'll understand. It's just that she has no idea I need access to the money."

Cronin decided he ought to massage the awkward silence.

"Dan's got a bit of a *cash flow* problem at the moment," he said, frowning all over the word like it was really unfair to call it that, but let's just say it and move on. "A government contract, of course. He did the sewers and can't get Will County to pay his goddamn bill. You've seen this kind of bullshit, Augie. Appropriations on the county board—the Joliet Democrats are holding it up because the Bolingbrook Republicans are a bunch of cocksuckers. That kind of deal."

Cronin sometimes took the edge off delicate issues by peppering his speech with casual obscenities. Boys-night-out bonhomie. It was one of the things Flood liked about him without knowing why he liked it. Cronin was so good at it: As if this hole dug by his client's incompetence—or malfeasance—was actually other people's lack of consideration, minor inconveniences that were nonetheless, say, keeping everybody off the golf course for the time being. *Christ, we could be on the back nine by now if it wasn't for these goddamn baseless allegations of embezzlement. Honest fucking mistake, of course. It'll all be straightened out in no time, and we'll just push our tee times back a bit. No sweat.* Cronin was a master of making a fiasco seem like the prelude to a victory parade.

"Anyway, Dan's in a jam," Cronin said. "Happens all the time, but it's just that it's happening at a bad *time* for Dan. He needs to tap into that account to make ends meet till Will County cuts the goddamn check."

The way Cronin saw it, Flood would make a few phone calls, talk to a couple of Marcy Westlake's lunch partners, and run down the phone number of the condo she was borrowing in Scottsdale or Fort Myers or wherever. Have it wrapped up by end of day. But something about Westlake made Flood anxious. He couldn't quite place it. And he didn't like the way Cronin was sitting there on the edge of his seat, trying to look like this wasn't an idiotic way to go about things.

"What have you tried already?" Flood asked Westlake.

Westlake frowned purposefully and began to stroke his ring finger with the thumb of the same hand, spinning the gold signet ring he wore.

"Tried her cell, of course." Flood noticed that Westlake's speech was a little different every time he said something, as if he didn't know which was his own voice. Now, he was authoritative but fidgety. He sounded like the first George Bush. "Left messages everywhere. Dropped by the house and the place she was staying before. When we separated, she moved in with her friend Pam in Hinsdale. It's close by. Pam's divorced and had plenty of room. They're good friends. But, you know, that can be a hassle. So she moved home a month ago, and I moved into some rental property we've got in Lemont. I just moved back to the house this week. Pam *says* she hasn't seen her. Brandon, my son, says he hasn't talked to her, either."

Flood saw Cronin's eyebrows go up. He hadn't known this much.

"Are you sure she's OK?" Flood asked. "Maybe something happened to her. Isn't it odd that her friend and your son don't know where she is?"

"It is," Westlake said, as if he was now a judge reluctantly allowing a questionable remark into the court record.

"And what about her cell phone? Don't you think she would have gotten those messages?"

"Oh, I didn't leave a message there. Can't. She never set up the voicemail," Westlake said, again as if the very suggestion was questionable. "She hates the cell phone, and she's a klutz with the thing. Unless the caller ID says it's my son, she might never check. She's just that way about it."

"Is she close to your son?" Flood went on, letting the cell phone thing pass for the moment. "Isn't it strange that she hasn't contacted him?"

Westlake was silent. Holding something in. His cheeks began to puff out, as if he was straining to keep this one quiet.

"Brandon says he hasn't heard from her," he finally said.

"*Says* he hasn't," Flood said. "You don't believe him?"

"I don't know. They've always been close. Closer than to me."

"Well," Flood went on, glancing at Cronin. "What about asking your son to relay a message to her?"

"I've done that. Told him I just needed to talk to her. He says he hasn't heard from her. Brandon's version is that we should be worried."

"But you think he's bluffing," Flood said. "I don't know, Mr. Westlake. I have concerns, from what I've heard."

"That's just it," Westlake said. "You don't know a lot about my wife. Trust me. She's just gone off somewhere."

Flood looked at Cronin to watch him fidget. His boss wanted to get up and pour a Scotch. It was all over his face. But he couldn't because it was barely nine in the morning. It wouldn't be a tension cutter; it would be weird.

"Is she having an affair?"

Westlake's expression didn't change. He'd been anticipating the obvious question. Cronin had probably asked that one already.

"I don't know. If she is, it's a fling. My wife is a very attractive woman and has no trouble getting men interested." The mirth in his voice was barely detectable. As if all that was just a nuisance.

"You want a private investigator," Flood finally said to Westlake.

"Al said you were much better than that. More professional. Said you worked all kinds of cases in the FBI where you had to track down missing people."

"More like fugitives," Flood said in a correcting tone. "Anyway, I had different resources at my disposal then. For instance, subpoena power. Access to phone records. Bank records."

Cronin chimed in again. "We'd like you to give this a try, Augie.

You've got a nice touch with people, with delicate situations. If you were to find her it would be important to talk to her in a sensitive way, to make sure she understands Dan's not trying to pull a fast one."

Flood wrinkled his brow but kept silent.

"Would you say you always found the people you were looking for, Mr. Flood?" Westlake asked. His tone had changed. He seemed a little desperate.

"I wasn't always looking for the people, Mr. Westlake," he said, mocking him a little. "But I almost always found what they were hiding."

Cronin grimaced as that hung in the air. Westlake smiled nervously and looked down at the dark carpet.

Flood finally gave Cronin a defeated shrug. He didn't have much of a choice. But he could at least set the rules.

"Here's the thing, Mr. Westlake. Brandon is clearly the first step. I'll talk to the girlfriend first because she's close, but I need to get some information from your son."

Westlake shook his head.

"No, it's too risky. To tell you the truth, we're not on great terms. I know he'll tell her."

"So what? You said she'll call in if she gets the message."

"Well, I'm not sure Brandon would give her the message straight," Westlake said, as if it should make sense to everybody.

Flood shifted in his seat. "Where is he? College?"

"In Champaign."

Flood leaned back and thought a bit. Champaign was a two-hour drive. He trolled through everything he'd been told so far, looking for the right piece of it.

"OK," he finally said. "You said Brandon is talking like he's worried about your wife, right? And you were, I take it, fairly dismissive of that, right?"

Westlake nodded.

"I need to look through his things. Especially his phone bill. If he's making contact with your wife, there should be some record of it."

Westlake nodded again, sort of dumbly.

"Who pays his room and board?"

"I do. It's a house he rents with friends."

Flood nodded. "So, it's really your home that he's living in?"

Westlake's eyes glazed over for a second before he saw what Flood was saying.

"Right."

"And you pay his phone bill?"

"He just has the cell phone."

"And you pay it?"

"So, it's really my phone?"

"Close enough," Flood said, wheels turning. He wanted to get this over with. "Can you get him up here to talk about his mother? Talk to him about why he thinks something's wrong."

Westlake grimaced, looking like it would be difficult to assign him a more unpleasant task.

"Whatever," Flood said. "Just get him up here overnight, and get me a key to his place, and I'll go down and check it out."

Chapter Two

Before he left the office, Flood wanted to dig up a little information about Daniel Westlake. He started to sign on to Lexis/ Nexis to look up property and court records, but there was a problem with the computer. He leaned out his office door and asked Jamie, who leaned back in his chair like he was suddenly in charge.

"Tough titty, Boss-man," Jamie chirped. "Nobody can get on. Something's wrong with the account. It forgot all our passwords or something. They say it won't be fixed till tomorrow afternoon."

Jamie looked spiffy and officious as he said it, as though disappointing people gave him pleasure. He was the only man Flood knew who bought new clothes every season. It was all off the rack discount department store stuff, but he was always up to date. In his solid lapis blue shirt and striped silver and peach tie, with his hair moussed and sculpted, he looked like a child dressed by a fussy mother. The heavy designer glasses lent a contrived accent of grown-up gravitas to his fashion magazine look.

Jamie had a short neck that gave him an artificially sturdy appearance. He was a 30-year-old towhead, constantly involved in domestic-grade mischief. His mouth was set hard in a smirk and his glasses were heavy black rectangles with soft corners. When they first met he struck Flood as a cross between a young Truman Capote and a very old Cary Grant—not the suave screen idol version but the bent, white-haired guy who sat silently smiling with Dyan Cannon at the Oscars in the 1970s. It was the glasses and Jamie's crackly Cary Grant voice, with a little gay drama thrown in.

Flood went back and sat down. He was itching to snoop in Westlake's back pocket. He picked up the phone and called Reece. His friend since high school was a reporter, and the newspaper staff had unlimited access to the database.

"Later," Reece said. "I'm on deadline. Do you know what I'm doing?"

"Who'd they indict?"

"Not Bepps. I'll tell you later."

"Come on, let me come by. I'll proofread and make sure you spelled all the FBI names right. I'll be your confidential source on government agent spelling."

Reece grunted happily. He was having a good day. "You can be the source of my beer money at the Goat later. Come by around 8:30. I'll put you on Nexis for an hour while my story's getting the final edit. We'll get beers after."

Flood went home and changed into a pair of jeans and finished off the leftover coq au vin. It always improved after a day in the fridge. He had helped Reece more than once when he was still an FBI agent and the reporter was getting settled covering public corruption in Chicago after five years in Boston. Reece had been two years ahead of Flood in their Jesuit high school, and while Flood was warming the bench of the Boston College football team—his dreams of Fiesta Bowl glory fading much faster than the bruises he suffered as a tackling dummy on the practice field—Reece was cutting his teeth as a reporter at the Worcester Press-Telegram and then at the Globe. The only classics major on the football team, Flood felt a little out of sorts in those years and had cherished the nights that his poorly paid friend from Chicago had showed up at his dorm in

Chestnut Hill with just enough money to buy them three pitchers of Rolling Rock.

Flood walked the two blocks to the Tribune Tower, picking up two cups of coffee on the way. Reece sipped at it immediately as he led Flood to his high-walled cubicle in a secluded corner of the fourth-floor newsroom. Most of the reporters toiled in noisy pods of desks scattered across the floor. But Reece was on the investigative team, clustered in a back room with six-foot partitions that lent them a taste of privacy and privilege.

As Reece disappeared into a hive of people working at the city desk fifty yards away, Flood started tapping into Nexis and soon found records of Westlake's home in Burr Ridge, an affluent suburb of newer subdivisions just off the Stevenson Expressway southwest of the city. He and his wife, Marcella A. Westlake, had bought the house for $600,000 with a $550,000 mortgage. Not much equity. He almost missed the most recent transaction, a second mortgage. For the owner of an ostensibly successful small corporation, Westlake didn't seem to have the sort of assets he'd expect.

Flood moved on and found records for Westlake's business property, too. There was a second and third mortgage on the property, and a lien held by a company called Happy Time Enterprises. Flood typed in a public records search for Happy Time and came up with corporate filings listing the company's president as George Kajmar, with an address in Bolingbrook, another suburb off the Stevenson but ten miles farther south from Westlake's home.

Flood had never heard of Kajmar, but he could probably find out who he was in a few seconds. Reece had taught him the value of having decades of newspaper stories at your fingertips. He tapped into Nexis's news archives and entered Kajmar's name.

The most recent articles were five years old: Bolingbrook

businessman George Kajmar resigned his seat on the Illinois Tollway Authority after it was revealed that contractors hired to work on the tollway roads were leasing earth-moving equipment from an implement rental firm owned by his wife. Kajmar argued that his wife's business was not his concern and there was no conflict of interest. But his fellow board members turned on him, judging from the story, and said they had been unaware that he was connected to any enterprises other than his chain of thirty *Jake's* hot dog and Italian beef takeout restaurants and seven currency exchanges in the western suburbs. George Kajmar was definitely somebody in the world of Illinois and Chicago politics. The Tollway Authority doled out hundreds of millions of dollars a year in contracts, and a seat on the board was a sign of hefty political clout.

Flood closed the file and then punched in Daniel Westlake's name. Nothing. Then he tried "Westlake" and "contractor," and sure enough, a brief story of about 150 words popped up, written from the Will County Board meeting for the paper's suburban section three months before. Just as Cronin had said, Will County was south of Chicago, on the edge of the suburbs. Its northern half was filling in with housing tracts while the southern end of the county was still mostly farms. The county seat, Joliet, known for its two state prisons, had been a dying Rust Belt town built on stone quarries and steel mills. But it had been making a comeback in recent years by annexing thousands of acres of new commuter subdivisions being built out along the Stevenson Expressway. Westlake was no doubt hired to build storm sewers along some old country road that was becoming a main suburban thoroughfare.

The story said board members argued over another delay in approving a $425,000 payment to Westlake Plumbing and Sewer for work to improve a county road. However, it didn't seem to truly be a case of political bickering, as Cronin had described.

Some board members argued that the contractor needed to be paid. But the highway committee chairman, from Bolingbrook, actually, claimed the work was not completed to specifications and wanted more time to review what remained to be done. There was talk of hiring another contractor to do the job right.

So Westlake was in debt to a politically connected hot dog tycoon, and he was being accused of shoddy work by a local government. Flood printed everything he'd pulled up and folded it into his coat pocket for his fledgling Westlake file.

He guessed this lien Kajmar owned was the heart of Westlake's crisis. He had probably borrowed money from Kajmar, put up a piece of his business as collateral and was unable to pay it back. Now the wealthy businessman was leaning all over him, probably wanting to sink his claws into the contracting business and take control of Westlake's livelihood. It made sense. Westlake's business apparently thrived on road contracts and Kajmar's time on the Toll Authority would give him all sorts of connections to those contracts. Flood wondered whether there was any significance in the fact that Bolingbrook was home to both Kajmar and the Will County Board member holding up Westlake's payment. Either way, Westlake seemed to be getting squeezed.

Reece appeared in the cubicle door, squinting and grinning.

"Story's in the can. Let's drink."

The U.S. Attorney's filing of a criminal complaint charging people in the case allowed the papers to finally lay out the whole scenario. With a tinge of hangover, Flood sat at his dining table the next morning sipping coffee and reading the next morning. Reece's story said the city had been close to approving the casino to be built on the Chicago River, right in the middle of the city. Right in the middle of gallery-chic, tourist-rich River North, at the west end of Flood's own neighborhood. There were gambling boats way out at the edge of the suburbs, in Joliet, Aurora and Elgin, and across the Indiana line in Hammond and forlorn Gary. But there were none in downtown Chicago, at the epicenter of eight million people. The profits could have been unprecedented.

After years of lobbying and negotiating and hand-wringing by all of the mayor's people, West Bank Casino Venture, LLC had finally been in the works. Casino operators had been lobbying for years for a site downtown. The mayor had resisted. He did not like the image, he said. Chicago was a major-league metropolis; it did not need to resort to gambling for tax revenue. It was a city of museums and concerts, ballparks and beaches. Not slots and dollar drinks. But the mayor had gradually come around over the last couple of years. First, he dropped the absolutist rhetoric and went from saying there would never, ever be a casino in the city of Chicago, to saying that he did not like the idea of a casino. Then he said the circumstances would have to be perfect, and a tangible benefit for the whole city would have to be shown. And so it went. Eventually his people were on board. There was talk of using some gambling revenue to rebuild the poorest neighborhoods, like Englewood and Lawndale. Gambling in the city took on the sheen of civic responsibility. Progress was made. Laws were passed in Springfield to make it possible.

But it didn't last long. The whole process had been rigged, it turned out. The limited partnership that won the casino license from the Illinois Gaming Board did so with bribes, blackmail and hookers—and all of it marshaled by mob boss Nicky Bepps himself. Allegedly. None of that had been proved yet, but nobody was surprised. It was perhaps the biggest nightmare City Hall had faced in decades.

A grand jury had heard evidence for months. Bepps had not been charged just yet, but the feds were close on his heels. They had rounded up most of the players. His brother-in-law would surely make the list, along with the officers of a suburban bank that financed the bid. Two gaming board members were toast. They seemed to have the most dirt on board member Art Callahan. He was accused of accepting bribes to sway votes in West Bank's favor. He had resigned from the Gaming Board on the strength of the rumors alone. An insurance consultant by profession, Callahan lost his biggest client—the state university system—because of the bad publicity.

In the first round of charges, the government alleged Callahan sold his vote for more than two hundred thousand dollars. A hundred thousand before, which the feds had traced to a Bahamian bank account. And a hundred thousand after, which they had found in a suitcase in the trunk of his BMW 740, along with a Mapquest printout with directions to a marina in Miami Beach, a hotel confirmation number and the phone number of a fishing charter written on the same sheet, according to the criminal complaint that prosecutors filed in court. Reece was able to take things a step further and report in the paper that the boat turned out to be owned by a limited partnership controlled by Bepps.

Flood took another sip of coffee. He sat back when he'd finished the story and looked out the window. The towering black IBM building obstructed part of his view west. He couldn't quite see all the way to the bend in the river where they were going to build the mob's casino. Thinking of all the public excitement that the scandal would generate didn't make getting started on Daniel Westlake's domestic troubles any more enticing. Flood resolved to avoid Keefer's bar and only skim the headlines until he had located Marcy Westlake and informed her that her jerk husband needed her nod to tap into their little Caribbean tax dodge.

When Flood got to the office, he opened his Westlake file, dropped it on the desk and dialed Marcy Westlake's friend, Pam

Sawyer, and told her he needed to talk to her about her friend.

"Are you a private investigator?"

"No, I'm a lawyer."

"Dan's lawyer?" she asked with a fresh edge of suspicion. Another reason, as far as Flood was concerned, why he shouldn't be doing this. It was deceptive. He really was acting like a private investigator. He decided to come clean.

"Yes, I was hired by Mr. Westlake. Or, at least my boss was. They pulled me into it because I used to be a federal investigator. All I'm doing is looking for Mrs. Westlake."

She paused and thought. Things weren't clear-cut for her, Flood gathered. She was conflicted.

"I'll talk to you," she finally said, sounding as if she was talking to a telemarketer. "How long will it take?"

"Well, I could leave in twenty minutes and be there by about 9:30. It would probably take an hour."

"We can't just do it over the phone?"

"Are you too busy?"

She hesitated. "No, of course not."

"I'll leave right now."

"And not here. I don't want to meet at my home. There's a Starbucks right when you get off 294 at Ogden."

Flood frowned as he stopped at Jamie's desk after hanging up, headed for the door in his overcoat and black watch cap.

"Tonight's the night," Jamie said.

"Hmm?"

"Don't 'hmm' me. Silver Cloud. 9 P.M. You're meeting and falling in love with my friend Jenny."

"Oh, I forgot. Let's reschedule."

"No. Not acceptable."

Flood didn't say anything. He wasn't playing Jamie's game.

"Why so disgruntled, Boss-man?"

"Pam Sawyer wants to meet me at Starbucks in Hinsdale."

"So?"

"So, I want to see her house. That's where the mysterious Mrs. Westlake was living for awhile."

"Well, cancel and then just drop in unannounced. Official business." He thumped the desk with his hand. "Swing that big swinging dick."

Jamie occupied an ill-defined position of paralegal, office assistant and fabulist for Flood's end of the corridor at the law firm. Technically, Flood shared his legal research services with another lawyer. But the woman didn't get along with Jamie, who thought she was homophobic, and so she rarely called on him for anything but envelopes and paper clips. Flood, on the other hand, ran him ragged finding case law, writing and editing briefs, vetting deposition questions, anything he could think of. Flood needed the help, but he was also trying to get Jamie sufficiently fed up with the abuse to actually go to law school himself instead of playing the aggrieved plebeian. A hundred years before and this would have been his law school; he'd be about ready to join the bar.

Jamie wasn't quite there yet. He was still reveling a bit in playing the long-suffering lackey. He still took comfort in cracking wise about all the asshole lawyers afoot and then heading home at five with no responsibilities, staying out in the Halsted Street gay bars until two in the morning and then stumbling in five minutes late for another day of work.

He also liked to juxtapose the actual Flood with the cardboard cutout of heterosexual machismo he thought ought to be standing in the shoes of an ex–football player, ex–merchant marine, ex–FBI agent.

Jamie always called Flood boss-man, but the *swinging dick* references were wearing a little thin.

"Just show up at her door and give her the business," Jamie growled on. "Maybe knock her around a little. Old School."

"With my luck, she'd be off getting a pedicure or a face lift or something."

"Palm readings. A high colonic."

"Exactly."

"You know how these rich suburban divorcees are," Jamie said, switching gears, ready to make fun of anyone.

"Values corrupted by vanity and insecurity. Slaves to consumption." Flood egged him on as he shuffled pages in his Westlake file.

"Crazy bitches."

"Yes."

Ken Hunt was coming down the hallway with an exaggerated arch in his eyebrows. He squeezed past.

"Sorry, to interrupt, fellas," he said as he passed. "I think he was telling you about somebody's dick, Augie."

Hunt never said Jamie's name—never addressed him by name or referred to him by name. He was certainly homophobic, but his antipathy toward gays was a convenient vehicle for his resentment of Flood. Hunt graduated from DePaul Law School a year ahead of Flood, but he was now only 28, and Cronin and Drew treated him like a summer associate compared to the work they entrusted to Flood. Hunt didn't care that ten years of age, another career, and the experience that went with it might be worth something in the practice. He had been a lawyer longer than Flood, and he wanted to be treated like a senior guy. The other two attorneys in their little firm were the same way. They'd been out of law school longer, but Flood just seemed more seasoned, and that was how the partners treated him. Because of it, Flood didn't have much to do with the rest of the staff in the office. He dealt with Cronin and Jamie, and occasionally Marty Drew, and that was it. It did not bother him in the least that he was not part of a law firm fraternity, but it pissed him off that they took out their resentment of him on Jamie.

Jamie frowned and sighed with tired annoyance as Hunt continued on down the hall.

"He's just inadvertently venting his repressed gay feelings, right?" Flood said to Jamie.

"God, I hope not. I hope he sticks to beer goggles and chubby girls who only get laid on St. Patty's Day."

"He's got a girlfriend?"

"I saw him with her at Miller's Pub—don't ask why I was there. A beaming young woman who looked like she'd just been elected student council president at Mother McAuley."

Flood rebuttoned his overcoat. "Well, whatever. I'm off to Hinsdale."

"Nine o'clock. Silver Cloud. Your destiny."

"I'll try to make it."

Flood really did want to get a look at Pam Sawyer's condo, hoping to spot some clue to Marcy Westlake's whereabouts. But she was adamant. So, he pulled into the parking lot of the Starbucks by the 294 exit just before ten in the morning on Friday.

He bought a small coffee and put half and half in it. He preferred to drink his coffee black, but Starbucks was so blasted strong he had to cut it with milk. He sipped at the rich coffee and peeked at the crowd. It was a suburban Friday morning gathering place. The parking lot was full of SUVs and Volvo wagons, and the tables were crowded with groups of chatty women in expensive turtlenecks, Kate Spade purses and lined suede coats; middle-aged men hiding their post-forty guts behind supple leather jackets the color of the coffee bubbling out of the urns. Flood fought the urge to feel superior. If he hadn't called off his engagement, he might be here, too, by now. He'd have been married four years, and Lizzy would have probably had a baby or two by now, and he'd be at a place like this, on a Saturday morning, driving a four-wheel-drive Infiniti around town trying to find some time alone, meekly fidgeting against his suburban dad role, taking his time with the sports section, swilling milky coffee and eating cinnamon scones, feeling well-heeled in the land of the lost, a place that could have been anywhere in America—Cleveland, Atlanta, New Jersey. Maybe he was jealous that these guys had an archetype to fulfill, a place in the order of things. Flood was still living alone in a high-rise apartment in a slightly soulless little section of Chicago between the Loop office buildings and the touristy night life of River North. And now, he was running a fool's errand into the purposeful suburbs to track down the wayward wife of a guy who looked like these men of Starbucks. If he did find the mysterious Mrs. Westlake, he might ask her for the secret to living a meaningful life.

Pam Sawyer looked like all the other women there. She wore sumptuous casual clothes, had well-fed good looks and had hair dyed the same tint of blonde as the women at other tables. But she spotted him right away—looking fit in his charcoal flannel suit and green and brown striped tie. She nodded at him, picked up a skim latte and walked over.

"You found it OK?" she said. Some of the wariness of their phone conversation had wilted as she sized him up in person.

Flood nodded and started to get up as she set her coffee on the table.

"No, don't get up," she said, sitting. "You know, I almost didn't come. I thought about calling you to cancel."

She left it there for him to judge both her guilty feelings and her ambivalence. He shrugged.

"I'd be skeptical, too," he said, trying not to fray her nerves any further.

She tried to come off as easygoing about this meeting, but he sensed there was some anxiety that she couldn't quite keep down.

They sipped their coffee silently. Neither was quite sure how to start. Outside the window an intermittent spray of gray slush rained down from Ogden Avenue over a concrete retaining wall. Flood had not been outside downtown Chicago for nearly a month, and he felt out of his element.

He would start from the beginning.

"So how'd you meet Marcy Westlake?"

Pam Sawyer gave a *let's see, now . . .* squint, an instinctive stall reaction to a simple question. She nodded, as if she had tracked down the file in her head that held all pertinent information about Marcy Westlake.

"I bought a car from her."

Nearly seven years ago, Pam's marriage was coming apart and she went to buy a $40,000 Lexus as a knife in the ribs of her philandering husband. Marcy was a soft-sell specialist, and she and Pam just started chatting, about husbands, and distant, adolescent sons and soon Pam was upgrading to the top-end stereo and a 250-horsepower engine. They were fast friends and went out for dinner the night Pam picked up the car. Tuscany, in Oak Brook.

"I put $300 on Richard's platinum card that night."

"Your ex?"

"Mmm hmmm." The memory still gave her pleasure.

They moved on. Danny Westlake wasn't a bad husband, she said, finally getting around to the point. He just wasn't in Marcy's . . . well, her league. She was too good-looking and too smart, and her taste was too good. "It's not like Marcy's an intellectual, or a snob," Pam said, but she was . . . clever.

"Danny was a nice enough guy who made a little money as a contractor, but the bigger the business became, the more stressful their relationship got," she said, studying Flood to see how this was playing. He was working for Westlake, after all. "Marcy thought it might work out if she went to work for the business, but Dan didn't want that. I think maybe he was afraid of how smart she would be at it."

She said that last part in a dying voice, as if she regretted letting it out but couldn't stop the words. It seemed like the first truly honest thing she'd said.

". . . So, anyway, Marcy went out and got a job selling expensive cars—did really great at it."

"And Dan's business started to hit some bumps."

She shrugged and looked at him with a little embarrassment. She didn't want to be the one to say that. Flood didn't know why—she was supposed to be a friend of Marcy, not Daniel Westlake.

"Not good for the marriage," he said.

"It's like they were suddenly in two different worlds," Pam said, recovering her confidence a little. "I mean, two different lives that had little to do with each other."

"But I gather Marcy's no longer selling cars."

Pam wagged her head.

"Why'd she quit? It seems like she needs the income. They split. He's losing his shirt."

"You'd think," she said, as if she shared his skepticism. "We didn't talk about money. I don't know."

"You're comfortable?"

She smiled. "That's a nice way to put it. I had a good lawyer, and, yes, I don't need help from anyone. And Richard's life is a little less than half as fulfilling as it was before the divorce."

"What's he do?"

"Anesthesiologist at Good Sam."

"Sounds lucrative. Did Marcy ever borrow money from you?"

Pam Sawyer wagged her head again.

"Did you have any kind of financial relationship?"

She quickly squinted. "Of course not. We're friends, not . . . business partners."

She stopped and drank some more, touching up the lipstick smudge on the plastic lid of her cup. Flood didn't like drinking from the plastic lid, so he'd taken his off and now his coffee was cold. He offered to buy another round.

"Decaf," she said with a nervous smile, as if another cup meant secrets were about to be spilled.

Flood bought the coffee and leaped forward in logic when he sat back down.

"Did she meet someone through the dealership?"

Pam put both hands around the cup like she was trying to steady it. She made real eye contact with him for the first time. She did not try to deny it, but she gave him a *damn you for asking* look.

"Danny doesn't know any of the particulars," she said. "You see, this is where Danny doesn't get stuff. You're just guessing, but you've already figured stuff out about Marcy. I don't think Danny knows this much. He will now, I guess. Please don't give him the impression I said he wasn't very bright. It's not what I mean."

Flood nodded.

"Did she run off with him?" he persisted.

"I can't imagine," she said, frowning. She had a healthy, full face with a wide jaw and sharply drawn flat lips painted pinkish brown. "I think she thought it was what she was missing when it started, but then it turned into a fling. In fact, I think it had sort of fizzled. But it's possible. I don't think she was coming back to Dan, and I don't know what her other options were. She could have met somebody else, too. Marcy's a real knockout, and not just for a 43-year-old woman. She looks ten years younger, and if she walked into a bar on Southport, 25-year-old guys would be all over her."

"Wouldn't you know if she met someone knew?"

The question surprised her and she wasn't ready for it. "Oh, I don't know."

"Did you two have a falling out?"

She made a face and said, "Of course not," too quickly. Flood bored into her with his eyes, knowing the scrutiny was making her nervous. He was going on instinct now.

"So who is he?"

She nearly jumped, and looked embarrassed.

"Who?"

"The man you know about. The first one."

"Oh. I really don't know," she said.

Flood shook his head. "You must. It sounds like you were best friends. She was living with you."

"His name is Vick or something. I don't know his last name, and I never met him," she said. "I think maybe he was married, too."

Flood gave her a look. "You're her pal, she was living with you, and you don't know where he lives or where he works? What he does?"

"I think maybe he works in the liquor business," she finally said, as if it had just come back to her. "It seemed like from what Marcy said he had a warehouse somewhere and did business with bars."

"And she met him where?"

"Did I say?"

"I assumed it was the dealership," Flood said.

"It might have been. I think she told me that. I don't remember if he was a customer," she said. "Or if they met through a business contact of some kind."

"The liquor business," Flood reminded her.

"Yes, I don't remember what exactly the connection was."

She wasn't a half bad liar, he decided.

"How long had it been going on—the affair?"

"I don't know. A few months maybe," she said. That seemed to be the truth. Flood was picking his way through her responses now, labeling each one true or false. Trying to figure out why some of the time she felt the need to fib.

"When did she quit selling cars?"

"About six months ago."

"Was he supporting her?"

"I don't know."

False. She knew something.

"And you never met him?"

"It was discreet," she said, glaring at Flood, as if he had accused her and Marcy of being tramps. "And it's not like we did everything together. She only moved in with me four months ago."

"And Dan doesn't know?"

Pam smiled. "Well, as I said, he's sort of thick-headed. The affair wasn't the issue in their marriage, anyway. The issue was that they really didn't have much in common after twenty years."

Probably true.

Flood was a bit steamed. Too much game-playing out of Pam, and now it was clear that Westlake had told him less than all he knew. As if it wasn't shameful enough spending the better part of a Friday morning in the Hinsdale Starbucks pumping soap opera secrets out of strangers. He also had the creeping sensation he was being used in a chess match between the possibly sleazy friend, Pam, and the perhaps dimwitted husband, Dan. Whether it was just a game of keep-away, with Marcy Westlake as the ball, was unclear. Flood felt a growing sense of disgust with himself for being involved in something so petty. Any alarm he'd felt the day before about whether the woman was actually missing had melted with Pam Sawyer. It seemed this was all about something else. A mystery man the woman was seeing, and something Marcy had done to anger her friend and necessitate cutting off all contact with her estranged husband.

"So, you haven't said where you think she is," he said, tired of fooling around.

She got rid of the smile. "I really don't know. If she needed some time away to think, I just wish she would have told me."

False. But what part of it was a lie? Did she really not know, or would Marcy Westlake not confide in her?

"You think she's off thinking somewhere?" he asked.

She was flustered, as much by the quick succession of questions as by the challenge in his voice.

"She must be. What else could it be?" she said.

"Well, she could have run off with the liquor-business man."

"I guess, but he's married."

"You know that for sure, now?"

"I'm pretty sure."

"But you don't know much about him, right? Maybe his marriage is breaking up."

It was a simple point, but her response surprised Flood. She looked suddenly like she felt backed into a corner. Like she was running out of things to throw in front of her. Very curious. He decided to keep pressing.

"Where did they usually meet?"

"I don't know," she answered quickly.

"Well, if he's married and she's married and she never brought him around your place, it must have been a motel or something. In the months she was with you, how long was she away at night? Did she stay out all night, or come home to go to bed?"

Pam looked around and then said, "I don't know."

He thought suddenly of the businessman with the lien against Westlake's office building and decided what the hell: "Do you know George Kajmar?"

"Who?" She wrinkled her nose immediately. "I've never heard of him."

False.

She was addled and back on her heels. Flood was starting to be glad they'd met in a public place. She was getting self-conscious and was afraid of causing a scene in front of the assembled Hinsdale café society.

"It's OK," Flood said. "Relax. Just take a breath. There's nothing to be afraid of, Pam. But some of these things you must know a little more than you're saying. Did she spend the night with him a lot, or was she coming home?"

Pam swallowed hard and looked at Flood. She was frightened now and trying not to fall apart.

"She always came back to my place."

"Did they ever go on trips? Maybe down to Florida for a few days or something?"

Flood believed the location of Marcy Westlake's hideout was buried just beneath the surface, and he'd found the spot in the dirt to dig.

"No," Pam said. "She always came back. They didn't go away. I don't think it was like that. It wasn't a real relationship like that. The only time she was gone overnight recently was a couple of trips to Champaign to see Brandon."

Disappointing. But at least it had the ring of an honest answer.

"OK, Pam. So, where did they meet? Was it a hotel?"

She nodded. "Yes, I think so. West. I don't know where, really. But sometimes she'd hit Oak Brook or Yorktown on the way home at night and do some shopping, so out that way."

"What about restaurants? Did she ever talk about eating out with him?"

"I don't know."

"Does she have some favorite places to go, where maybe he would have taken her for dinner?"

"I don't know."

"You mentioned Tuscany. In Oak Brook?"

"Yes, but that was my idea. That's my favorite."

"OK. But think. There must be some other places. Maybe she brought receipts home and left them on the counter, or something."

Pam was finally warming up, but he couldn't tell if she was upset or just reveling in the acting role. She leaned over the table, looking like she was struggling for something.

"Why are you doing this?" she whispered. "What does Dan want? Doesn't he know it's over? Why is he sending a lawyer? There's nothing he can take from her. She doesn't have anything."

Flood thought about this for a minute. If Pam knew about the Cayman account, and Marcy's control of it, she'd have figured it out and would probably be giving Flood a smug, pitying look. She must not know about it, he concluded. It made him think two things: Either Pam Sawyer was of limited further use to him because she didn't know; or, possibly, Westlake was making up the Cayman account story and he had some other motive for looking for his estranged wife.

It was the first he'd thought of it. And how was he going to figure it out? Demand to see bank statements? Cronin wouldn't go for that demand any more than Westlake would. Flood sat wondering about where Pam Sawyer sat in the scheme of things. What did she really know about the secret boyfriend, and what did she really know about where Marcy was, and what did she know about why Dan Westlake wanted so badly to find her?

This was the lousy part about being a private lawyer. He was working for somebody without knowing the motives. At least with the government the motives were ostensibly enforcement of the law, and if there were politics involved he usually understood it up front and could deal with it. Here, he was working for a man whom he didn't believe he understood and whom he certainly did not trust.

A question popped into his head: "How'd Dan find out that Marcy was having an affair?"

Pam had used the pause to begin to recover her composure.

"She probably told him."

"Does her son know? Could he have told his dad?"

She laughed.

"Brandon would have enjoyed keeping the secret from him. He adores his mother and does not like his father."

"Why not?"

"Brandon picked sides, and picked the one who loved him."

As he parted from Pam Sawyer in the Starbucks parking lot, Flood told her he was going to run into the gourmet grocery store next to the coffee shop to grab a few things. He didn't want her to see him get into his car. She said goodbye and headed for her blue BMW SUV. She'd apparently moved on from the Lexus Marcy Westlake sold her. Flood watched her pull out of the lot and then ran to his car. She pulled out onto Ogden and headed west. He waited a few seconds and then followed. A purple Cadillac pulled out of the lot going the same way, and Flood stayed behind it, using it for cover. He was going to get a look at her place whether she liked it or not.

They headed downhill on Ogden toward the York Road intersection. On the left they passed a Ferrari dealership and then a Land Rover dealership. She went straight through the intersection and then turned off into a wooded subdivision nestled on the side of a knoll. The Cadillac made the same turn, but then made the first left and headed off down a tree-lined lane, leaving Flood unshielded as he followed her. She lived in a complex of townhouses that formed a chain of saltbox-style facades on a curve in the street. They were all dusty blue with white-trimmed windows and black shutters. The thin strip of common yard in front was landscaped with box elders and bushy bunches of prairie grass that were supposed to look like beach grasses. They were yellowed and limp in the deep freeze of winter. All of the townhouses had their own front driveways and two-car garages.

Flood followed to the end of the block to watch her turn into her driveway as the garage door slid open and she pulled in. The other space was empty. No Lexus belonging to Marcy Westlake.

Flood sat thinking for a minute about what he should do next. So far, Pam Sawyer had done little for him other than confirm the seemingly obvious notion that Marcy Westlake might be having an affair. As he looked up and down the placid Hinsdale street, his thoughts returned to the police. Flood felt strongly that the first step should have been to contact the local police to see if they could find anything out, or if they knew anything suspicious about people involved in Marcy Westlake's life. But the husband was adamantly against it, and Flood believed that was probably from a sense of embarrassment, or at most, because he did not want to draw the attention of law enforcement to his finances—the reason he needed to find his wife in the first place.

The client was the boss, but this did not sit well with Flood. He didn't trust the Westlakes, and he was not about to risk getting drawn into some eventual ethical, or even criminal, morass over it. He pulled out his cell phone and decided there was nothing wrong with looking up an old acquaintance when he was in the neighborhood. He scrolled through the numbers saved in his phone until he found Jake Pialetti. Flood's entry was followed by *DUPSAO,* his shorthand for the DuPage County State's Attorney's Office. Pialetti was in investigator with the office. He picked up on the third ring.

"Pialetti."

"Jake, it's Augie Flood."

"Hey, long time. How are you, buddy?" he said, with genuine surprise in his voice.

"I'm good. And I just happen to be wandering around in your neck of the woods and wondering if you've got time for lunch. I'd love to catch up, and I've actually got something I'd like to run by you."

Pialetti apologized, put him on hold for a minute, and then came back and accepted the invitation.

"Where are you?"

"Hinsdale, just off Ogden."

"Can you make it to Ballydoyle from there without getting completely lost?"

"I think so. See you in a half hour?"

"Great. Looking forward to it."

Flood figured Pialetti was out of the office somewhere because the State's Attorney's office in Wheaton would be a half-hour drive to Ballydoyle. The place was a favorite of cops, especially federal agents who worked downtown but lived in DuPage County. It was a slick Irish pub in the old village part of Downers Grove, one of the county's many sprawling, affluent suburbs. Flood had been there several times and remembered roughly how to get there—heading west on Ogden and then veering down Maple for a few miles. In downtown Downers Grove, Flood parked and walked into the bar.

Pialetti was standing at the bar dumping cream and sugar into a mug of coffee as he chatted with a young bartender he seemed to know well. Pialetti was a big man, a couple inches taller than Flood and at least 250 pounds spread evenly around his frame. His brown hair was thinning but still represented in most places on his scalp, and he wore an ample cop's mustache. He wore a dark blue dress shirt and a blue striped tie. His parka was off and draped over a barstool, leaving the black semiautomatic handgun strapped to his belt in plain view. His badge was clipped to his belt next to the gun.

They greeted each other and tried to remember the specifics of their last meeting. They decided it was a retirement party for an ATF agent at this same bar, right before Flood left the Bureau. Pialetti recalled that Flood was the only "Fibby" who had bothered to show up. There wasn't a whole lot of love between the FBI and the rest of the law enforcement community. Everybody regarded the FBI as arrogant and elitist because the Bureau was the biggest agency, with the most resources and reach. ATF, DEA, and the Marshals always felt they were fighting for the FBI's table scraps, and most local police harbored a grudge that the FBI would let them do all the grunt work on an investigation and then swoop in at the end and take credit because the case was headed to federal court. Flood had made plenty of friends in local law enforcement because he never showed much of the FBI arrogance.

Pialetti gestured to the barstools.

"You want to sit up here?"

"Actually, Jake, let's get a table or a booth someplace quiet. I do have a little business I need to talk."

They sat in a booth and looked at the menus while going over the latest on the handful of people they knew in common. They ordered sandwiches and then ran out of friends to talk about.

"So what brings you out to the 'burbs?"

"Weird job. That's why I'm asking. I have a client who says he can't get in touch with his wife. They've separated, but he claims they're working on it. He's got some personal finance issues they need to work out, and I'm supposed to track her down. They live in Burr Ridge, and it seems their whole world is out here. He didn't want me contacting coppers, so we're not having this conversation, but I just want to run it by you."

Pialetti seemed interested. "I'll look into it."

"Her name is Marcy Westlake. Short for Marcella. Husband is Daniel Westlake, plumbing and sewer contractor."

"OK. Doesn't ring a bell, but I can nose around a bit." He pulled out a small notebook and asked Flood to spell the names. When he finished, he hesitated a moment and then said, "Just out of curiosity, Augie, what's this woman look like?"

"Well, I haven't seen her myself, but I'm told she's very good-looking. Tall, slender blonde . . ."

He stopped because Pialetti had a look on his face, suddenly grave. His eyes turned hard and stared straight ahead, studying Flood's face.

"What is it, Jake?"

"Last seen when?" Pialetti asked.

His tone made Flood immediately nervous as he thought of the answer to the question.

"Um, nobody I've talked to has seen her in a couple weeks. But that doesn't really mean anything. She's on the outs with them."

"How old?" Pialetti asked.

"Well, she's 43, I think. Jake what are you getting at?"

Pialetti's expression was now agitated and tinged with a hint of amazement.

"Augie, I don't know how to tell you this. But we've got a Jane Doe who fits that description. Her body was found Wednesday morning along Roosevelt, just west of York."

Flood searched his face for understanding. "What do you mean?"

"A homicide victim is what I mean. Blonde, slender. But her face is unrecognizable. She was beaten with something after she was dead. Coroner is still working on her . . . Flood, tell me more about your woman."

"I don't know much about her, Jake. Jesus. She and her

husband are separated, and he says there's been no contact for two weeks. They've got one kid—son who's a senior at U. of I. What happened to *this* woman?"

"She had duct tape adhesive on her wrists and ankles, but the tape was removed by the time we found her. Ligature marks around her neck. She had been raped . . . more than once. No biologicals from that, apparently. Um, bruising on her arms, hip and a big one on her scalp—back of her head." Pialetti exhaled. "And then the face bludgeoned post-mortem."

"And you have no leads on IDing her?"

Pialetti shrugged. "She was nude, no personal effects. We found her rolled up in a carpet remnant—" He hesitated.

"Prints?"

He nodded. This was what he hesitated over.

"None to take. Her fingertips were snipped off. With a garden shears or a big scissors, or something. Post mortem. Meticulous. It's fucked up."

They both glanced around to make sure no one had overheard.

"Jesus, Jake, are you sure this is his first time? Sounds like a serial."

"That's what we're afraid of. But we don't have any like it that we know of."

"Have you asked the Bureau for a profiler?"

"That's our next step."

They sat for a minute, thinking it all over.

"What are you going to do?" Flood said, meaning about the knowledge of Marcy Westlake missing.

"Well, it's not technically my case, or even our case. It's Lombard P.D.—but you know, it's all hands on deck across the county. So I don't know. But, Augie, you understand that I have to tell Lombard about your woman, and it'll be their call how to handle it."

Flood felt sweaty. Their food came, but neither of them touched it. Flood was not hungry. He was stewing—this was suddenly out of his hands, and Lombard detectives would soon want to talk to Daniel Westlake. Flood had followed his instinct to do the ethical thing, even if it was against his client's wishes, because he was sure he could control the situation and keep his inquiry quiet. But no sooner had he opened his mouth than he stumbled into a mess. Not that it would matter much if Marcy Westlake had been abducted, brutally raped and murdered. His train of thought brought him around to Westlake's demand to keep the police out of it. Flood had wondered since he met Westlake whether he knew more than he was letting on. That hunch took up much more ominous implications with the possibility that Marcy Westlake had been savagely murdered. Flood broke the silence.

"Jake, you think you can keep them from talking to the husband immediately? If it's not her, I'll be in a jam for coming to you with it. Maybe we can all run down more loose ends this weekend and know more by Monday."

Pialetti shrugged.

"Not my call, but it makes some sense. Can you get us a DNA sample?"

Getting a strand of Marcy Westlake's hair would be complicated. He would have to get into their home, he figured, and be able to look around her bathroom. Not likely.

"It would be a lot easier to get the kid's hair. Is that OK?"

"It'll either rule her out or get close enough to break the possibility to the husband," he said. "We'll go from there."

Where they would go from there would be an uncomfortable topic, and Pialetti stopped short, leaving the rest unsaid. He would have talked about making Daniel Westlake a suspect in his wife's murder, but Flood was Westlake's lawyer. But it did not really bother Flood at this point. He was hired to find Marcy

Westlake, not to defend Daniel Westlake against the suspicion he killed her.

Pialetti changed the subject.

"Either way, we wouldn't get the fucking crime lab to lift a finger and run DNA over the weekend anyway."

Pialetti eventually ate half his sandwich, but Flood had no appetite. The waitress asked him twice if everything was OK and offered him a take-home bag.

"No, sorry. Just take it away."

As Flood drove back downtown in swelling afternoon traffic on the Ike, he worried. The chances of a coincidence were not good. DuPage County had more than a million people in it, but the likelihood was low that one good-looking blonde woman was missing at the same time that a different good-looking blonde woman of roughly the same age was found murdered in the same area. If he were dealing with black women on the violent, drugged-out zones of the South Side, he would fear they were the same woman. In placid, middle-class DuPage, it seemed almost a certainty. But before Westlake and Cronin found out that Flood had gone to law enforcement against their orders, he needed to find out more about Marcy Westlake, the man she was sleeping with, and the life she was leading away from her family. The next step was Brandon Westlake's phone and email records in Champaign. He couldn't do much more about that until the next morning.

Flood was frazzled and wanted a drink. He decided he would keep his promise to Jamie.

Chapter Three

Jamie had a booth halfway back in the bar. The woman with him was beautiful, and they were drinking whatever the "martini" of the moment was. Something pinkish with a squiggle of orange zest floating in a cocktail glass: not really a martini at all, but it was hard for Flood to complain about the names of drinks he would never order.

He had taken a cab to the Silver Cloud bar and arrived twenty minutes later than he said he would and wandered halfway back across the wood floor of the bar. He was scanning the back of the room for Jamie when the shrill, tipsy voice called out from the booth to his left.

"Hey, Mr. Private-dick-man. Over here."

Jamie was snuggled into the seat that faced the back of the bar with this woman who smiled in a way that showed she was years past being embarrassed by Jamie's behavior. When Jamie got drunk, sometimes he acted like a teenager swooning under the weight of his first breath of Southern Comfort fumes—obnoxiously self-absorbed with the qualities of his drunkenness.

The bar was crowded, all of the booths and stools taken, and Jamie's shout brought befuddled smirks from a handful of people. As Flood sat down, the woman fingered Jamie's ribs playfully.

"Do you need a time-out, Jamie?" she said, making eye contact with Flood. Jamie was going to be their little joke.

"Let's take him into the women's bathroom and wash his

mouth out with soap," Flood said.

"Everybody here hates gays. I can sense it," said Jamie, attempting to brood. He didn't have a serious bone in his body tonight.

Flood reached across the table to take the woman's hand, making a show of it to mock Jamie for not being on top of the introductions.

"How do you do? I'm Augie."

She gamely put out her hand.

"I guess we'll have to introduce ourselves. I'm Jenny. It's very nice to meet you."

Jamie just waved to the passing waitress.

"This man hasn't started drinking yet, and he's got an unpleasant disposition to begin with, so it's sort of an emergency," he said. "And at the end of the evening he'll be taking the bill."

The joke sparked when the waitress didn't get it and asked Flood for a credit card.

Flood had thought a good deal about Jamie being gay. They had clearly become friends since Jamie was hired and he'd never really been friends with someone who was gay before. In the end, the only thing that bothered him was that Jamie had stunning taste in women that went completely to waste. Until now. Flood had dismissed the possibilities of meeting Jamie's friend days ago. That was before he saw her. Flood raised his pint of Bell's when it came, but he couldn't say just exactly what he was thinking, so he said, "To Jamie's friends, may they continue to see past the façade of the besotted little fairy he shows the world and appreciate the besotted little fairy he hides on the inside."

Jenny seemed to think that was funny. Flood didn't care what Jamie thought. She had a beautiful face with big brown eyes that seemed to be apologizing for some private joke she was enjoying. Self-possession, Flood thought, then discarded it as not quite right. Some sense of curiosity that lit up her eyes. It would stay with him for days.

She was slender but strong-looking in a way that suggested she just worked hard and didn't take time to eat much rather than spending lots of time in a gym. She confessed to smoking a little—just five cigarettes a day—as she pulled one from her small black leather purse and held it up before Flood for an objection. He shrugged and slid the ashtray closer to her. If he'd been holding a book of matches he would have given her a light.

The smoke drifted from her lips, not blown, and seemed like mist in a greenhouse, enveloping all the lovely blooms around. Flood thought this even though it was a bit corny, and then justified it to himself because of the collar of her blouse. She wore a fitted black v-neck sweater that hugged her tight over a starched white blouse with a long straight collar that rose from the sweater, opened like an orchid, framing a generous expanse of her neck.

"Jamie said you can cook," she said, changing the subject.

"A little, but Jamie's impressed by anything that doesn't come sealed in cellophane."

Jamie rolled his eyes. "What was that ducky thing with the orange peel?"

Flood shrugged. "Duck with orange peel. I don't think it really has a name."

Jamie gave Jenny a grave look, like what he was about to say couldn't be true but was.

"He just makes the shit up as he goes." Then he looked back at Flood, "You've got to cook for Jenny. She loves to eat."

"I'd like that," he said.

Flood changed the subject away from food and asked about Jenny's job. She had a good job she liked at the Art Institute taking care of paintings in the permanent collection. She and Jamie had been friends as college students at the School of the Art Institute before he dropped out. She finished, while Jamie floundered around for a few years smoking pot and hating himself for being gay before he finally came out for real and landed back in school, finishing at UIC with a degree in communications, disappointed but relieved.

Jenny gave no hint of being anything but satisfied in her work. She had been a good painter, Jamie said, but she just shrugged and said she liked her job. Then she brought up politics.

"Jamie said you have a friend at the Tribune who's covering this casino thing."

"Keith Reece. We went to high school together."

"They're lovers," Jamie said. "Or would be, if only they could cut through all of the repression and buried feelings."

Jenny was practiced at ignoring Jamie.

"I can't believe this city," she said. "They bought off the whole process. You can bribe anybody. It's amazing."

"It's what Floodie and I do for a living," Jamie said. "Bribe people to get business with the city."

"It is not," Flood shot back.

"OK, just you," Jamie said, bug-eyed. "I'm only your lackey."

Jenny laughed, but Flood felt compelled to explain.

"The law firm we work for does a lot of City Hall lobbying," he said, sounding too much like a sales pitch. "But I don't get involved in it, and as far as I know nobody's paying bribes and setting up hookers to win re-insurance contracts."

He sort of regretted saying it. Once it was out of his mouth like that, he began to think about it and he felt immediately that he did not know if that was true. He could not swear that his bosses did not deal in bribes of one kind or another. In fact, it was entirely possible. Cronin was such a glad-handing bullshitter, after all.

"How much do you know about the mobsters?" she asked.

"A fair amount. I know who Nicky Bepps is. And I know roughly how he works. I didn't know he was manipulating the casino business, and I'm still not quite sure how he did it. But I'm not that surprised, I guess."

"So much for gambling being a legitimate business," Jenny said.

Flood smiled at her.

"Las Vegas has stopped marketing itself as a place to take your kids," he said. "Remember that? Roller coasters and water parks. They wanted to make it like Disney World. But they've gone back to saying come lose your shirt and cheat on your wife. We won't tell."

"Thank god," Jamie said.

"What else does Bepps do?" she asked.

"He's diversified pretty well, I think. A little trucking. He's got some garbage hauling contracts in the suburbs and some construction trucking—hauling gravel and dirt. His name's not directly on any of it. I know he owns a lot of residential property on the North Side. I think he built a bunch of strip malls in DuPage County in the early seventies. That laundered several million dollars and gave him a legitimate base to work from. But he just can't stay straight. He's got a hand in some strip clubs and massage parlors—you know, the *health spas* that advertise in the Sun-Times sports section. That's all a front for prostitution and it's mostly cash. I don't know if they move drugs, but I suppose so. Or at least put up the capital."

"Wow. It's like this whole alternate universe under our noses," she said, clearly fascinated by the notion. "You know what I mean? Like how far removed from all that crime are we? It seems so foreign but then this happens and suddenly it's like, this bank is involved and city officials are involved. You know, I've met some of those people who work for the mayor's office.

They come to museum parties."

Flood liked her a lot. The story of the casino had revealed a layer of the city she didn't know existed, crime and corruption as something palpable in her life. She was the odd person who was paying attention and connected dots to her own life. She knew some of those City Hall hacks, and now the whole thing seemed relevant, and it frustrated her that she did not understand the world as it really was.

"Is he a real gangster?" she asked, fully engaged in the conversation and focused on Flood in a way that made his heart race a little. "Or is he, like, just sort of a shady businessman."

"No, I think he's a real gangster," Flood said. "Well, gangster's a funny word, I guess. Let's put it this way, he's definitely at the top of the organized crime structure in Chicago. It's the real Outfit."

"Do they kill people?"

"We think he ordered the murder of a guy named Franco Devaney who got shot outside a diner in Franklin Park two years ago."

Jamie perked up. "Listen to you," he said to Flood. "*We*. You said *we*. You don't work for them anymore. You hate it."

"Hate what?"

"That you're not one of them anymore."

Flood laughed. "I certainly do not hate that I'm not one of them anymore."

Jenny didn't join in. She just smiled and let them bicker. Jamie had surely told her he'd been in the FBI. Maybe Jamie had told her he thought Flood was conflicted about it and she wouldn't ask because it was none of her business and, anyway, she could just sit back and let him whale away at Flood.

"You say 'we,' all the time," Jamie went on.

"I still talk to people I worked with. It's a habit."

"We," Jamie said, as if it would be the final word in the discussion.

"I'm hungry," Flood said. "Let's order some food. Jenny, Jamie said that you like to eat. Is that true or is it another one of his lies?"

"The baked goat cheese and the spinach dip," she said without hesitating.

"You don't even need a menu."

"That's how much I like to eat."

Flood's phone rang. He couldn't hear it, but he felt it vibrating in his pocket. He stood up and pulled it from his pocket to look at the number. A DuPage County area code. Westlake. He grimaced and excused himself. "I have to take this."

He walked outside into the cold and answered the phone, straining to hear over the street noise on Damen Avenue. But the call was already gone. He'd missed it. While he thought about calling back, the voicemail signal beeped. Flood called for the message, which was indeed from Westlake and said, "The key is in the mailbox at the end of the driveway. Just pick it up." And it went on briefly saying Flood should be in Champaign in the morning because his son would likely head back to school in the afternoon. Flood figured the son, Brandon, would want to spend as little time as possible alone with his father, no matter what the subject matter of their discussion.

He flipped the phone shut and headed back inside, relieved that he didn't have to actually talk to Westlake and dodge the issue of the murdered Jane Doe who might be his wife.

When Flood sat back down, he realized Jamie was talking about the missing Mrs. Westlake, illuminating it for Jenny as the ridiculous soap opera that it seemed to be.

"Tell her about the rich divorcee today, Floodie." Flood had told Jamie about Pam Sawyer but he didn't share his talk with Jake Pialetti. Nobody knew about the Jane Doe.

"Jamie, you're not discussing privileged client information with a third party, are you?"

Jamie went all bug-eyed. "No names," he exclaimed with conspiracy in his voice, and then clasped Jenny by the wrist. "I think Floodie's hot for you. He called you a 'third party.' "

Jamie held up his hands, as if to touch something precious hanging in the air over the table.

"Feel the unleashed testosterone," he said, "cutting the cigarette smoke and washing over us."

Flood flagged down the waitress and pointed at Jamie. "Miss, could you mix another metaphor for my friend. And whatever she's having, and a Bell's for me."

Chapter Four

It was still dark when Flood got out of bed. He showered and shaved, put on a pair of jeans and a thin wool sweater and his black winter jacket. He filled a flask with coffee, pocketed a plastic sandwich bag and a cotton swab for his promised DNA collection, and went down to the garage for his car. The sun was just beginning to rise above the silver water of the lake as he slipped down into the caverns of Lower Wacker Drive and then headed southwest on the Stevenson Expressway. There was little traffic on the highway and he could smell bread baking on an industrial scale as the highway arced through the Bridgeport neighborhood. The drive took him through a landscape of gravel pits and huge rail yards stacked with cities of boxcars. The surroundings gave way to trucking terminals and then to groves of trees and then he left the highway and drove into Westlake's subdivision. The house looked roughly like all the others on the block—a hulking chunk of red brick with a tall column of windows revealing a two-story entrance hall. The place was still dark. A white Honda Civic was parked in the driveway. A blue and orange college bumper sticker told Flood the son was there.

The mailbox was within reach of the driver's seat as Flood pulled to the curb. He opened the box to find a shiny new key taped to a thick sheet of paper. When he picked it up, he found that the paper was a print of three digital photos. In the margin, Westlake had written a note: "So you'll know what M looks like." Flood pocketed the key and dropped the photos on the passenger seat.

The key was shiny, and its teeth were still jagged with tiny filaments of steel that had not been smoothed over with use. He didn't want to linger at Westlake's driveway, so he kept driving, out of the subdivision and south on the Stevenson. As he drove he began to focus on the photos, taking his first glances at Marcy Westlake.

In the first photo, the Westlakes were with friends someplace, and everybody else had been cropped out. The image of her wasn't very clear because it had been doctored and enlarged. But she was clearly a beautiful woman. Tall, he was judging, maybe a half-inch taller than her husband. She wore a brown cocktail dress with spaghetti straps that revealed elegant shoulders and slender, toned arms. Her blonde hair was styled fairly short, but not cropped. It was still femininely curled. It framed her face well. Nice cheekbones and a full mouth. She had a full bosom and filled out the rest of the dress more like a good-looking woman in her late twenties than a mother in her forties. He studied the look on her face a long while. She half smiled, amused, understanding maybe that this scene wasn't quite what it seemed. Flood wished he had the rest of the photo.

The second photo was a formal family portrait. Marcy seated on an iron garden bench in the backyard with Daniel Westlake on one shoulder and their son, Brandon, who was tall and thin and took after his mother almost completely, at the other shoulder. Westlake himself looked a bit like the third wheel.

In the last photo, her face filled about a third of the frame. She seemed to be leaning over the kitchen table, wearing a big wool turtleneck. She looked different. The coy amusement in her mouth in the other photos was absent. Here she looked earnest and affectionate. The photo was much older.

He looked at the first picture again and wondered if her bare neck and shoulders might give the DuPage coroner's office enough to compare with their Jane Doe. Maybe, but it wouldn't be scientific enough for anybody to care. He tucked the sheet of photos into his Westlake folder and left it on the passenger seat. But the last image of her, probably ten years old, would stick with him. The light in her eyes was so different. Innocent. Their son would still have been a little boy, learning how to behave, funny and awkward. Her husband's business would have been apparently strong. Perhaps she had just started working herself and was having fun, feeling independent and part of something exciting for the first time in a while. Her world could have been growing in the right directions all at once. He was making this up based on what Pam Sawyer had told him, of course, so who knew if it was true. But she seemed happy in the photo. She was the light of the room, responding to the careful attention of the photographer, who was probably her husband.

The photograph was close-up and clear as a bell. It exposed her face to fine scrutiny, and the face triumphed with uncomplicated beauty. Flood wanted to see a close-up ten years later, as it looked now. What lines and creases of new and different experiences would be reflected in the light? He wanted to see for himself.

He shifted his attention back to the road opening before him. Because it was so early, he could cut cross-country on smaller roads and make it back to Interstate 57 without much delay. He took Route 53 down through the middle of Joliet, past the taquerias and old steel mill bars out by the original prison, down past the new casino on the banks of the Des Plaines River, past the restored Rialto Theatre and the Will County courthouse and jail, past the junkyards on the south end of the city and the mammoth new NASCAR track with its grandstand rising from the prairie like a butte, and then south to Wilmington, along the Kankakee River and across little Bourbonnais, back to 57, which headed straight south to Urbana-Champaign, home of the state university.

His mind trundled up the events of the night before, Jamie had gotten drunker and more difficult to understand, so Flood and Jenny just talked, like they were getting to know each other. He asked her about painting, and she talked about artists she liked rather than herself. At the end of the night Flood insisted they all share a cab even though he would end up getting stuck with big chunk of fare because he lived back downtown. He said he wanted to do it to make sure Jamie, stupid drunk by this time, got home safely. But as he drove south toward Champaign, he admitted to himself that he really just wanted to ride around with Jenny a little longer.

When he arrived in Champaign, Flood sat outside Brandon Westlake's house in his car for twenty minutes just watching for signs of life. The shabby white house was still. Westlake had promised that the place would be empty, and his voicemail last night had guaranteed no one would be back yet from Christmas break. He decided to wait another ten minutes just to be sure. Finally he got out of the car.

It was a medium-sized, ramshackle two-story house with a covered porch and dirty white aluminum siding. Like many of the old houses on the street, it looked like a smallish farm house transplanted to town. Unshoveled snow had accumulated on the steep walk in a hard-packed chute that had nearly turned to ice. A legless, collapsed green sofa sat on the porch, waiting patiently for the kegs of spring to bring it back to use. On the other side of the porch, a neglected propane grill sat listing to one side and chained to the porch rail. The floor of the porch was littered with flattened cardboard Busch and Milwaukee's Best cases.

Flood put the key in the lock, but the door didn't give, so he gave it a bump with the toe of his boot and it skidded open, revealing a cavern of dim quiet. As his eyes adjusted, he saw mismatched carpet remnants covering the worn-out wood floor, which he followed from the small entry hall to the living room. It was a typical college house. There were three buckled and torn couches of about the same quality as the porch furniture. A coffee table made of veneered pressed board, now warped by absorbed beer, supported three empty pizza boxes and several wads of aluminum foil and white paper; judging from the stale smell of pork grease and chili peppers, they were the detritus of burritos consumed at three in the morning. It was unclear how many hours, days or weeks the trash had been sitting there. A dozen empty beer cans and one moisture-damaged biochemistry textbook rounded out the menagerie of the coffee table.

Everything looked so perfectly in place that it took Flood a second to register the pair of eyes watching him.

She was sitting on the end of the couch. She had long brown hair tousled from bed, and she was clothed only in a tattered t-shirt. It had been white once but had turned grayish with age and was full of small holes, printed in rough letters with the name “The MUDHENS”, and then below was a small cartoon of a skinny chicken wearing a fedora, with more script below: “have mercy!” written small. It was a curious t-shirt, and it distracted Flood from the trouble that its wearer presented. She looked at Flood and took him all in. Too old and unfamiliar to be a student, even a law student. Not old or distinguished enough to be a professor. All Flood could think was that Daniel Westlake had once again given him unreliable information—this house was not empty.

“Who are you?” she asked.

He could tell she had been crying. Flood tried to think fast.

“Augie. I work for the lessee,” he said. Doubletalk. Nonsense. But it was before 8 A.M. on a Saturday morning in a college town, and she was half-naked and crying.

"Who?" she repeated, but meekly.

"Who are you?" he shot back, smiling as if he knew something she didn't.

"Alison."

"Alison, are you on the lease?" Now he used an earnest, puzzled tone, like he was trying to be nice but her unauthorized presence wasn't adding up.

"No," she said, plaintively, almost begging for it to be OK.

"Who is?"

"Joey."

"I know that," Flood said. "But where is he?"

"Asleep."

"OK, Alison," Flood said. He wasn't sure who he was supposed to be, other than pretending to be acting in an official capacity on behalf of someone in authority. But there really wasn't much official capacity to be had in a college flophouse. Nonetheless, it was working.

"Alison, are you OK? You look sad."

Her face melted and she shook her head slowly, like she couldn't even find use in seeking sympathy.

"It's nothing," she said.

"Joey?"

She nodded.

"You just need some time to think," he said. "Listen, I need to check the pipes in Brandon's room. I'll just be about twenty minutes, OK?"

"Should I get Joey?"

"No, let him sleep. You just sit here and take it easy," he said.

She nodded. "What's your name? Andy?"

"Sure," he said. "I'll see you in a few minutes."

She nodded and put her head down on the arm of the couch. She looked drowsy.

As he tiptoed to the stairs, he cut in half the time he had allotted himself to scour Brandon Westlake's room for clues to the whereabouts of Mrs. Westlake. Ten minutes and out, he said to himself, thinking of the aforementioned Joey, and doubting he would be as pliant as his fragile girlfriend. There were four bedrooms, and Brandon's was at the very end of the hall, according to Daniel Westlake's recollection. The door faced him as he soft-shoed down the hall trying to avoid creaky floorboards.

The room was well-ordered compared to the rest of the house. Brandon's bed was unmade, but his desk was in working order and there were no remnants of food or alcohol containers scattered across the floor like there were everywhere else. His desk was a cheap door from a lumberyard laid over two plastic sawhorses. His laptop computer occupied the middle of the desk and the rest was taken up by stacks of textbooks, workbooks and scattered copies of *BusinessWeek* and *Fast Company.* The computer was open and appeared to be on, although the screen was dark.

There were no posters on the wall, and his stereo was a very compact portable that sat on top of a stack of wire baskets that served as a clothes chest. The closet door was open, revealing one dark suit, a navy blazer, a pair of pressed khaki pants on a hanger and three pressed shirts draped in dry cleaner plastic. It looked like it would take him about twenty minutes to pack his belongings and move out.

Flood sat down at the desk and began to look around. There was a plastic file box on casters under the desk and he rolled it out and opened the drawers. Bank statements were clipped together, as was a stack of correspondence from the university registrar. Letters and documents from the business school were in an actual file folder. Underneath the top folder was another labeled "apps." He opened it and found copies of applications to business schools. Before he closed the file, he noticed a pattern. UCLA, USC, Berkeley, Pepperdine, UC San Francisco, Stanford, UC San Diego. All of them were California schools. Brandon Westlake had his mind made up. He was heading west.

There were more folders, marked for different courses. Inside those were papers he'd written. Most of them marked with As and B+s. No phone bills. Flood shut the drawers and rolled the little cabinet back under the desk.

He looked at his watch: five minutes gone. He ran his finger across the mouse pad and the screen came to life. He opened Microsoft Explorer and found himself on Yahoo. From the row of asterisks in the password box, he could see that Brandon had it set up to click right in. First he went to Brandon's Internet bookmarks and found Sprint. When the page popped up, as he had hoped, this username and password were also saved and he clicked into Brandon's cell phone account.

As he searched, Flood wondered if he was making a big mistake. Everything he touched was potentially evidence if Marcy Westlake turned out to be the Jane Doe, and her son Brandon was one of the last people she had contact with. Her last words with Brandon might contain clues to her death that Flood wouldn't understand. Even if he didn't mishandle anything, the case might eventually reveal that he had been here, snooping around in Brandon Westlake's private property. He used the fact that Daniel Westlake was paying his son's bills, but that was a very gray area, at best. He decided the thing to do was push forward—find out as much as he could about Marcy Westlake in the next forty-eight hours. If he had to tell Westlake about the body in the carpet on Monday, he wanted to know as much as there was to know about Marcy before then.

In another moment he was able to pull up the most recent bill, and he began to scan through the numbers. Most were local calls with a 217 area code. Then he spotted several from the same 630 area code. He pulled out his little notebook and opened to the page with information he had gotten from Daniel Westlake. All of the 630 numbers he saw were from Marcy Westlake's cell phone. He kept going. There were several with a 708 prefix. Flood checked his notes again—Westlake's office. Next he found an 847 number, the north suburban Chicago area code. It was a possible. Flood noticed that there were not half as many calls from his father—maybe one for every third call from Marcy Westlake. But he was not seeing anything helpful. He went over the small clumps of calls from Marcy one more time and finally saw it. Second from the last in a group, a 630 number that looked nearly the same.

In the hallway outside, a bedroom door opened abruptly, creaking heavily as it swung. Flood froze. Heavy bare feet padded toward him. Then they stopped. Another door, closer, slammed. Joey up to take a leak. Flood muttered an obscenity under his breath and waited. He wanted to hit print and get the hell out of there, but he was afraid the noise of whirring electric motors churning paper and squirting ink would be clearly audible from the bathroom. He waited. The toilet flushed. The feet padded back into the hallway and stopped. He could feel Joey standing out there in the hall. What was he thinking about? His girlfriend leaving his bed to whimper downstairs. Some noise he'd heard coming from Brandon's room? Something not quite right in the morning air. Flood sat perfectly still, thinking about what he'd do if the door opened. He thought about not hitting print at all. But he wanted the bill. You never knew. He began looking around the room for exposed pipes. That was his cover story. The heat register was in the corner under a metal cover. It would be a ridiculous explanation.

The feet shuffled on the bare wood. Away from him. The bedroom door slammed. Flood reached for the pillows to pick them up but then stopped himself. He bent over the bed and inspected the pillow and sheets. Nothing. Then he turned it over, and found a three-inch hair on the sheet. Using the cotton swab he had brought, he picked up the hair and eased it into the plastic baggie, sealed it and put it back in his coat pocket.

Flood then picked up the pillows from the bed and set them on the floor in front of the door. Then he took the comforter and draped it lightly over the printer and hit print on the laptop. He could barely hear the paper feeding and gears whirring himself. He clicked out of the phone bill, out of Explorer. In a hurry, he was about to get up, but then remembered the Yahoo password and decided it was worth risking another minute. He clicked into Brandon's email and started to look for an address that might be Marcy Westlake. He saw nothing that fit the bill and opened a few randomly, to no avail. He scrolled into a second screen and was two weeks back now. From what Daniel Westlake had said, it was likely Marcy did not even have an email account. But one address in the inbox caught his attention. Pamswy@ . . . He opened it and, yes, it appeared to be from Pam Sawyer.

B—

Try not to be mad. Things are just so crazy right now. Nothing makes sense. But this wasn't what you think. I do care for you . . .

The hair on the back of Flood's neck bristled.

. . . I had strong feelings, and I gave in to them when I was feeling very vulnerable because of what happened. That was wrong. But it doesn't change how I feel about you. I didn't use you to get back at her. You have to believe me.

Oh, for Christ's sake, Flood thought. Her email was a response to a message from Brandon, and Flood scrolled down to see it.

This all makes sense now. I was just a way to get back at her because she stole that sleazeball away from you. Thanks a lot, you bitch. Leave me alone. I'm sick of all of you.

Flood could see there were more messages in the string, but he didn't have time to read them all. He hit print again and the whole string reeled off in three pages as he exited Yahoo and Explorer.

He restored the bedding and folded the phone bill and the emails into his jacket pocket.

He waited a minute and then opened the door. The hallway was again empty, but he had twenty feet of creaky floor to cross to get to the creaky stairs. He closed the door and walked along the wall; less creaking at the edge of the floor. He was just at the top of the stairs when the voice called out from behind the bedroom door.

"Allie?" Plaintive, and somehow hurt. Joey was a schmuck, Flood decided. Calling out to his girlfriend, who'd gotten up to cry by herself in the cold living room, trying to make up but too lazy to drag his ass downstairs to get her. Flood wanted to stop in the living room to check on her, but when he stepped onto the first floor, he headed for the front door. He had to keep moving. There were probably just seconds before Joey, now alert, heard her addressing Flood.

"Hey," she said, lifting her head from the couch. "Did you fix the pipes?"

"Everything's in working order" Flood said, pulling hard on the front door. "Thanks. Take care of yourself, Alison."

Flood skipped down the steps and steadied himself on the icy walk, striding as fast as he could out to the street and then jogging the half block to his car. He got in, started the motor, wheeled around and headed away from the house. He made it. He drove about five blocks without paying any attention to where he was going before beginning to get his bearings. He was south and east of the Interstate. He was also hungry. It was 8:30, and he was headed west through the corner of campus on Green Street, past a number of bars and cheap restaurants, convenience stores and t-shirt shops. He came to a stoplight. A white cinder-block Steak-n-Shake diner sat on the corner at his right. Flood changed lanes and pulled in. The place was fairly empty, and he took a booth at the back with no one at the surrounding tables. He ordered coffee and bacon, eggs and wheat toast, and then pulled the notebook and his cell phone from his jacket. He had two phone numbers. He dialed the 630 number. While it rang, he thought about what kind of a path Marcy Westlake had gone down. She had looked like the ideal of suburban prosperity in those photos. Good-looking, and aging well, affluent and the mother of a son who packed off to a good school to study business. But along the way things had really gone haywire. First the mystery man, and the apparent trouble with Pam Sawyer over whose man he really was, and then something sordid involving Pam Sawyer and Brandon Westlake. Her disappearance, and now an unidentified woman with a shattered face, lying on a cold morgue slab after being raped and strangled.

Thinking about it was making him sweat again, as it had the day before when Pialetti first told him about Jane Doe.

The phone rang five times, and he nearly gave up. Then came a rapid, difficult to grasp greeting in a young female voice. But Flood caught all he needed to catch. "Inn-n-Suites," the woman said.

Flood smiled. "What's your address?"

She gave him the name of a road that meant nothing to him, but then volunteered that it was just off I-88 about a mile west of Route 59. He wrote it down and thanked her. Flood looked at the address as he ate breakfast and idly watched the first of the campus hangovers stumble in to recuperate. Marcy Westlake called Brandon from a motel close to where she lived. The likely explanation for her staying there was an affair. It was progress.

Chapter Five

On the drive back to Chicago, Flood had more than enough time to think about what little control he had over his own conduct. Taking on a case at his boss's insistence that had almost immediately landed him in the middle of a horrible crime in which he should have no involvement. And this was all about some shady contractor dodging bankruptcy? He spent a moment trying to convince himself this escapade might help keep certain skills sharp. But why would he ever need such skills again? He'd left all that behind. Once the adrenaline had worn off from his little covert operation, Flood started to feel a strong sense of dread over what would come next.

Flood was home by eleven-thirty. He parked his car underground and rode the elevator to his apartment. The Saturday papers bored him; he was too antsy and tired. The printed words kept blurring into a gray mess, yet he didn't feel like he could sleep. Running might help, he decided, so he put on his heavy sweat pants and a fleece pullover covered by a hooded anorak and an expensive cap from the store where he bought his running shoes. He disliked expensive, faddish gear, but the hat had turned out to be a splendid asset for shielding his sweaty head from icy winds off Lake Michigan. He stretched in the elevator on the way down and then some more in the lobby before heading out on the streets. It was probably about fifteen degrees outside, brutally cold even with the midday sun high in a clear blue sky. In the summer he would have headed east on Illinois for the lake. But it was better to stay out of the wind as much as possible, so Flood started running up Rush Street. As he ran and the blood began to flow through his body more rapidly, with exertion, he began to feel the adrenaline percolating. It was a sensation that always played tricks on his mind. He was taken back to his youth, running on a field, making tackles, catching balls, running to catch someone, running to escape. Now running was supposed to be a time to clear his head, but there was always so much muck to get through first. Flood felt himself on a football field, running hard, timing his steps to fill a gap at just the right moment. It was dark, and the field was lit by bright lights, the grass was hard beneath his feet, the thuds of players running into each other vanished in the moment of his speed. He ran for the gap, seeing the fullback with the ball turning into the hole and accelerating. Flood ran and reached for him, extending, and missing. He sprawled on the grass, watching the fullback run on. It played in his head like this every time.

Flood ran about three miles north, through Division Street and the posh Gold Coast lakeside streets, into Lincoln Park, sticking to the secluded paths along the west side of the park and the zoo. He was sweating and felt loose. He sped up and was back on the field again. Another try, and he raced for the gap, linemen shoving each other, grinding the grass into black dirt beneath their cleats, opening the hole wider. The fullback turned, Flood dove, closer this time, but he just clipped him in the hip and he didn't go down, but kept scampering with the ball. Feeling around inside himself for momentum, Flood found himself leaving the FBI. It was the biggest decision of his life, a complete change of direction, abandoning the organization, the government, law enforcement, striking out on his own. It made him strong, but still he had missed something. He had not quite taken the right tack, had not hit the hole hard enough. He landed where he landed, with this law firm, taking orders, and getting stuck with the Daniel Westlakes of the world.

Just north of the zoo entrance Flood stopped in the Conservatory to get warm in the botanical garden's humidity, use the bathroom, and take a drink of water before heading back. The burbling fountain felt warm on his frozen lips. He started out again down the sidewalk that lined Lincoln Park West, through the winding paths of the zoo. He was really warm and relaxed now, running hard without effort. The blocks passed by in a blur. Another cut at the hole, he could feel the turf flying by under his feet; he saw the crossbar of the fullback's face mask earlier this time, sized him up and timed it two steps back. The fullback turned the corner with the ball and Flood lunged in, lowered his shoulders and hit him square in the belly, wrapping his arms hard and driving through him, sending them both skidding across the grass on a slick film of sweat and nylon. Perfect. Flood smelled the sweet damp earth close to his nose and felt the ache in his shoulder. He raised his head and turned and saw the good things, this city, this run, a table in a warm bar on a cold night, and a beautiful young woman sitting next to Jamie laughing, looking right at him with light in her eyes.

The thought startled him. He had barely met her, and here she was already, dropping into his thoughts—both the doldrums of the long drive and the adrenaline-fueled daydreams of his run.

After six miles in the cold his cheeks were chapped and numb, but he felt good, relaxed and tired. Back in his apartment, he took off the running clothes and dumped them into the washing machine. He walked around the apartment naked for a few minutes to let his body air dry and then put on a rumpled pair of jeans and a dirty t-shirt and lay down on the couch in the living room, spreading a throw blanket loosely over his torso. He fell asleep immediately and dreamed not of Jenny, but of Marcy Westlake.

The woman in his dream treated him with predictable suspicion—the agent of a lousy husband. All they had in common was Daniel Westlake and they both knew he was a bad connection. In any event, Flood was on the wrong side of that equation, working for the guy. One more man coming after her. In the dream, she kept shaking her head as Flood talked to her, trying to get her to believe that he was OK and her husband was being honest, that there was not some hidden agenda. She kept shaking her head and Flood felt ashamed and humiliated. It was hard to tell where exactly they were. It seemed like maybe the lounge of an old bowling alley somewhere. They weren't drinking, but there seemed to be a lot of cigarette smoke clouding things up. They were boxed by dark veneer paneling, and there was a lot of orange carpet and vinyl around. Flood thought it must be some place from her past, and he knew he was not even being granted access to the current Marcy Westlake. She was showing him some anachronous version of herself. Then they seemed to be driving together, in some decrepit white van with rattling floorboards and a loud engine. It was bitterly cold, and the van, he realized, seemed to be open to the wind, no heat, windows down, doors all open, or even missing, as they rode. He looked at her and she was blue and looking ahead at something so intently that Flood found himself following her eyes, and realizing, with a start, that she was glaring at the roadside, into the tan weeds of a vacant lot along Roosevelt Road just west of York. Exactly where Pialetti said the body had been found.

He awoke with his heart pounding, feeling the blurring between what was dream and what was real. The sensation that he had fallen asleep suddenly seized him in the context of the dream, but it did not help him from feeling a little sick. That there had just been a glimpse of the woman in the brown cocktail dress and knowing smile, that he had been privy to some communication from the dead that had grabbed him and then let go of him as he awoke, vanishing in the light that now bore down on him through the windows, magnified by the canyon of skyscrapers lining the river. He wondered for a minute about the rattling white van, but Flood did not believe in dreams that way. He stood up and rubbed his face. The light on the facades of the buildings across the river was blinding, but they cast deep, angular shadows down the side streets that divided the buildings. He was awake and she was gone.

Flood thought about calling Westlake to give him an update and to ask him if maybe, just maybe, Marcy bolted because her best friend was fucking her son to spite her. And he wanted to listen to Westlake talk, just to see if there was any whiff of knowledge hanging over the man's words. He asked himself how much Westlake really knew about what had happened in the last two weeks of Marcy Westlake's life. He did not believe Westlake had told them everything he knew. This was a mess. He'd have to sit on that until he was sure of it. He felt that understanding how Marcy Westlake responded to finding out that her friend had slept with her son to spite her could provide critical clues to what happened to her. But Flood did not yet possess enough pieces of the puzzle, and if there was some simple explanation for all of this, he would really have made a mess by suggesting it to Westlake. He would stick to telling Westlake that he'd made it in and out of the house without major problems, other than the unexpected girl on the couch. But, even this update, he decided to put off for a bit.

In the meantime, as he sat sipping fresh coffee, Flood was still curious about Westlake's Cayman account and why he needed the money so badly. If he was not a very good business-man, as Cronin and Pam Sawyer had seemed to suggest, then how did he amass his offshore stash in the first place? It bothered Flood because, as an FBI agent, whenever he ran across money stashed in offshore accounts he traced it back to ill-gotten gains. Drug money or extortion money. But that wasn't really fair because Flood and his FBI colleagues would not have been looking at the accounts in the first place if they didn't think crooks were involved. Maybe the offshore account was well within the realm of legitimate tax dodges. But Flood couldn't help it—it seemed a little shady. He wondered how Westlake had gotten the money down there in the first place and what role the missing wife had played in that. Vacation, probably. They'd been sunning themselves in the Caribbean and decided to open a bank account while they were there. Set it up so they could wire funds there whenever they wanted. Wired there, or maybe Westlake would make a brick of hundreds and bury it in his Tommy Bahama collection in a suitcase on their next vacation.

Flood went to his office, the smaller second bedroom, where he'd installed an old green-steel schoolteacher's desk and a couple of filing cabinets, a computer and combination copier, printer and fax machine. He picked up his Westlake file and went back to the living room and sat down.

He leafed through the financial documents. The lien held by George Kajmar troubled him because Cronin hadn't mentioned it. Flood didn't know who Kajmar was until he read the little newspaper blurb about the Tollway Authority. But Kajmar was a political powerbroker, and Cronin would have been likely to know all about him.

He looked at his watch. It was two-fifteen. He wasn't hungry, but he felt like he should be out somewhere having lunch. He needed to bounce ideas off somebody. He would go to the Inn-n-Suites that night to try to find out why Marcy Westlake called her son from the motel, he decided. He didn't want to go during the day when it was more likely to be busy with check-ins and check-outs. Plus, if Marcy Westlake was having an affair there, it'd be more likely to be noticed by the night staff, he figured. He took the elevator down to the street and walked over to the Billy Goat Tavern. A bank of filthy windows at knee level framed neon beer signs and then a heavy red door swung back at the corner of Lower Hubbard and Lower Michigan to reveal more steps down into the tavern. The Goat was, first of all, subterranean. It was a bar that looked like an old lunch counter in a bomb shelter, done up in grimy tile, faded Formica and paneling covered with black and white pictures of forgotten newspapermen and obscure beauty queens. It had become the only steady hangout for journalists in Chicago. A staircase outside went up to Michigan Avenue, directly across the street from the Tribune Tower. In the other direction, the Sun-Times building was about a hundred yards west, and the City News Bureau, Associated Press office and several television stations were all within walking distance.

Flood walked down the steps and scanned the L-shaped bar, which bent from his right down the wall to a TV set hung in the corner and then turned and continued to the end of the room. The tables in front of Flood were half full, mostly tourists, outfitted with souvenir paper hats like the grill men wore, eating cheeseburgers and watching college basketball. Illinois was playing Michigan State in East Lansing. It was almost halftime and the Illini were winning. Bouch, the Moroccan waiter, tapped Flood on the elbow.

"Hey, man, you want Jack on rocks?"

It was what he usually drank, and Bouch had an astonishing ability to remember the usuals of even casual customers. It was his pride. If he got it wrong and you ordered something else—say Bouch said Old Style and you corrected him and said Heineken was your usual—he would give you a look that seemed to say, *OK, pal, now you're changing your drink after all these years and, just so you know, that complicates things.*

Bouch got it right, but Flood didn't want a drink. On Flood's left the grill counter had a short line of people waiting to order burgers and potato chips. There he found who he was looking for. Reece was wearing an untucked white button-down shirt and blue jeans and had no coat. He was reading from a manila folder, lost in documents. Flood's tap on the shoulder roused him, as if from sleep.

"Come on, I'll buy you lunch," Flood said, waving toward the door. Reece shrugged, not the least bit surprised to see Flood and gave up his spot in the burger line. They headed for the exit.

Bouch, grinning, followed them to the door. "You steal my customers, damn you," he said, wiping his hands on the folded apron tied around his waist. "You bring him back."

"Don't worry," Flood said. "I'm going to get him food that won't kill him so he can come back and drink himself to death later."

Outside in the bitter cold, Reece closed the manila folder and tucked it under his arm. He wasn't wearing a coat because he had intended just to walk across the street from his cubicle at the Tribune, pick up a burger and a Diet Coke and go back to his piles of documents.

"What are you reading?" Flood asked.

"Where are you taking me to lunch?" Reece asked, ignoring him. "I've got a one-block limit. It's fucking five degrees, you know."

"Shaw's. And it's at least fifteen degrees. What are you reading?"

"Shaw's? You must want something," Reece said. "Listen, this can't be a four-bloody-mary-lunch again. I'm working, as I'm sure you understand from your sophisticated grasp of the news cycle."

"The story has legs, as they say," Flood said, smiling.

"Long, fast ones," Reece replied.

"I saw this morning's, but I don't read the Sunday paper until Sunday, what have you got in it?"

"Nothing huge, your former employers seized documents from Art Callahan's house on Captiva. Sun-Times had it, too."

"Know what's in the docs?"

"Why don't you find out and tell me. You should be taking them to lunch and me to dinner. The paper will pick up all the tabs."

"They don't like me talking to you," Flood said, which was a pointless fib. His colleagues had always known when he was going to call Reece and what he was going to tell him. Because Flood knew him and trusted him, they chose Reece for the occasional useful leak. Reece had other sources inside the office, but no one knew who they were. Flood was a known conduit. If it suited the FBI's purposes to have some little tidbit out there as events unfolded, then the official policy of no comments about an ongoing investigation would be circumvented with Flood and Reece having a whisky somewhere late at night. Although Flood had left the Bureau, it still happened, but less frequently, and with less sensitive information. Reece had been heartbroken when Flood quit.

They took a booth in the informal bar side of Shaw's Crab House. The barroom was better lit than the dining room and was decorated like an old-timey New England oyster bar. Flood ordered a Guinness. Reece wanted one but ordered a Diet Coke instead. As if he was on a date with a very traditional girl, Flood ordered. He asked for a dozen oysters to share, two small Caesar salads and cups of clam chowder. Reece dug into a dish of giant oyster crackers on the table and started to munch away at them.

"I'd heard they were going to toss Callahan's beach house," Flood said, when the waitress had gone. He had run into an agent named Feinberg at lunch Thursday at the Berghoff bar. By that time a handful of details had emerged, and Feinberg had been in the mood to gossip. "I thought it was on Sanibel, but same difference."

"Why didn't you call me?" Reece said, wincing. "I could have broken it alone."

"I've been busy. I'll see if I can find out what they picked up," Flood said, knowing he should never admit after the fact that he might have been able to help Reece out with a scoop.

Reece fidgeted, holding his tongue but peeved. This was a very important story. It was not just a story about public corruption. It was a story that brought organized crime dangerously close to a mayor who had been politically untouchable for more than a decade. Mayor for life, it seemed. He had the entire city council under his thumb. He was never seriously challenged at the polls, and he was a part of a family legacy that seemed quintessentially tied to Chicago's identity.

But now the casino scandal. The mayor had backed the idea of a casino in downtown Chicago. He had the state legislators, whose puppet strings he controlled, write new laws to make it possible and twisted the governor's arm to make it happen. He appointed committees to study proposals for a site and to scrutinize the backgrounds of potential developers. His people drew up the specifications for applications in concert with the Illinois Gaming Board, a panel of appointed officials who regulated the gambling industry. Gambling in Illinois had traditionally meant horse tracks—mostly trotters—and church bingo. But in the last twenty years, Illinois had embraced the nationwide riverboat casino craze. At first the boats, anchored on navigable waterways, would cruise out into the slow currents of the Mississippi, Ohio, and Illinois and a half dozen other rivers across the middle of the country. Gradually, the laws changed. At first, gambling could only take place when the boats were cruising. Then the boats left the dock just once a day, and gambling took place even when docked. Then they didn't go out at all except for special occasions. Eventually, the meaning of a riverboat had morphed into riverside buildings with boat-like appendages that dipped into the water. Gambling went on twenty-four hours a day. In the Chicago area, the state had granted casino licenses to operations out on the edges of the suburbs—Joliet, Aurora, Elgin, even famously forlorn Gary, across the state line in Indiana—all the old, atrophied industrial towns that cried out for some miracle of economic rebirth. Casinos had been a haphazard boost to those local economies. They built swanky new downtown convention centers and parks that amounted to little more than temporary sources of construction jobs. Dreams of packing the places with Wayne Newton or James Taylor on tour disintegrated. More likely the pavilions would settle for hosting community college graduations and hot rod car nights, where middle-aged men in sleeveless t-shirts opened the hoods on the chromed cams of their '72 Barracudas and sat in lawn chairs sipping beer they'd brought from home. Some boost to economic vitality.

Meanwhile, the casino companies raked in hundreds of millions of dollars a year, most of it frittered away at the slots by unemployed factory workers and old people spending their prescription premiums as they unfixed their fixed incomes. Politicians had sold legalized gambling to Illinois voters with the promise that a chunk of the revenue would go to funding public schools. But that never worked out quite as well as they'd promised, and the schools were still a mess in the towns that needed help.

All the while, Chicago had avoided the casino industry. The big city had enough going for it, the argument went, and it didn't need to be stealing future members of Gamblers Anonymous from Joliet and Gary.

But the mayor hated being left out of the gravy. If there was a cash cow penned up somewhere else in Illinois, Chicago must eventually slaughter, butcher and hang the meat of that cow for itself. After a few years, so it was. And with the mayor's political weight behind the idea, the partners who got the license turned out to be . . . the Outfit. The process was fixed. The whole deal was as crooked as an old-time aldermanic race. How perfectly Chicago.

According to Reece's sources, the scandal had unraveled like this. A former state senator named Puska—a very undistinguished lawyer from the Northwest Side of the city—was hired as a consultant to be City Hall's eyes and ears at Gaming Board staff meetings as the policy wonks and bean counters drew up the specifications for applications to run the casino. About a third of the way through the process, after Puska got cozy with everybody and knew how it all worked, he quit to take a job at a law firm. A week after Puska started his new job, the firm was subcontracted by the lawyers who represented West Bank Casino Venture, LLC, one of five partnerships that was bidding to run the casino.

There were three main named partners in the West Bank venture: Lyle Soppel, who was the son of a Las Vegas casino magnate; Mikey Moutard, a former Chicago hockey star who now owned a popular restaurant in River North; and Andrew Flaherty, a wealthy businessman who owned a suburban manufacturing company that made replacement windows. Their efforts were managed through a suburban bank, called Sovereignty Savings and Trust, whose chairman, Samuel J. Pistenich, owned a minority share of the partnership. That's where the fun began.

Once the FBI was onto Puska, they went after everybody

involved in West Bank. They seized documents everywhere, and among Pistenich's private papers they hit the jackpot. A secretly executed contract between himself and John Castle, who happened to be the brother-in-law of Outfit kingpin Nicky Bepps.

Anyone might have argued that it was only a coincidence that the bidder that won the license from the Illinois Gaming Board happened to be West Bank, which had hired the lawyers who hired another law firm that had just hired the politically connected former state senator who advised the city on the casino plan. But that anyone would have been naïve.

Perhaps no one would ever have been the wiser, so the unfolding story went, except for a smart lawyer from New York who represented one of the license bidders who lost out. He had watched the process like a hawk, and, prejudiced by an outsider's respect for Chicago lore, had harbored a gut feeling from the beginning that his clients weren't going to get a fair shake. This was all according to Reece's sources. Then one day the New Yorker walked into a Gaming Board hearing and ran into a woman he'd known at the University of Chicago Law School.

"Kate, what are you doing here?" he asked.

"I'm working for Don Powell."

"Who's he?"

"The city's liaison to the Board."

"To the Gaming Board?" the lawyer said, raising his eyebrows.

"Mmm hmm."

"What happened to Howard Puska?"

"I think he went into private practice."

"Now?"

"I know," she said. "Weird timing."

Weird timing, indeed. And it had happened without anybody saying a word publicly. The lawyer from New York started looking for Puska. When he found him, he asked him what kind of work he was doing, and Puska, who never had much of a poker face, started sweating and mumbled something about estate planning. So the lawyer tore through every one of his competitors' casino license applications again, went through every piece of paper he could get his hands on. At last, he found that copies of a piece of recent correspondence in the West Bank application file had been cc'd to a partner at the firm that had hired Puska. The feeling in his gut getting harder, the lawyer from New York paid a visit to the U.S. Attorney.

According to Reece's sources, the federal prosecutors started digging. They found out a lot of things, but the big one, eventually, was that gaming board member Art Callahan had recently bought a house on Captiva Island on Florida's Gulf Coast. Callahan had made a $125,000 down payment in cash, and the feds couldn't find any records of it in his financial statements. Eventually they traced it to a cash deposit made to a bank account in the Bahamas. They had a pretty good idea that it came from Bepps, but they did not know how, physically, it got into Callahan's hands.

Reece wanted to know, too. He and Flood ate the oysters. Reece's cell phone rang. He whispered into it.

"I need to know that," he insisted. Then long silence while he listened. "It's going to come out sooner or later, and it's not like they don't know they're being looked at, right? They've gotten, like, three different subpoenas."

More listening. Flood knew that Reece had other sources inside the FBI, but they were lower down in the food chain than the people who sometimes used Flood to pass things along. They didn't always have the whole picture, and they couldn't go looking for it without raising eyebrows inside the office. So there were limits to what they could help Reece with. Some of their stuff was unusable scuttlebutt.

"I really need to know. This worries me. You understand? It

really worries me."

He snapped his phone shut and dropped it back into his shirt pocket, where its weight tugged at the collar and made one side of the baggy shirt sag.

"What do you need to know?" Flood asked.

"Who gave Callahan the money? Where, exactly, it came from. One of Bepps's businesses? One of the brother-in-law's businesses? Where? Who was the bagman?"

"I don't know if my guys know. I think that's still the big question," Flood said. When he said his guys, he meant the people in charge. Flood heard the same gossip Reece heard from the underlings, but when he helped his friend, it was with information from the top.

"Can you ask?"

"Well, I'll ask if they want to tell you. But, you know how that goes."

Reece nodded.

"It's driving me nuts."

They finished the oysters and then ate the salads. Eventually, the chowder came and the salad plates were taken away.

"What are you so busy with?" Reece said, blowing on a spoonful of soup.

Flood groused about it but sketched the basics. He left out the weird sexual games involving Brandon Westlake. And he left out Jane Doe, for the moment.

"What's the guy's name?" Reece asked.

"Daniel Westlake."

"Never heard of him."

Flood suddenly realized this was out of line professionally, talking about a client. But he didn't care.

"Forget I told you the guy's name, OK?"

"OK." Reece took another big spoonful of chowder. "I don't give a shit about it."

"I feel slimy. I don't know why the family hasn't reported her missing."

"Why don't you?"

"Everybody says I just don't know her, and they do, and she's fine. She's just taking some time for herself."

"D'you call her cell phone?"

"Not answering. The husband says she never set up her voicemail. Dingy that way, I guess. The message just keeps saying customer unavailable."

"So, what do you do next?"

"I make a mess of the whole thing," he said, grinning. "I think she's got a boyfriend. I'm sure he can fill in lots of blanks, and I'm going to find him and ask him. He's probably married, so that will be real pleasant for everyone. Lawyer for asshole-estranged-husband calls family man to look for mistress. I'd like to be done with this and go back to the exciting world of high-stakes insurance defense."

"Weird."

Flood decided to loosen the strings a bit.

"Hey, do you know whether you guys have written anything about a Jane Doe murder victim in DuPage?"

Reece immediately saw the connection, put down his spoon, and said, slowly and quietly, "Augie, what the fuck are you into?"

Flood shook his head. "I'll let you know when I find out."

Chapter Six

Flood went back to his apartment after lunch and paged Rob Feinberg. He returned the call in ten minutes.

"I just saw Reece," Flood said. "Anything they want to give up about the Callahan search?"

"I was going to call you, actually," he said. "Nothing about that, as far as I know, but we do have something."

"Am I going to need to write this down?"

"No, it's short. It's about Callahan. When he wasn't serving the interests of organized crime on the Gaming Board, he was a consultant to the University of Illinois board," Feinberg said.

"Right."

"Tell Reece we're investigating Callahan's activities on campus—say it like that, *activities on campus*—to see whether it played any role in the casino license award."

"That's it?" Flood said. "That's pretty thin."

"I know. That's how we want it."

"What if it's too thin for him to put in the paper," Flood said. "I really don't want to spend the rest of my day on the phone shuttling questions and answers back and forth. Like, what do you mean by *activities?* You know there are already call girls involved in this scandal, you're going to have the parents of ten thousand coeds flipping their lids with that. And which campus, Chicago or Champaign?"

"That's it," Feinberg said, firmly. "Just say what I told you."

Flood thought about not doing it. He really didn't think it

was something that Reece could publish without asking a million follow-up questions. But he made the call anyway. The investigator's motive was to create some kind of spark in the small group of people they were investigating. To make them nervous, and maybe spur them to react in some way the agents could see. But they didn't want to give away too much, nothing too firm. It served their purposes much more than it served the public's desire for information. It was a mildly sleazy way of shaking the tree—to see what would fall out. Flood guessed the feds didn't know the answer to Reece's burning question: Who was the bagman handing off sacks of cash to Art Callahan? They were guessing the exchange had something to do with Callahan's job with the university system. Leaking something vague might prompt a meeting, or a cell phone call, that one of their wiretaps might pick up. There were a lot of maybes there, and it seemed slightly desperate to Flood.

"They're investigating Callahan's activities on campus, and no, he wouldn't be more specific than that," Flood said, bracing for a cranky response.

He was met with silence.

"You there?"

"I'm here," Reece said.

"It seems thin to me," Flood said. "I thought you'd be more annoyed than anything."

"They're talking about the bagman. It's got something to do with the payoff," he said. "It must have happened at the university."

"Maybe."

When he finished mediating the exchange between Reece and Feinberg, Flood was rejuvenated enough to return to his own strange task. It was close to four in the afternoon and the light was fading outside his windows. A hard wind was blowing off the lake, rippling the green river in small skirmishes, slowly pushing the big trapezoids of white ice through the channel below. The few pedestrians on the street hunched and leaned against the wind as they crossed the Wabash Avenue Bridge. Flood needed to touch base with Westlake. He wondered if Brandon was still there. He decided to call the house. Westlake picked up on the second ring.

"It's Flood. Can you talk?"

"Not really."

"Your son still there?"

"For a bit."

"Call me when you're free. You have my mobile?"

"I do. OK." He hung up.

Flood flipped on the TV and sat down to wait for the call back. Basketball highlights rolled by on the screen. And then two hours rolled by on the clock and there was no call back from Westlake. He called and got the machine but didn't leave a message. Annoyed, Flood threw on his jacket and headed for the garage. But when he got to the elevator, he stopped and thought about his ultimate destination that night—the Inn-n-Suites. The way he dressed mattered. He went back to the apartment and changed from his jeans and boots to a pair of flannel pants, a starched shirt, gray V-neck sweater, olive corduroy jacket and an alpaca wool overcoat. He looked more distinguished when he returned to the elevator and rode down to the garage.

It was after seven and pitch dark when he pulled onto Westlake's block. He stopped at the curb around the corner from the house on a side street, but because there wasn't a single mature tree in the entire subdivision he had an unobstructed view of Westlake's front door. The driveways were so big that six cars could fit on them, and there were no cars on the street. The road was dusty with salt and the curbs were trimmed in old ridges of plowed snow. The white Honda was gone from Westlake's driveway, but there was a polished sky-blue Lincoln Town Car in its place. Westlake drove a Lincoln, but a Navigator, a huge SUV—according to motor vehicle records Flood had tracked down through Nexis. He took out his notepad and wrote down the license plate number of the Town Car. Then he called Westlake's number again. Westlake answered.

"Hey," Flood said. "I couldn't get ahold of you."

"Sorry." Westlake offered nothing more.

"Well, I'm in the area checking some things out, and I wanted to stop by and talk to you about what I found and get some more information about your wife."

"Tonight?"

"Now," he said firmly. "I'm just a few minutes away. I tried to get ahold of you."

"Um," Westlake sounded frazzled. "OK. Like twenty minutes?"

"More like ten. I'm pretty close."

Something was going on. There was a kind of tension in the house, Flood could tell. He wanted to see who came out and got in the Town Car.

"OK. I'll see you in a few minutes. Will this take long? I have some things to do later."

"No. Just a few minutes. I'm getting off the Stevenson here."

"I'll see you in a few."

Flooded waited a minute to see if the owner of the Town Car came out. The door never opened. So he started the car and backed down the street, turned and went around the block, and pulled up in front of Westlake's house as if he was just arriving. Westlake came to the door immediately and let him in. The foyer was marble-tiled and a bit grandiose, Flood thought, though it was probably typical for the neighborhood.

Westlake looked so exhausted and anxious that Flood wanted to offer him a drink. They went into the kitchen, which was messy with used dishes, empty frozen dinner boxes and a floor badly in need of sweeping. Westlake did not offer him a seat or a drink.

Flood was thinking about the Town Car in the driveway. He scanned the kitchen. There was a small glass breakfast table under a hanging light in a bay window nook that looked out on the back yard. There were two rings of moisture on the table. A glass on the counter between a stack of junk mail and some dishes looked like a weak whisky and water. Flood figured the other drink was in the hands of the Town Car owner, somewhere in the house.

"I'm sorry," Flood said. "Do you have company?"

"No," Westlake said with a start. "What happened today?"

Flood was again getting the impression of being told to mind his own business. So he eased on with the business at hand.

"First, the house wasn't empty," he said, trying to show good humor. "There was a girl inside when I got there. She thinks I work for the landlord."

Westlake shrugged; not interested in the unexpected difficulties of the assignment.

"I have some phone numbers to run down."

"Can I see them?" Westlake asked, looking suddenly engaged.

Flood pulled out his notepad and flipped it open, quickly moving back a page from the Town Car license plate.

"There were a lot from your wife's cell phone. A few from your phone. Most were local calls down there. But these two stood out, partly because they both appear just once. One's a residential number in Northbrook. The other is a motel off I-88."

"A motel?" Westlake looked a little perplexed and embarrassed, like he hadn't expected it to unfold this way just yet.

Flood nodded. "It could be anybody. One of his friends."

"What about the one in Northbrook?"

"I don't know. It's registered to a Paul and Mary Ellen Jensen. Ring a bell?"

"Jensen. I think that's Brandon's girlfriend. She's from up there somewhere. Northbrook or Northfield. Deerfield. I don't know."

Flood wanted to change the subject. Westlake knew damn well that the motel number was the lead. It was very likely his wife was meeting somebody there. But he didn't want to talk about that, and that was fine with Flood. The less he had to talk about with Westlake, the better. He had come here for more on the marriage. The more he gathered, the less he liked being on Westlake's side.

"Also," Flood said. "Do you have any photo albums or scrapbooks with pictures that your wife may have put together of your family?"

Westlake's reddish eyebrows arched. His eyes were such a washed-out blue that it almost pained Flood to look at them. They were tired and confused eyes and there was something pitiable about them.

"Why? I gave you those photos on the sheet. You know what she looks like."

"I know," Flood said, feigning embarrassment. "I was never a real profiler, but I know the basics. The more images I see of her, in different situations, the more I'll understand about her. Things so common that it might not occur to you to tell me about them. But they might tell me something about how she behaves and what she might do next."

It barely made sense, and Westlake looked confused. Flood himself knew he was fishing, looking for any overlooked detail that might lead him in the right direction, either to the man she was seeing, or to the peril that put her in the hands of a killer.

Westlake grimaced. He was put out by the whole thing, but he told Flood to wait there and he left the room and was gone several minutes. Flood took the opportunity to drift over to the little kitchen secretary desk in an alcove left of the refrigerator, with a phone on the wall next to a cluttered cork bulletin board. As he scanned the desk, he spotted several scraps of notes in a woman's handwriting. Lots of phone numbers and dates and times scribbled in black ballpoint. He sighed. Any one of these scraps could give up her whereabouts. A good investigator would run through all of it, but he wanted nothing to do with them. Nonetheless, when Westlake came back toting a vinyl bound album, Flood asked.

"Can I take some of these notes? They look like her writing. I should run them down."

Exasperated, Westlake sloughed over to the desk and began pointing at the notes pinned and scattered about.

"Dry cleaners, gynecologist—let's see—Pam's number, a different dry cleaner. The Lexus dealer—service department." He kept jabbing a finger at each one dismissively. "I know what all this shit is. Waste of your time."

He walked back to the granite-topped island in the middle of the kitchen and picked up the album.

"Here. She made this. It's pictures," Westlake said, like he was being forced to participate against his will in a hokey game of charades at a dinner party he didn't want to go to in the first place. "Listen, I'm going to have to get going. OK?"

Flood took the album and tucked it under his arm. Westlake was behaving very strangely, as though this search for his wife had been an imposition rather than the result of his own insistence.

"Sure. Absolutely. I'm sorry to drop in like this, but—you know—I'm trying to find her quickly."

"Right, of course," Westlake said, ushering him back toward the door. "I really appreciate it. Let me know on Monday what you find out."

In an instant Flood was over the threshold, and the heavy front door was closed behind him. Any nascent thoughts he had about coming clean and telling Westlake everything he knew were moot. The cold air felt clean after the staleness of Westlake's house. Flood went back to his car and drove off, but he circled the block, killed the lights, and returned to the spot where he'd been watching before. He parked and slouched down behind the wheel. He wanted to see who was in that Town Car.

After about ten minutes the door opened. A man taller, older and looking in much better health than Westlake strode out, with his host trailing behind. The man had gray hair that was longish for someone who looked about seventy. He dressed like a younger man as well, in black pants and shiny black shoes with floater soles and a black leather jacket that was tailored like a long blazer that draped almost to his knees. It looked like it wasn't enough coat for the weather, but he did not appear to shiver in the slightest or hug himself against the cold as he walked toward the Lincoln. He was talking and looked impatient, but Flood couldn't make any of it out. The old man pointed a finger back at Westlake, who stood there with a puppy-dog look on his face. Westlake put his hands up defensively for a moment. The man in the jacket was ten feet away and waved dismissively at Westlake, and then turned and got in his car.

When he was gone, Westlake stood in the driveway looking up and down the street, as if he expected someone to be watching. Flood sat very still. Finally, Westlake turned his back and went inside. Flood waited a while longer, willing to follow Westlake if he did come back out. He waited twenty minutes and looked at his watch. It was five to nine. He thought about the night shift at the Inn-n-Suites. He should probably get going.

As he was putting his car in gear, the garage door of Westlake's house began to open, revealing a red Lincoln Navigator shifting into reverse.

Chapter Seven

Flood followed Westlake's hulking SUV back out onto the Stevenson, heading southwest until they took the Tri-State north, a path from the industrial corridor of the southwest suburbs into moneyed DuPage County. Keeping a distance of about five car lengths, Flood tried to stay in a different lane. He didn't expect Westlake to be an expert spotting tails, but he might as well be cautious. Traffic was light, and he didn't have much trouble. Westlake signaled after a couple of miles and began to drift across traffic toward the Ogden Avenue exit. Hinsdale.

Flood had a feeling. Glancing at his watch, he saw it was almost nine-thirty. They cruised west on Ogden, and then Flood's anticipation grew stronger as Westlake signaled for a left turn, the turn that led to Pam Sawyer's condominium development.

Now that they were on side streets, Flood worried more about being seen. He slowed down and turned a block before Pam Sawyer's townhouse. He went around the block driving fast, and when he came around at her place from the south Westlake was in the snow, using his remote to lock the doors of his SUV as he trudged toward her door. Flood drove slowly past and pulled over. The street was nearly deserted. Parked across the street and up the block about a hundred feet was a white pickup with a business name on the door and a dark-colored Cadillac parked behind it. Flood adjusted his side mirror to watch Westlake arrive at the door, but it was very dim. He turned around in his seat and watched. His car purred in idle and the window radiated coldness as he faced the glass. Before Westlake even made it to the door, he could see it open. There wasn't much to recognize beyond a flicker of blonde hair.

Flood fumed and cursed out loud. Westlake was screwing Pam Sawyer now? Flood felt he was the idiot whose professional services were being cuckolded, so to speak, by this philandering ass of a businessman who was direly searching for his wife on Friday and fondling her best friend on Saturday. He picked up his phone and contemplated what profane message he would scream at his boss, Alan H. Cronin. And then he thought of Jane Doe, again, and took a deep breath. He tossed the phone onto the passenger seat and pounded the dashboard with his fist.

He idled down the street and went around the block. Flood's car was a Ford Taurus, and he had bought it partly because it was hard to find anything so common, ordinary and serviceable. It was as nondescript as an automobile could be, out of place nowhere. That was the instinct of an investigator, but now he was a private attorney. He could have bought something slick, like an Audi or a Land Rover, but cars like that did not appeal to him. He preferred not to stick out on the road. He drifted slowly around the block and came up the street from the south again. This time he pulled over before he passed Pam Sawyer's front door. It was ten o'clock. He sat and waited, watching the house. It seemed every lamp in the place was on. Light beamed from every window. If they were having an affair, they were doing it with the lights on, and Flood bet Westlake wouldn't go for that.

So, as Flood's rage subsided slightly, he began to ponder why the hell Westlake was here if he wasn't going to bed with her. Why did Westlake need to see Pam Sawyer in person at ten o'clock on a Saturday night? And what did the old man in the Town Car, dressing down Westlake, have to do with it?

At ten-thirty the front door opened and out came Westlake, walking briskly down the driveway, through the heap of plowed snow at the curb and back into his Navigator. He started it up and didn't wait for it to warm before plunking into reverse and backing into Pam Sawyer's driveway to turn around and head back the way he came.

Flood wondered where he'd go next and gave Westlake a block head start before easing off the curb himself and turning his headlights back on. They retraced their path, it turned out. Westlake peeled down Ogden to the Tri-State and headed south. Flood figured he was headed home, but he was beginning to feel that thoroughness would be essential to keep him out of trouble. He wanted to know exactly what Westlake was up to.

It was after eleven-thirty when Flood finally decided he had Westlake tucked in for the night. The lights were out, except for the blue glow of the television in an upstairs bedroom. Flood headed back out onto the expressways, which still hummed with high-speed traffic. At this hour, there were no jams, but there was still a city's worth of people flying through the night in carousels of red taillights. It took him a half hour and ninety cents in tolls to travel the twenty miles out to the western edge of DuPage County to the sprawling expressway-side office park anchored by the Inn-n-Suites, a compact, tidy two-story motel with no restaurant or bar, just a small, spare lobby.

Flood had been thinking about what sort of ruse to attempt in order to get information and decided on posing as Brandon's obsessive, annoyed dad, irate about the phone bill he was paying, and armed with a confusing but convincing tale of suburban peril. Coming straight out and saying who he was, even if he offered to pay something, would likely get him nowhere, he decided.

The motel parking lot was about half full. Flood sat in the car for a minute to scope out what was going on inside. The night manager was the only soul in sight. He was a middle-aged man wearing a white dress shirt with pink stripes and a navy sweater vest with the motel logo stitched on the chest. He was thin in a way that suggested cigarettes and a nervous stomach. His bronze hair, clipped short except for a curt wave of forelock, was bristly, and may or may not have been real. A bracelet of gold links hung from his wrist.

As he opened the lobby door and made first eye contact with the night manager, Flood put on a face of exasperation turning to hope—that this man's man behind the counter might be his port in a storm.

"Hey, I'm hoping you can help me with something," Flood began, putting out his hand to shake with the manager over the counter. "My name's Augie Flood, and I'm trying to get to the bottom of my kid's cell phone bill."

The manager arched his back and nodded in a way that said he didn't get it.

"This is probably your oddest request of the night, especially at this hour."

The man nodded hesitantly, and said, "I'll certainly try to be of help, sir."

"I need to know who called him from this motel," Flood said, making his last-second improvisation. "The boy's in college, and some of his roommates got in a bit of a pickle with the local yokels in Champaign over a party they had and a car accident one of their friends got in that night, and I'm trying to make sure my boy's telling the truth."

"Hmmm," said the manager. "Not sure how I can help."

"Well, the kid told me his story and I'm just trying to check out every detail," Flood said, his speech becoming more folksy and good-ole'-boyish with every syllable. "I'm trying to make sure my ass is covered. That's what I'm really doing, if you want to know the truth."

"And you want to know if somebody called him from here?"

Flood laid the phone bill on the counter.

"Who," he said pointing to the motel's phone number. "I know *somebody* called. See, right here. This is the night of this damn party they had. January 7. Now, I'd like to know who called him just to make sure it's not anybody who was mixed up in this wreck. It was some kids from Minnesota who were driving down to Champaign for the party. The boy's at U of I. Can you believe these kids: Minneapolis to Champaign for one night of drinking?"

The manager shook his head, chuckled in agreed amazement and leaned over the counter. He recognized the phone number where Flood's index finger pointed and nodded.

"You said your name was Flood?" he asked, crinkling his freckled brow. "The bill's for a Westlake."

Flood gave a pained look.

"Tell me about it. Kid takes his mother's maiden name after the divorce, but it's still OK for the old man to pay all the bills."

The manager started to shake his head in an exaggerated wag.

"Say no more. Been there, done that," he said, chuckling. "Now, let me understand, you want to know who made that call from here?"

Flood nodded. "Is that even possible to do?"

The manager straightened again.

"Oh, hell yeah," he said defiantly, and then leaned forward with a conspiratorial dip of his chin, and said out of the corner of his mouth. " 'Tween you and me and the wall."

Flooded nodded. "It never happened."

The manager nodded and went stone-faced serious. As Flood sized him up at first sight, he had banked on the manager being the sort of man who did not like to say he didn't have the authority to do something. He was old enough, and in his own way, macho-looking enough, that Flood guessed—correctly, it turned out—that the night manager would be reluctant to admit he'd have to wait for some suck-up day manager to say it was OK for him to pull the name of a guest out of a file sitting right in front of him.

"I just got to take a minute to remember how to pull that up. What number was called?"

Flood handed him the bill and pointed to Brandon's phone number at the top. The manager took the bill into the little office behind the counter and sat down out of Flood's sight. He heard tapping on a keyboard, and the manager humming and talking to himself.

"Goddamn computers. Hmm hmm hmm. OK. Hmm. January 7. Hmm. Time, let's see, 19:22. Hmm. Aha, yes. Here. Room 215."

"Sounds like you've got it," Flood said from the front desk.

"Getting there. Got the room, now I've got to switch to another one of these files. Hmm. Here. Huh. I'll be . . ."

He sounded surprised, but when he came back with a slip of scrap paper he'd written on with a pencil, his face was inscrutable.

"Like I said," he whispered.

"Didn't get it here," Flood whispered back, completing the sentence.

The slip of paper slid across the counter.

In pencil scrawl: *Vincent Tortufi.*

Flood looked at the name. It seemed Marcy Westlake's world of intrigue and peril was opening up before him. It meant nothing concrete, but the possibilities of the name seemed endless.

Vincent Tortufi. Vincent. Vinny. Vince. Mr. Tortufi. Who was he and what had he done to her?

The manager leaned across the desk.

"Between you and me again," he said. The man had a mishmash accent, part Chicago ethnic white man, but also something rural. More farm-town downstate Illinois than southern. Maybe Iowa or Kansas. He wasn't originally from Chicago, and Flood imagined a steady string of failures that had brought him to the overnight shift at the Inn-n-Suites.

Flood quickly looked up from the name to study the manager's face.

"I don't think this guy's a college boy from Minneapolis," the manager said. "This guy's a regular here. He and a lady friend, if you know what I mean."

"Huh," Flood said, acting the befuddled father. "Well, my lawyer will be happy."

"Your boy know Mr. Tortufi?" the night manager persisted. He seemed as interested as Flood now that he had placed Tortufi.

"I can't imagine," Flood said. "I've never heard of him."

"This guy's about fifty, I'd say."

"What about the woman? Who's she?"

"I don't know her, but I wouldn't mind, my friend, if you know what I mean," the manager said. "A very well preserved forty-something. I mean *very* well preserved. I mean. She. Is. A. *Very.* Fine. Looking. Woman. They're pretty regular, but I ain't seen 'em in a couple a weeks."

"Hmm."

"Is that your ex, maybe?"

Flood grimaced; having fun now. "No," he said, drawing it out. "Last couple of years my ex's turned into a real pig. Can't be her."

The night manager grinned, as if he preferred to keep the

realm of possible identities open and undefined for Vincent Tortufi's mystery mistress.

Flood started to reach into his pocket.

"I'd like to give you something for the trouble," he started.

"Well, that's not really necessary," the manager said slowly, unsure of how to respond. Flood slid two twenties across the counter, and they shook hands.

The adrenalin was throbbing in Flood's chest as he left the building and climbed back into his car. It was a mix of feelings—the sudden triumph of pulling off a con, and the relief of all the fear of failure being released into the night, and dread. He dreaded where this piece of information would lead him. Who was Vincent Tortufi, and what had he done? The night manager said he had not seen Tortufi and his mistress in a while. Had he taken Marcy Westlake to some other location? Had the sex turned kinkier, stranger, more daring, and had something gone wrong? Had Marcy Westlake protested, or had Vincent Tortufi been toying with her all along? Had he bound her and tortured her? Had he placed a rope around her neck and killed her? Had Vincent Tortufi done these things, or had someone else?

As Flood put the car in reverse and backed out of the parking spot, he looked up and saw that the night manager was watching him closely as he left.

It was midnight by the time Flood was back on the highway and felt sure enough of his whereabouts to make a phone call. He called Reece's desk at the Tribune. It was absurd at that hour but he had a feeling.

First ring: "Reece."

"Jesus, Keith. It's midnight on a Saturday. You have a serious problem."

"I'm working on something."

"You're always working on something," Flood said. "You

need a woman."

"I had one of those once," Reece said. "And are you settling in with the wife and kids at this hour? What do you need, doctor, I'm busy."

"Can you run somebody through Nexis for me?"

"Gimme a sec."

Flood could hear him sigh softly as he twisted in his chair and started clicking his mouse.

"Name," he said.

"Vincent, and spelling the last name: T-o-r-t-u-f-i. No middle initial or town. But Illinois."

Flood could hear more clicking and tapping.

"Looks like two of them," Reece said. "One in Oak Brook, wouldn't you know. And one on Lake Shore Drive."

Both because he was a journalist and in spite of it, Reece indulged the occasional prejudicial thought when certain variables were put together. In this case Flood's interest in Tortufi, plus the Italian surname, plus a suburban Oak Brook address, equaled possible mobster.

Lots of mobsters did live in Oak Brook, or at least they had, and Flood thought the same thing, but as a former cop—not to mention a reluctant investigator who was not sure he wanted this missing person to be any more complicated than necessary—he looked for something more concrete, less made of conjecture. But he also doubted that his Vincent was the one with the LSD address.

"Wait a second," Reece said. "Looks like they're one guy. The LSD address pops up under the Oak Brook entry and vice versa."

"Hmm," Flood said, making Reece chuckle.

In his most exaggerated, vinegary Chicago accent, Reece said, "My friend, I'm guessing your mystery man is an Oak Brook wise guy with a Gold Coast pied-a-terre for banging broads." *Pee-ed-AY-terray fer byeean-g-ing brahtz.*

"Why's he need a motel in Naperville or wherever the hell I just came from?" Flood said. "Hey, run him nationwide. Maybe my guy's a traveling salesman from Columbus."

Reece deleted the "IL" from the field and ran the name again.

"Two more. Westwood, Mass. And Jersey City," Reece mumbled as he clicked open the entries on the screen. "Doesn't look like it. The Boston guy's DOB is 1982, and the Jersey City guy . . . 1926. Lover boy would have to be either a kid or almost eighty."

"Damn. How old is the Oak Brook guy?"

"Born in '53. That sound right?"

"I'm afraid so."

"Want me to have the morgue Autotrack him? I can fax it to your apartment."

"That'd be great. I'll owe you."

"That's the way it works, old friend," Reece said.

Flood nearly forgot the old man in the Town Car.

"Hey, don't hang up. You there?"

"I'm here."

"Run this plate for me."

There was a moment's delay of the computer working its magic. And then another moment's delay of Reece's confusion.

"Flood," he said, sounding like his suspicion was aroused. "What the hell does George Kajmar have to do with your missing wife?"

"Is that who it is?" he said, trying to mentally reconnect the dots. Kajmar was the ex–Tollway Authority honcho and hotdog mogul, who had a lien on Westlake's holdings. He was the tall gray-haired man hiding in the den while Flood waited in the kitchen of Westlake's house?

"He's involved with this guy Westlake, who I'm working for. What do you know about Kajmar?"

"Know about him? Jesus, Flood, what are you in the middle of? Kajmar was a casino bidder. He lost out to Bepps."

Flood reflexively took his foot off the gas, letting the car drift off the seventy mile an hour mark.

Reece again: "Why are you running his plate? Where was his car?"

"In Westlake's driveway tonight. I was there, and Westlake kept him away from me, but I stuck around afterward, sitting down the block, and saw this old man come out and get in the car."

"Well, your guy Westlake is involved in the casino business, then. Did you know that?"

"No," Flood said, dumbly. He felt stupid but it all sort of made more sense, suddenly. His boss, Cronin, caring enough about Westlake to get involved in this ridiculous search for Mrs. Westlake never really added up. But if Cronin believed he had a shot at doing some of the legal work for the proposed casino, he would gladly have ordered Flood to ride across China on a skateboard to secure his place at the table.

"Well, he is," Reece went on. "I guarantee you that anybody having a disagreement with George Kajmar right now is disagreeing with him over some angle of the casino. That's all he's got on his mind. With the Bepps indictments, they're starting from square one, and Kajmar's back in the thick of things."

The newspapers had not named Kajmar as a casino bidder because he wasn't the front man on the bid. He was always one of the investors in the "group of investors" led by someone else, Reece said. But since the scandal broke, Reece said he'd been digging more carefully into the also-rans, and he'd figured out that Kajmar was really the first among equals in another group of investors.

Now Daniel Westlake's quest for the nest egg in the Cayman account seemed a little more understandable. Perhaps he was investing in the partnership bid and needed to remain a solvent businessman in order to keep the bid untainted. If Kajmar were successful, Flood's bosses, the firm of Cronin, Drew and Guzman, would have a professional connection to the most lucrative casino in the Midwest.

"Why didn't Cronin tell you this guy Westlake was wrapped up in the casino stuff?" Reece asked.

Flood was angry.

"That's an excellent question."

He happened to be skirting along the edge of Oak Brook on the expressway when he hung up. He gave a quick thought to finding Vincent Tortufi's house, but he was tired, and there wasn't much point. He'd learn a little more from Reece's database search, which would collect addresses connected to Tortufi, automobile registrations, possible relatives, dozens of neighbors and possible phone numbers.

What would he do with them? All that information about a man he did not know. He had let himself be hired by one man he did not know—hired to stalk, basically, a woman whom he did not know. And now that endeavor had led him to another man he did not know. And all the while there was a body on a slab in the morgue that looked a lot like Marcy Westlake.

Flood began to perspire again, just as he had when Pialetti had told him what he knew. The moisture on his brow turned cold immediately and sent a chill through this body. He felt not only that he was descending deeper into the problems of a man telling lies, but also that his own bosses weren't telling him the truth, and everybody was playing with matches because the Outfit was involved. He felt like he had spent too much energy working up his disdain for this job and the people who ordered it, and he should have been paying closer attention to the warning signs that something was deeply, darkly amiss.

Chapter Eight

Flood was still stewing when he got back to his apartment. He poured a large whisky and dropped a couple of ice cubes into the glass, and then stood at his windows looking out on the glittering nightscape along the river. Ice clinking against glass was the only sound in the room. Flood tried to put a few pieces together. He was tired, but he had a few more minutes of concentration left. He had to learn what sort of man Vincent Tortufi was. Was there anything in his past that suggested he might be capable of a horrible crime? That idea immediately became trapped in the logical assumption that Tortufi was the man involved with Pam Sawyer, as well. If he killed Marcy Westlake in the middle of a sexual encounter that got out of hand, he must know that Pam Sawyer, not to mention Brandon Westlake, would quickly lead police to him. It didn't make sense.

And how would Westlake respond to this? Flood now understood that his poor behavior was probably the byproduct of extreme preoccupation with the biggest opportunity, and the biggest risk, of his life. Everything he had likely was riding on the coattails of George Kajmar's casino bid.

He went back over the likely scenario of Westlake's scheme. Westlake was in debt, partly to George Kajmar. He was desperate to lay hands on the $350,000 he said he had stashed in the account in Marcy Westlake's name. With the Outfit's West Bank venture in an FBI-induced sling, Kajmar now had pole position in the new process for the casino license. Kajmar and Westlake quarreled tonight. Westlake went off for a late-night visit to his estranged wife's best friend.

Flood gave up on Westlake again. It was bizarre and shocking to learn that his client might be involved, or at least be angling for involvement, in the casino business. But he really didn't care at the moment. All he could think about was Vincent Tortufi and what Tortufi could tell him about the last two weeks of Marcy Westlake's life.

He went into his study and pulled the search results Reece had sent him off the fax tray. There were about twenty pages, ordered oddly by the priorities of a database. The documents started off with the most likely address for the subject, in this case the address in Oak Brook. Then it seemed to jump into information about other people—names with similar Social Security numbers, people who used to live at that address in Oak Brook, neighbors. Then it looped back into Tortufi himself, other places he'd lived in the past, his cars—a Cadillac Escalade, a Lexus and an '86 Camaro.

It listed his spouse as Cara Tortufi, then listed a Cara Durdala, and a scroll of information about other people named Durdala. Her maiden name. In the last few pages, there were more addresses after a section on the Lake Shore Drive place, but it wasn't clear whether they were Tortufi's or they belonged to someone who had once crossed his path. There was an address in Fontana, Wisconsin, and a second in Las Vegas.

The numbers and names, and parts of Social Security numbers X'd out, made his head ache. Flood had one last sip of whisky in his glass, but he felt his eyes getting heavy. He put the boring papers down and picked up the photo album Westlake had given him that night. Its first pages held baby pictures of their son. Earlier photos of them as a young couple had either been replaced or had never been included, Flood gathered. The album followed the general course of the son's growth. Baptism and First Communion, Little League games, vacation photos that looked like Wisconsin. There were a handful of photos of the three of them in snorkeling gear on a boat that could have been in the Caymans. There were very few photos of Marcy and Dan Westlake as a couple without their son. Most of what pictures did exist without the boy appeared to be at social functions—weddings, retirement parties, it was hard to tell. To Flood's eyes, neither of them looked particularly happy in the photos. Westlake looked like he was trying to affect a tough pose in most of them, and Marcy just looked like she was thinking about being someplace else.

He flipped through the plastic-covered cardboard pages until he found the most recent picture of her, in a snug black cocktail dress with a scoop neck; taken at some event that looked like a fundraiser, with Westlake standing next to her in a double-breasted suit with padded shoulders that made him look like a refrigerator. He removed the photo, slid it into his file folder, and then set the album down. He wasn't careful and put it down on the edge of the desk. It immediately flipped and fell to the floor. As he leaned over to pick it up, he saw something sticking out from the bottom of a page. It was a photograph that had been stuck up between two pages, as if hidden.

Flood tugged at it gently and it slid all the way out. It was a photo of Marcy Westlake in a negligee, clearly taken in a studio. It looked like the sort of photo women have taken as anniversary presents for their husbands, or as desperate attempts to spice up their marriages. She was reclining on her side, wearing a see-through black strapless camisole. The definition of her breasts was clear, the delicate circles of her nipples and the dimple of her navel were all visible through the sheer fabric. Her left arm draped over her hip and her long bare legs stretched out in a gentle, inviting bend, one delicate foot draped over the other. Flood studied her face for a clue about why in the world this photo was taken. Was it what it seemed, the gift to her husband with a somewhat desperate hope of rekindling the romance of their marriage? Or was it something else—something that contained a clue to where Marcy Westlake had ended up? Flood had more questions. Why was it hidden between the pages of the photo album? And why was it in the photo album at all?

Eventually the question faded, but his interest in the seductive image of Marcy Westlake did not subside. He looked at it for a long time, and then he leaned his head back, just for a second. He closed his eyes, just for a second. He felt himself begin to float away. He felt the six hours behind the wheel, and the anxiety of fearing a hung-over college kid might open the door, and the stakeout and his deception of the sad, proud motel night manager, the image of a big house in a gated community where Marcy Westlake's lover lived, and the supple flesh of Marcy Westlake's body, open to suggestion, and ultimately vulnerable to something terrible, all began to scatter behind him, leaving only dark road ahead.

Flood slept hard until ten Sunday morning when the phone rang. Jamie was calling.

"Wanna go to brunch?"

"With you?" he said, still a mess of grouchy, half sleeping, fully relaxed synapses.

"No," Jamie sneered, "with your girlfriend. Oh, wait. You don't have one. You might have a date if you bothered to call Jenny, but you haven't shown the balls for that yet. So you can just eat brunch with us homos."

"How many gay guys, other than you?"

"Three. That's five total counting you—an odd number, if you didn't get it—so it won't be a weird thing where it's like couples and you're some man's lover."

"What time is it?"

"It's ten. Meet us at eleven at Wishbone."

"Which one?"

"West Side! By Oprah."

"Hmmm."

Jamie had already hung up. Flood tried to go back to sleep, but the harsh white winter sun was high and bright coming in through his bedroom windows. He rolled out of bed and stumbled to the shower. Afterward, he wiped the foggy mirror to shave and then put on the jeans and sweater he'd worn the day before, along with an old pair of running shoes and his black watchcap and jacket. He made sure there was cash in his wallet and rode the elevator down and caught a cab on Wabash at Hubbard.

Wishbone, the original, was a hipster version of a Southern-cooking restaurant just west of the Loop, a couple of blocks from the complex of green buildings where Oprah Winfrey's television production company was headquartered. Oprah's headquarters were Jamie's landmark for the entire Near West Side of Chicago. Everything of interest to him—the row of chic restaurants on Randolph Street, Greektown, the big Helix photography store, the UIC campus—were all, more or less, *over by Oprah* to him. It was funny to Flood, because Jamie always said *West Side,* with a little hip-hop inflection. While the neighborhood he was talking about was, indeed, west of the Loop, it was still the domain of middle-class white people. The true West Side really began beyond Ashland Avenue, with the ruins of the Henry Horner Homes as a gateway. The real West Side was a place where Southern cooking meant blocking off the street and making a charcoal fire in one end of an old 55-gallon drum to cook chicken wings and rib tips. And the West Side to Flood, and anybody who knew the city like a cop, meant the shooting-gallery high-rises of Rockwell Gardens, East and West Garfield Park (the murder capital of Chicago), Lawndale, the birthplace of the Vice Lords street gang, and Austin, one big open-air drug market where people from the suburbs furtively jumped off the Eisenhower Expressway and rolled their SUVs and minivans down the side streets with the neighborhood junkies to buy crack and heroin in little plastic and foil packets. The West Side had caught the overflow from the South Side of the black migration from the Mississippi Delta. And because it developed later, and more quickly, none of the great black social institutions—like the South Side's Bronzeville business district—had developed there. It was desperately poor, overcrowded and violent from the beginning. Flood was pretty sure Jamie had never been to the real West Side.

Flood was early and put his name in for the group, and then went to the bar and had his first cup of coffee. The smell of cornbread and fried potatoes spiced with paprika and cayenne filled the air. It smelled good, but Flood was a fastidious breakfast eater who rarely touched anything but coffee, orange juice and bread before noon. His bacon and eggs the morning before were an aberration. At the moment, bitter black coffee with real cream was all he needed to feel whole. He sat facing the front door and thought about Daniel Westlake.

Westlake's premise, that the need to track down his wife was the result of a misunderstanding, was unraveling. She had become entangled in an affair with a married man, who already had been having an affair with her best friend, and that path of secrecy, deceit and sex looked like it had led her down some even more dangerous way. Maybe Westlake did not know all the details, and maybe he did not know his wife put herself in a position to be raped and murdered, but he could not possibly have believed she just wanted some time alone somewhere.

Beyond all of that, Westlake and Pam Sawyer had both misrepresented their relationship with each other. Clearly, Flood was not getting the whole picture. And now Westlake's real motive would seem to be the chance at a piece of the downtown casino, rather than just keeping his plumbing and sewer contracting business afloat.

He wondered about Brandon Westlake. If the emails meant what Flood thought they meant, then Brandon had been through a very strange few months himself. He'd gotten tangled up in whatever strange behavior his mother was involved in, and then fell in deeper when Pam Sawyer came knocking on his bedroom door. If the kid did not like his father, as Westlake had implied, he might be a decent soul. In any event, he sure as hell was getting screwed in this family circus. Flood wished he could talk to him about this awful mess. What would he really say about his mother if Flood asked, and not as Westlake's lawyer? Flood had a hunch that Brandon might eventually provide more accurate clues to what had happened to his mother than her husband ever would.

It was fifteen minutes until Jamie and his friends were supposed to show up, and they were usually late. He flipped open his telephone and called Westlake's house. He would gauge the reaction to Vincent Tortufi's name. It rang over to the voicemail. Flood told him to call. Then he called Westlake's cell phone. Voicemail picked up there, too. He closed the phone and let the pretty bartender pour him another cup of coffee.

Jamie and his entourage breezed in at ten after, but they still waited another twenty minutes for the table. Flood knew them all fairly well and, for the most part, they treated him like the understanding, straight big brother they wished they had. They stood around him drinking mimosas and bloody marys while he sipped more coffee, and Jamie said ridiculous things about how Flood was onto a huge case that was going to alter the way society viewed the institution of marriage, and the sewer contracting business, forever.

One of them was George, a short, muscular redheaded Irishman from a prosperous Catholic family of Connecticut Republicans. Sainted mother, distant Wall Street father—the whole bit. Flood would have guessed anyway, but Jamie confirmed, George was pretty much still in the closet at his investment banking firm and with his family. The secret must be wearing thin; George was thirty, good looking, successful—Colgate and Wharton, and now his business card said *principal.* He was gregarious but never took a woman anywhere. Still, he used none of the gay affectations that the others had picked up and made their own. He would have seemed straight to anybody who met him on the street, except for the company he kept. It gave him a nervous, slightly sad, edge. And he, more than the others, was drawn to Flood. Flood was his conduit between his secret gay reality and some remembrance of feeling a part of the heterosexual mainstream, or of just not feeling different. It was a dynamic that manifested itself awkwardly, with George seizing on Flood's erstwhile football days at BC, insisting on talking Big East sports. It was a vestige of the preppy, Catholic world he had grown up in. Jamie said George was surely in love with Flood. That didn't bother Flood in the slightest, but he hated talking about sports.

"What's Jamie talking about, Augie?" George said, in his best locker room tone.

"As usual, Jamie only knows a third of the story, and it's the third you'd leave out if you were pressed for time in telling it." Flood suddenly found that he was willing to talk, at least about part of it. He set it up like they were playing a game.

"Tell me this," he began. "Why does a middle-aged man who's been dumped by his hot wife, who is out of his league, apparently, go see the wife's best friend—a divorcee of some affluence—at ten o'clock on a Saturday night? He stays one half hour, the lights are on, and she has previously suggested to me that she's got little use for him."

"He's boffing her anyway," said Peter, who had started the mimosa ordering.

Several dismissals whistled out of the group.

"He's threatening her because she helped the wife do something, screwing him over," said Jamie.

Flood shrugged.

"He's begging her for help," said George.

"Why do you say that?" Flood asked.

"It's late, and he's not screwing her," George said. "He's spent the whole night thinking of other solutions, and he's hit bottom. He's out of his wits and out of options."

Admiring silence from the table. George was proud of that one, and Flood thought it sounded pretty good.

"What does he need?" asked Alan, who was older than the others, and fat and rich and very sad most of the time. Flood thought he must be getting tired of hanging out with carefree men in their late twenties. But he had nobody serious in his life.

"Money," Flood said, answering Alan's question. "He's broke, and the wife has access to a pile of money that he needs."

George nodded some more. "He's begging the divorcee for help getting to the wife and the money."

Flood thought about that from a few different angles. Not only was everybody involved in the case pretty much lying to him if George was right, but it would mean that Westlake and Pam Sawyer had no clue what had happened to Marcy Westlake. They thought she was OK somewhere. Not that he had thought much of the potential for either one of them to have sexually assaulted, bound and strangled her, but if George's theory was correct, they'd both be in the clear for her murder.

They were sitting at a round table now and Flood couldn't drink any more coffee. Everybody else ordered huge omelets with ham steaks and grits and eight or nine other fried things. Flood had a glass of orange juice and an order of cornbread.

"You're not eating?" George asked.

"I won't starve."

"Watching his hunk figure," Jamie said. "I'm setting him up with Jenny, and he's been sporting wood ever since he laid eyes on her."

Howls of laughter.

"She's such a little hottie," said Peter. "What's the story, Flood? What kind of rap have you got with her?"

"Lovely woman," Flood said. "Jamie's making all the arrangements. I think he's rented a church and a room at The Drake. In June, I guess. You're all invited, of course. You're all groomsmen except for Jamie. He'll be the maid of honor."

More howls.

"You haven't even called her yet, I happen to know," Jamie said. "You think she's just sitting around with nothing to do? Guys are all over her."

"If you were straight . . ." Flood offered.

"If I was straight, I'd be all over that shit," Jamie said.

Flood's prospects with Jenny aside, it raised an interesting point about Jamie. He loved her more than as a friend. He was, in his own way, in love with her. But he was as gay as a room full of roses and sunshine, and he didn't know what to do with this overwhelming affection for a woman, especially a young, beautiful woman. His answer, oddly, seemed to be to steer her toward Flood.

A disaster in the making, for sure, and when Jamie first proposed a meeting, Flood had quickly consented, believing that a stance of passivity followed up with indifference and inaction would take care of things. He had even planned to dominate the conversation Friday night talking about football and guns, if necessary. But Jamie was right about Jenny. Flood had been, avoiding the vulgar description his friend had given, at least thinking about her since they met Friday night. He was able to avoid the issue because of the immediacy of his work. But given everything that was going on, it was remarkable he was thinking of her at all. Passive indifference was not really what he felt for the dark-haired museum curator. Still, it was perplexing.

George had gone off to the bathroom, and the others delved into conversation on some topic Flood couldn't really grasp, so just he and Jamie were talking.

"So why do you think she needs your help finding a man?" Flood asked him. "She's gorgeous."

"She doesn't need my help. But listen, I've talked you up big-time."

"Why?"

Jamie was uncomfortable with the question. Why did it even need to be asked? Didn't a man want to be with a woman? Weren't they both alone? And weren't they compatible? Jenny: artistic, talented, funny and beautiful. Flood: sensitive and literate, athletic and—what—honest?

It was so central to Jamie's frame of mind, apparently, that he was having trouble sharing the thought.

"I love her," he said, awkwardly.

"Meaning what?"

"Meaning just that. I'm gay, so I don't want to be with her—like that—but I love her more than anyone I know. She's always been there for me."

"That almost sounds like a challenge to your gayness."

"It's not, really. But I don't really understand it."

"So?" Flood asked, demanding a more exact account of what Jamie's platonic devotion to Jenny had to do with him.

"So, you are an honest man."

"You mean you trust me with your girl?"

Flood was trying to be a little funny, but Jamie wouldn't have it. He didn't answer. No more banter.

"I don't know, Jamie. I wouldn't put much stock in my romantic commitments."

Jamie could talk like this.

"You don't deceive people."

Flood thought about this. He really wanted to dismiss it with a joke but, at this point, Jamie would be offended.

"I stay un-entangled. You know me. I don't get close enough to care enough about how the upshot of the truth will change things. It's easier to be honest when you're not really involved."

Jamie raised his eyebrows. Drawing out all the words, he said, "That's. Utter. Bullshit."

Flood shrugged. He had never said anything like that before. Jamie was really shocked, and he now looked like he had gotten something honest out of Flood in a way that did seem to matter. Flood couldn't run away from that admission now that he had said it.

"She deserves a man she can count on," Jamie said.

"I'd fall short of your expectations," Flood said. He could not stop a small, humorless smile. "And we're not even talking about her expectations yet."

Jamie wasn't hearing it.

"If you fell in love with her, you wouldn't let her down."

Flood felt almost that he wasn't even in the room for a moment. It was Jamie talking to himself, or talking to the world, or God, or the wall.

"Who am I to you?" Flood said, trying to show how puzzled he felt. "Jamie, I've been falling short of people's grand expectations my whole life."

Chapter Nine

Homicide investigators learned not to underestimate the obvious. Even when a case seemed to be surrounded by mysterious loose ends, the reason behind someone's murder was usually the most easily identifiable conflict in their lives. In Flood's relatively small professional experience with homicide, the murder of a man could most often be traced to money owed or stolen, and the murder of a woman could usually be traced to an angry asshole of a man she knew. Flood knew of three men in Marcy Westlake's life: The husband who had hired him to find her, the only-child son in college, and a married stranger with whom she had an affair. He supposed Daniel Westlake could be involved in some crazily elaborate ruse that involved murdering his wife and then hiring someone to search for her in an effort to cover it up. But, partly because of the logic George had presented about Westlake's motivation for visiting Pam Sawyer the night before, Flood doubted Westlake killed her. Alternatively, it was not completely out of the question that the son had deep psychological flaws, because of the way he was raised, and snapped in some fit sparked by feelings of abandonment when his mother left home and took up with another man. That scenario, too, was a stretch. It was somewhat less of a stretch to believe that her death was somehow connected to the risky behavior of an affair with Vincent Tortufi, a married man who had apparently been having an affair with Pam Sawyer when he met Marcy. But the means by which she died made little sense as Flood tried to connect Tortufi. The police investigators feared they had a murderer with serial killer tendencies. Such a killer would have been unlikely to have a relationship with Marcy Westlake first and to be known to other people she knew.

Flood again went through the file of records and documents he had gathered. Printouts on the house and contracting business from public records, information about George Kajmar's hot dog fortune. The photo album of Westlake family pictures, including the hidden portrait of Marcy Westlake in a negligee. He found he kept lingering on the picture, thinking not altogether businesslike thoughts. He finally set it aside and went out to the living room and looked down on the frozen water and the skyscrapers across the river.

Flood picked up his cell phone. He was going to tell Westlake about the body found in the suburbs. He didn't care about the consequences. He scrolled and hit redial. When the call went through, he got voicemail again. He just left another message to call. It was news that needed to be explained in person.

He put the phone down on the dining table and just looked out at the city, watching the shadows shift in the afternoon light. About ten minutes went by before he was jolted back to the moment by his phone vibrating against the hard wood. A tingle of fear went up his back. It was probably Westlake. Flood suddenly could not imagine how the words would come out.

He picked up the phone. Caller ID showed "Private Number." It was not Westlake. He answered, wondering which cop it would be.

"Augie, it's Jake. Where are you?"

"Home." Flood could feel the agitation and excitement in Pialetti's voice. He knew this was it and Pialetti was going to tell him one way or the other.

"Marcy Westlake is not our Jane Doe."

The words made his head swim. He had been putting all of the pieces of information in place to try to learn who had killed her. Flood had been bracing himself to tell Westlake the news, and in an instant Pialetti had turned all of Flood's anxiety and expectation on its head. "What happened?"

"Well, we're pretty sure we know who it is. Prostitute from one of the massage parlors on Lake Street came forward this morning and told us her friend has been missing since last Monday morning when she left the place at three A.M. Polish immigrant. Late thirties. We're comparing hair and looking for dental records to compare. No DNA yet, but the hair is looking like the same woman under the microscope."

"Who is she?"

"As best we can tell, her name is, bear with me, Celinka Kieslowski," he said, fumbling out the syllables. "A fairly recent arrival from some city in southern Poland: Katowice."

"She's a prostitute?"

"Friend says she only gives massages, you know. Ever been through one of those places?"

Those places were a handful of massage parlors that did business in unincorporated DuPage County, many of them along the corridor of Lake Street, a broad thoroughfare that cut straight west through the western suburbs. Unincorporated areas were subject only to the local control of the county—not municipalities—and therefore tended to have less stringent guidelines for adult businesses. They were often connected to organized crime of one flavor or another.

"I had a pen register on the phone at one of them one time," Flood said, making the point. "Can't remember which. Money laundering operation, but I don't think we ever charged it. Who runs your woman's place?"

"I don't know yet. But I don't think this is mob-related. This is a sex crime, Augie. Our guys are collecting security video from everything in the neighborhood. Probably, most of them are going to be recorded over by now. But I think now that we know what we're on to and it makes more sense, we'll get there."

Flood's mind had stopped listening to Pialetti for a moment. Now he was thinking about something else. Marcy Westlake was alive somewhere.

He rejoined his friend's thoughts.

"This means I'm still looking for a runaway wife, Jake."

"I'm glad to say it does. I'm afraid this would have been messy for you, Augie."

Flood sat down hard in his reading chair. He stared out the windows and felt the breathless sensation of just having dodged a bullet or a wreck or something else that might have ruined him in an instant. He kept thinking the words he'd said to Pialetti. *Marcy Westlake is alive. Out there somewhere.* He felt exhilarated and relieved for a moment, but then it gave way to a hint of desperation. What was really going on? He was lost and confused. All of the strange things that had seemed marginal in the context of Marcy Westlake's brutalized body sitting in the morgue, now came rushing back to him. They were the details that mattered. Flood stood up again and started pacing his apartment, turning meandering circles through the living room and kitchen, with a new urgency beginning to catch up to him and take hold of his mind.

On a whim, he called Pam Sawyer's again.

To his amazement, she answered.

"I'm at my sister's in Milwaukee, Mr. Flood. What do you want?" she said, sounding annoyed, or at least impatient.

"I didn't know you were leaving town."

"No, you didn't," she said, curtly.

He'd said it just to see how she reacted, but he couldn't read much into her tone of frustration.

"OK, I need to talk to you about Vincent Tortufi."

"Mr. Flood, I'm here for a family event and I'm busy. If you want to talk to me when I'm back on Monday, give me a call. But I have to go now."

"Vincent Tortufi."

He could hear her huff on the other end.

"That sounds about right," she said. "I said Victor but it could have been Vince. Now good-bye."

He noted the way she said Vince instead of Vincent.

"Don't hang up, Pam. I need you to tell me about your relationship with Tortufi."

"What are you talking about?"

"I think you understand that Marcy Westlake probably dropped out of sight for awhile because of what happened over Vincent Tortufi."

He couldn't tell if it was anger or frustration or fear as she raised her voice. "Listen, I don't have any idea what you're talking about, but you're way off base. I don't know anything about Marcy. I don't know that guy, and I don't have to stand here and listen to this."

She hung up. The first thing Flood thought was that she had gotten mad before he had said anything explicit. He hadn't said she'd had an affair with Tortufi or that Marcy Westlake had stolen him from her, and he had not gone anywhere near suggesting Pam had retaliated by seducing Brandon Westlake. Yet Pam had blown up at him like he had accused her of that. She knew that he knew.

Flood wondered whether Westlake had any inkling of this end of things, especially that Brandon was involved. He thought about whether he would ask such questions directly. Not that it mattered at the moment.

In the meantime, he needed to deal with the fact that he could not get ahold of his client. Flood called Cronin, reminding himself that the tryst was only the latest development he was still withholding from his boss. At the same time, Flood felt emboldened by the fact that he had just spent a day and a half thinking that Marcy Westlake had been raped and murdered. And he thought about what a mess it would have been if he had told them about that right away. He felt like he should trust his judgment in keeping other possibilities close to the vest until they were proven.

"He won't call me back, Al. Do you know where he is?"

Flood also did not let on about what he presumed Cronin already knew—Westlake's likely interest in Kajmar's casino bid. He wanted to see if Cronin would offer it up. His boss did not mention it.

"Flood, don't worry. The guy's all stressed out. He probably drove up to Wisconsin to go ice fishing or something."

Ice fishing?

"Whatever," Flood said. "Listen, if you hear from him, let him know I need to talk to him."

"What have you found?"

"Nothing much, yet. I just need to run a couple things by him."

"Like what?"

Flood regretted calling. He didn't want advice from Cronin and didn't want him back-seat driving his inquiry.

"He gave me a photo album, and I want to know who some of the people in more recent photos are. Maybe there's a connection there."

Cronin grunted, as though that sounded like a waste of time. It would have been. It was just a lie because Flood didn't want to tell Cronin about Vincent Tortufi.

They hung up, and Flood went through his files and picked up the Tortufi printout from Nexis, which had phone numbers listed for both the Oak Brook and Lake Shore Drive addresses.

He called the LSD number first. It rang several times and then a machine with a generic prompt picked up. Flood decided he had nothing to lose.

"This is Augustine Flood. I'm an attorney in Chicago, and I am trying to reach Mr. Vincent Tortufi. Please call me . . ."

He then called the Oak Brook number. A teenage girl answered.

Flood identified himself again and asked for Mr. Tortufi.

"Um, he's not here."

"Do you expect him back soon, I'd like to leave a—"

"No. He doesn't live here now."

"I'm sorry," Flood said, a bit confused by the *now.* "Do you know where I can reach, um, is he your dad?"

"Yeah. He's living downtown. We have a condo on Lake Shore. He's there," she said, matter of fact. "I can't give out the number."

"That's OK. I think I have it," Flood said. He hesitated before asking, but really wanted to know. "I'm sorry, but can I ask when your dad moved out?"

The girl breathed a beat, as if weighing whether that was a question to get mad about or just answer. She decided not to take offense. "Couple weeks ago. It's only temporary. I have to go now. Bye."

She hung up and Flood folded his phone and put it on the dining table. From the conversation, he surmised that Mrs. Tortufi was perhaps on to the affair with Marcy Westlake and had given her husband the boot.

He didn't have a lot of ideas about what to do next. Finally, a thought occurred to him and he looked at his watch. Five-thirty. He put on his coat and headed down to the lobby. He walked down the building's driveway ramp to Wabash. He didn't see any cabs, so he took the stairs down to Hubbard, and crossed the street diagonally toward the entrance of a restaurant called

437 Rush. There were always cabs idling around the steakhouse, and he motioned to a driver. He got in and leaned into the window.

"Do you know how to get to the Napoli Tap?"

"Of course, but what'sa matter?" The cabbie grinned and jerked a thumb at the blue awnings of 437 Rush. "This place no good?"

"It's dandy, but I'm feeling poor."

The cabbie shrugged and laughed, pleased with his jokemaking. They went west a few blocks and then crossed the river going south into the Loop, then west again on Adams, over the Kennedy expressway and through Greektown to Racine. Soon Flood was dropped in front of the Napoli, which looked like a well-kept corner bar that spilled over into a couple of dining rooms. It was a popular real-Chicago joint with southern Italian cooking, huge "family-style" servings and lots of tile and Formica.

Flood got to know the Napoli Tap when he was an FBI agent working regularly with Chicago Police officers assigned to federal task forces to fight drug traffickers and street-gang money laundering operations. The cops and DEA did most of the heavy lifting, but the FBI was always on the lookout for a money laundering angle, and Flood was often the guy they attached to those kinds of investigations. Most of the manpower was CPD, but using a federal task force gave the cops working the case more power and resources to go beyond the city limits as deputized federal agents, and if they made the bust there were bigger federal conspiracy crimes to prosecute the traffickers with. Flood had become a team leader because he had a way of diffusing all the inter-agency bickering and competition.

One of the police department's gang specialists was a brawny guy who always wore flannel shirts and always had some new idea where Flood should dig next for the buried assets of drug kingpins. His name was John Lambert, and he liked to meet Flood for dinner at the Napoli Tap. Lambert was not a task force member, but he had cultivated a relationship with Flood nonetheless, and they met occasionally to trade information. Flood never talked about open investigations with Lambert, but he would trade general things he'd heard along the way and let Lambert run on with tips about this and that. At first he figured Lambert was trying to ingratiate himself with the feds. He thought the guy was a political operator who was thinking about his career ten years down the road. The neighborhood where the Napoli was located was called Taylor Street, but since the state university campus had expanded and swallowed most of the old Italian neighborhood, there wasn't much left to the area except Taylor Street itself. The Napoli was one of the few places left to go that wasn't on the main drag. It was basically a tavern with a dining room. There were no menus, just a couple of chalkboards on the wall. The floors were old tile and the tables were brown Formica. Mexican bus boys slapped red plastic baskets of bread on the table when you sat down. The waitresses told you to watch how much you ordered because everything was served in giant dishes. One bowl of pasta, one plate of lemon chicken and a "salad for two" could easily feed three people, four if two of them were skinny women. Or it could barely feed two if Lambert was at the table. He started with a plate of calamari, a salad layered with paper-thin slices of salami and provolone among the greens and tomatoes and peppers. Then he ordered a bowl of penne with red sauce and a short link of sausage. Finally, he asked for either the pork chops or the chicken piccata. If it was the platter of chicken, Lambert would say he was not very hungry.

Flood liked the food but hated Lambert. Besides the gluttonous eating, he was always coming up with eight or nine different theories of what Flood should look into next, who might really be controlling the money, when the next truckload from Mexico might roll in, or in which Logan Square or Little Village garage it might be cut and packaged for the street. Lambert was full of ideas, but the problem was, they were all pretty general when it came to the when and where. They already knew the who. It was a matter of catching them with a load of the stuff. Flood finally deduced that Lambert's enthusiasm and scattershot ideas were fishy. One night as they were leaving the restaurant, Flood went to the bathroom between the bar and the kitchen. When he came outside into the dewy spring air, Lambert was outside talking on his cell phone with his back to the valet parking stand, and he did not immediately see Flood come out. Flood heard him describe a gas station on Fullerton Avenue far out on the West Side and then say, "gimme a half hour."

Deeply suspicious to begin with, Flood left the Napoli ahead of Lambert, hit the Eisenhower and flew west, beating Lambert there. He parked a block away, changed his coat to a ratty jacket he kept in the trunk and walked back and stood in the doorway of a liquor store catty corner from the gas station. Lambert's Crown Vic pulled in and parked by the tire pump. A few minutes later, a pearl-colored GMC Denali with flashy chrome rims eased up to his car. A short Hispanic in a sleeveless San Antonio Spurs jersey got out, put a quarter in the slot and left an envelope on top of the pump and then started to fill a rear tire with air. Lambert got out of his car, walked to the pump, slid the envelope off the top, walked back to his car and drove off. The man in the jersey dropped the air hose and returned to the back seat of the truck. It left in the other direction as Flood took down the plate and followed the Denali out into the suburbs on a forty-minute drive that ended at a townhouse in Carol Stream.

Flood ran the SUV's plate, did a little digging and came up with the names of three gang members, two of them high-ranking leaders suspected of collecting street taxes and ordering shootings. Flood started watching Lambert and found out he had a place in Vegas in his wife's name. He called a colleague in the Vegas field office who checked it out and found a golf course condo that should have been a little beyond the reach of a detective's $75,000 a year, considering that Lambert still had a mortgage back in Edison Park and his wife was at home. Flood took it to Ridgeway, who set up his own investigation of the gang faction paying off Lambert and left CPD task force members off the case.

Ridgeway had intended to bring CPD internal affairs and the superintendent's office up to speed before they arrested Lambert, but one night agents unexpectedly caught Lambert on a wiretap and video taking money and giving up the identity of an undercover DEA agent. They couldn't wait, and they had the whole thing wrapped up, so they pulled him over and locked him up. It was bad enough that CPD officials did not know one of their own was under investigation in a drug conspiracy case, but that night somebody tipped a Channel 5 reporter that Lambert had been arrested and it was blasted all over the ten o'clock news before police officials had a chance to scramble up a response. The media played the story as though the FBI did not trust CPD to investigate a bad cop, and the fact that Lambert was accused of giving up an undercover federal agent made it even worse. The whole thing turned into a political nightmare. Relations between the bureau and CPD chilled to a new low, and for some reason the special-agent-in-charge of the Chicago office decided he was catching hell from the cops because Flood had in some way screwed up. Flood hadn't done anything wrong, but the SAC got reports that he had worked the case on his own for a couple days—including involving the Las Vegas field office—before notifying a supervisor. So it became convenient to tell the police brass that most of the reason they were bushwhacked was because Flood was a cowboy, which was untrue.

Flood did not actually get a reprimand of any kind, but the group coordinator above Ridgeway kept dropping hints that Flood needed to rehabilitate his reputation as a team player. His seeds of discontent were planted. He had four semesters of night school left at DePaul Law, which he was paying for himself, and he started to think about life after law enforcement.

Lambert was charged, convicted and packed off to a federal prison in Michigan for twenty years. The case and everything to do with the dirty cop had left a bad taste in Flood's mouth about a lot of things. But he still managed to have a soft spot in his heart for the Napoli Tap. In addition to the food, those days had yielded him a bartender who was something of a weather vane for the shifting climate of organized crime in Chicago.

Barry McManus was about forty and he'd been tending bar at the Napoli since he was about twenty. One night Flood was sitting at the bar waiting for Lambert, who never showed. He was sipping a club soda; even before he figured out Lambert was a crook, his sleaziness had made Flood want to play the altar boy. McManus, skinny and going gray, put his long arms on the bar and cocked his head at Flood.

"Hey, ain't you that guy who played linebacker at Ignatius and then got made a safety at Boston College?"

Flood's jaw dropped.

"How in the hell did you know that?"

"I recognized you from pictures in the paper and TV."

"That was fifteen years ago, and the team was terrible."

"Yeah," McManus said, sheepishly wiping the bar with a wet rag. "But I follow the high school ball pretty close. And I got a pretty good memory."

Flood stuck his hand out.

"Augie Flood. Nice to meet you."

"Barry McManus."

"We look about the same age. Were you at Ignatius?"

"Bogan. I'm a few years older, too, I think."

If you were white and Irish in Chicago, where you went to high school was sort of like what country club your parents belonged to, for those who kept track. Flood didn't, but he went to the best one. Of the seven or eight Catholic high schools in Chicago, Saint Ignatius was the top of the heap, the most expensive with the best academic reputation. That was good and bad. It made you a potential elitist, a bit apart from the South Side fraternity of boys who went to Brother Rice or Marist, not quite part of the North Shore clique of Loyola Academy. Bogan was the public high school that served many of the working-class white neighborhoods on the Southwest Side. In the Irish-Catholic hierarchy it was a full step down from the least of the parochial schools. Flood always wanted to qualify things by saying he went to Ignatius tuition free because his dad taught there.

McManus seemed to be mob-free. It was hard to tell in a place like the Napoli. But at the same time it made sense for the owner of a place like that to have a guy at the front of the house who was not too close to the thick necks wearing Miami casual who sat at the rear of the dining rooms talking the language of the new mob: recycling fees, towing contracts and whether the same old municipal lawyers they used still had the pull to arrange yet another tax-increment financing district.

On Sunday night at six, when Flood got out of the cab, the Napoli was pretty empty. There were three chubby old farts sipping red wine and watching a Bulls game at the end of the bar closest to the street. At the other end, a man in his twenties was trying to impress his date—a skinny stack of blow-dryed brown hair, big mascara, a fake tan, and tight low-rider jeans stretched over a narrow set of hips and thighs. The guy's ammunition seemed to be that he was pals with Dante, the Napoli's head waiter, a nephew of the owner, Pasquale "Paddy" Bernini. Dante always told everybody he was going to open his own place next year, and it was going to be just like the Napoli, only better and in the suburbs. Uncle Paddy didn't seem to feel threatened. He spent most of every night standing silently in the wide threshold between the bar and the dining room. Always with an ugly frown on his face, he watched to make sure that the customers he didn't know didn't get in the way of his regulars, most of whom were either mobsters, relatives of mobsters, cops or other city officials of some significance. He especially kept a wary eye peeled for anyone who looked like they might try to pay with a credit card. The Napoli was a cash business in the most comprehensive sense of the term.

The girl date was looking bored. She kept peeking at her watch and then asked her boyfriend to get her another Bacardi and diet. This was not the sort of place she wanted to spend the balance of her evening. Flood sort of wanted her to look at him, not because he thought she was cute, but just because he wanted her to show the dopey date some disrespect.

After McManus poured another drink for the fake-baked bimbo, he sauntered over to where Flood was sitting and raised his hands, as if to express his hurt feelings that Flood had not been by in months. He had a way of looking like he was setting aside all of his other duties to make a customer feel like the most important guest in the house. He tossed aside his damp white bar rag and shut the lid on the ice bin by the service bar.

Flooded ordered a beer and then waited patiently as the illusion of McManus on break dissolved with an order for a carafe of Chianti and a Manhattan from the dining room.

When McManus returned, he leaned on the bar with his elbows.

"What's up?"

"How are things in this neck of the woods?"

McManus smirked.

"I figured you'd be around, with all this stuff going on. But you quit the G. You're still out of the game, right?"

"Very much out of it. But I happen to be curious at the moment."

"Well, as you can imagine, it's been a bit tense." He hissed out the last syllable and made a face for emphasis. "Nobody wants to be mistaken for a casino investor, you know what I mean?"

Flood kept his voice very low, using the chatter of the Bulls telecast as cover.

"What do you know about a guy named Vincent Tortufi?"

McManus made a new face and seemed genuinely surprised.

"Yeah, I know him. Odd time to ask about a guy like that. He's a friend of Nicky Bepps."

Flood's suspicions, and Reece's early conclusions, were right. Tortufi had mob connections.

"What kind of friend?"

McManus shrugged. "There's a zillion people Nicky Bepps knows, smiles at and maybe remembers their kids' names. There's maybe a dozen who are his friends. That guy's one of his friends, you know."

"Any business ties?"

McManus started to chuckle. "You sure you're not back with the G?" he said. "None that I know of, but that's not really the sort of thing that gets talked about in front of me."

McManus nodded at Paddy Bernini, who was standing fifteen feet away in the doorway with his back to them. McManus pulled a toothpick from his shirt pocket and began to nibble on it.

"Keep your voice down, too. Paddy don't like people asking

that kind of shit about his regulars. This place is supposed to be a haven from such worldly troubles."

"Tortufi's a regular?"

McManus hesitated, looked at Flood and smiled.

"Semi-regular for as long as I been here."

Flood asked, and McManus told him the last time Tortufi had been in was about a month before, around Christmas.

"Brought his girlfriend."

"What'd she look like?"

"A hot forty-five. Blonde. Nice tits. Nice everything. Not Italian. *Very* not Italian. Very much *not* Mrs. Tortufi," he said, describing Marcy Westlake. She'd clearly made an impression. The light of another thought came into his face. "A little better looking than the last aging blonde beauty he had. But she wasn't bad, either."

Flood knew he must mean Pam Sawyer. "Names?" he asked.

"Don't know. Just two good-looking blondes in their forties, put together and respectable looking. Not the typical goomahs, you know. Not thirty with the wheels starting to come off."

"Remember when he switched girls?"

McManus half looked at the ceiling and squinted.

"Probably less than a year. Six months."

Flood nodded.

"Any chance you can remember exactly when he was in here last with the better-looking one? Is there anything else about that night that sticks out and could help you place the date?"

McManus shrugged.

"Not offhand. Why's it matter?"

"I can't say, other than it's really none of my business, so I have to be careful."

McManus shrugged again. Flood leaned close.

"I'm trying to get ahold of him."

"For what?" McManus sort of snapped it back at Flood, involuntarily.

"I know. It's completely out of left field, but I'm looking for a woman he knows."

"One of them?"

"The second one."

McManus leaned back and exhaled. He shook his head, as if Flood should know better than to court trouble. Then he cracked a half-smile.

"You wanna eat?" he asked. "The marinara's fresh."

"Sure. Give me a little salad and some linguine."

"Meatball?"

"Just marinara."

"Another beer?"

"Chianti."

As he ate, Flood thought about things. He believed he had figured out what was on Marcy Westlake's mind. She had been restless in her marriage to Westlake while her divorcee friend Pam was involved with a married wise guy. Her son was finishing his college education and getting on with a life of his own, and what was there for her? She had put her own wants and needs aside to raise Brandon. And now, she was left with a tedious husband who was probably going to run his business into the ground, a big stupid house in a rootless rich suburb, and not much else. She got bored and curious, and soon had the attentions of Pam's friend Vincent. The danger and intrigue was fun, she decided, and what right would Pam have to feel betrayed, anyway? Vincent was a married man. For the sake of argument, Flood guessed maybe Pam didn't know for a month or so that Vincent was cheating on her with Marcy. When she figured it out, some set of circumstances must have presented itself and given Pam the idea to get even instead of getting mad. Brandon was around for winter break. There was a lot of Christmas-party alcohol flowing, and something interesting happened. Flood wondered where. How would Brandon and Pam have ended up drinking in the same place? For some reason, he believed it had to be that way. He doubted Pam would have hunted Brandon down to seduce him. He really did not know the first thing about Brandon, so he could not say whether the kid had pursued his mother's friend. Maybe he had gone to her for some other reason.

He needed to make sense of it before he presented his theory to Westlake on Monday.

She probably might not care about Vincent Tortufi, but drawing her son into a sordid sexual warfare between herself and Pam Sawyer would have turned everything upside down. He figured she was disgusted with everybody, including herself. He figured she did not care much about her husband, but that she could not face her son. That much made sense.

Flood had purposely not told the brunch gathering the real details of his search for Marcy Westlake on Saturday. He saved it for a Monday morning talk with Jamie. His mind was spinning circles around itself in the last few days because he had too many things going on that were rapidly moving beyond his control. One of them was Jamie's friend Jenny. After Sunday morning's talk, he knew Jamie would come back at him. He did not want to talk about it, so he kept pressing forward with the Westlake business. The inquiry, as Jamie called it in a poor imitation of a middle-class British accent, was not leading where Daniel Westlake had said it would go.

"What are you going to tell Westlake?" Jamie asked, grimacing. "That his wife was banging some sort of grease ball named Vinnie, who she stole from her best friend, who started fucking their son to get back at her?"

"Not in so many words, but essentially, yes," Flood said. "It's his money and his information. And I think that's why his wife blew town."

Jamie teeter-tottered his head back and forth as he attempted to envision the road map for where this fiasco would go next.

"What if she killed herself?"

"Suicides don't go missing. That's really unlikely."

"Sort of grim," Jamie said, taking a sip of coffee.

"Well, that's the least of it," Flood said.

They were in Flood's office. Outside, a Green Line train ambled past on the elevated tracks, silenced by the plate glass. It was even colder than the week before. Too cold for snow, the weathermen said. Flood kept talking, building up to his full indignation over the fact that seemingly everyone, including his own boss, had deceived him about what was really going on here.

"And it looks like the real reason Westlake is so desperate is that he's involved in a casino bid."

Jamie's eyes widened.

"THE casino? The scandal?"

Flood nodded. "After the feds finish with Nicky Bepps, the state will likely start over looking for someone to operate the casino. All the bidders who lost out will be back in the running, and it looks like Westlake is a fringe player in one of those partnerships."

"Jesus. Now what do you think?"

"I think it's a small town, and everybody who's an idiot is mixed up in the same crooked shit sooner or later. I wonder what Marcy Westlake will say when she finds out her husband's betting the nest egg on a casino bid he's helped steal from the Outfit. Tortufi's probably the key to finding her. I'll have to find out more about the guy. At this point, all I know is that he seems to have a fair amount of disposable income. If he's keeping her on the side, and she wanted to get away from her life for a while, then she could be at one of his vacation places or at the apartment on Lake Shore."

"What about something more sinister?" Jamie asked. "I mean, Westlake probably really thinks she might steal his money, doesn't he?"

"Could be. But all I see right now is a broken marriage, a good-looking woman who's seen her affluent life headed for the rocks because of her husband's shitty head for business, and an affair with a married man rolling in cash. And then she splits. So far, all of the bad things have happened to my client, and he brought them on himself."

"Well, the kid's lost his mommy."

"True. This kid's lost his mommy," Flood conceded. "Well, maybe. I wish I could talk to the kid."

"The kid didn't lose his mommy?"

"I don't know, but I wouldn't be surprised if he's still in contact with her."

"What about the phone bill?"

"Hmm?"

"You made a copy of his cell phone bill, right?"

Flood hadn't thought of that. He'd been so wrapped up in looking for numbers he could trace Marcy Westlake to that he didn't think to figure out if they were still talking. He reached into his bag, took out his Westlake file and laid it flat on the desk. Jamie stood up and looked over the printout with him.

Flood pointed to a 630 number. "This is her cell phone. See, all these calls. Then this is the motel number."

His finger slid down to the Inn-n-Suites number that he'd circled. Then, in the two weeks of phone records since, there was nothing.

"No more calls from her cell," Jamie said. "She really is AWOL, if you're right about her and the kid being so tight."

"Looks like it." Flood felt stupid for not thinking of checking the rest of the phone bill before.

His phone rang with an inside call. Flood leaned forward to read the LCD panel. Cronin's extension. He picked up the phone and was summoned to the boss' office.

Despite his spindly legs, Cronin was a fat man. His body teetered a bit with all that unruly weight belted around his torso. He ate a lot of steaks and drank a lot of Chivas, ostensibly in pursuit of business, but mostly because he liked throwing money around at Gene and Georgetti's.

With his beefy, telegenic personality and his casual disregard for who was wrong and who was right, he would have made a good Fox News moderator, Flood thought. He wore a simple, unapologetic smirk that seemed to be set in concrete on his pale face. The smirk was his insider's dismissal of all the outsiders. Flood could not help but assess himself in the terms of how Cronin probably saw him. A semi-insider, but not really. Really, Flood was an outsider who got stuck on his path to the inside and never quite made it over the threshold. An Irish name, eight years of Jesuit education, the FBI and then DePaul law school were lovely insider credentials in Chicago, but Flood had gotten stuck somewhere. It was his own lack of ambition, or desire, or his lacking the need to be liked by anybody, perhaps, but it left him floating in the margin between those who toiled for others and the people who got things done and made piles of money.

Flood had never seen Cronin without the smirk; until now. Flood stopped in the doorway to the office. Cronin was standing behind his leather swivel chair, grasping the high back with his pink fingers. His posture told Flood this meeting would not last long. Flood's stopping in the doorway seemed to annoy the boss.

"Come in and close the door," he snapped.

Flood stepped in and gently closed the door. He remained standing.

"Did you find her?"

It was not a request for a progress report, but for an admission of success or failure.

"I have not."

"What the fuck, Flood. How hard can it be?"

Cronin's explosion came out of nowhere, and Flood mustered his own frustration with his boss and fired right back.

"Listen, Alan, it's a ridiculous job and if you don't like it, then you shouldn't have made me take it. I'd be more than happy to drop it. But don't take this tone with me. I'm not your caddy."

Cronin retreated a bit. He knew he was overreacting.

"I told Westlake this would be easy pickings for you," he finally said, and then uttered another half syllable, as if he wanted the words back.

"Tell me this, Alan, when were you going to tell me this was about you getting a piece of the casino bid?"

Cronin looked away almost instantly. "What are you talking about?"

"Come on," Flood said. "Westlake's under the thumb of a guy named George Kajmar. I'd never heard of him, but I'm sure you have. Kajmar was at Westlake's house Saturday night and they had a fight. Are you going to tell me you didn't know Kajmar was lurking behind Westlake? Are you going to tell me that you really put me on this because you believed Westlake is trying to save his contracting business? I think Westlake told you he's got a shot at a piece of the casino now that the bidding is open again, and he told you he could get you a piece of the work, but it'll be fucked up if he doesn't get to his offshore account and keep the bank from foreclosing on his shop."

Cronin had turned to his corner windows and wasn't looking at Flood.

"Nothing's definite," he finally said. "Have you asked Dan about Kajmar?"

"I would, but I can't find him, suddenly."

Cronin turned around. "What do you mean?"

"I mean he hasn't returned my phone calls. I called him several times yesterday and this morning. Voicemail everywhere, and he hasn't called back."

"What about his office?"

"There was no answer when I called. I'm going to call back in a bit."

Cronin sat down and frowned, lost in his own thoughts.

"Listen, Alan," Flood said in a softer tone. "There's nothing wrong with helping this guy on this stupid wild goose chase after his wife if you think it'll lead to handling business for the casino, if a casino ever gets built. But, Christ, be straight with me."

Cronin nodded and looked apologetic. But he didn't say anything.

"I'm going back to my office," Flood said. He turned and started for the door.

"Augie?" Cronin said sounding beaten.

"Yes."

"What did you find out? About the guy's wife."

"Nothing much," he said, with expert nonchalance. "She was screwing somebody. Don't know who he is. And I've got no clue where she went."

Flood walked back to his office and closed the door. Cronin had pissed him off, and he felt he was getting him back a bit by withholding Tortufi's name. He picked up his desk phone and called the FBI office. McManus's information about Tortufi had only whetted Flood's appetite. He wanted more specifics.

"Ridgeway," the hushed voice on the other end said.

"Hey, it's Flood. What d'you know?"

"I know you're making more money than me," Ridgeway said. "When are you going to come back to the poker game so I can take some of it?"

"I'm broke."

Special Agent John Ridgeway snorted on the other end. He spent his life chasing people who had lots more money than him, and he'd developed a complex about it that had permeated every level of his life. As a supervisor in the organized crime unit, he was Flood's former boss, and Flood called him because he could enumerate the branches of the Chicago Outfit's family tree in his sleep. If somebody was connected to the mob in Chicago, however tangentially, Ridgeway would know all about him.

"I want to run a name past you," Flood said.

"I'm not in the mood to help out your reporter buddy," Ridgeway said, meaning Reece.

"It's not about that," Flood said. "This is completely different. A guy I ran across doing somebody a favor."

"Hmm. What's the name?"

"Vincent Tortufi."

"Tortufi," Ridgeway repeated slowly. There was a pause on the other end, a confused silence.

"Have you heard of him?" Flood finally asked.

"Not especially."

"Not especially?"

Oddly, the response seemed to have the same tone as McManus's response. It was a defensive response that seemed full of skepticism. Flood felt as though he was being accused of something dishonest.

"Who is he?"

"He's, uh. He's just a name to me at the moment. I'll have to get back to you," he said, then added after a pause, "It might take me a couple of days."

"A couple of days? Why?" Flood was used to getting this sort of information immediately.

"The person who would know is out of town," Ridgeway said. "Why do you want to know about this guy?"

"Came up in a case."

"Really? What kind of case?"

Flood started to feel something else. There were more angles in play than he knew.

"A marital dispute; not his," Flood finally said, bending the facts a little.

"How's he involved?"

"I don't know. I don't think he really is, Ridge. But his name came up and my worst instincts told me to call you. Let me know if you find anything. Thanks buddy, I've got to run," Flood said in one breath, allowing no space for Ridgeway to ask another question before he hung up.

Jamie half knocked and walked in.

"Two things. First, look at your watch, boss-man."

"Shit, the dep."

"In forty-five minutes."

"Did you call Patrice?"

"All set up."

Flood stood up and started looking for something on his desk. Jamie came in with the file he was looking for. He took it and put his coat on.

"What's the other thing?"

"The Cayman Islands," Jamie said, grinning.

"Yes?"

"Well, maybe she's there. Christ, if I had any reason to go there in the middle of January that's where I'd be."

"Do you want to start nosing around?"

"Can I run up the phone bill calling hotels?"

"Absolutely. I think probably just Grand Cayman."

Flood had a deposition in an insurance case that could not be postponed. The eleven o'clock interview with the plaintiff was scheduled at a personal injury law office on Erie, just east of Michigan. Despite the cold, he decided to walk for the exercise and to clear his head of all the Westlake trouble before doing some real work. But on the march up Michigan, facing a bitter wind, Flood's thoughts kept coming around to the start he gave Ridgeway when he mentioned the name Vincent Tortufi. This wasn't just a guy with possible mob ties, it was somebody whose name threw Ridgeway for a loop right now. It was time to stop beating around the bush, Flood decided. He needed to see Tortufi.

When Flood arrived at the bland office building where the plaintiff's lawyer worked, he rode the slow elevator to the seventh floor and found the stenographer he'd hired already waiting in the reception area. They greeted each other, and Flood sat down. The other lawyer was making him wait a while, which he thought was a bit cheap. That was not the way to throw Flood off his game. But he ended up not minding. There was piped-in music playing, and as he sat there on the sofa staring at a really bad piece of framed office art that matched the carpet, he recognized the music as one of the tracks from a Count Basie record that his parents used to play. It reminded him of Saturday nights when they were having some teacher friends over for dinner. The memory was festive. Damp from a bath and sheathed in cotton pajamas, he was briefly shown off to the dinner guests as they arrived and sipped High Lifes or glasses of burgundy from a Carlo Rossi jug on the kitchen table. The smell of beer and wine breath swirling in his head, he was then packed off to his parents' room to watch *McMillan and*

Wife or *Columbo* on the black and white TV, well past bedtime, while the laughter of adults and a hint of cigarette smoke rolled up the stairs. It was a good memory, and he wondered for a moment why it had registered so strongly.

He was pretty sure this was the right Count Basie tune. He looked at the young receptionist.

"Excuse me, is this a disk you're playing? Isn't it Count Basie?" He pointed at the ceiling.

She gave him a blank look of indifferent ignorance. "I don't know where it comes from. There's no disks here."

"Never mind."

The door to the offices opened and a middle-aged woman in flannel slacks and a black jacket stepped toward him.

"Mr. Flood, sorry to keep you waiting," she said. "Mr. Safar will see you now."

She said it like an appointment with *Mr. Safar* was not an easy thing to get. From her tone, no one would guess that his name was Bernie and it took him an extra year to get through Northern Illinois law school and two whacks at the bar to get his license. Flood nodded and smiled and headed through the door after the stenographer.

Luckily, Flood had prepared most of his deposition questions a week ago, before he'd ever heard of Daniel Westlake. The plaintiff was anxious and easy to handle, while Bernie Safar interjected the wrong objections in the wrong spots. Flood was finished in an hour. He shook Bernie's hand and called him Mr. Safar, and then walked the stenographer to a cab, and started back down to the Loop.

He couldn't hear it, but he felt his phone vibrating in his chest pocket. He ducked into the vestibule of the Burberry's store so he could hear. On the other end, Reece was excited and breathless.

"Jesus, Flood, you've got trouble."

“What now?”

“Tortufi. He’s a target of the casino investigation. The feds are looking for him.”

“What do you mean, a target? Who told you?”

“Somebody I talk to with the Marshals Service just told me. He only told me because he’s pissed that the FBI won’t let them help find him. He says they’ve been looking for Tortufi for a few days and can’t find him but they won’t ask for help.”

“Typical.”

The tension between the FBI and other federal law enforcement agencies was legendary. There was no denying the FBI’s arrogance, or the resentment from the other agencies. The Bureau routinely turned down offers of help and froze the others out. He could imagine how this case must have annoyed Reece’s marshal source. They prided themselves on their ability to hunt down fugitives quickly, and on the biggest corruption case in town, the FBI couldn’t locate a key person but refused to let anybody help. So they were letting the press know about it.

In any event, it was clear now why Ridgeway stammered when Flood asked about Tortufi. He must have thought Flood was playing games. This changed everything. If Marcy Westlake’s boyfriend was involved with Nicky Bepps in the casino deal, and her estranged husband was involved in a competing casino venture, then Westlake might not even be after the Cayman account money. He might be chasing his wife to talk to her about something related directly to the casino.

“What are you going to do?” he asked Reece.

“Try to confirm with somebody inside the FBI or inside the U.S. Attorney’s office. I can’t go on the word of a pissed-off marshal,” he said. “But what are *you* going to do?”

“Well, I was going to talk to Vincent Tortufi. But if the Bureau can’t find him, I might have trouble, too.”

The immediate question was what to tell the law firm. But now he did not trust Cronin. First he had not told Flood that Westlake was involved in the casino bids. Now, it turned out that the wife had connections to the mob's bid. He did not know if Cronin knew that, but if he did, and he hadn't told Flood, it would be the end of him working for Cronin, Drew and Guzman. Flood was being played for a fool by somebody while being cast blindly into the teeth of a massive federal investigation.

He figured that there wasn't much use in calling Tortufi's apartment, but he had nothing to lose.

Chapter Ten

"Christ Almighty. I called fifteen hotels in Grand Cayman. There's another fifty-some to go. Nothing." Jamie looked dazed as he sat down in Flood's office.

"Don't bother. It sounds like a waste of time."

There were no blinking lights on Flood's phone, and Jamie had not taken any messages. No Daniel Westlake. No Pam Sawyer and, certainly, no Vincent Tortufi. The one place he had not checked lately was Westlake's business. A woman named Joan answered.

"No, Mr. Flood. He's not here."

"You still have not heard from him?"

"No. I thought you knew. He went out of town for a few days."

"Where?"

"I really don't know. He said he'd be back tomorrow afternoon."

Flood thought about things for an instant.

"OK, Joan. Thanks. Hey, changing the subject, but do you know where Dan and Marcy stay on Grand Cayman. A friend is looking for recommendations and I remembered that Dan said they love it down there."

"Oh, yes," Joan said. "They went every year until the last few. I made the arrangements with their travel agent a few times and it was always the Marriott. It sounded very nice."

"On Grand Cayman, right?"

"Oh, I think so."

"Thanks, Joan. If Dan checks in, make sure he knows he needs to call me."

Flood hung up and started tapping his keyboard.

"You devious bitch," Jamie said.

"What, I didn't lie. You are looking for recommendations of which hotel in Grand Cayman to call."

Flood Googled the Grand Cayman Marriott and came up with a number. He didn't like using speakerphone, but he'd make an exception so Jamie could listen.

He asked for the front desk and a got a woman with a sunny, Caribbean voice that filled him and Jamie with an instant longing for rum and sand.

"Hello, I'd like to see if Marcy Westlake is checked into the hotel. The last name is spelled—

"Oh, sorry, sir, but Mr. and Mrs. Westlake have checked out already."

Jamie made a silent scream face and stood up shaking his fists. The part that stunned Flood was the Mr. Westlake sighting.

"You saw them leave?"

"Well, I checked Mr. Westlake out myself, actually. I'm afraid that's all the information I have, sir."

He thanked her and hit the speakerphone button to hang up and slunk back in his chair and cursed. Jamie was walking around the room like he had too much energy surging through his body to sit still.

"You busted his ass! He's telling you he can't find his wife, and then he's on vacation with her. Ho-lee shit, boss-man."

"This has gone far enough," Flood said. He stood up and walked down the hall to Cronin's office. The door was closed and his secretary Mary Pat looked up from her computer.

"Not here. He's still at lunch."

Flood looked at his watch. It was three-thirty. He walked back to his office and called Cronin's cell phone.

He could hear the noises of billiard balls knocking in the background.

"Sorry to bug you, but it's important."

"It's OK, I'm shooting pool with Jerry Lawrence at the University Club. He's finally ready to talk about switching law firms. What's up with Marcy Westlake?"

"Well, Jamie came up with the idea that maybe she was in the Caymans, so we figured out where Dan and Marcy stayed when they vacationed there and called."

"Are you going to tell me you found her?"

"The front desk at the Marriott said Mr. and Mrs. Westlake had just checked out."

There was silence on the other end.

"Are you shitting me?"

"She said she checked Mr. Westlake out herself."

More silence.

"I'm really pissed off and sick of this, Al."

The other thing Flood was thinking about was Vincent Tortufi. If Dan and Marcy Westlake were back together, he wondered where Tortufi now fit into the scheme of things. Then an idea started to take shape. He kept quiet about it.

"Augie, do me a favor and sit tight. I don't know what's going on, but I want to sort it out in person. Don't call Westlake. I'll have him come in when he gets back to town and the three of us will sit down and we'll figure out what the hell is going on."

If that was the way Cronin wanted to handle it, that's what they would do. He would have to tell his boss about the Tortufi connection before that meeting happened, but not yet.

Jamie was waiting impatiently for their conversation to resume.

"Well?"

"I'm to leave Westlake alone until he gets back, and then Al says we'll ambush him."

"OK, so what's this mean?"

"I think it means that Dan and Marcy Westlake are scamming the mob together, and we're a part of it. But god knows how."

"What's the scam?"

"Our man Westlake is somehow involved with a guy in the suburbs named George Kajmar, and that guy was a bidder for the casino license and lost out to the Outfit."

"Oh, shit," Jamie said. "He's not just a cheesy douche-bag lying about losing his wife?"

"Not just. And it doesn't stop at him. I don't know how to connect it yet, but she was into something screwy, too. The guy she was, or is, sleeping with is a mobster."

"It's all connected? The wandering wife, Vinnie the grease ball, and the whole great big fucking casino thing?"

"Maybe."

"It sounds like Marcy got inside the Outfit by striking up a romance with Tortufi. She found out how they were rigging the process with the Gaming Board, and then they probably tipped off the feds."

"I thought some other lawyer figured out that West Bank had the liaison guy—Puska—in their pocket and he told the feds."

The New York lawyer who connected the dots. That was the story Reece and the other media had reported, and the feds had not contradicted. But maybe it was what they wanted people to believe.

"Maybe the lawyer did figure it out on his own, but I bet the feds were already working this. I bet Dan and Marcy had already tipped them off."

"So why scam us, too?"

"Maybe it's a cover story. If Bepps gets curious about who sold him out, he may suspect that it was Marcy because she's an outsider. But if his ear is close to the ground, he'll maybe hear that her husband has hired a lawyer to find her because he doesn't know where she is."

"But how could they be sure Bepps would know that?"

"Maybe Dan was pretty sure I'd find out about Tortufi. He didn't seem all that surprised when I told him about the motel room she called Brandon from. So he figures I'll find out about Tortufi, ask Tortufi where she is, and bingo, it's back to Bepps."

Jamie rolled his eyes; not at Flood, but at the elaborate scheme.

"Well, now wait a minute, sister. Let's count the ways you could do the same thing, but easier."

"Persuade Nicky Bepps that your wife is not screwing one of his guys to get inside info about stealing the casino license?"

"Right. He could have covered his tracks some other way, right?"

"I suppose. But creating the illusion that you don't have anything to do with your wife and that she is avoiding you would seem fairly effective to me."

They sat for a while and thought about it. If Daniel and Marcy Westlake had decided to scam the mob together, it was extremely bold. But what had been the impetus for it? Flood kept going over the traits of the Daniel Westlake he had seen in the last few days. He just did not believe the man was audacious enough to do such a thing. Maybe Marcy Westlake was that sort of woman. Her friend Pam Sawyer had said she was "clever" in ways that Dan was not, but this was a complicated scheme—one that could easily get both of them killed. His thoughts popped back to Brandon Westlake, the son. Why had

Daniel insisted that Flood not talk to him? The tension that Flood sensed from Westlake about the dynamic between his son and wife seemed very real. None of the pieces added up. But he believed the woman at the Marriott in Grand Cayman was not mistaken when she said she had just checked Daniel Westlake out of the hotel and that he had been there with Mrs. Westlake.

"Well, I still think it's bananas," Jamie said.

Flood's thoughts had shifted again. He still wanted to lay eyes on Vincent Tortufi.

"There's one way to figure out whether their scheme is working: see what Vincent Tortufi says when I tell him Dan hired me to track her down."

"But Tortufi's hiding, right?"

"We'll see."

Flood was in a cab heading north on Lake Shore. He took three twenties out of his wallet and put them in his coat pocket. The Lake Shore high-rise where Tortufi had an apartment was among the dozens of distressingly plain glass-and-concrete towers strung along the Drive just north of Belmont Harbor. Ugly buildings like Tortufi's stood out because they shared the lakefront skyline with so many old beauties with flourishes of terracotta and gray stone. Flood got out of the cab and stepped into the bright lobby lined with floor-to-ceiling glass and honey-colored paneling. Two elderly black men in worn blue blazers staffed the lobby. One was standing near the elevator banks. The other sat behind the reception desk. Flood walked up to the desk and took out a business card but didn't hand it over yet.

"Sir, my name's Augie Flood. I'd like to see Mr. Tortufi in 1813 if he's home."

The man moved slowly. He was sparely built and his skin was papery and dry. His eyes were tired and bloodshot, and a gray speckled mustache covered a harelip. He frowned and slowly picked up the phone, shaking his head, as if he and Flood had been talking a long time and he was tired of Flood's stubbornness. "He ain't home. I'll check, but he ain't here."

The man sat and listened to the phone for a bit and then put it down.

"No, sir. He ain't here. You with the gov'ment, too?"

The way he said it, it registered with Flood that he must mean the U.S. Attorney's office. If the FBI had paid a visit, he would have said FBI.

"They were here earlier?" he asked.

"Mmm hmmm. About an hour ago."

Flood leaned over the desk.

"Mr. Tortufi talk to them?"

Now the man behind the desk was looking askance at Flood. "So, you're not with the government then, sir?"

Flood handed him the business card.

"I am not. I'm a private attorney."

The old man shrugged.

Flood pulled a folded twenty and the photograph of Marcy Westlake out of his pocket together. The money sticking out from behind the picture didn't appear to impress the guard, either.

"I'm actually looking for this woman, as well. I think she's a friend of Mr. Tortufi."

"Mmm. Hmm," he said, barely amused at the edge of a bill sticking out from behind the photo. "You looking real hard for this woman."

"Have you seen her here? With Mr. Tortufi?"

"Mmm," he said. He folded his arms over his chest and bent slightly from the waist. "You a friend of Mr. Tortufi, then?"

"Not really," Flood said.

The man gingerly extended his creased fingers and touched

the edge of the photo, as if to steady Flood's hand. "You might have to look a little harder than that, young man."

Negotiation. With his ears reddening, Flood switched the photo and folded bill into his left hand and pulled another twenty from his pocket with his right hand, tucking the bill in with the other.

"Mmm. Hmm," the guard nodded. "Saw her once. About a month ago. Come in here late with Mr. Tortufi—she was in this same dress. Beautiful woman. Real woman. Not a child he picked up out of a nightclub."

Flood nodded. "You're sure. Even though you saw her just once? How can you be sure it's the same woman?"

The guard smiled. "Well, sometimes Mrs. Tortufi stay here. Whole lot' o' Neiman-Marcus bags, you know what I'm saying?"

Flood smiled, letting the two twenties slide into the old man's hand.

"OK," he said, tucking the photo back into his pocket. "But you haven't seen her since? And just that once? For instance, she wasn't here last week, was she?"

"That's right."

Flood turned and faced the front of the building, with the windows and landscaped circle drive out front, traffic racing by on Lake Shore Drive beyond. This was not much help. He turned back.

"Did the government people ask you about her?"

He whispered back. "Not me. Jonesy over there." The man nodded in the direction of the other elderly guard in a blue blazer standing over by the elevators. "Asked about a woman, but didn't have no picture. I guess maybe they meant the same lady. I don't know the name. Jonesy don't know, either."

"Mind if I ask Jonesy if the government people had a name for her?"

The old man scowled, not liking the way this exchange was growing into new shapes after money had been exchanged. He nodded in a different direction and Jonesy, perceiving all, slowly ambled their way. When he arrived, the man behind the desk scowled again.

"This man asking questions about the government people here this morning. He a lawyer looking for Mr. Tortufi."

Jonesy sized up Flood skeptically and looked back to his colleague, who just shrugged. Flood didn't know how much information was conveyed in the shrug, but he assumed more than met his eye.

"Mr. Tortufi not here. What about it?" Jonesy asked.

"When they asked if you'd seen a woman with Tortufi, did they use a name for her?"

Jonesy looked like he was thinking about it a moment, but then frowned. "I don't know. Bunch of fools, sounded like to me."

Jonesy seemed perturbed and a bit angry, maybe about being called over by the other guard without knowing how much to say or what might be in it for him. Flood turned his back on the seated guard and brought the photo of Marcy Westlake out of his coat pocket again, with the last twenty peeking out from behind the print. He held it close so that Jonesy could see but the other man couldn't. Jonesy grunted a little, disappointed, annoyed, resigned. All of it.

"Hell, all a sudden bunch of white men in suits want to find this woman," he said, as if to his co-worker but not loud enough. "Yeah, that's her. They didn't have a picture or anything, but that's got to be the lady. I remember her."

"Did they ask for her by name?"

"No. They didn't have no name. Asked me and him," he said, nodding to the man behind the desk. "We don't know her name. Good-looking woman belongs to Mr. Tortufi, all I know. That's too much, judging from all the attention she's getting."

Flood nodded at him and said thank you. The prosecutors were trying to put the pieces together but did not know who was who. All the feds knew, Flood decided, was that there was a woman involved in Tortufi's life that might matter. That wouldn't last. They were closing in. And then things would really turn into a mess. Flood's client and his so-called missing wife were about to be exposed for their role in scamming the mob. If Marcy Westlake knew about illegal things, she'd be a witness. And Bepps's defense lawyers would crucify the Westlakes, trying to make it look like the mobster was nothing more than a victim of their scheme. Flood decided he needed to stop nosing around for the time being.

"What are my chances of catching a cab?" Flood asked the man behind the counter.

"Jonesy."

The old man turned and ambled off toward the front door, digging in his coat pocket for a whistle.

The cab crawled along the curves of southbound Lake Shore. Out the left window the lake was endless and gray, frozen here and there inside the jetties. The beachfront was deserted and there were just a few well-bundled joggers and dog walkers on the path. Diversey Harbor was on his right. Its slips were empty. In the summer it would be full of motorboats and cabin cruisers, any vessel that could pass under the Lake Shore Drive Bridge. Lincoln Park widened south of the harbor, and the sheer black slopes of the John Hancock Tower loomed over the approaching bend in the Drive. As the taxi made its way back downtown, Flood flipped open his cell phone and called Pam Sawyer's number in Hinsdale. No answer. He left a message.

"Pam, it's Augie Flood, Daniel's lawyer. I've got a couple of things I want to run past you. Still no sign of Marcy, right? Call me back, if you would."

He snapped the phone shut. She must be in on it, he figured, if Westlake was visiting her late Saturday night. Maybe Marcy Westlake was holed up there after all.

It was six o'clock and pitch dark. The office had emptied, and Flood had a headache because he'd skipped lunch. He had run out of options for the moment, until Westlake returned and Cronin set up a meeting. At this point the only thing that really interested him was actually meeting Marcy Westlake and Vincent Tortufi. The more he thought about it, the more he figured this was all her idea. Even if the Westlakes were the ones headed for serious trouble, some of their problems could be Flood's as well. As the lawyers in the case dug into what they had done, Flood's role working for Daniel Westlake would no doubt be probed. He had not committed a serious crime, but the means by which he came across the knowledge that Vincent Tortufi and Marcy Westlake were involved was suspicious. He had bent the law slightly by invading Brandon Westlake's home and files, and he had flat-out lied to the motel manager to obtain the phone records revealing Tortufi's identity. Reece would probably have to write about it. TV would probably have fun with it, and that public attention might prompt the Attorney Registration and Disciplinary Committee to look into his conduct. He felt a sense of anger brewing, part of it directed at the Westlakes and part of it at Cronin. But most of his anger and frustration was reserved for himself. He knew better than to get involved in this stuff. When Cronin put him on the spot, he should have said no. He should have insisted they get somebody more suitable—a private investigator—to do it. But he had been just bored enough with his work, and just self-destructive enough, to jump in. It was a mistake and now Flood could face real problems because of it.

When he needed to deal with stress, he did one of three things: he drank whisky, ran eight miles, or cooked. Whisky seemed altogether the wrong way to go at the moment, and he was in no mood to face the cold in running shoes, so he caught a cab on Wabash that dropped him at Fox & Obel to look at fowl. The store smelled of expensive food—good fresh bread and cake, the clean salty smell of an impeccable fish counter, pungent cheese, tart brine keeping olives, and meat roasting for people who didn't want to cook. He wandered around the warmly lit store before heading to the meat counter. Back by the cheeses and olives, in the soft brown light, he found a woman among the shoppers, standing with her back to him, hands on hips in a way that suggested she was scolding the Stilton for being $25 a pound. She looked familiar from behind. Then it dawned on him that she was Jenny. As if the recognition had been voiced out loud, she turned around and looked at him. A smile appeared on her lips.

"Augustine Flood," she said, as if it was the answer to long unanswered question. "What a surprise."

"Hello."

"Hello."

"You called me Augustine. Augie's fine."

"I like saying 'Augustine,' " she said. "There's something festive about it."

"I don't think my parents were shooting for festive. More like contemplative. Or at least tortured and lonely."

"Hmm. Hippo, right? Augustine of Hippo?"

Flood nodded, "You have an ecclesiastical vocabulary, it turns out."

"Art history. It ventures into the sacred, you know."

"So where was Hippo?"

"What do I win if I get it right?"

"Well, you could choose between the pair of jet skis and the trip to San Francisco."

"Not Egypt, but Africa on the Mediterranean. I'll say Libya."

"Close. Algeria."

"I should have known that."

They smiled at each other some more. Jamie was right about her. He couldn't believe he was thinking that. Flood pointed at the cheese.

"The cheese has upset you."

She shrugged. "Stilton. It's expensive."

"You can get domestic blue for a third of the price, but it won't be as creamy."

"See, and I like creamy."

"Just get a few ounces."

"Maybe a quarter pound."

"That's plenty. A pound would kill you."

She laughed at the thought of dying from a pound of cheese.

Flood remembered how hungry he was and figured a dinner invitation wouldn't be completely out of line.

"So, you win the consolation prize for guessing so close to Algeria."

"Really—what's that?"

"I'll cook you dinner."

"When?"

"Now."

She hesitated, looking like a schoolgirl being offered her first cigarette.

"You know," he reassured her, "it's just down the street. And I've got wine. Lots of it."

"Well, it's getting more tempting," she said, nearly talked into taking a puff. Definitely wanting to light up. "What are you cooking?"

"A chicken. Straight into the oven. It'll be ready in 45 minutes. We'll have half a bottle of Bordeaux and a salad put away by the time it's ready."

Flood was suddenly at the height of his powers. What woman could resist the reformed jock, ex-cop, bachelor lawyer's promise of a succulent meal straight out of a Julia Child episode whipped up under an hour?

"What the hell," she said.

She bought her four ounces of cheese, and Flood picked out a very small chicken after receiving all sorts of unsolicited promises that the bird had lived a dignified, uncrowded, steroid-free life and died a humane and sanitary death. They took a cab back to Flood's building. Apart from a few untidy piles of newspapers, his apartment was clean and orderly, and she looked around a bit while he seasoned the bird. It took a few minutes for the oven to heat before the little bird for two was actually cooking. But after that he was in rare form again. He opened a closet between the bedrooms that held a floor-to-ceiling wine rack and took out a good bottle of Bordeaux. He poured two glasses, and Jenny sipped and smiled. He sipped and smiled. Greens came out of the fridge, were torn, washed and spun. Flood sliced four little waxy potatoes as thin as potato chips and set them to simmer in a pan of half and half, butter, salt and nutmeg. When they were tender he turned them into a small enameled dish with a handful of shredded Gruyere and several grinds of black pepper and then slid them in by the half-cooked bird.

He took a half-pint container of brown ice out of the freezer and popped it in the microwave for five minutes.

"What's that?"

"Duck stock."

"Where'd you get it?"

"From some ducks."

"You made it?"

"In November."

"I see."

Her eyes slowly widened. At this point it didn't matter if none of it was edible. The fact that he appeared to have a plan and was executing it, on a moment's notice, was somehow priceless.

"Good God," she said. "What are you doing?"

"Haven't you ever seen a grown man cook before?"

"I have seen meat scorched over fire, and I have seen bad pies baked to make a point. But I don't know that I've seen . . . this." She sounded almost frightened. "It appears that this is how you eat. Is this how you eat?"

"More or less."

The mingling of flesh, herb and heat was beginning to perfume the apartment. It was half past seven. Flood gave Jenny the task of setting their places for dinner, tablecloth and all, a single candle. He refilled both of their glasses. She picked out some music and put it on low. They sat and waited for the chicken and potatoes. Jenny looked like she might start giggling.

"So, tell me why you cook."

He shrugged and took a drink. The question made him happy, for some reason. How many things in the last three days had been so badly out of his control? His job—the assignment to find Marcy Westlake—had managed to intrigue him in a serious way, while, at the same time, infuriate and humiliate him, before eventually making him a professional cuckold.

Jenny wanted to know about his personal refuge.

"Because I can," he said. "Because I should eat. Who tells you that? *You should eat.* Your mother tells you that. Your grandmother, and an overweight aunt, any Jewish woman over forty who fears the unknown."

She laughed and said, "Just answer my question. You could eat anything. You're single and successful. You could be out with friends ordering steaks and eating pomegranate-apple foam. You could have great Thai food delivered from a different place every night of the week. Why do you go to the trouble to cook well?"

"It puzzles you."

"It fascinates me."

"You haven't tasted anything yet."

"I can smell what's coming."

"OK. I cook well because I'm suspicious of strangers and their capacity for casual misanthropy."

"The chef's going to spit in your bouillabaisse syndrome. I'm sure it's a very real danger."

"It happens. I cook because I've eaten bad food too often. Because I've settled for the wrong things too often."

She arched her eyebrows playfully. "Interesting. A window into your deeper psychology."

"I cook because I like the smell of roasting meat and the heat off the oven, and I love a really goddamn sharp knife."

He was going on his own now.

"Because I like eyeballing how much broth and wine to pour over the beef, and guessing how long to sear it in how much oil, and getting it right. Because I love lifting the lid on Beef Bourguignonne when it's ready to eat, and mashing potatoes by hand with butter and cream, and cooking a piece of fish in five minutes in a 500-degree oven.

"I like mixing oil and vinegar. I like adding mustard to things and watching it vanish. I like cast iron, and I like working with fire. Most of all, because most days I leave my office and wish I was someplace else. How's that?"

"Persuasive," she said.

They drank more wine, and she stretched out a little, her feet, sheathed in black leather boots with narrow heels, tucked under the coffee table and her back arched a bit against the arm of the couch. She seemed pleased that she'd accepted his invitation. She wore blousy black slacks and a fitted gray turtleneck that looked soft enough to be cashmere. There was something easy about her beauty that had Flood by the collar. Her slender hands tapered into delicate fingers with nails that were manicured, but not elaborately. The only jewelry she wore was a silver watch. There were two or three strands of gray in her long brown hair, and she didn't bother much with makeup other than a hint of drama around her eyes that showed she paid some attention to her power to turn a man's head and set him to thinking.

Flood looked at his watch and got up. He took her to the kitchen and, with mock ceremony, removed the well-browned chicken, glistening and speckled with pepper, from the oven. He set the golden-topped crock of potatoes gratin next to the bird to rest, dressed the salad and then seated her at the table in a chair that faced the glittering skyline through his windows.

With a ten-inch chef's knife he divided the chicken into quarters and then halved the breasts, and put it all on a small platter with a remaining sprig of uncooked rosemary. He drained the fat out of the roasting pan and then set it on a high burner and splashed in the thawed duck stock and a splash of cheap white wine he kept on the counter for cooking. He carried the dishes to the table while the sauce reduced and placed a thigh and piece of breast on Jenny's plate with a spoonful of potatoes. He came back with the sauce in a coffee cup and spooned some over the meat on both of their plates.

She took her first bite of chicken and smiled at him.

"Good God."

"Don't sound surprised. There's no reason it shouldn't be good."

She laughed and dug into the potatoes.

"Come on," she said. "The way you just throw everything together. It could have been god-awful. But it's really amazing.

These potatoes are fantastic. You're going to make me fat."

Flood shrugged and sat down, liking the idea that he'd have her for enough dinners to make her fat.

"So when I met you Friday night Jamie was talking about some guy whose wife you were supposed to find," she said, changing the subject.

"That's right. I'm Flood, private eye."

"So you did it?"

"I did something."

"Have you found her?"

"I have not. I think she'll find me in the end," he said. "I'm feeling a bit bush league at the moment. My client won't even return my phone calls."

"That's weird. So where do you think she is?"

Flood wanted to tell Jenny everything, partly just to be telling her anything because he felt a growing desire to sit there talking to her all night long, and partly because he wanted to bounce the story off a fresh set of ears, hoping for a sliver of insight. But he caught himself. As bizarre as the whole scenario and arrangement was, he had rules to play by. It forced an embarrassed smile to his lips.

"I just realized that I can't really tell you. This guy's still my client, and I shouldn't be talking about his business, no matter how asinine it seems."

"Can't you pretend he's a just a hypothetical guy and his hypothetical wife?"

"Only if you promise to believe none of it really happened."

"I don't know the guy's name."

"Good point. Let me think about it."

She ate all the potatoes on her plate and cleaned the thigh bone of every morsel of meat. She left a smidgen of the breast portion, for decorum's sake.

Flood ate everything and poured more wine.

"I'm sorry," she said, grinning. "I can't let this go. Tell me just this: Do you think the wife doesn't want him to find her, or is it possible something bad happened to her?"

With Marcy Westlake's abrupt disappearance from her son's phone records, it had become something to think about until the call to the hotel in Grand Cayman that afternoon. His mind wandered for a moment—from wondering what the son knew about all of it, to thinking about the photos of Marcy Westlake he'd seen and all that he had tried to interpret from her expressions about what was really going on in her life. It had all seemed like lies kept up to preserve the notion of a successful, well-off suburban family. The photo in the negligee had puzzled him the most, but now it made sense. It was what it appeared to be.

"I'm sorry," Jenny said, miffed at Flood lost in his thoughts. "I think I asked the wrong question."

Flood snapped back to attention.

"No," he said, embarrassed.

"I'm being nosy."

"No, it's all just a pain. I think it's all been over nothing. It looks like the husband may have found the wife, himself."

Or never lost her in the first place. But he left that out. He did not know whether their entire story of marital discord was invented for the purpose of the ruse to rip off Bepps, or if they really had been separated but then reconciled over their plan. He had been so convinced of the logic of Marcy Westlake really leaving her husband. He wondered how much of that was just that he disliked Westlake personally and found her to be every bit as attractive as most men did.

"Pretend you're married to my hypothetical client," he said. "He's in his late forties, runs his business into the ground while he's living in a $700,000 house in the burbs and driving a $50,000 truck. He's overweight but slightly vain about his appearance. Carefully sculpted beard, a little hair color, Rolex, more jewelry. If you were leaving him, what would be your chief reason?"

This sat her back in her chair with a new grin.

"Well," she said. "Where do I start? How did I get married to him in the first place? He must have been a bit more dynamic when he knocked me up at twenty-one."

"How do you know he knocked her up?"

"Just a feeling," she said, taking a big sip of wine. There was a twinkle in her brown eyes, candlelight catching slightly in the flinty golden specks of her irises. They were inviting eyes.

"I don't know," she went on. "How old is their son?"

"Senior in college. So, I guess about twenty-one."

"How old is she?"

"Forty-three."

"When'd they get married?"

"Not sure. I guess it could have been a shotgun wedding, in her early twenties."

Perhaps Marcy Westlake had been waiting for this year for the last twenty—patiently waiting out her commitment to their son, to see him through college. It would take that kind of marital fatigue for them to decide that she should start sleeping with Tortufi in order to play the part convincingly. People who were really in love wouldn't carry out this sort of plan. This really was a hypothetical question if the Westlakes were really still together, or reunited.

"A bad marriage from the start," Jenny said. "Doesn't it make you sad?"

"It would if it was my marriage."

"All those wasted years."

"She got a son out of it."

"That's true," she said, weighing it, considering whether a child would make a bad marriage and the sacrifice of those young years worthwhile. "I don't know how I would come out feeling in that."

"Probably much better than if there were twenty years of misery and no child. If there's a kid, the question's probably moot in a way we don't get."

He winced at himself a bit just as he said it. He didn't know Jenny well enough and had no clue what she thought about children. She was thirty years old.

He looked back into her eyes: "So how have you avoided a husband?"

"I haven't," she said, smiling a little triumphantly. She knew more about him than he did about her. "I was married for three years."

Jamie hadn't told him, the little shit.

"When?"

It was a couple of years after the Art Institute. He was a *serious* artist. Flood couldn't tell if she said it like that to mock her own artistic ambitions, or if she said it with resentment of his mocking of her ambition. They had been an off and on item as students, she said. Things became more regular as he struggled to make a name for himself in the Wicker Park scene. She was a solid foundation for him. He sold a few paintings, got a big foundation grant. Things changed.

"Thank God it didn't go twenty years," she said. "Thank God there was no baby or it might have."

"Why'd you marry him in the first place?"

"Suspended reality," she said. "I was in love with him, and then I was sort of, I don't know, dependent on him being around. Or me being around for him. It gave me a purpose when I was looking for one. I couldn't imagine how it would ever be different."

He asked her how the marriage ended.

"An epiphany," she said and laughed.

"Really."

"Sort of. I was running one morning. Every day I did the same run, across North Avenue to the lake and back. Every morning for, like, a month, I was crying as I ran. I just ran and thought about things and cried. And the thing that always made me cry was that I was accepting being unhappy. I wasn't crying over James. I was crying because I wouldn't do anything about it. I never considered how it could be different. I had given up on being happy with James, but I didn't see how I could survive on my own again. It was the same thing every day—at about mile two," she said, smiling. "And then one morning, when I got to the lake—mile three—I sat down on a park bench and just sobbed and sobbed, out loud, really loud. And several people—mostly women but not all—came up and asked if I was OK. And after a while I was just sitting there. I stopped crying. And people stopped coming up and asking if I was OK. It was late fall and cold out in the mornings, but I wasn't cold sitting there for the longest time. Even though I was sweaty and had just enough layers on to stay warm as long as I kept running. And then I finally started to get a chill and I thought, OK, it's time to get up and get moving again because I'm getting cold.

"And that was it. I don't know, really. I guess I was just ready. I told him that night. That was the hard part. He had not really paid any attention to me in two years. But suddenly I had his attention. I thought for a second that it was the beginning of mending things and maybe saving the marriage, but I was listening to him, and it was all about him, how *he* needed me, his *work* needed me. I was his rock. But it was like he needed to be able to take me for granted. He needed to have me present without having to pay me any attention."

"It's amazing," Flood said.

"What?" she said with a puzzled smile.

"That you had that moment on your run. That you figured it

out on your own."

"I told you. It was an epiphany," she said, smiling again.

"A good, hard thing."

She shrugged.

"How about you? Jamie said you were smart and had an epiphany before you tied the knot."

It was clear whose side that little bastard Jamie was on. He was in the dark while she knew his life story. Flood looked down at the table.

"I didn't want her life."

"And what was that?"

"Oh, it was sort of about buying into an idea. Her family. Huge family. It was like a corporation," he said. "You ever know somebody who works for a big company or a new company, and they wear the golf shirts with the company logo and talk about how great the company is and they have this look in their eye, like it's . . . religion? You need to buy into that to be successful and climb the ladder to make vice president some day, and all the while just deciding that you believe in the whole thing, that it has integrity and they all love you and would never let you down. And her family was like that, like buying into something to fit in and get ahead."

"They wanted you to be a company boy?"

"Yes. And I sort of respected it, I guess. That family was the most important thing to all of them, Lizzy and everybody, and that's the only way for a family like that to survive—to think it's the greatest, most dynamic family in the world."

"Are you saying you don't have family values?"

"Maybe not."

"So what happened?"

"I was lucky, I guess. It was so extreme. There were so many commitments and so much pressure. And I was bad at it. I didn't play soccer with the nieces and nephews, and I found excuses to skip grandma's birthday party at the club. It was like I weeded myself out."

"All that was more important to her than you?" she asked, as if it was too much to be believed.

"Well, it was sort of like your husband. I was important, but my critical role was to be there to be taken for granted. Any Irish Catholic boy with a resumé could have played the part."

"So . . ."

He laughed.

"So, no, it didn't end well. She didn't understand any of that. And I couldn't figure out how to say it any other way than, *honey, your family is insane and I don't want anything to do with them.* So, that's where I made a mess. I never really said that, and it made her really angry because she didn't understand. But she had already bought into the family, and she couldn't survive without it, so I decided understanding me was less important to her than not having that whole idea challenged."

"Do you still think that?"

"No, I think I was chickenshit. But I'm not going back."

"I take it they were rich."

"Very."

"You could have been on easy street." She smiled.

"That's one way of looking at it. But try this image instead. It's what I saw: a 45-year-old Percodan addict, trying to feel up the babysitter as I drive her home through the streets of Winnetka, and crashing into a tree instead. An embarrassing lawsuit follows. An eventual headline. I wasn't cut out for making the family look good."

"Vivid," she said, lifting her wine glass again.

"Isn't it."

"Why Percodan? Why not alcohol?"

"I love booze too much to make it my demon. Pills, on the other hand—I could have been hooked. My illustrious football career ended with a hyper-extended knee that nearly made me an opiate addict."

"I have a hard time seeing you as a serious jock. Jamie told me you played for, like, a big time college team."

"Oh, I could have been great, really," he said. "If I wasn't small and very slow."

She laughed.

"I played a very cerebral game."

"Is it a very cerebral sport?"

"Football? Not in the least. There's a lot of memorization, but it's really all instinct and timing. Mostly instinct. And speed. And size."

"You're not small," she said, mock flattering him. Having fun. "You're . . . strapping."

"I'm a big clumsy oaf in the real world. But on a Division 1 football field, I was wee, worthless and weak. I was big enough to play the position they put me in—safety. But I was about eight steps too slow. I needed to play linebacker or end to be any good, and I was two inches and fifty pounds too small for that."

"It's a strange game."

"Yeah, well, we're a strange people."

She shrugged.

They sat for a moment. Jenny looked out on the glittering skyline of the north edge of the Loop along the river. None of Chicago's signature buildings were in the line, but it was a stunning view anyway, and Flood loved it. It was one of the reasons he stayed in his shoebox apartment in a high-rise with no balcony or deck where he could put a lounge chair or grill. He didn't even have real windows to open, just panes that would crank open a few inches.

Flood looked at her beautiful face. The room smelled of wine and rosemary. He didn't know what he was thinking about—

maybe everything at once—Marcy Westlake, his jilted Lizzy Sheil, James the serious artist. What kind of a man made his wife call him James instead of Jim or Jimmy? Jimmy was a great name, a great shortening of a name. He could see a Robert not wanting to be a Bob, it was a judgment call, but not wanting to be a Jimmy was somehow wrong. James, on second reference, was pompous. Flood hated the precious bastard.

They killed the bottle of Bordeaux and she eventually cocked an eyebrow and held up her wristwatch.

"I should go home," she said.

He nodded. "So, I think I passed muster."

"Mr. False Modesty. I'm pretty sure I owe you a dinner someplace fancy. I sure as hell can't cook like this."

"Are you asking me out on a date?"

"I'm too traditional for that."

"Let's do something Friday."

They were on their feet now and he was helping her with her coat.

"Do you have my number?" She started to dig in her pockets looking for a pen.

"Jamie gave it to me. Come on, I'll give you a ride home."

"No, I'll get a cab. It's a five minute ride for me."

They rode down to the lobby in the elevator and walked silently toward the turnaround, the heels of her boots echoing as they clicked on tile.

Outside, a cab pulled forward into the turnaround when Flood raised his hand.

"I had a really nice time with you," she said.

"Get in before you freeze."

She started to get in, but then leaned over the door and put her hand on his shoulder. She pulled him close and kissed him. Flood felt the electricity shoot from his lips to his belly and back up his spine. It had been a long time since a kiss had been anything but a courtesy or a formality. He put his hand to the side of her cheek and held her there just as long as he could stand it, then finally let go. He felt drained and blurry eyed for a second. Jenny folded herself into the back seat and closed the door, keeping her eyes on him as the cab lurched down the drive toward Wabash Avenue.

When Flood returned to his warm, empty and quiet apartment, he realized he had not bothered to check his messages. There were three, all from Keith Reece. The reporter would never leave specific information on voicemail. All the messages just said to call him because he had important information "on what we talked about before." Flood called Reece's office number, but there was no answer and it went to voicemail. Then he tried Reece's cell phone, and his call went to voicemail without ringing. He left his own message and hung up.

It brought him back for a moment to the realization he had made before running into Jenny: he was potentially in for some trouble once the feds started investigating what Dan and Marcy Westlake were up to. Flood was too happy to think about it at the moment.

His apartment seemed less lonely. Its silence seemed temporary, and suddenly the place vibrated with possibilities. Flood saw Jenny curled up on his couch with him, sliding into his lap as he read in his easy chair. Walking out from the bedroom in nothing but one of his dress shirts on her way to the kitchen for a glass of cold water. Eating his coq au vin with a glass of wine at the table as the river and the skyscrapers faded in the twilight like ships sailing into the mist. He poured a bourbon and ran a thimble full of tap water over the ice before sitting down in his chair to look out at the office lights sparkling back at him. He just wanted to stay connected a few moments longer to the thread of this night.

He finished the whisky and stared off into space, thinking

about nothing. His mind came to such a complete stop that he caught himself falling asleep. He lifted himself up and stumbled to the bedroom. He had shed all his clothes when the phone rang.

Chapter Eleven

"It's McManus."

Flood rubbed a little of the coming sleep out of his eyes and said hello.

"Listen, guess what?" McManus said, not waiting for a rhetorical answer. "The certain somebody you asked about last night, well, he's in here right now."

Flood felt his body wake up immediately with a jolt of adrenalin.

"Tortufi is there?"

"In the flesh. He's been sitting here about a half hour. Told me he's meeting somebody, but I think he's been stood up. Now he's just sitting here at the bar. Watching the front door in the mirror. Every time somebody walks in, he gets off the stool and walks into the kitchen 'til they're in the dining room. He's jumpy as all hell."

Flood was pulling his clothes back on. "I'll be there in a few minutes. If he starts to leave, call me back. Do you mind?"

"No, man. You got it."

Flood hopped on the elevator and rode down to the garage, thinking about how he would approach this and what he would say if Tortufi asked him how he knew to show up at the Napoli just then. The world was full of enough dumb luck, he decided, and didn't worry about it. He raced the car around on Lower Wacker, jumped off and then onto Monroe, across the expressways and past UIC to Racine. He knew he should just leave the whole thing alone at this point, but he wanted to know how Tortufi would react when asked if he knew where to find Marcy Westlake. He wanted to gauge Tortufi's level of surprise and credulity. In a way, it was playing along with Westlake. As soon as Tortufi heard the question, Flood could be assured that it would get back to Bepps, which was what he guessed Westlake wanted to happen.

As Flood turned off of Racine and idled down the side street, past a row of houses before reaching the restaurant, his phone rang. It was McManus again.

"He's paying his tab and buttoning his coat."

"What else is going on?"

"I can't really tell. This guy Chucky who hangs around here walked in and used the can about two minutes ago, but then just walked back out on the street and disappeared. I think Tortufi noticed him, and that's when he paid his tab. Chucky's a connected guy. You close by?"

"Pretty close. What's he wearing?"

"Camel hair overcoat."

The restaurant was closing down for the night. It was after ten-thirty and the valets were all across the street in the university basketball arena's sprawling empty lot where they parked cars. Flood pulled to the curb and watched as the man that had to be Vincent Tortufi stepped out into the cold night from the restaurant vestibule. He would be waiting for his car for a minute, so Flood shifted into park. Now was his chance to get out and approach him. But something on Tortufi's face made him wait a beat. Tortufi closed the top button of the camel hair coat, appeared to take a deep breath and walked away from Flood to a black Town Car that was parked at the curb. He stopped at the back passenger door, where the window slid down as Tortufi approached. The man bent his big body for a few moments, as though he was listening intently to someone inside, and then he slowly turned his head and looked down the street toward Flood as a pale blue Ford Econoline van pulled past Flood's car and eased up behind the Town Car. Tortufi stood up and lingered for a moment before turning and walking slowly toward the van. The side door of the van slid open, and a young man in a black leather jacket stepped out with his back to Flood. Tortufi did not make eye contact with the man and just got in the van. He had a look on his face that struck Flood. He looked drained—fatigue mixed with dull resignation. The man stepped back behind Tortufi and slid the door shut.

The Town Car left first, making a U-turn and driving back past Flood toward Racine. Flood didn't turn his head. He was slumped back in his seat so that the darkness and the door frame obscured his face from full view. Then the van pulled away from the curb and made a slow right turn down another side street. Flood waited a beat and then followed the van. As he pulled past the restaurant, he looked over into the university lot and saw a pearl-colored Cadillac Escalade parked there, the only vehicle left. Flood recognized it from the motor vehicle records he'd pulled on Tortufi's family. He caught up with the van as it turned left on Taylor Street. Most of the restaurants were closing down after a slow Monday night. Older couples and groups of men who looked like business travelers ambled slowly into their waiting cars under the weight of heavy Italian food, oblivious to the strange circumstances passing by in a baby blue van. The van traveled east a couple of blocks to Halsted Street and then turned right, heading south. Down through Pilsen, over the South Branch of the river and into Bridgeport, the van drove slowly, carefully slowing and stopping at yellow lights before they turned red. They went far enough that it would have made more sense to take the expressway. But they stuck to Halsted, easing through the stretch of Bridgeport bars, and the signs telling them to turn left for Sox Park, down to

Pershing Road and the industrial area around the vast spaces that used to be the Chicago Stockyards. After heading west a couple of blocks on Pershing, the van slowed and turned into the drive of a large garage next door to an auto impound lot. As if the building had been anticipating the vehicle, the garage door rose loudly, and the van pulled in. Flood drove by, trying to look inside as he did, but it was dark. He saw a car parked inside but could not make out what kind. He turned around at the end of the block and pulled to the curb and waited.

There was little traffic on Pershing other than the occasional heavy truck rumbling by and a few rickety old sedans ferrying slouched young men back and forth from one street-gang battlefield to the next. Pershing runs across the South Side almost five miles from downtown, from middle-class black neighborhoods on the lakefront, through the old ethnic white outposts of Bridgeport and Canaryville, into Mexican and Polish neighborhoods, and eventually the tough, corrupt suburbs of Cicero and Berwyn. The garage was in the middle of the Pershing Road corridor, amid blocks of grubby machine shops, salvage yards and small factories. It wasn't a pretty neighborhood, but it was dirty and tattered from industry, not neglect.

He waited, wishing he had coffee because he'd had so much wine earlier. He did not want to risk going around the corner to an all-night diner for a cup, so he just sat and yawned and tried to stay awake listening to the erudite but increasingly cranky and right-wing Milt Rosenberg on WGN. Flood's father had been a devotee of Rosenberg because the University of Chicago social psychologist had the smartest show on radio, probably anywhere. The guests ranged from writers and scientists to former Cabinet members, to private detectives, ghost hunters and historians of everything from baseball to the Restoration. But Rosenberg was becoming increasingly a political reactionary in his old age, and the folly of the Clinton administration had sent him over the edge. On many nights, he sounded almost like Rush Limbaugh with tenure. As Flood sat there listening, Rosenberg was taking the President's evangelical fervor at face value. Eventually he turned the dial and found an abrasive, shrill sports talk show and turned it down to provide just a murmur of background.

As time passed, a number of tow trucks came hauling cars and trucks to the impound lot. They dropped them off and then headed back out on the streets for more easy revenue. Flood wondered how many of the cars weren't even illegally parked. The towing contractors did it all the time, figuring—correctly—that the owners would just accept their fate and pay the $150 rather than fight the faceless corruption of the auto towing industry in Chicago.

An hour passed in silence on the street. Then, just after one in the morning, the garage door finally opened again. The van did not come out. Instead, a brown GMC Denali emerged and turned east on Pershing. He did not catch a glimpse of the two people in the vehicle, but he could see down the road that the SUV crossed Halsted and kept on eastward. They were not going back to the Napoli Tap, which meant they were not returning Tortufi to his car. Flood figured they were headed toward the Dan Ryan Expressway instead, probably south or all the way to the North Shore. Flood decided not to follow them. He got out of his car and walked to the garage. It was dark, but around the corner, the lights were on at the impound lot office, awaiting the outraged and the merely drunk, who would come to claim their towed cars.

Flood listened but heard nothing at the side door of the garage. He gave up and started to walk back to his car. Just as he turned his back, the garage door started to rumble again and a diesel engine chugged to life inside. Flood ran for cover behind a parked car a few lengths ahead of his and watched as headlights cast a milky glow over the parked cars on the street in front of the garage. He heard big gears shift, and then a dump truck eased out of the garage and turned the same way that the brown Denali had gone. Careful to stay low and out of sight, Flood scrambled to his car, started the engine and followed, eyeing the open garage as he passed. Inside he saw a parked dark-colored Cadillac as the door was sliding shut.

The dump truck rambled about a mile across Pershing to the Dan Ryan and onto the southbound ramp, with Flood behind. Despite the hour, there was traffic on the expressway, and they even slowed to a crawl around the split for the Skyway toll road. Eventually, the truck veered into the split onto I-57 and drove down south another fifteen minutes, through Blue Island, over the Cal-Sag Channel and the Tri-State overpass to 159th Street. The landscape turned to middle-class suburbia, first older housing tracts in Oak Forest near the interstate, then a long line of strip malls and big box stores surrounded by newer subdivisions. Flood followed all the way through Orland Park and into the southwestern fringe of Chicago's sprawl, where subdivisions and farm fields were still hop-scotched together. He kept his distance now because the area was wide open and deserted in the middle of the night. He'd be noticed if he got too close. The truck turned south at the intersection ahead of him, and Flood turned off his lights when he reached the stop sign and watched the red beads of its taillights as it traveled about a quarter mile and then pulled into the gravel access drive leading to a construction site of several new homes. He continued to idle in the darkness and squinted at the distant dump truck, seeing a person jump down from the passenger side. Then he saw a form move into the wash of the headlights at the closed chain-link gate to the development. The man appeared to unlock the gate and then swung the fence doors back. The truck drove into the development, leaving the gate open.

Flood wanted to follow, but he wasn't about to drive his car in there. He drove down the road slowly—lights still off—once the truck had disappeared deeper into the curving streets of the new subdivision. He stopped about a hundred yards beyond the gate, where he found a dirt turnoff, which probably would someday be another street into the same development. He parked his car and got out, climbed the eight-foot chain-link fence, which had probably been put up to keep thieves from stealing construction supplies. It was pitch dark, and the frozen clods of turned earth under his feet were difficult to walk on. He started to jog carefully over the mounds and chunks of raw, upturned dirt, weaving through the shells of framed-up houses, jungle gyms of raw blonde wood, as he followed the distant white rays of the dump truck's headlights. As he ran, he heard the diesel take a breath and grunt, and then heard the steady beep of its reverse alarm. The truck was backing up to something. Finally he arrived at the corner of a short concrete block wall that was a house foundation. He looked over the wall into a poured concrete pit. These houses were having their basements poured, one by one. He crouched and looked over at the dump truck backing up to the edge of a big rectangular hole in the ground at the next site over. There was no concrete lining the hole yet, just black earth. The man from the passenger side jumped down from the cab again and ran around the back. He shouted directions at the driver, who kept inching back.

Flood wanted to get closer to see what was at the bottom of the hole. From where he crouched, the truck was on the far corner of the hole. There was a Bobcat earth mover parked at the opposite corner of the hole. If he could get to it, he'd have cover to look into the hole, but there was a lot of open ground between his current perch and the cover of the Bobcat. He waited. The truck kept inching back until the man standing said, "Ho!" and started to walk toward the cab, disappearing from view. It was Flood's chance. He sprinted over the open ground, careful not to stumble on clods of dirt or ruts and made it to the Bobcat undetected. From there he could see into the hole. The ground at the bottom was smooth and compacted, except for one spot, the corner below the dump truck. There was a deeper hole, about four feet by eight feet, and maybe four feet deep. Flood knew what it looked like.

Now the man came back into view and stood at the edge of the basement. The reverse lights illuminated him, and he shone a flashlight down into the extra hole in the basement. Then the sound of the truck's diesel hiked up a pitch, and the hold of the truck began to incline slowly under the smooth power of pneumatic lifts. Eventually, the back gate swung open a little with a rusty whine and a little loose dirt began to pour out of the truck, then more, and finally a large bundle wrapped in black plastic sheeting slid out and tumbled down next to the larger hole.

The man shouted "Ho!" again, and then jumped down into the basement as the truck's hold began to ease back to its level position. Now another man appeared at the back of the truck, although he stood outside of the reverse lights' glow and Flood could only tell that he was large and was holding something long. It could have been a gun or a shovel. Down in the bottom of the basement, the other man toiled in darkness. He dragged the big bundle into the larger hole and then the other man dropped the object down next to him. It was a large flat shovel. The man picked it up and started filling in the pile of dumped dirt over the package. He shoveled for about ten minutes, until the area was smoothed over. Then the fat man threw down a piece of plywood, which the other one placed over the area and jumped up and down on, moving it around, trying to make the freshly covered area smooth and compact like the rest of the foundation dirt.

Flood looked around at the construction equipment parked around the site, and he presumed that a new concrete basement would be poured into the hole when the weather warmed up in the spring. It would cover the buried package forever. Finally the man tossed the shovel and the plywood back up onto the ground and climbed out of the hole. The two of them stood there at the edge of the basement for a moment, shining the flashlight over the burial spot. Satisfied, the fat man holding the light then turned it on the surrounding area, searching the house frames and the open ground. Flood ducked down and made sure he was completely shielded from view by the back wheel of the Bobcat. The light finally washed over the Bobcat, lingered a moment, and then moved on, inspecting the other areas around the house site. Then the light went out and Flood peeked again, watching the men turn their backs and climb back into the truck. The reverse light went off and the truck churned loudly into gear and began easing away, back into the dirt road. Flood turned and ran back the way he had come, making sure to stay low and in the dark, well out of the path of the truck and its headlights.

Flood sprinted across the hard, dark ground, watching over his shoulder as the truck made its way out to the gate. He needed to get back to his car and take off before they had a chance to see it. He wondered what would happen if they turned toward his car instead of heading back the way they came. The truck was at the gate and the thinner man was out again shutting the gate when Flood's foot hit a big clump of dirt that rolled out from under his boot. He tripped and went sprawling. When he regained his feet, the truck had turned. It was coming at his car, its high-beams on, lighting up the dusty black Taurus. Flood's stumble had ruined his chances of getting there in time. They would beat him to the car. All he could do was lay flat on the ground and watch.

The truck eased down the road, as if cautiously, and came to a stop behind Flood's car. It shifted into idle for a moment, the high-beams brilliantly illuminating his rear license plate. Finally, the younger man jumped down from the cab with his flashlight and approached Flood's car. He shone the light on the interior as he slowly walked around. Surely they would be able to trace it to him through the plate later, but he racked his brain to remember if there was anything lying out on the seat that would arouse their suspicions further right now. It should be clean. The man crouched at the driver's door, shining the light. Flood worried for a moment that he was picking the lock or using a Slim Jim to get in and go through the glove compartment. Flood felt his head begin to sweat under his watch cap. Finally the man stood up and used the flashlight to scan the surrounding area. He looked up and down the ditch, and then swung the light over the ground inside the fence. Flood put his face down against the dirt and held his breath. If the light fell on him, he would present nothing but dull black fabric, except for his blue jeans, but they'd be behind him and difficult to see. The light finally went out without shining on his body, and the man walked slowly back to the cab. The truck idled another minute, and Flood wondered if they were making phone calls trying to figure out what to do. Eventually the truck ground into gear and turned back into the road, making a herky-jerky U-turn and heading back north the way they had come. Flood waited in the same position, lying flat, until the truck had made the turn east and was out of sight.

Then he cursed himself and stood up. He jogged back to the fence, climbed over, and then stood at the back of his car. He was torn between getting the hell out of there and going back to confirm his suspicions. The feeling in his gut told him he was already in too deep to play it safe, and he could not make himself leave.

He popped the trunk, where he kept a toolbox, and took out a flashlight, a box cutter and claw-hammer, which was the best thing he could find to dig. He went back over the fence and jogged back to the site, looking back at the road constantly to make sure they did not return. He walked around the edge of the basement hole to the spot where the men had stood and then jumped down beside the freshly filled dig. Wearing his black leather winter gloves, he began to scrape away the dirt until he had it loosened up and could shovel it away with his hands. About a foot deep, he found the tip of the black plastic. He brushed away more dirt until he could get his hands around the package.

"Damn," he said under his breath, in frustration and horror. It felt like hard shoes and ankles. The package was a body. But the wrong end of the body. Flood's heart was racing and his breathing was out of control. His lungs hurt in the cold air and he felt confused and dizzy. He managed to turn himself around and start digging at the other end of the hole. He uncovered the end of the plastic wrapping and took out the box cutter, steeling himself for what he'd find on the inside. He looked around again, to make sure there was no one there. And then he gingerly began to slice away at the layers of black plastic. The first thing he saw was gray flesh and deep-red congealing blood. There was a straight line of crimson across the flesh. The man had been garroted around the neck. The shirt collar was soaked in blood. Flood sliced up the plastic to the top of the head and peeled away the sheets. For the first and last time, he was face to face with the man he had wanted to see—Vincent Tortufi. There was a bullet hole above his left ear, but not much blood around it. Flood figured it was a shot after he was dead just to make sure.

He brushed away more dirt and cut down through the plastic around Tortufi's torso. There were two gunshot wounds in his chest, both of these drenched in blood. The massive amount of blood finally was too much for Flood. He stumbled away from the grisly grave and sat back on his haunches gasping for air. He ran through the evidence in his head and figured they had probably killed Tortufi in the van, maybe right after he got in. Somebody probably just turned around from the front seat and shot him in the chest twice, and as he reeled from those wounds another killer wrapped the wire around his neck and finished him off. The garage in Bridgeport was all about cleanup and disposal.

Flood picked up his tools and ran back again to the fence, hopped over and put everything in the trunk. He got back in the car and started to drive back the way he came, but then thought better of it. He turned back around and headed south again; eventually he found a road heading east and took it. As he drove, Interstate 80 was in sight to the south, running parallel to the road he traveled. The road came back out of farmland onto a major artery and he headed north toward the lights of Orland Park again. He needed to report what he'd seen, but he did not want to be involved in an investigation. He drove across 167th Street until he came to a large gas station with a pay phone outside. He left his car running and parked out of view of the store clerk, took a packet of handy wipes from the door and then walked to the phone and called 911.

"I need the Orland Park Police Department, please."

A dispatcher came on and said, "What is your emergency?"

"I just witnessed two white males bury a body in the unfinished basement foundation of a house site in the Meadowridge Glen Farms development. You need to send investigators there immediately," Flood said. He thought a second and then added, "They had a key for the padlock on the gate and let themselves in."

"Sir, what is your name and location, please?"

Flood gave the plate number of the truck and then hung up. He wiped off the phone receiver, put the wipes back in his coat pocket and then returned to his car and drove off toward the city.

Chapter Twelve

It was three-thirty in the morning when Flood passed the Chinatown/Lake Shore Drive split from the Dan Ryan Expressway. He took the Congress exit and before he headed underground on Lower Wacker, he called Reece's home number. Half-asleep, Reece croaked an obscenity into the phone when he answered.

"Meet me at Pat Haran's in ten minutes," Flood said, and he hung up. He couldn't think of any place else nearby that was open at four in the morning. Flood parked in his garage and walked the block to State and Hubbard. The bar was dark, smoke-stained and sprinkled with very serious drinkers. Flood bought a Johnnie Walker Black at the bar and took it to a back table and waited, his hands shaking when he held the glass.

Reece looked remarkably composed when he walked in ten minutes later. He had caught a cab at the Holiday Inn. He stopped at the bar and got himself a whisky and then joined Flood. He didn't bother to protest. He knew it was serious.

He sat down and said, "What happened?"

"I saw Vincent Tortufi murdered tonight."

Reece did not say anything, but his eyes were locked on Flood, and Flood saw fear flickering in them. He told Reece the whole story, starting with the phone call from McManus, whom he did not name.

"What do you want me to do?" Reece asked when he had finished.

"Watch the morgue. Don't let Tortufi's body slip by unnoticed. And have some suburban reporter stumble ass-backwards onto what happened tonight. Just cover my tracks and your tracks, but make sure there is attention on this thing immediately. Don't let anybody sit on it for a week."

"Because whoever they were, they saw your car, and they're going to be looking for you and trying to figure out what to do about you?"

Flood nodded.

"If they think it's just me and them, I think they'll be more inclined to decide they can take care of me," he said. "I also want to have a legitimate reason to know about it. At least for a little bit."

Reece nodded, and they drank their whisky. The reporter was probably thinking about Flood's last statement and whether it pushed him into an ethical compromise. He had just been told astonishing information by the eyewitness to a murder, and he was agreeing not only to not publish the eyewitness account, but to keep the secret in part so that the eyewitness could mislead the authorities about how he knew that Tortufi had been murdered. The bartender murmured out a last call, and Flood smiled weakly at Reece.

"I don't think we've ever closed Pat Haran's before."

"Strange times."

When they walked out of the closing bar a few minutes after five, the streets were beginning to come to life again. Cars were backing up at the lights and filling parking garages, and men in suits and overcoats and warm hats were trickling up from out of the Red Line subway stop at Grand and State. Sleep was out of the question, so Flood walked home, showered and shaved and put on a fresh suit. He was starving and walked down to the Renaissance Hotel and ordered a full breakfast of poached eggs, bacon and an English muffin. He drank several cups of coffee and looked out the window at the frozen river. The ice, green and frosty white along its cracks, struck him funny and looked to him for a moment like a piece of broken glass that someone had spilled cocaine across, as if they had been doing lines on a coffee table and had a fit. All sorts of nonsense spun through his head without reason or focus. He had brought the morning papers along, but they lay unread and still folded neatly on the table. Flood was in a bit of shock.

As he thought about the ice and drugs and cut throats and the glow of fluorescent lights at a suburban gas station lighting up the night, his mind hovered over the fragments of Dan and Marcy Westlake's life that he had collected in the last few days. The taciturn businessman with the suspicious motives, the beautiful woman and doting mother, unfaithful wife, the mobster's mistress, her disappearance, the scheme, Grand Cayman, three bullets and a garrote line across Vincent Tortufi's thick neck did not bode well for the Westlakes. But Flood did not know what might happen next. He wondered if they were scared, hiding, sorting our their plan and the mess they had made of it by Marcy bedding down with a grade-A wise guy who was involved in the sort of thing that eventually got him whacked.

None of the pieces really fit together, and he just sat there in a muddle. He knew he should go to Ridgeway and the FBI, spill all and ask for help, but something kept him from doing it. He was telling himself his responsibility was to his client, and that he and Cronin needed to confront Westlake and find out what was really going on before talking to anybody else about it. Flood kidded himself that he had satisfied his legal requirement of reporting the crime he'd seen last night by calling the Orland Park police and telling them where to look. Of course, that was nonsense. He'd witnessed the crime unfolding, which certainly carried more responsibility than phoning in an anonymous tip. He was a lawyer and an officer of the court. But something made him stall. Flood did not want to give up on this and turn it all over to the authorities. He needed to understand what all this meant to Daniel and Marcy Westlake before he just offered it all up to the FBI. If he went to Ridgeway now, it would all be taken away. The investigation would be all over Daniel Westlake's and his wife's ties to Tortufi, and Flood would be frozen out of whatever they found. The client would certainly not be served, he thought. And yet, he decided he would not tell Cronin about what he'd seen last night, either. Cronin would be given the same dilemma Flood was now moving through—the officer of the court's obligation to report a crime.

He would acknowledge what he knew in a couple of days, but he first needed to figure out how it fit together, and whether it had any impact on his client.

Oddly enough, the only person Flood could trust was Reece. As a journalist, he operated in a gray area of responsibilities. Flood knew Reece would protect him not just because he was his friend, but because he was his source, and he was producing information that Reece could not get anywhere else. Flood had floated into some critical, uncharted vein of the biggest story Reece had ever covered.

Flood's head ached and he was very tired. But his mind was focusing now on what came next. He remembered that he had called Ridgeway the day before to ask about Vincent Tortufi. If Ridgeway was not already aware of the murder, he would be soon, and that would surely mean he would be asking Flood questions.

As Flood paid his bill and headed back to the street toward his office, he was left thinking about what they would say to Westlake. For the moment, it was not a terribly pressing problem. Flood had left numerous messages for him in the last two days and saw no reason to keep trying. On this point, he agreed with Cronin that they should just wait.

Flood more or less turned over the current insurance case he was working on to Jamie so that he could focus completely on writing a report for Cronin. That begged the next question: what to tell Cronin about Tortufi.

He started with the affair, writing that it was clear from his interview with Pam Sawyer that Mrs. Westlake was involved in a personal relationship with Vincent Tortufi and that he believed her whereabouts were probably related to . . .

He stopped. There was only one place to start, and it wasn't the stuff of memos. Flood erased the file he'd started on his computer and sat back to think. Reece would have the information about Tortufi on the record and developed by midday. Then it would be logical for Flood to know about it, and he could turn around and tell his boss and Westlake. But he had to wait a few hours playing dumb.

Outside his open door he heard Jamie say hello to someone and could hear the alarm in his assistant's voice. Flood closed out of Word, opened the Internet and started browsing headlines. He was scrolling though the latest news on the 9/11 Commission when the two men in suits appeared in the doorway. Ridgeway and Feinberg trudged in, looking heavy in their overcoats and brown suits, closed the door and plopped down in the chairs in front of Flood's desk.

"Hi, guys," Flood said, feigning a warm welcome.

Ridgeway just looked at him. Feinberg looked at Ridgeway. Flood smiled.

"And?" he said.

Ridgeway acted like they were already getting the runaround. "Vincent Tortufi."

Flood nodded. "That brought you over to see me? Did I ask

about the wrong guy?"

Feinberg looked harder at Ridgeway.

"Don't fuck with me, Augie?" Ridgeway said. He had a way of growling out questions sometimes that never really had the menacing effect he intended. "What do you know? And why are you asking?"

"Well, why are you asking, John?"

Ridgeway leaned forward and was already fuming. Flood had not really recognized all the tension wound up inside the agent when he arrived.

"Maybe you didn't hear me the first time, Augie. Do not fuck with me. I came down here to see you as a courtesy. I could have dragged you up to the office with no notice and taken the rest of your day."

The fact that he hadn't, if he was really as angry as he was acting, meant that Ridgeway did not know what to do. The unfolding events had him completely flummoxed. Flood decided not to push him.

"A client of the firm asked me to make contact with his estranged wife," he finally began. "She's cut off contact with him, and he says he does not know where she is. I learned that she has some kind of relationship with Vincent Tortufi. Something about him made me wonder whether he was connected. I didn't remember the name, but what do I know. I didn't work Outfit cases. So I called you. John, I called just as much to say hello. I didn't really expect you to have heard of the guy."

Feinberg's face said nothing, and it was impossible to tell what he was thinking. On the other hand, Ridgeway now looked like he was losing his patience.

"Who's the client?" he said, in a terse, clipped voice.

"John, I'm serious, too. If you want me to talk about a client's business, you need to give me a little more reason than the fact that you're pissed about something. You need to tell me what this matters to my client."

"We can have this discussion at 219," Ridgeway repeated. Flood did not want to go to Ridgeway's office, but he believed Ridgeway really didn't want to take him there, either. So Flood wasn't going to budge until he heard a bit of what Ridgeway knew, and he knew how much Ridgeway was willing to tell him.

Ridgeway sat back, pissed. He wouldn't dignify Flood's demand himself, so he glanced at Feinberg, who now spoke up. He was much more congenial toward Flood than Ridgeway.

"Well, Augie. This guy Tortufi, as you've probably figured out, has some organized crime ties. And then the other thing is that . . . well, now he's dead."

Flood wasn't going to feign surprise; that would be lying, and eventually they'd know he was lying. So he just sat there stone-faced. He did it well because he'd been anticipating the words *Vincent Tortufi is dead.* After a bit of silence he shrugged and leaned forward.

"What does this have to do with my client? My client is not a mobster; his wife is not a mobster," he said. "How was he killed? Do you have some reason to think my client would have any connection, or would know anything, about him being killed?"

Feinberg took a quick glance at Ridgeway, didn't get waved off, and so went on explaining.

"Murdered. Mob hit. Throat cut and shot. They dumped him in—"

Ridgeway held up his hand to cut off Feinberg. "That's enough."

Oh, wouldn't Ridgeland be surprised when the media contact got a call from a reporter about the body in the fresh basement in Orland Park, Flood thought. Ridgeway stopped Feinberg because he thought Flood was of limited use, he guessed. He didn't want to get into the details of the murder.

"I've let you know why we're here," Ridgeway said. "Now you tell me who the fuck your client is."

Flood thought about it and realized he didn't have much cause to hold out any more. He'd learned a little about what Ridgeway was after. It felt like he just wanted to clear the decks of any possible entanglement from Flood.

"OK, John. My client is a guy named Daniel Westlake. He is a plumbing and sewer contractor who's separated from his wife. She controls some money that he needs to use at the moment to pay bills and payroll so he doesn't lose his business. He has a cash-flow problem at the moment because a government job he did hasn't been paid off." Flood paused and took a breath. "In searching for his wife, I learned that she had what I presume to be an extramarital affair with Mr. Tortufi. He seemed my best bet for contacting her, but I was tiptoeing around that, for obvious reasons. I don't even know if they were still seeing each other, John."

From the look on Ridgeway's face, it seemed this wasn't exactly what he had anticipated hearing. Now Ridgeway looked like he was chewing on a question and trying to decide whether to ask it. Flood hoped he would because he could tell he'd learn something from it.

"Why's he in a bind right now, financially?" Ridgeway asked.

He was fishing for the right reason and didn't want to say it himself. Flood knew the real reason was Westlake's entanglement with George Kajmar and the casino bid in which he wanted to invest. But it wasn't clear whether Ridgeway knew. Westlake had not actually told him that, so he decided to stick with what Westlake had told him the day they met.

"He told me it's a run of the mill shortfall. I think he's just over-extended. Borrowed too much money and the littlest thing—this sewer contract in Will County—getting hung up by local politics has put him in a spot. Between you and me, John, bad management. But it's not my business to tell the guy he's a lame businessman."

If this answer wasn't good enough, Ridgeway wouldn't leave it here. He'd keep pressing for Flood to say something about the casino angle. Flood started pushing in the other direction.

"John, I'm not sure I'm seeing why this has got your attention right now. My client didn't know Tortufi. He didn't know his wife was having an affair. I haven't found her to talk to her about it. Is Tortufi part of the Bepps investigation?"

Ridgeway rocked nervously in his chair. "Why do you say that?"

"Because you're in the middle of nailing the biggest case of your career, and you're spending part of your day here with me grilling me about the guy."

"We can't talk about it."

Flood smiled. "I'm not a reporter, guys."

They both rolled their eyes, as he knew they would. They didn't need to say Reece's name for him to know that's what they were thinking. They figured anything they told him now that he was no longer an agent would be likely to end up in Reece's notebook. Flood thought about how they would react later in the day when the Orland Park cops and the medical examiner called, asking what they should do because a reporter was asking them about Vincent Tortufi's body.

CHAPTER THIRTEEN

Flood was certain that Dan Westlake would be hauled in for questioning next as soon as he got back from Grand Cayman. When Ridgeway and Feinberg were gone, he made another call to Westlake's cell phone. The voicemail again.

"Dan, it's Flood. You really need to call me. Things are happening, and I need to speak to you. I'm sure the FBI is going to pay you a visit. Probably today. It's about your wife and a man named Vincent Tortufi."

Jamie had kept his distance for a few minutes, but he couldn't stand it anymore. He came to the door, looked in and raised his eyebrows.

"What?"

"You look like you haven't slept."

"Not so much," Flood said. "Wanna get coffee?"

They went down the street to a coffee shop and found an empty table.

"I have a problem," Flood started.

"Did you talk to the Westlakes?" Jamie said, frowning.

"No."

"Tortufi!" Jamie said it triumphantly. "You talked to him?"

"Not exactly. I saw him."

Jamie's eyes narrowed. He stirred his coffee for further dramatic effect, and then gave up on hoping for an insight.

"So now what?"

"I don't know," Flood said. "Nothing, I think, until I figure more of it out, or until we confront Westlake."

"What else can you do now? That Tortufi guy's not going to talk to you about Marcy Westlake."

"No, he's not. He's dead."

Jamie spilled latte on the table.

"Dead?"

"Murdered last night."

"Jesus, Floodie."

The old feeling of being used by other people with more power and secret agendas was so strong that Flood barely noticed it. He had been so used to it for so long that it merely felt like the status quo of his world. He thought he had rid himself of that sickening feeling three years ago, but now it was back, stronger than ever. The feeling had crept in days before as nothing more than self-pity, but over the last few days it had grown into a lump lodged in Flood's gut. Why him? Why not hire a private investigator? Why not some other lawyer?

He was sitting in his office staring at the wall when his cell phone rang. It was Reece.

"It's starting to make sense," Reece said. "And you have a more serious problem with Tortufi."

The tone jolted him a bit. "What?"

"West Bank."

"How was he involved?"

"Majorly," Reece said. "I just got off the phone with a guy. Tortufi worked for Nicky Bepps and the feds have a late-breaking theory that he was the bagman between Bepps and the Gaming Board. They think he was in charge of putting the cash in Art Callahan's hands."

"Did your source tell you Tortufi was dead?"

"No. I think he was trying to find out if I knew he was dead, but I just kept asking if he'd been subpoenaed yet. I'll call him back in about a half-hour when our reporter in Orland is done making his calls."

"Hmm. But it's weird that they didn't have him wrapped up by now. It's like they're just figuring it out after they've started charging people."

"Shaking the tree. Indict a handful of people and it scares the shit out of the rest and they start cooperating. That's what they do. That's what you did."

"I guess."

"I guess," he said.

"Please connect the dots."

Reece held the phone closer to his mouth so that his voice was suddenly a little warmer and blurrier. He said Tortufi owned two businesses—one that put video poker machines and juke boxes in bars, and one that recycled auto fluff, which was an industry term for all the soft parts of a car once they're put through a huge shredder—upholstery, seat cushions, dashboards. The vending business was no doubt what Pam Sawyer was talking about when she said Marcy Westlake's mystery man was in the liquor trade, Flood figured. Video poker was notoriously a front for illegal gambling run by the Outfit, but in this case the feds were interested in the recycling business because their forensic accountants had traced it to Bepps. The company leased its land from a bank trust landlord. And the beneficiary of the trust turned out to be Aldo Beppo, brother of Nuccio Beppo, a.k.a. Nicky Bepps.

On its own, this was a tenuous link between the Outfit boss Bepps and Tortufi. But there was more. One of Reece's sources had let him see a transcript of a wiretap in which Bepps asked Tortufi if "our professor friend" was happy. Aside from his role on the gaming board, Art Callahan was an insurance consultant. But the mobsters apparently called him "the professor" because he worked almost exclusively for the state university system's board of trustees.

"Keith, who gave you that?"

"Source."

"Jesus, your source is going to be the subject of a Dirksen Building witch hunt if you publish it."

"Listen to you," Reece said, mockingly. "Mr. Law and Order."

"Just be careful with it."

In any event, Reece had tidied the story up considerably. Somehow, Tortufi had been the one to supply the bribe to Callahan. He was at the center of the whole scandal. So where was his girlfriend when this was going on? And if Tortufi's role got him killed, what did Nicky Bepps think of Marcy Westlake, whether or not her husband put out the word that they weren't getting along?

Flood had swiveled in his chair so that he was looking out the window. The plate glass was thick enough to blot out the rumble of the trains, wailing truck and taxi horns and the occasional crashing iron sounds of Dumpster lids and garbage truck lifts from the alleys. All bounced off the glass while he sat sealed in quiet comfort. A couple of pigeons huddled at the corner of the thin concrete ledge. It sucked being left out in the cold, he thought. But then again, they could fly away, and they just sat there. They must know what they were doing.

"Well, was Tortufi just the bagman or did he have a stake in this?"

"Hard to say," Reece answered.

"We might never know. I mean, did they figure out a way to deal themselves into the revenue stream? Invisible but legit-looking. I don't know if the investigation got that far. Bepps probably would not have really set it up until the casino was actually operating."

"Maybe Tortufi was just going to take his dividends home in paper sacks."

"Unlikely. That's not how it works."

"How does it work?" Reece asked, now playing the student.

"Well, Tortufi already has his recycling business with Aldo Bepps," Flood said.

"Then he'd just take his rewards out of that?"

"One way or another. They'd build some new revenue stream into the business, which would actually be casino profits. Fifty thousand a month for slot machine cleaning fluid, or something ridiculous like that . . ."

"From an auto-fluff recycling business?"

"I bet it has a subsidiary. A license to do something that could be construed as a service to the casino." Flood fell silent.

"What are you thinking about?"

"About Marcy Westlake. If Tortufi and Bepps thought she was really with them, there must have been some money in it for her. She wouldn't want to be played for a fool. I don't think she could have played the naïve head over heels type."

"What makes you say that?"

"Just something about the looks of the guy."

"Wiseguy?"

"He looked like a mid-level manager for the Outfit. Expensive clothes. He'd moved on from leather to cashmere. But at the end of the day the guy was still a thug who spent too much time eating on Taylor Street," he said. "He didn't look like my missing woman's soul mate. I think if she had played it that way he'd have gotten suspicious."

Reece chuckled.

"OK, so now Augie Flood is investigating the casino scandal. Your woman would only have been a one-time payment though, right? She wouldn't have gotten cut in as anybody's partner."

Flood nodded. "Yeah, they wouldn't cut her in, officially. I'm seeing a manila envelope."

"How much money do you see in that envelope?"

"It depends on what all she did," he said. "I think she's a worker. All she'd ask for is enough to get started—a down payment on a business. Maybe fifty grand. Enough to get away and get started."

"You think this is the story she was telling Tortufi?"

Flood didn't know. He had two competing scenarios playing out in his head. The likely truth and the cover story. He couldn't decide which one was more plausible, or less absurd.

"Get away where?"

Flood thought of Brandon's business school applications. There was something about the singularity of applying only to graduate programs in a state two thousand miles away. It seemed part of a larger plan.

"Probably wherever her son ended up. California."

"How do you know that?"

"The kid. He's planning to move to California this summer."

"Now what are you speculating?"

"I don't know. I'm mixing up my facts. I'm sort of lost."

Chapter Fourteen

He worked on cases he had been neglecting for the rest of the afternoon, trying to put the Westlakes and Tortufi out of his head. Cronin dropped by his doorway, but he was busy with other things, as well, and had resigned himself to the idea that they could put all this aside until Westlake showed his face again. But Flood needed to tell him about Tortufi. He said he had discovered the name of the man Marcy Westlake was having an affair with—Vincent Tortufi—and now something had happened. In the version Cronin got, Reece called Flood to tell him that a suburban reporter had learned from the Orland Park Police that there was a body in a housing site, and that it was Tortufi. Cronin turned white and closed the door.

"What do we do?"

"We sit tight a little longer. We really need to pin down Westlake on what's going on."

Flood told him about the visit from Ridgeway. Cronin nodded and sat still like a child. He was so far out of his depth, he practically begged Flood to make it all go away.

In the early evening Flood took a cab back to the Napoli Tap. Tortufi's Escalade was still there in the parking lot. Nobody had reported it, and the agents hadn't tracked it down. Ridgeway's office would presume Flood knew about Tortufi by now, he figured, even if they didn't suspect he tipped Reece to it. Reece had been on the phone with the FBI and U.S. Attorney's press offices all afternoon. So Flood called Ridgeway's office as he stood in front of the restaurant. He got Feinberg.

"I talked to Reece. He said Orland Park had a body in a hole in the ground, and it was looking like Vincent Tortufi."

"Now you understand Ridgeway's mood."

Feinberg never bothered giving Flood the nasty attitude that Ridgeway used. He liked Flood too much.

"Bring your client in when you talk to him, Augie. We really need to talk to him and his wife." He paused. "You know, Ridgeway's not just being a dick. He is very angry about all this."

"I know. But I really didn't know Vincent Tortufi was anybody when I called John." Flood was looking at Tortufi's Escalade as he talked. The big, glossy white truck seemed to be looking back at him. He and the empty vehicle shared a secret about what had happened to the driver and who had seen it. Flood decided to buy a little good will.

"Feinberg, I've got something for you."

After he hung up, he decided not to go into the restaurant. In a few minutes the agents would arrive to process the Escalade, and probably start interrogating everybody at the Napoli. He did not want to be a part of that. Flood walked down the street, retracing the path from the night before when he followed Vincent Tortufi to his death. When he got to Taylor Street, he thought about catching a cab, but he didn't know where to go. He didn't feel like sitting in his apartment, but he also did not relish stopping into one of his regular bars around his building and seeing people he knew. At Taylor and Halsted there were a handful of students hauling backpacks, walking north and south, and a group of gray-bearded professors dressed not warmly enough came hustling around the corner, heading for one of the restaurants on Taylor. Flood stood there looking east at the soaring black right angles of the Sears Tower, which loomed just a few blocks away and felt so intimately close from this vantage because there were no tall buildings in between. The collective fluorescence of the thousands of lit windows seemed to tint the dark sky from black to deep green. For some reason, standing on Halsted and looking up at the Sears Tower from this angle always brought Flood a glimmer of hope. He didn't know what for, exactly, unless it was just a sense of possibility. He stood there feeling the cold of the night seep through his dense wool overcoat when the Number 8 bus rumbled up to the curb. He decided to get on, and even found a CTA fare card in his wallet that still had money on it. Flood sat down next to a woman who was struggling with two small children and several plastic grocery bags. She begged them to calm down in Spanish, but they only took it as encouragement and made more noise. Flood smiled at the mother, who seemed to be suddenly embarrassed by the children because there was a gringo in a suit watching. The bus was not crowded. Most of the filled seats were taken by heavy black women in office clothes. Most looked tired and stared out the windows at the miles of Mexican and white neighborhoods that would have to pass by before they reached Englewood and Auburn-Gresham fifty blocks south. Flood closed his eyes and thought of nothing.

He got off at Cermak and started to walk east, through a low canyon of old red-brick factory buildings that were now lofts, then under the expressway and over the drawbridge crossing the South Branch of the river, and into Chinatown. The aimlessness of his walking felt good, and he began to feel hungry. He stopped into a Walgreens and bought the papers, then crossed the street and looked in the windows of Lao Sze Chuan. The dining room was not crowded, so he went in and took a table. A Chinese soap opera was playing on two hanging televisions at opposite corners of the restaurant, and there was a distant din from the huge kitchen down the back corridor. Flood ordered Szechuan fish filet, a plate of stir-fried potherb, and a Chinese beer.

As he was reading the paper and sipping beer, his cell phone rang. Caller ID said it was McManus.

"Barry, what's up?"

"Were you just over here?"

He had seen Flood lingering around outside the Napoli.

"I was. I'd planned to come in, and then something came up and I had to take off."

"Too bad, you could've seen a circus. The feds just showed up here. Augie, Tortufi's truck is still here. Did you talk to him last night?"

Flood had not thought of this consequence. The FBI was processing the scene where they found the dead man's car, and that was going to involve talking to all the restaurant employees about what they remembered of Tortufi the night before. McManus was now in a spot. Should he tell the agents he'd called Flood to tip him that Tortufi was there, and that Flood had said he was coming in a hurry?

"Have they talked to you yet?"

"Yep. I told them what I saw with my own two eyes in this bar. Not what conversations transpired over the phone. If I called you last night, it was about getting together for a steak and a couple of beers sometime. Not about this, and I have no idea what you did with your evening after our conversations. Understand?"

McManus was adamant. Flood couldn't tell if he was angry that Flood had nudged him into a tricky spot. Whether or not he was mad at Flood, he was watching his own back. If anybody knew he was feeding Flood information about Tortufi, he was finished. Certainly at the Napoli, and maybe in more ominous ways.

"That's fine."

Flood's food arrived, and he felt it getting cold. His appetite was up in the air.

McManus whispered, "The rumor is he got killed last night. You know that?"

"I do. It's not a rumor. Someday we'll talk about it, but I'm in my own tricky spot at the moment, so why don't we just agree that we'll meet for that steak next month and leave it at that for a while."

"Sounds good. But here's something else. I don't know what you're in the middle of, but I'm assuming it's legit. I don't know if this would help you or not, but I told the feds about it because they were pressing all the right buttons, so I'll tell you. Now, this is like six months ago, but Tortufi and his girlfriend, they had dinner with Bepps. I hadn't thought of it earlier because it was so long ago."

"And this is the same blonde we talked about?"

"Yep. Anyway, I think she was maybe married because she came out to the bar at one point to use the washroom, and this other guy sitting at the bar gets up and goes over to her. I think he'd been waiting for her to go to the can. It was sort of a scene. She was real embarrassed because she's with old Vince that night, and here's her husband showing up at and sitting at the bar like he's keeping tabs on her."

"What'd he want?"

"Well, he pulled out this piece of paper and wants her to sign it, and she won't and they're standing there bickering when Bepps comes around the corner and sees them. So then she's got to introduce her husband to the boss of the Chicago Outfit, and then they're just standing there all awkward and shit. Bepps starts to get that look that he gets. Like he's completely out of patience with everybody and he's decided to lock the doors and burn down the building with everybody in it."

"Hmm. Did you see how Tortufi reacted?"

"Don't know if he knew it even happened. I'm sure Bepps busted his balls about it later for not keeping his woman in line you know. But he never came out while the husband guy was there."

"What did the guy look like?"

McManus described Westlake fairly accurately.

"Huh," he said. "Weird."

"Anyway, for what it's worth." McManus sounded disappointed, like he'd gone out on a limb to tell Flood and he didn't even sound interested.

Flood thanked him and hung up. Six months ago, he thought. What was Westlake trying to get his wife to sign that long ago, and why did they make a scene like that at the Napoli? Was it part of a plan? He could not imagine that it was, but what did that mean about everything else that had happened? The pieces were not fitting together. He thought about Pam Sawyer again and did not like the fact that Westlake had gone there late at night Saturday, and then apparently turned up in the Cayman Islands the next day with his allegedly missing wife. Pam Sawyer was holding out on Flood, he figured, and he might be able to break her. He remembered how flustered she had become when he started to press her about Marcy Westlake's affair. He decided he would go see her again if Daniel Westlake did not turn up by morning to explain what was going on.

The unresolved questions did not help his appetite, and he ate about half of his meal before paying the bill and leaving. The restaurant was at the end of a new outdoor mall development, and Flood walked down the brick thoroughfare dividing the two long two-story buildings of the shopping and dining center. Nearly all of the people were Chinese; there were very few tourists or white visitors. Flood crossed Archer and Wentworth and skirted a parking lot to the Red Line station. He waited five minutes for a northbound El train. There were no seats, so he stood by the door. His cell phone rang again.

"Hello."

"Hi. It's Jenny. Are you around?"

"Around where?"

"Around that fancy French restaurant you call an apartment," she said. "I'm in your neighborhood and wondered if you wanted to get a drink?"

Flood looked at his watch. Nine o'clock. All day he had not known what to do next.

"Sure. Where?"

"How about the Inter-Continental? Ten minutes?"

"The bar or the lounge?"

"The lounge. I think there's a singer."

"Ten minutes."

He hung up and pondered the prospects. She called him and wanted to meet in a romantic spot where the music would preclude much talking. Now Jenny was tossing him a life preserver. It brightened his thoughts as the train descended underground in the Loop. Flood got off at Grand and walked over to Lower Michigan. He was about to climb the stairs to Michigan Avenue when he noticed a car that had caught his eye a few minutes before as he had walked past the block of his own apartment building. It was a blue Cadillac, but the shade of blue was peculiar, almost a purple. It appeared to be circling the area. When Flood saw the car, it was across Lower Michigan turning onto Hubbard and then immediately pulling to the curb. The windows of the car were dark. For some reason, it registered. Had he just seen it parked down the street at the Napoli? He had seen it somewhere, he thought. He wasn't going to stop, so he trotted up the steps to the sidewalk, turned north and crossed the street to the Inter-Continental. Two uniformed doormen were negotiating a tanned, blonde woman and her two children into the back of a hired black Town Car. All of their cold weather clothing—parkas, hats, scarves, mittens, boots—looked newly acquired from a fancy outfitter.

Wealthy Sunbelters who had prepared for a trip to Chicago in January as if it was an Everest expedition.

He watched them pack off into the night, and then turned and looked through the windows of the hotel. Then it hit him. The purple Cadillac. He'd seen it twice, both times in Pam Sawyer's neighborhood—the first time he met her, it was leaving the parking lot ahead of him as he tailed her to her home. And the second time was Saturday night; it was parked on the street outside her place up the street from where he'd parked. Flood felt a tingle on his neck. Who was it? He thought a moment and looked south on Michigan to the other stairwell across the avenue, in front of the Walgreens store. Flood had the walk light and dashed across Michigan and up the half block to the stairs that went down to Lower Michigan and Hubbard. He didn't descend the steps, just crouched at the top and peered down. The spot on Hubbard where the Cadillac had been parked was clearly visible, but the car was gone. He went down a few steps but saw nothing. Maybe it was a coincidence, he thought. He gave up and crossed Michigan again in front of the Tribune Tower and walked back up the block to the Inter-Continental.

On the other side of the windows the lounge was dark, but sparkling here and there with candles on cocktail tables. He could see the faces of people as they sat back in the deep, cushy lounge chairs. Back in a corner, a woman in a blue evening gown leaned against a baby grand piano, bathed in soft blue light, holding a microphone while a gray-haired black man in a black suit sat at the piano, eyes down as he concentrated on the keys. It was all a silent tableau to Flood as he walked to the doors. He scanned the dark room, and then the lighted doorway to the lounge, where he saw Jenny waiting for him, her eyes tracking him across the pavement, a smile on her face. She had seen him come toward the door and then turn in an instant and run across the street. Now he was back.

She was wrapped in black and immediately looked different to him. Her soft curls had the same, casual, swept back look. But her usual look of a slightly bohemian professional had been replaced by something he liked better. She was wearing a tight black turtleneck sweater, a tighter, knee-length black skirt that, like the sweater, left little to be imagined of what was underneath. Her slender legs were sheathed in black stockings and she stood a little taller than usual in black high heels.

"What have you been up to tonight?" he said when he came through the lobby to meet her. "You look like a million bucks."

She smiled wider and maybe started to blush a little.

"What was that?" she said, pointing outside. "I thought for a minute you had second thoughts and ran away."

He didn't have a ready answer, so he just gave a limited accounting.

"I thought I saw somebody I needed to talk to, but it wasn't them. Stupid," he said. "Where have you been? You really look terrific."

"Boring gallery opening. I need you to save my evening from being a complete snooze."

Flood thought about giving her a greeting kiss. After all, she had kissed him just last night when they parted after dinner. But he just took her arm and guided her into the lounge, and the hostess found them a sofa and coffee table near the windows, far from the singer and her accompanist. Flood had already had one beer, and he thought about what he should have next after half a Chinese dinner. He wanted a bourbon, but feared it would set him on a path to sloppiness. She ordered a glass of white wine, and he said he'd have the same. When the drinks came they sat silently with the rest of the crowd listening to "Someone to Watch Over Me" and then "Crazy." The singer was half way through a halfway peppy "Fly Me to the Moon," when Flood's eye was drawn to the window facing Michigan. Out on the street, two men had moved into view. They stood facing each other, talking. One was about fifty, burly—no, fat—and rough, tucked into a short, puffy leather jacket and wearing a tweed cap over stiff hair that was streaked with gray and white. He had a long, red nose and watery gray eyes. The other man was young, late twenties probably, tall and broad-shouldered but skinny at the hips. He had a three-quarter length black leather coat on with a thickly rolled gray turtleneck underneath. His black hair was slick. Like the Cadillac, he looked vaguely familiar. A doorman walked up, and the younger man put his arm around the braided shoulders of the man's coat. They talked for a moment, and then the older man reached out, as if to shake the doorman's hand, but it was an awkward handshake and looked to Flood like something else—slipping the guy money. The doorman tipped his cap and then turned and walked away. The two of them chatted some more and finally the older man turned and walked down Michigan, out of view. The younger man walked on an angle toward the hotel. It looked like he was headed for the lobby.

The congregation of torch-singer fans in the lounge was tipsily reverent, focused on the woman at the microphone. But Flood was thinking about the pair outside, wondering if they belonged to the idling Cadillac. He was trying to dodge his way through a rocky landscape of thoughts. A second glass of wine was halfway to his liver. Jenny was purring happily next to him, stealing the occasional glance. His gut was divided between gathering desire for her and all the anxiety of his day. His heart and his future bent against the mystery of the Westlakes, some twisted casino scam he didn't yet grasp, and the rebukes of his former FBI cohorts, with the goombas outside playing referees. He had to decide right now, at least for the rest of the night. If Daniel Westlake decided to return one of the dozen messages

Flood had left for him over the last three days, then maybe he'd refocus his attention. But this was silly. He had a beautiful woman at his table, and she was very interested in him.

Jenny leaned over and whispered in his ear.

"My night is saved," she said. "I like being with you."

That was that. Flood turned his face to her and laid a gentle kiss on the corner of her lips. They both sat back and thought about how much more of this music they should listen to.

It was about eleven when they headed for the door, the music still gently drizzling from the piano. The lobby was empty, and as they crossed the creamy marble tile Flood caught a glimpse of the other bar, through the next open archway. Sitting at the end munching on snack mix and sipping a Budweiser was the young man from the street, looking right at Flood with dull-eyed directness. Flood kept moving but took his hand off the small of Jenny's back. He felt a brief impulse of need to turn and walk over to the guy and knock him off his barstool and squeeze his Adam's apple until he coughed up what the hell was going on. But he dove into the revolving door behind Jenny instead. They spun slowly into the cold air outside, and the soft sounds of jazz evaporated and were replaced by the squall of the street.

Maybe he should have been thinking about the mystery thugs, but he had Jenny standing in front of him now, looking at him to see how bold he'd be. He ran through the mental list of bullshit excuses for getting her back to his apartment—call her a cab, one more drink, show her his signed first edition copy of *The Moviegoer*—and then just smiled and said, "I'd like you to come with me."

She turned without a word and started to walk down Michigan, toward his apartment building.

Chapter Fifteen

Since he broke off his engagement, the women Flood had slept with fit roughly into two categories. There were the rudderless babes looking for a moral rock. They took Flood's inconsiderate refusals to tell them lies that would have made them feel better as a sign that he might be the one. Then there were the cold-edged carnivores attracted on first impression by his decent looks and confidence, his resumé and prospects. It was easy to take his decision to leave the intrigue of the FBI for private law practice as an inclination toward making a lot of money. It was only when they had sunk into him a bit that they realized he wasn't nearly as ambitious as they thought.

Flood would not have seen these categories, but they were real, and as he and Jenny tenderly grappled with each other they were very much at work in his head. His mind was subconsciously attempting to decide into which category she should go.

The way she stripped away his suit coat, pulling it off his shoulders to his elbows and suggesting for a moment that he was bound evoked the carnivores. Then when she hugged him tight as he slipped his hands to her back to unfasten her bra, maybe she belonged with the sweet searchers.

But the real question was not really who Jenny was. It was too early to know. The essential thing that Flood needed to decide was whether the version of himself that emerged after sex would be not only honest but open.

Slowly but surely he did everything he knew to please a woman. He ignored his own body until she, on the verge of coming, took matters into her own hands. The whole encounter felt utterly unfamiliar, not quite natural, slightly terrifying and completely exciting. If they had taken a breath they might have wondered whether they would be too embarrassed to look one another in the eye when it was over. But the sex was breathless and dreamy, with an uncontrollable swimming-underwater feel about it.

They lay at angles on the rumpled bed, her head resting on the hollow under his ribs. His hand warmed the cool skin of her belly, and she had curled her wrist around the back of his knee.

"Aside from you, and I haven't quite figured you out yet, I really needed that," she said.

"You don't look like you need anything."

He felt her almost laughing.

"Is that why you like me? Because I don't look needy."

"Well, it's a pretty good start. But I like you for a lot of reasons."

"Tell me all of them." She pinched his calf a little, and he felt a tingle that told him they were not altogether finished, at least if he had anything to say about it.

"It all starts with your mouth," he said.

"Well, then you must be pleased with the way this night's gone."

He pinched back.

"I like the way it looks, and I like what comes out of it."

"You haven't heard me sing."

"Maybe you could hum a few bars."

They lay silent for a while.

"Aren't you going to ask what it is that I haven't figured out about you yet?"

Flood groaned.

"Oh, I think I can guess. 'Am I worth the effort?' It's an excellent question."

"Are you offering any insight other than praise for the question?"

"All I can tell you is that I'm not lying here thinking of how I'm going to get out of this."

She started to giggle and said through the laughter, "That's got to be the lamest compliment I've ever gotten lying in bed with a man."

"Well—"

"Well, nothing. For some reason, it seems like a good thing." She was still laughing.

After Flood served orange juice and coffee in bed, Jenny caught a cab home at eight in the morning. She'd be late to work, but Flood was in his office by nine. He picked up his newspaper on the way out and unfolded it as he walked south on Wabash. Keith Reece's story was tucked into the left-hand side of the front page, not the lead across the top, but above the fold, so it was still prominent. *Casino 'Witness' Slain.*

The lead byline belonged to Dennis Hamill—the suburban reporter, Flood thought. The second byline was Reece's. He had done it that way to protect Flood. This way, it looked like it was Hamill's scoop, picked up on a routine check of the morgue, with the expert Reece brought in to give the story context once they figured out what they had. Ridgeway probably would see through it, but Flood would have deniability.

It went like this: "The body of an Oak Brook businessman, whom the FBI wanted to question in the widening West Bank Casino investigation, was found early Tuesday in a hastily dug grave at a construction site in Orland Park.

"The apparent murder is a shocking turn in the casino scandal, which has so far led to the indictments of three Gaming Board members, the vice president of a suburban bank, and a lawyer who was at one time the mayor's appointed liaison to casino negotiations.

"Investigators believed Vincent Tortufi, 49, had intimate knowledge of an alleged bribe paid to a member of the Illinois Gaming Board in order to win a state license to operate a casino in downtown Chicago, according to an affidavit reviewed by the Tribune. The affidavit was filed under seal last week in federal court to support an FBI request for a wiretap of Tortufi's phone.

"Tortufi's body was discovered by Orland Park Police in a shallow hole partially covered with dirt at the bottom of a newly excavated basement in the Meadowridge Glen Farms subdivision, Orland Park police said. The housing developer, Peter McFadden, said Tuesday he had no idea how the body ended up on his property, where he is building a 500-home subdivision in a still-agricultural area along Wolf Road in the southwest corner of the suburb. None of the homes is occupied yet, McFadden said, and the area is deserted and secured by locked gates at night. Tortufi had been shot once in the head and twice in the chest with a .22-caliber firearm, and his throat had been cut, apparently with a piece of wire, a spokesman for the Cook County Medical Examiner's office said.

"Federal prosecutors have alleged in court that the West Bank Casino Venture, LLC, was secretly controlled by reputed organized crime head Nuccio 'Nicky Bepps' Beppo. No charges have yet been filed against Beppo or members of his inner circle, but sources close to the investigation say the 67-year-old resident of suburban Melrose Park is the focus of a federal grand jury investigation. State records indicate that Tortufi operated a business in Hodgkins with Beppo's brother, Aldo Beppo. Neither of the Beppo brothers could be reached for comment . . ."

Flood rolled the paper back up and walked into his building.

The most interesting thing was that they had not asked a judge for a tap on Tortufi's phone until last week. No wonder Ridgeway seemed to know nothing about Marcy Westlake, they were just starting in on Tortufi. Flood could not help but think that it was poor investigating, and he would have turned up the guy's name earlier if he had been on the case.

Jamie was already at his desk, clacking away on his keyboard when Flood walked down the hall.

"Cronin here?" he asked Jamie.

"Nope. Won't be in until after lunch."

Flood silently waved him in to his office. He closed the door as Jamie came in and sat down.

"I need to leave the office for a few hours. I've got a conference call at eleven. Can you patch it to my cell phone?"

"Sure."

"And . . ."

"I'll handle everybody else," Jamie said, getting up to leave. You never had to tell him you were done with him. He always knew. He even closed the door on the way out without asking. Flood thought about whether he should have said something about Jenny but decided against it. He wanted to see whether Jenny would tell Jamie all about it first.

He picked up the phone and dialed Pam Sawyer's number. He had hoped she would fall apart on him, but he would need to be in her face. She did not answer until the fifth ring. He exhaled audibly. Finally, he had somebody on the phone.

"It's Augie Flood. I've been calling you for days. Where have you been?"

"I've been very busy, Mr. Flood. Sorry." She sounded peeved, and Flood supposed that was justified. He wasn't her boss. Then again, she had a lot of questions to answer.

"I need to speak to you in person, right now, Pam. I'm coming out to Hinsdale."

"You know, Mr. Flood, not today. I'm very tired," she said, and sounded like it. Her voice was raw, as if she'd been talking instead of sleeping the last couple of nights. "How about tomorrow?"

"I'm afraid it won't wait."

"Well, I'm sorry. I'll have to call you tomorrow." The doorbell rang in the background. "Listen, I've got somebody at the door. Really, I promise, I'll call you tomorrow."

She hung up. Flood cursed. His questions for her: Why was Daniel Westlake, whom she described as a pathetic fool, coming to see her in the middle of the night Saturday? And why was she playing along with the idea that Marcy Westlake had really vanished?

Then Flood thought of something else. She probably had not bothered to read the paper or listen to the news, so it was unlikely she knew Tortufi was dead. He stuffed the paper back into his overcoat pocket. Dropping that on her coffee table would get her attention.

Flood put on his coat and left the office. He caught a cab back to his apartment building and went to the garage for his car. It was late morning, and traffic on the Eisenhower was still pretty light. He made the trip to Hinsdale in less than half an hour. He took the Ogden exit from the tollway, passed the Starbucks where they'd met for coffee just a few days before and kept driving west to her building. He spotted Pam Sawyer's driveway by the blue BMW SUV. The other drives, on either side, were empty.

Flood parked on the street and looked at his watch. It was almost eleven. He waited and then his cell phone rang. It was Jamie forwarding his conference call. He sat there in front of Pam Sawyer's condo talking to a lawyer in Florida and an insurance adjustor in Hartford for twenty minutes. Finally it was over. He got out of his car and walked up and pressed the doorbell. There was no answer, and after about thirty seconds he rang it again. Nobody in the suburbs went anywhere by means other than their car, especially in January, so she had to be here. Still, no answer. The midday quiet of the suburb was eating at him, and he started to have a bad feeling. He walked around the complex to the back of her place to see what he could find. There was a wooden privacy fence, but the latch was not locked and he let himself in to her backyard. He walked up on her little patio, which was enclosed by a shake-shingled wall. The space was just big enough for a round patio table and chairs, a chaise lounge, and a small gas grill. The doors were small-paned French doors and he peered inside, seeing nothing at first. He scanned back and forth, from the counter of the open kitchen through the dining area and into the den to his left. The home was not particularly well-kept, but that was to be expected under the trying circumstances of recent days. He kept looking. Then he spotted something. He'd almost missed it because it was white on white: white plastic on cream carpeting. It looked like part of a cordless telephone. The back and the panel that fits over the battery compartment. And there was a set of batteries wrapped in white plastic—like the battery packs used in cordless phones—lying underneath. It was all broken in pieces. Flood put on his gloves and turned the door handle. The lever handle turned all the way down. He gave the door a bump with his shoe, and it opened with a crackle as the heavy aluminum separated from the weather stripping. Flood wiped his feet vigorously on the straw mat outside and then stepped into the home.

"Pam," he called out, and when there was no answer, he repeated it louder. There was no one in the kitchen, or in the living room. He peered over the sofa. The rest of the telephone was in four or five more pieces on the floor. From the looks of things, the phone had been slammed down on the heavy greenish glass of the coffee table. Flood looked in the front hall and rooms. A cane umbrella stand was turned over on the hardwood floor, and a Burberry umbrella had spilled out and slid across the floor to the front wall. He studied the front door and found that the chain was snapped and there was a dent in the door jamb about chest high, but the door was closed and locked. There was a small sitting room off the foyer, and then a small office on the other side. Both were empty. He called out Pam's name again as he set a foot on the first carpeted step leading upstairs. There still was no answer. He climbed the steps. There was a red leather Mephisto clog lying on its side on the third step. He did not touch it. Halfway up he saw a smear of crimson, a faint droplet on the carpet. It was the only one on the steps, but then he got to the top of the stairs and found a quarter-sized spot that was clearly blood. There were a few more droplets leading into the bedroom.

Once he reached her bedroom, the body was lying in plain sight. Pam Sawyer was on her back on the carpet. Her shirt was torn open to expose her bare chest, which looked to Flood to be a clumsy attempt to make this crime look like a rape gone from bad to worse. Her blank, dead eyes open, her face relaxed, no longer showing any of the terror of the last moments of her life. Her mascara had run all over her face, however, carried by streams of tears that had since dried. She'd had time for the terror to really sink in, he thought. She'd had time to beg for mercy.

There were two bullet holes in her head—one that had torn away part of her cheek and one straight into the bridge of her nose that had created a gruesome bulge between her eyes. Two shots to the head, from a gun he guessed to be the same caliber that killed Vincent Tortufi. There was blood smeared on her upper lip that looked like it had come out of her nose. A ripped-up embroidered pillow lay on top of her splayed blonde hair. It had been thrown down after she hit the floor. Her body was crumpled and bent back on itself, with her legs folded under her hips.

Careful to stand in exactly the same place, Flood stared at Pam Sawyer's lifeless body for several moments, looking for clues. He barely knew her, but he doubted she was quite bad enough to have warranted this treatment. Nobody deserved to be shot in the head in her own bedroom. Flood was confused. He did not understand where Pam Sawyer fit into the scheme of things. He thought of the men in the Cadillac. He knew he had seen the car near her home twice, but he did not understand why. He looked her up and down one last time. He was in a hell of a fix now and needed to get out of there and figure out how he was going to call the police without getting himself arrested. For the second time in two days. Why was he finding all the bodies?

He noticed something in his last look at her hands. Her fingers were bent in different directions. He leaned closer. He wanted to pick up her hand and look, but he knew he couldn't touch. But it was clear now. The fingers on her right hand, which was curled against her belly, were all broken. Every last one of them. Even the thumb was twisted askew in such a way that the bone couldn't have gone along without snapping.

He pieced together the puzzle. She had opened the door with the chain on. Whoever did this immediately used a crowbar or the like to break the chain and come into the house. Pam had probably turned and run back to the den, fumbled for the phone to try to call 911. The killer caught her, broke the phone to pieces and then dragged her kicking and screaming upstairs. A bit of a feat, Flood thought. She was a strapping woman of forty who worked out every day. If he was going to kill her, why not just do it in the living room? More than one killer? And perhaps they needed information, so dragging her to the bedroom would maximize her fear of what was coming. In the struggle the umbrella stand had been knocked over, and she lost a shoe on the stairs. At the top of the stairs the killer had finally hit her hard in the face and broken her nose, causing the splash of blood and then the little drops that trickled into the bedroom, where she surely begged for life and offered them anything they wanted once she saw the gun that was used to shoot her in the head.

This wasn't just a hit. Whoever killed her had taken some time and tortured her first. Maybe they didn't care what others would think later, and they ripped her shirt open to make her fear she'd be raped. When that didn't work they set in on her fingers. Why? What did she have that somebody needed? Flood stared at the fingers and then found himself going back over his last conversation with her. Nothing came to mind.

Flood looked past her body. The mutilated body of a woman in the room had a way of obscuring everything else, and he had to ignore it for a moment. He began to inventory the bedroom. The bed itself was made and clean. The nightstand held a couple of paperbacks and a prescription bottle and the base of a cordless phone. Framed seascape prints on the wall. Nothing out of place. He turned around and looked at the other side of the room, immediately seeing the thing that didn't fit. A suitcase on wheels, handle still extended, stood next to the armoire. Her carryall bag lay on the floor next to it, open and partly spilled. Flood took two careful steps across the carpet and bent down over the open bag. He poked into it with his pen. Makeup kit, wallet, hair clips—the usual things. Tube of sun block. Flood studied it for a moment as it slowly registered as, again, something out of place. With the pen he poked into the open wallet. The stub of a United boarding pass slipped out. It said O'Hare to Grand Cayman.

"Well, what the hell?" he mumbled to himself.

Underneath the wallet lay a blue passport book. Flood opened it with his pen and saw the lovely face of Marcy Westlake, and her name, place and date of birth printed to the side.

The questions were melting away. He guided his pen back into the wallet and opened it wider to expose the driver's license in its clear plastic pocket. It belonged to Pam Sawyer.

The whole thing finally hit Flood in the face. In his effort to figure out where Marcy Westlake was, they had confused the issue with the dumb luck of his conversation with the Marriott clerk in Grand Cayman. Marcy Westlake had not been in Grand Cayman with Daniel Westlake. Pam Sawyer had gone in her place. Flood had already come to believe he was being used as a cover story—but he had misunderstood what he was helping cover. Westlake was not trying to convince the Outfit he was on the outs with his wife. He was trying to convince anybody paying attention that he was concerned about her whereabouts and doing everything he could to find her. If he and Pam Sawyer had taken off to Grand Cayman so quickly to impersonate Marcy Westlake and withdraw the money, then he had a pretty good idea about what had happened to his wife. Flood felt the cold, numbing realization of just how far he had been misled and how deep the trouble was.

When Bepps started to get nervous about the feds, he looked around to decide who his problem people were. He must have realized that it had not been wise to let Marcy Westlake, an outsider, get involved. He had given Tortufi too much latitude to handle the bribes, and he had unwisely chosen to involve his girlfriend to cut her in on the action. So Marcy Westlake disappeared without a trace. Tortufi had probably even helped. But then people got interested in Tortufi. The feds were nosing around and even Flood, a private attorney working for the girl's husband who had ties to federal law enforcement, was asking about him. Flood wondered if his involvement had contributed directly to Bepps's decision to kill Vincent Tortufi. And he even wondered if that had been part of Daniel Westlake's plan.

In any event, Flood saw Tortufi murdered and kept that from becoming another unexplained disappearance. The press got it, and now things were getting crazy. Pam Sawyer was murdered recklessly. What next . . .

Flood stood up. Marcy Westlake's passport in Pam Sawyer's bag, along with a used ticket to the Cayman Islands, where Daniel Westlake had a bank account he couldn't withdraw money from without his wife's authorization. He saw his role to play in the deception a little more clearly, and his week's worth of mild humiliation turned instantly to anger. His hunch all along had been that this Westlake affair was somehow worth digging through. He had started this by giving in to Cronin and feeling it would be an act of self-flagellation that might make him see the future more clearly. Help him get off his ass, in other words. But once he was in it, and the logic of everything started to break down—and Westlake's connection to the casino became apparent—then he started to feel the urgency. To what end, it was unclear. All he knew was that the roadmap through this mess increasingly was being drawn in blood. There was more than just hundreds of millions of dollars at stake; the survival of organized crime's most powerful criminals seemed to lie in the balance.

Now Westlake's deceit made more sense.

The concerned husband hires a lawyer to find his missing wife. And not just some hack with a private investigator's license, but a former FBI agent. What could be a more genuine show of concern? But Westlake had a pretty good idea all along where his wife was. She'd been disposed of by people who were experts at disposing of people. Marcy Westlake was dead, and her body was ash or smoke or vapor by now. Or maybe she was in a grave beneath another new house in Orland Park. In her place Westlake had inserted a poor substitute—Pam Sawyer.

Daniel Westlake had failed to get Marcy Westlake's consent to access the account six months ago when he ambushed her at the Napoli Tap, in the incident McManus had described to Flood the night before. So Westlake eventually moved on to Plan B: have Pam Sawyer pose as his wife at the bank. Flood wondered whether Pam had been involved from the start with Westlake's plan to invest in George Kajmar's casino bid. Now, had Westlake been successful in getting his money out of the Cayman account with the human facsimile of Marcy Westlake? Probably. And where was he?

It was time to call Ridgeway and throw up his hands in surrender. But something occurred to him. Now there were at least two people dead, and it certainly looked like Marcy Westlake was dead rather than missing. Westlake might be next on the hit list, which Flood really didn't care much about, even if the guy was still his client. On the other hand, the hit men—Flood figured it had taken at least two to drag Pam Sawyer up the steps—could be cleaning up a different part of the mess that didn't directly involve Westlake. Killing Pam Sawyer wasn't necessarily about Westlake's attempts to finagle his way into the casino deal, it was about what Marcy Westlake knew. Pam knew enough about what Marcy was involved in to double-cross her friend, Flood decided. That's why she was murdered. Who else would know?

He thought about what Marcy Westlake's role would have been. The payoff to Art Callahan. He remembered what Feinberg had said in the leak to Reece. *Tell him the FBI is investigating Callahan's 'activities on campus'.* On the University of Illinois campus. Brandon, Flood thought. The kid knew.

"The next loose end," Flood whispered. He turned and retraced his steps out of the bedroom and went down the steps as fast as he could, carefully avoiding the blood smears. He opened the back door and left. His footprints were in the snow, and he didn't bother to try to hide them. He ran around to the front of the complex, figuring that in such a densely populated block, at least half a dozen people had at least noted his presence, even if he did not look suspicious to them. He jumped in his car and did a U-turn and headed back to Ogden, sped through a yellow light and onto the Tollway again, this time headed south, to I-57 and Champaign.

If he called the police now, he would have to stay and be questioned and processed like a piece of bloodied furniture. If he called Ridgeway to ask him about Brandon, it would take forever to cut through the muck of the agent's stubbornness and his suspicions about Flood. He did, however, want to call Brandon Westlake to warn him trouble could be headed his way. He did not have Brandon's cell phone number with him. Flood had been carrying his Westlake file with him everywhere for days but had left it behind today when he ran out of the office. It was sitting on his desk.

Chapter Sixteen

He called Jamie for the cell number, and then called the kid. Brandon's voicemail picked up. The boy sounded nothing like his father. His voice was rough and direct. The message was the kind that is as brief as possible. Most personal voicemail greetings fell into two categories. Some people made voicemail messages that rambled with introductions, apologies for not being available and suggested options. Others barely left their names, seeing no need to take up time explaining what to do. Brandon's was that kind. When the beep sounded, Flood rambled a bit. He had a lot to explain. He described himself as an investigator working for Brandon's father and hoped that would not prompt the kid to do the opposite of whatever he asked. He told him it might not be safe to go home and that he should go to the campus police and call Flood back.

He put the phone down and drove, figuring what the chances were that this was an unnecessary trip. It made him think about what he would say when he reached Brandon's house in Champaign and found a half dozen young people hanging out, watching ESPN and drinking beer. Young Westlake did not know who Flood was or what he was doing. How would he explain that he was working for Daniel Westlake, but something was amiss and now he didn't trust his client? He also did not know what he would do with Brandon. If the killers who took Pam Sawyer's life were not there, it did not mean they were not coming to get Brandon at any moment. Flood would need to persuade the son he needed protection, and he would have to explain what was going on to the authorities—namely, Ridgeway. Nobody else would be in a position to even begin to believe Flood knew what he was talking about.

Flood sped through the tail end of the southern suburbs on 57, heading south into the country again, the Illinois landscape spreading out before him flat as a map in the weakening light of a gray winter afternoon. The farmland looked dead in winter, the raw black fields and brown grass speckled with old snow that looked like decay. Farmhouses and barns in the distance looked abandoned, as if the highway traffic had driven off the farmers years ago. There was little traffic on the road and most of it was semis headed to and from Chicago. Their numbers thinned even more as Flood made his way south, past Kankakee.

Flood was avoiding calling Ridgeway, so he called Reece instead.

"We got lucky with the M.E."

"I saw. What's the reaction?"

"Well, the FBI is very edgy, and the U.S. Attorney is trying to do damage control over the fact that Tortufi needed to be questioned. I think they're worried about Tortufi's death becoming a defense lawyer's dream. Everybody will claim Tortufi pulled off all the bribes himself, for himself. They'll say the whole scheme started and ended with him and your Mrs. Westlake, and Nicky Bepps, or anybody else, wasn't involved. So the feds are trying to distance the investigation from him. But everybody's rattled. And it's made this a national story. I've gotten requests all day to do CNN, MSNBC, Fox—all of them."

"You can't do TV. You need to stick by a scanner."

"Scanner? I wouldn't even know how to work one any more. What do you mean?"

"Figure out how to listen to the Hinsdale police frequency

and listen to it for the next couple of hours."

"Is somebody else dead? Weren't you talking to somebody in Hinsdale?"

"I'm walking a fine line here, Keith. Just listen," he said. "I'm still figuring it out."

And that was the truth. He assumed that Tortufi led the killers to Pam, at the very least, and then the killers knew to torture her to find out who else knew about the bribe money linking Bepps to the gaming board.

He couldn't put off the call he really needed to make any longer. The agent picked up on the first ring.

"Ridgeway."

"It's Flood."

He could hear the gathering rage.

"You know what your little leak cost us? These fuckers are battening down the hatches like you wouldn't believe."

"Shut up, John. It's not like they were inviting you in for coffee before the public information contained in the medical examiner's report was made public. They've been battening down the hatches for weeks. It's called murder."

"All I know—" he started to say. Flood cut him off.

"Listen, John. The case that brought me to you—Marcy Westlake. It took me somewhere else today that's going to piss you off even more."

"I told you to stay away from this thing."

"Well, this wasn't really about Tortufi. At least, not at first."

"What the fuck is it?"

"Does your family tree on this case have a woman named Pam Sawyer in it?"

"No! Why?"

"Well, you should have met her when she was still alive. There's a crime scene in Hinsdale you need to go see."

Just south of Kankakee, Flood needed gas. He was still more

than an hour from Champaign. As he sat in the car listening to the gas flowing and the wind whipping against the giant flat gas station canopy, he thought about Jenny and the fact that what he really should have done was call her today and ask her to lunch. They had spent the night together and now the better part of the next day had gone and he had not even called to tell her he was still thinking about her. He was not the sort of person who sent a woman flowers the morning after going to bed with her. Something about that seemed distasteful. But he should have called, more than once. Instead she had heard nothing from him. It gave him a sickly feeling in his belly.

The clock on the radio said three-thirty. He picked up his phone and called Jenny's office.

"Who?" she said. "Do I know an *Augustus Flim Flam?* I don't think so. I bedded down with some guy last night, but that was such a long time ago."

"I should have called earlier. I'm having a very weird day."

"I thought maybe you were dumping me as soon as you scored," she said, now coquettish. All was well.

"Mmm. I'd like to get you in the sack about a hundred thousand more times before I move on, I think."

"How tender," she said, laughing. "Why's your day weird?"

Flood thought about what to say.

"Can I tell you about it tomorrow?"

"Oh, all right. Does this mean I have to entertain myself tonight?"

He hung up, feeling completely frustrated and stupid.

His phone rang, and the caller ID said "private number," which meant most likely that it was a cop.

"You're telling me you were in this crime scene?" Ridgeway replied to Flood's wary greeting. Flood envisioned him standing in Pam Sawyer's kitchen.

"I was," Flood said. "I went looking for her to talk. Her car was there, and the back door was unlocked."

"Goddamnit."

"I know how to tiptoe through a crime scene. Don't worry," he said. "You there now?"

"Yes."

"Did you notice the broken fingers?"

"What did they want from her?"

"I think they wanted to know who else knew."

"Knew what?"

"About the route the money took from Bepps to Callahan."

Flood was quickly piecing together the fragments of Marcy Westlake's last known whereabouts into a story. She was looking to stray. She met slickster Tortufi when he came shopping for a Lexus. She started sleeping with him. Or maybe that was a story Pam Sawyer fabricated. Perhaps, Pam met Tortufi and became involved with him, only to have Marcy steal him away. He got her involved in some end of the casino deal with Bepps. She got too close to it. The whole scheme blew up in Bepps's face. And now there were loose ends to clean up. Marcy disappeared, the proper way, with no body to be found and no evidence. But then the indictments started coming, and Bepps had to act quick. He tried to get rid of Tortufi efficiently, but Flood lucked out and saw the whole thing unfold. Once that was screwed up, they got reckless and didn't clean up the mess they made of Pam Sawyer. Brandon could be next if Flood didn't get there first. He thought about calling the Champaign police. But he feared how that would go. He knew nobody in the department, of course, and had no proof that Brandon was in any danger.

"I don't understand perfectly, but I think Marcy Westlake was the bagman. I think Tortufi put her up to it, and I'm betting she was the first one to get killed."

"Goddamnit, Flood. You told me you were chasing an unfaithful wife."

"I was. And I thought that was all she was," he said. "Then Vincent Tortufi happened."

"So who's this woman? Looks like she wasn't hurting for cash."

"She was Marcy Westlake's friend." He left it at that.

"What's her deal?"

"I don't know exactly where she fits in. But make sure you look in her bag."

"Where the fuck are you? I want you back downtown. I want this all on the record. Goddamnit, Flood, I warned you. You're gonna get fucking disbarred for this."

"Calm down, John," he said. "You need to know something else."

"What?"

"I think they broke her fingers to get her to say who else knew something. And I'm betting they stopped at one hand because she told them something. I think the thumb did it. I think she told them about Marcy Westlake's kid, Brandon."

"What about him?"

"He's a student in Champaign. I think he knew something about what his mother was doing. I think she came down here to make the drop to Callahan. I think he witnessed it, or saw the cash, or something. And I think Pam Sawyer told Bepps's boys about him."

It was almost dark now, and Flood was cursing himself for not calling sooner. A soft dome of dark gray-yellow sky loomed in relief against the blackening night. Champaign-Urbana was just ahead, to the east of the ribbon of highway in front of him. Bepps's killers would have had some work to do to figure out where Brandon lived. There was no phone listing for him. But some crooked whiz somewhere in the mobsters' crew would have tracked it down for them. Flood wondered if he would be in time. If a call to the police would be in time.

"Why the kid? Why not his mom?"

"I told you, I think his mom's dead already."

"And why do you think that?"

"Because she would have been the first to go. She made the drop, and she had no other value to Bepps."

"But where's her body? These two have been left for us to find."

"Just Pam Sawyer. It looks like they were trying to conceal Tortufi and screwed it up." Flood was careful not to give Ridgeway any clue that he had been the one to see it and phone in the tip.

"Maybe. Where's the kid?"

"In an off-campus house near the university. Can you have the locals pick him up?"

Flood heard voices talking to Ridgeway and a radio chirping in the background, and he no longer had the agent's full attention. He tried to hear what was being said in the background, but it was mostly murmurs. He thought he heard somebody say, "the plate comes back . . ." and somebody else say, "white, ES . . ." The rest was unintelligible.

"John, are you there?"

"I gotta go, Flood. You're in deep shit. I don't think they were after the kid. I think it's the mom. We'll talk later."

He hung up. Flood was curling over the cloverleaf ramp at about twenty miles an hour faster than he should have been. His tires squealed in protest and gravel pelted the undercarriage of the car as he screamed in frustration, cursing Ridgeway. He hurled the phone down on the passenger seat, took the wheel in both hands, and floored the gas pedal, fishtailing and then straightening up at sixty miles an hour coming off the interchange, feeling the suspension heave lightly as he accelerated toward the University of Illinois campus.

Flood took an exit for Lincoln Avenue and started south toward the campus. Out by the highway there were several new complexes of student apartments, all blocky, cheaply constructed buildings with tiny balconies.

His phone rang, and he nearly drove off the road stretching to pick it up. It was Reece.

"Hey, where are you?"

"I'm in Champaign, trying to get to this lady's kid before Bepps has him killed."

"Where is he?"

"I'm hoping he's at the library like a good boy. I'm afraid if he's home I might be too late."

Reece didn't say anything. The silence meant something, and Flood knew it wasn't good.

"What is it?"

"They found her car."

For a moment he wanted to say, *Whose? Pam Sawyer's? I found it.* But he knew Reece was not talking about Pam Sawyer. He was talking about Marcy Westlake.

"Where?"

"Sanitary and Ship Canal. Willow Springs. I just got a tip."

"How'd they find it?"

"I think they figured it out since you told them about Marcy Westlake," Reece said. "I think they started going back over their wiretaps looking for things they didn't understand before, and somebody said something on tape about a car in the canal, and they're just now understanding what they heard."

Coast Guard was trolling the bank and snagged it. "White '02 Lexus ES 300."

"I thought your sources were clamming up for the rest of the day."

"Me too. I guess they love me. Seems like everything is changing fast. Things are chaotic over there. I think they're pumping me for info as much as I'm pumping them."

Flood didn't ask if he was giving them anything. He assumed he was, and some of it was filtered information from Flood. It hardly mattered to him at the moment. It was worth it. At the moment, Reece was completely wired in to what was going on. It had been just a few minutes since Flood overheard Ridgeway getting the call that must have been about the Lexus in the canal, and Reece got the call almost simultaneously.

"They didn't find her?" Flood asked.

"No. No body," Reece said. "My guy said the driver side window was gone. I got the call right away. They just found it. Don't know about any other evidence."

"I think Ridgeway got the word five minutes ago when I was talking to him. He got some piece of news about a car and then hung up on me."

"I'm sure that's it."

"Shit."

"What are you going to tell the kid?"

Flood was beginning to think about it. If he found Brandon Westlake in one piece, he would have to tell him something. Kid, they just pulled your mom's car out of the canal. No body, but it'll turn up. Kid, they found your mom's car. Good news: she wasn't in it. Kid, I'm pretty sure your mother died a violent death.

"I really don't know," Flood said. "Thanks."

"Augie?"

"Yes."

"I need a favor."

"What?"

"I need to use you as a source."

"No."

"Come on. A source close to the investigation."

"To say what?"

"That she's Tortufi's girlfriend and Pam Sawyer's friend. Two dead bodies and the car of a third pulled out of the canal. It's news. You know it."

"You've got other sources."

"But you're the only one who really understands who she is."

Flood and Reece had made a deal early on in the professional end of their relationship. Flood would give him information, but he would never be referred to, even anonymously, in a story. It was only a tip to be confirmed somewhere else. Reece had never asked to change the rules. And Flood had never dreamed of being the source of a story. It was ironic that he was the only usable source on a story about a federal investigation, and he was no longer a federal investigator. He thought about the ramifications. Ridgeway and everybody else in the office would know it was him, and his plausible deniability would be gone. There would be no use in claiming he wasn't the source close to the investigation. But what was the harm? Rather, what was the further harm? Ridgeway was already threatening doom. All empty threats. Bullshit. He hadn't done anything wrong. And there was no stopping this avalanche, triggered by mounting bodies, tumbling down on top of the feds' casino investigation.

Then there was the matter of Cronin and Drew, his law firm. He'd probably get fired if it became publicly known that Flood was in the middle of the scandal and feeding confidential information published in the Tribune. Flood could hear Cronin already, using the media leaks as the wedge to separate himself from responsibility for forcing Flood into this mess in the first place. Flood didn't care. He believed Cronin would take that route and hang him out to dry, and it made him feel like he was already an ex-employee.

"Fine."

"Thanks, Augie."

CHAPTER SEVENTEEN

Flood hung up and drove slowly down Fourth Street until he could see the house in the next block. He pulled over and shut off his lights. The street was quiet. Two girls trudged toward him on the sidewalk, both carrying backpacks. They were talking at the same time, and the chatter of their voices was unnerving as he tried to listen for signs of safety or danger coming from the house. Clouds of frozen breath churned in their wakes as they passed his car. The noise drifted slowly away, leaving the snow-packed street silent again. Flood studied the lights of the house for activity. It looked like there might be a kitchen light on, not the whole room, just a small fluorescent under a cabinet or over the sink. The upstairs was dark. He looked up and down the street, hoping for something that stuck out, but he saw nothing. Finally he put his car in gear and eased down the street. He passed the house and looked back up at the upstairs window from a new angle and saw that there was a bedroom light on. He saw at least two figures silhouetted behind the drawn paper blind. They were big and distorted and moved a lot. Flood studied the forms for signs of violence. It was a definite possibility. He turned the corner and started to go around the block. When he finally took his eyes off the figures in the upstairs window, he came to a short stop. Dead ahead of him, parked on the left side of the street, facing away, he saw the car: a deep blue Sedan de Ville. He recognized it immediately as the same car he had seen around Pam Sawyer's condo. And as the car that had been idling down the block at Michigan and Hubbard the night before as he arrived to meet Jenny at the Inter-Continental. It stood out here like a sore thumb—a forty thousand dollar old man's car parked next to all the college-student beaters. It was empty.

The sight of the Cadillac turned Flood's stomach. Suddenly this race to Champaign was no longer a better-safe-than-sorry trip. Flood had believed he could be heading into danger, but he had not felt the danger. Now he felt it, in the form of a parked, empty Cadillac that had no business being there. The car was clean, probably washed the same day. It was a shade of blue that seemed extravagant—bold, neither dark nor light, but deep and bright. It was almost violet. In brighter light, it could look purple. It belonged to men who had come here to kill; men who were inside this college student's house right now. Somehow he knew he was in time. They had not killed anyone yet. The sick feeling fled, and Flood's fear turned to something else, a feeling tinged with terror but beyond it, welcoming it and reckoning with decisions he had already made and actions he would have to carry out.

He drove past and went around the block. He parked on the opposite side of the house, on a corner out of view of the upstairs window and out of view of the Cadillac. He got out and quietly shut the door and did not waste his energy wishing he had a gun.

The porch was exactly the same as he remembered it from just days before. Peeled battleship gray paint on the floor revealed bare wood that was wet in spots and frozen in other spots. The old sofa looked clean in the deep freeze of the January outdoors because it was far too cold for all of the bugs that would infest it in warmer months. Flood stood on the porch for a second, making one last decision about calling the local police. It would be a death sentence, he decided. These were bad men, and it was likely that Brandon had seen their unmasked faces. He wasn't leaving that bedroom alive unless someone surprised them before they were ready to kill him. Uniforms on the scene would have meant a quick bullet in Brandon's head and then these two wise guys shooting their way out of the house, taking the locals by surprise and probably winning a short, bloody firefight.

The front door was unlocked, and Flood gently pushed, remembering how it had stuck on Saturday. He held on tight and put his hip against the door until it opened just enough to slide through, and then he shut it silently. He looked up the stairs. It was dark, but he could hear voices. One voice was going on in a low plod, and then a loud, defiant retort. An "I don't know!" That was Brandon. He was up there. They were up there. Flood looked around for a weapon, but nothing presented itself. A screwdriver would have done. He decided to risk tiptoeing to the kitchen, hoping the floor would not creak. He picked his way along, gently putting one foot in front of the next, walking only on the balls of his feet across the dark, worn wood floor and the stained pieces of carpet. It took him a long time, but he reached the kitchen without making a sound. The light over the sink lit the countertops but revealed nothing of use to him. He tiptoed to the stove and opened the drawer next to it. Under the tongs and the rancid little paintbrush that smelled like old barbeque sauce was the instrument he had hoped to find. A heavy, ten-inch chef's knife with a white plastic handle. Restaurant-supply-issue, which somebody in the house had no doubt filched from the kitchen of the bar where they worked. The knife had a heavily beveled edge, the way that cheap restaurant kitchen knives are kept, ground often to a brutal sharpness that can draw blood with the slightest pressure. This knife was dangerous to anyone not accustomed to handling it. He gingerly lifted the other utensils out of the drawer and finally hefted the knife in his hand. It would be no use against a gun pointed at his chest, but if he got close he could nearly take someone's head off with it.

Flood tiptoed back to the staircase and mounted the steps. Suddenly, a woman cried out. She cried out again, wilting, "Please stop. We don't know anything."

Brandon's occasional girlfriend had picked the wrong time to resume the romance. Stop what? Flood wondered. Some form of torture was taking place. He wondered if they'd gotten to the finger-breaking stage yet. There were any of number of gruesome tricks they surely knew, but they'd have to improvise in somebody else's home, with somebody else's furniture and only a few tools available. Flood bet on a straightforward, old-fashioned beating. From the sound of her wails, at least, he could tell that the door was closed. He quickly ascended the stairs, keeping to the side to minimize squeaky steps. When he got to the landing, he turned and faced Brandon's door at the opposite end of the hall. There was light coming from under the door and more whimpering from the girl on the other side of it. He held the knife out in front of him like a fixed bayonet and started to walk down the hall, every step on the balls of his feet to keep his heels from clicking on the bare, dusty floor.

Halfway down the hall he came to a bare light bulb hanging from the ceiling. He unscrewed the bulb, put it in his pocket, and kept moving. He came to the last bedroom door before the bathroom, which was next to Brandon's door at the end of the hall. He pushed the door open and slid into the darkness of the room.

His plan would either be very lucky or disastrous and fatal. It depended mostly on the skill level and organization of his foes. Flood believed he was smarter than they were and better than they were, even after three years without formal FBI training. But would he be better than two of them? Could he separate them? There was a light switch just inside the door. Flood stepped to the middle of the room and lifted his hands, feeling blindly in the darkness until he found the hanging light fixture. This one had a glass shade. He stood on his toes, unscrewed the nut, carefully removed the shade and set it on the floor. He reached back up, again feeling blindly in the darkness, and removed the two light bulbs.

Flood took a breath and then was ready. He took the light bulb out of his pocket and tossed it in the middle of the floor, where it shattered. The response was immediate.

"What the fuck was that?" the low plodding voice said. "Who's here, fucker? Which one of your little roomies came back early?"

There was no answer, and Flood could imagine Brandon shaking his head, terrified.

"I'll check it out," he heard the other one say.

He heard the door handle turn and saw a blade of dull light partially lift the darkness in the hallway. He heard the click of a light switch but no light.

"Fuckin' eh," said the man, starting out into the hall. His footsteps were heavy and steady. Flood felt him coming closer to the bedroom. The light in the bathroom next door flipped on, then off as he found nothing. Two more steps and he'd be on the threshold of the bedroom. Flood leaned against the door, which he'd fully opened. He held the chef's knife tight, the blade facing inward. It was the man who stepped into the doorway, the young greasy guy from the night before who was sitting at the bar of the Inter-Continental watching him. The man reached for the light switch as he moved into the room. He flipped it. No light.

"Goddamnit. No fucking lights work in this house."

Flood was behind him and brought the knife up deftly so that it was suddenly pressed against the man's throat, drawing a trickle of blood. Flood pressed up against him from behind.

"I'll cut your throat," he rasped into the man's ear.

The man gasped slightly but didn't move.

"There's a shelf to your right, just above the light switch. Lay the gun on it very gently."

After a pause, Flood sensed the man's gun hand rising very slowly. At Quantico Flood had been a standout in the hand-to-hand training. He beat the shit out of everybody. He just had a knack for it. He was a good shot with a gun, but he hated guns and so he had always liked using his body, being able to disarm someone before they got the upper hand. He radiated power and violence when he needed to. Now, he needed to, and the man was outmatched by a mile. The man felt exactly how close that razor-sharp blade was to severing his jugular vein. Flood saw the glint of the gun's metal as it was laid on the shelf. He felt the empty hand go back down to the man's side.

The low voice from thc othcr room was starting to sound concerned.

"Chucky, what's out there? What the fuck?"

Flood pressed the knife a little harder. So it was Chucky.

"Quiet, Chucky," he whispered. He had him by the hair on the back of his greasy head now. Knife against throat, head pulled back. Chucky's head was about a foot from the door jamb. He stood there stiffly, frozen, confused and scared. They had planned only for possible interference from college kids, and now somebody with the skills of an Army Ranger had a knife to his throat in the darkness. Chucky did not have a chance. Flood planted his back foot then and jolted forward, slamming Chucky's forehead into the doorframe with a thud. He let go of the back of his head and wound up a fist and brought it down hard, a stunning punch to the crook of his neck. Chucky dropped to the floor like a sandbag.

Flood picked up the gun from the shelf and checked it—a

9mm semiautomatic, round in chamber, ready to go. He turned into the hallway silently and raised the gun. Through the open doorway he saw the fat, older guy from the night before. The man in the cap who had been talking to Chucky on the sidewalk in front of the hotel. He had his back to Flood, and a small gun trained on the bed. All Flood could see of Brandon was a pair of bare legs duct taped to a chair. A pair of bare woman's feet also peeked out from the bed, the ankles cut off from view by the doorframe. Flood waited silently, the gun trained on the fat man.

"Chucky!" the man shouted. Silence. Chucky was still out. Then the fat man began to turn slowly and look. He saw Flood standing in the dimly lit hallway, with a gun pointed right at his chest. Instinctively, the man began to turn his gun on Flood, an automatic self-protection impulse that was exactly the wrong thing to do. He should have dived out of the doorframe, but he was way too fat to move fast enough for that. As soon as the barrel swung away from the bed, Flood pulled the trigger. Three quick shots—two right of center on his fat chest and then one to the forehead that made a mess on the wall behind him. The fat man had tied up his last loose end. He fell like a plump angel, spread-armed, back over the edge of the bed. His head took a brutal wallop against the corner of Brandon's desk, not that it mattered. He was long gone.

The screams from the girl pierced the echo from the gunshots. Her feet pushed violently against the bed, twisting the white sheet into a sandwich of folds, and disappeared. Flood stepped into the room and when she saw him there, as much a stranger to her as the fat man and Chucky, she was halfway up the wall and all the way hysterical. She wore nothing but a bra and mismatched panties, and her arms flailed instinctively to cover herself. Brandon was shaking like a leaf, taped to the chair.

"Oh, God. Oh, shit," he kept saying, over and over. The tears finally began to roll out of his eyes. His face was bloody, and it looked like his nose was broken. His chest and belly were splotchy red and beginning to welt up. They'd been beating the hell out of him, but he'd been tough for his girl. Now he was out of gas. She looked unharmed other than being terrified and no doubt scarred for life, first by the promise of her own imminent death and then by seeing a bad man have his brains blown out.

Flood's head began to swim, and he sank into a chair and stared at the dead man. His vision fuzzed and brightened, and he watched it over again, a dozen times in an instant. Then it stopped, and he felt his mind pulling away from his sickened body, like the peel being torn from an orange in a single piece, the dry doughy tissue separating from the cool, smooth membrane in a million tiny snaps. All he could think was that he didn't know the fat man's name. He'd just killed a man without even knowing his name.

"Did he tell you his name?"

Brandon didn't get it. He was sobbing.

"What?"

Flood pointed shakily at the slumped, keeled-over corpse. He could see the dead man's open eyes, just open and focused close, on nothing, as if recognizing the folly of his last moment on earth.

"Him," Flood mumbled. "What's his name?"

"I don't know," Brandon spat out. His response spilled out in one unbroken sound, like a single German word with too many syllables. "I don't know—he was going to kill us—God, he was going to kill us."

Flood felt sick. He turned away from them and stumbled, suddenly feeling dizzy and disoriented. A wave of nausea crept through him, and his vision turned a little yellowish and blurry for a moment. He leaned against the wall. He'd never killed anyone before. The dizziness passed in a moment, but he still felt disoriented. Brandon and his girlfriend were unfazed by his stumbling confusion. It seemed appropriate. Flood's vision came back to him. The peel was fitting back around the orange. He took a breath.

The girl had slid down from the wall and huddled into Brandon's arms. Flood stood up and regained his composure. He took the chef's knife out of his coat pocket and cut through the duct tape.

"Brandon, my name is Augustine Flood. I'm a lawyer, and I was hired by your father. But I think your father is a crook. I'm here to help you and keep you safe. Do you understand me?

Brandon nodded, somehow Flood's bizarre explanation fit right in.

The girl finally spoke, through her tears. "Where's the other one?"

The other one? Chucky. Flood turned and faced the door, holding the gun firm and pointing it down the dark hall. He turned on the bathroom light to help him see and inched back to the bedroom. He could see well enough to see that Chucky was no longer lying where he'd fallen.

"Brandon, is there a desk lamp in this room?"

"Um. Umm. To your left. About three feet."

Flood went in and sidestepped and reached. He nearly knocked the lamp over but he caught it and switched it on. Chucky's blood was smeared on the floor, but he was not there. Flood stood looking at the smear, trying to judge where he'd gone, farther into the room—under the bed or to a closet—or out. If he'd gone down the hall and out, he had done so very quietly. The room felt empty, but Flood dropped to his knees and bent down on the dirty piece of gray-green carpet remnant to peer under the bed. There was a copy of Penthouse, a plastic burrito wrapper with just enough food matter left on it to attract roaches, and a heavy book with a glossy paperback finish titled "Financial Statement Analysis." He was on all fours, bent over, looking under the bed, the 9mm grasped firmly in the palm of his right hand. It wasn't his gun, he didn't have a permit to use it, and he had just killed a man with it. The awfulness of not caring about those factors right now, the exhilaration of holding the gun and being perfectly ready to use it again, was terrifying. Flood leveled the barrel in front of him as he got to his feet and braced to open the closet door. He yanked, and the door swung easily, revealing a closet so stuffed with clothes and junk—golf clubs, ski boots, coats, sleeping bags—that no one could have hidden inside.

He stood still, listening to the whimpers of Brandon's girlfriend, and light wind against the tattered old wood siding of the house. Then came the thud, a stumble, at the bottom of the stairs. Then the sound of the door opening and slamming. Chucky getting away.

Flood did not think seriously about going after Chucky. His mind trained wholly on staying with the kids and protecting them. He came back to the bedroom.

"Get dressed right now. We're getting out of here."

"What about the police?" Brandon said.

"We have to get out of here first."

He imagined Chucky coming back after rearming himself from the trunk of his car. And the cops showing up late, a standoff underway. He thought about picking up the fat man's gun, but decided to leave it because it was evidence that Flood was acting in self-defense. He did pick up the roll of duct tape lying on the floor and stuffed it in his overcoat pocket. Flood turned out the light and pulled the window shade back so he could see the street. Chucky's bent form was staggering up the street toward the Cadillac. He fell, then got up and kept going.

Flood turned back to look at Brandon and the girl. They hadn't moved. He shouted at them.

"Get dressed, goddamnit! We can't stay here. He's going to come back with a shotgun."

They squirmed into their clothes and shoes in seconds. Flood looked for coats and threw two at them. They stormed down the stairs with Flood leading the way. He dashed out onto the porch and down the steps to the corner of the front yard so he could see up the side street and keep them covered. Chucky was leaning against the Cadillac; he looked like he was digging in his pants pockets.

If Flood went after him, he would be exposed in the street and Chucky would have plenty of time to reach into the trunk for another weapon. Flood looked back at Brandon and the girl, standing on the walk. He pointed at his car on the corner behind them.

"There. The black one."

They ran across the empty street, sliding in the packed, wet snow, to his car and got in. He started it and roared into reverse, wheeling hard backwards and around the corner and then peeling through the slush and gravel back down Fourth Street, in the opposite direction from Chucky.

Chapter Eighteen

"Brandon, where's the police station?"

"Uh, shit," Brandon said, confused. "I don't—wait, yeah, go right on University. The light."

Flood stopped at the red light but then eased through it, drawing a honk from an oncoming car. He sped up and headed east on the four-lane street. He slowed but did not stop for another light.

"Where is it?"

"Um," Brandon seemed less sure. "It should be on the right. Just past the train tracks."

"What train tracks?" Flood shouted. He saw nothing but fast food places and gas stations for several stoplights.

"Shit," Brandon finally said. "I think it's the other way."

Flood braked and made a squealing U-turn and headed back west on University. They'd lost precious minutes, and Chucky was getting away.

There was more traffic at the next light, so Flood waited for green. Another minute went by.

"Not the next light, but the one after that," Brandon said.

As they approached, Flood saw the sprawling one-story red brick slab of municipal architecture, surrounded by ample un-landscaped lawn and a large area enclosed by a six-foot chain-link fence in back. His cell phone rang.

He pulled it from his coat pocket and flipped it open to look at the display panel. The incoming number was blocked. Cops always had their cell numbers blocked. It was probably Ridgeway.

"Flood," he answered.

There was a pause, as if his greeting was being analyzed.

"Mr. Flood. Glad I could reach you," came the voice, which was aged and thick and full of unsettling confidence. Flood felt himself begin to squint as anxiety crept up through him. The voice went on.

"Mr. Flood, I understand you've been busy tonight. I'm told you killed our good friend William and gave his assistant a terrible headache. Is that true?"

"Who is this?"

"Oh," the voice came, as if embarrassed by the question. "You don't know? I think you understand who this is. Is it true you killed our old friend William tonight, Mr. Flood? We go way back. He's like family, William is."

The voice's sickening combination of menace and humor had hold of Flood and he felt like he was treading very cold water. He was not about to answer the question directly. The only thing to do was play the game.

"Was William the fat one torturing the kids?" he said.

"Now, now, Mr. Flood. William was merely seeking to retrieve proprietary information. Information that people outside our circle of associates had no business knowing. He was performing a valuable service in our interest when you murdered him."

So, this was somebody close to Nicky Bepps. Maybe the boss himself. Now the question was how did he have Flood's cell phone number. He could guess what the ultimate purpose of the call was. In addition to getting his brains blown out, Fat William had ultimately failed on his very important errand. The proof of that was sitting in the back seat of Flood's car.

"What can I do for you?" Flood asked.

"Well, Mr. Flood, I'm sure that's a question you could probably answer yourself if you tried. But I'll tell you. I'd like you to drop those two people off for me. I've got a place in mind."

"I'm afraid I can't do that. I'm not really in the same line of work as William, after all."

"Well, we'll see about that."

The confidence in his voice was beginning to rattle Flood. What wasn't he seeing? There was danger around the corner There was a face card lying down about to be turned over, Flood knew, but what was it? All he could wonder was who gave them his cell phone number.

The voice just went on making plans with confidence.

"Here's where I want you to go. There's a little country road, it's on your way home, before you get back to the suburbs. Have you ever been to Peotone, Mr. Flood?"

"Can't say I have," Flood said. Peotone was a farm town just beyond the southern suburbs. The governor wanted to build a third Chicago airport there, fifty miles from downtown. That's all he knew about the place.

"If you want to meet me," Flood said, attempting to show as much confidence as the voice on the other end, "why don't we just find a place we both know? How about the corner of Adams and Dearborn?"

The voice laughed. It was the address of the Federal Plaza—the Dirksen Federal Building, home of the FBI, the U.S. Attorney and the U.S. District Court.

"No, Mr. Flood. I think you'll like Peotone. It's quiet, very quiet on a night like this. You can see the stars, and the land just stretches out for miles and miles. Really, it's lovely."

"I'll meet you somewhere public, in downtown Chicago, but I'm not going to Peotone."

The voice chuckled.

"I think we'll meet in Peotone, Mr. Flood," he said. "Here's my situation."

Flood felt the urge to scream at the repeated use of his formal surname. He squirmed in the driver's seat of the idling car, aware that Brandon and the girl were listening intently to his side of the conversation. Maybe they had been all along, but certainly they were riveted to it since he'd uttered the word torture and put a name—William—to their torturer.

That's what it had been then. Torture. But torture was something that did not happen in the experience of suburban college kids in the Midwest, or any other place in America. Torture happened in places like Afghanistan and Haiti and Syria. But good God, yes, they had been tortured. Brandon bore the physical marks from the beating, and his girlfriend bore the psychological burden of the experience, of sitting there in terror, knowing she was next and most likely in for something worse than a beating. They had been tortured at the hand of a fat man named William. Chucky landed the punches, but he took his orders from William. Chucky had been like a dog—a sleek Rottweiler, vicious, on a chain. The scary one was the fat one who held the gun and the leash. He did not look like a William. He looked like a Vito or a Bud, or a Max, but not the least bit like a William.

They hung on Flood's every word and what little expression they could glean from the side of his face and his eyes in the rearview mirror.

"Here's my situation, Mr. Flood," the voice repeated. "I was planning on just meeting you and having you do the appropriate thing by bringing along these people who have information about our interests that they, quite frankly, should not have. So the person here with me, I was just going to shoot her in the head and give her a proper cremation and be done with all this business. Normally, I would dig a hole in the ground. Well, not me personally. That's not the best use of my skills, but one of my friends. William, actually. But he's not here anymore to do such work, is he? But you seem to have a knack for finding holes in the ground, so maybe I'd just have somebody run her over to the mills in Indiana. But it's getting harder and harder to find an open steel mill in this part of the country, isn't it. It's these kinds of problems that I'm good at solving, Mr. Flood. But I'm digressing, and you've been kind not to point that out."

"Shoot who?" Flood blurted, thinking for a moment that Marcy Westlake was still alive and he was finally close to her.

"Careful, Mr. Flood. Don't scare the children. I'm sure they're there with you right now."

Flood felt himself sinking into a sickness, feeling the peel separate from the orange again.

"Shoot who?" he said low, in nearly a whisper.

"Well, perhaps an exchange is in order," the voice said. "I'll let her speak for herself."

He felt stupid, as if he had been wandering in a pitch black room, thinking he was in the basement, only to have someone turn on the light suddenly and show him he was in the attic. How could he have presumed things were not going to turn out just like this? They had seen his car parked outside the site where they dumped Tortufi's body. And he had seen them watching him at the Inter-Continental the night before. He had been on full alert and felt his defensive instincts pull taught as he left the lounge and crossed the marble lobby of the hotel, his hand on her back and seeing the young man at the bar who turned out to be Chucky. Why had he not seen that it was more than just knowledge of his whereabouts that could be valuable? What about her?

The voice went away and new breath came across the cell phone into his ear. The beautiful, terrifying breath of a woman, released in desperation, with the same force that he had heard it and felt it released into his ear the last night when it was not a gasp of fear but of pleasure. He did not want to hear any more, but he had to hear everything he could.

"Hello," he said.

"Augie?" It was Jenny's voice, but altered in a way that would haunt him forever. No matter what happened, he believed that he would never really understand whether that little extra pitch in her voice—"Augie?"—was from fear of what might happen or the scar of what already had happened.

"Jenny. Have they hurt you?"

"Augie, I'm so scared."

He could hear the tears in her voice.

"Jenny, where are you? I'm so sorry."

"I don't know where I am. I—"

The voice came back amid the sound of the phone being taken from Jenny.

"Peotone it is, then, Mr. Flood. What do you say, eleven P.M.?"

Flood's blood was boiling. He had made plenty of mistakes in the last twenty-four hours. He had not watched Jenny's back after knowing that Chucky was watching both of them. He had not gone after Chucky and stopped him in the street before he could check in with his boss after the mayhem in Brandon's house. He had not taken Brandon and the girlfriend straight to the local cops so that he would not now be faced with this decision. But he was not going to make the mistake of driving into the dark, cold grave dug for all of them in the farm town eighty miles up the road. He would not give another inch. It was no use to beg him not to hurt her. Either he would or he would not. Either it served his purposes or it did not. Flood would not even mention Jenny's name to this scumbag. He would not betray any feeling at all for her. This would look like as cold-hearted a business deal as the Bepps crew could imagine.

"Peotone, my ass," he said back to the voice. "We meet in Chicago, at one A.M."

The voice started to chuckle its confident, condescending chuckle.

"Fuck you," Flood said, interrupting. "I've heard the whole story. I know what this means to you—you sleazy, goomba-Outfit-fuckheads. I know you've got a choice to make—do you fight a corruption charge in federal court, or do you get three rock-solid murder raps pinned to your oily fucking foreheads to go along with it."

There was only one way to go, and that was to be in charge of this arrangement, and to say to Bepps's crew that he didn't give a shit about Jenny or Brandon or the girl, or anybody else, except himself.

"I've been a good boy to this point, but if you think one night in the sack with a woman is enough for me to put my head on your chopping block, you're an idiot. We're going to do this my way, or the case against Nicky Bepps is going to be over before it starts."

"I don't like your tone of voice, Mr. Flood."

"Listen to me. One A.M. Lower Wacker and Stetson. It's next to Columbus. If you don't try any bullshit, it will all go smoothly and you'll have half a dozen choices for directions home. But if you pull any shit, we're right in the middle of the city."

"Mr. Flood, I'm not meeting you on Wacker Drive."

"One A.M.," Flood said. "You can make a deal with me, but you can't kill me. Give me a fucking break."

There was silence. Flood waited. Brandon and the girl smelled the danger hanging in the air of the car and said nothing, waiting. Flood looked down the road ahead. He had either just regained the upper hand, or he had ensured the murder of this beautiful woman.

Finally the voice spoke.

"If you bring anybody else, you will watch her die a very horrible death," he said. "I have decided I don't like you at all, Mr.

Flood. I look forward to hunting you down and having your teeth pulled out before I cut your throat myself when this is over."

"Whatever makes you happy," Flood said, and disconnected the call.

Chapter Nineteen

"Where are we going?"

"Chicago. I'm taking you to the FBI there."

The girl was in the back seat crying uncontrollably. She doubled over and sobbed, muttering gibberish to herself. Brandon tried to console her.

Flood made his way blindly through the streets, barely noticing what lay ahead in the wash of his headlights. Somehow they made it out of the college town without running anyone over. The highway opened before him and drew him in like a dream. Flood drove for several minutes in a daze, but the monotony of the yellow ribbon down the middle of the road finally dragged him back to reality. He had killed one man but only bloodied the other one, Chucky, who got away. Now Chucky would likely be out on this same highway, how far behind or ahead he did not know. Flood thought about whether to just drive faster or to pull off at an exit and wait for Chucky to pass. That seemed silly. He just drove. He thought about taking a different road, but it might add as much as two hours to the trip.

The car was silent. The girl had fallen mute, and Brandon was keeping everything inside. He was now too much in shock to say anything. He was probably thinking. If he had almost been killed, it meant that his mother probably was dead. If she was alive, and he was in this much danger, she would have protected him somehow. What about his father? Flood had told him his father was a crook; surely, that wasn't news to Brandon.

Flood decided the son would not expect much from his father.

Flood tried to imagine the condition Jenny was in at that moment. Terror, confusion. That much was certain. But what about physical pain? What about rape? As he drove he could barely hear himself, but he was talking, muttering questions into the air, not really to himself. Whatever they thought, Brandon and the girl kept quiet, in their own terror. Flood's heart began to pound, and he felt his eyes swell up and spill tears down his face. He felt grief that surpassed any rage, as if it was already too late, no matter what had happened or did not happen to Jenny. Her voice on the phone was worse than bad enough. Flood sobbed for minutes before it was out of him. It was a process of emotions, from fear, to grief, to a different, more selfish fear, and then it moved on to the emotion he needed, to the one that would get him through this—anger.

The silence coming from Brandon felt like it could explode any second. It seemed Brandon wanted to ask, but feared everything: what Flood would say; what he would find out. Flood had abandoned his sensitivities. He was turning coldly into action. He would say what he had to say and do what he had to do.

"Brandon, I don't know exactly what's going on, but I have a pretty good idea."

Flood decided to put the hard part in the middle.

"This is about something your mother did for a man named Vincent Tortufi," he went on. "Do you know who that is?"

Brandon did not answer right away. It was as if he did not want to be involved, even to hear why his world had just been ripped to shreds. But he could not stay out of it.

"Sort of," he said.

"Your mother was seeing him regularly. You know that?"

"Yeah." It was a defeated syllable. He did not have the energy to deny that she knew a man named Vincent, nor even the implication of the word *seeing*.

"Did you ever meet him?"

"No."

"Vincent Tortufi worked for a man named Nicky Bepps, who is a leader of organized crime in Chicago. Bepps is in a lot of trouble right now for paying bribes so he could build a casino in downtown Chicago. Do you know about that?"

Flood did not glance in the rearview mirror trying to catch Brandon's eyes. He just listened for the response and measured the silence in the meantime.

"I don't know who that is. But my mom talked about the casino."

"What'd she say?"

"She said she was investing in it through her friend. Vincent."

"Did she ever come to visit you at school and have a meeting with anyone while she was there? About the casino?"

Flood waited for the answer but got only silence. Brandon didn't even respond by fidgeting in the back seat. Finally Flood had to turn around and look. He found nothing spectacular, just Brandon looking down at the girl's head in his lap. She had drawn into some kind of shell that was just short of shock. Brandon stroked the blonde hair from her temple into a stream that swirled gently around her ear. He did not look up, so Flood just waited.

"I saw some money. A lot of money," Brandon finally said as tears began to drip into his girlfriend's pile of corn silk hair. "She had it in a yellow envelope in her bag. I was looking in her bag for money."

He choked on a chuckle. It was sort of comic. He began to cry hard now and was having trouble saying the words through sobs.

"I was looking for a fucking twenty," he sobbed. "I was just looking for beer money."

He stopped, as if he could not go further.

"How much did you see, Brandon?"

"I don't know. It was all hundreds. Bundles of them. Like in a fucking movie."

"What did she do with the money?"

He shook his head violently. His girlfriend was coming back to life, from a coma into confusion. First, she did not know whether to roll over or sit up, then she did not know what to do for Brandon. Nothing made sense. It was clear this was the first she was hearing of anything.

"After I saw it, I was scared. I didn't let on that I'd seen it, and then she said she was going to run an errand. She said she was going to a pharmacy or something, but I followed her. She went to the Union and sat in the lobby. I watched from the hallway. This guy came in and sat down. And she got up and walked over to him and sat down in the seat next to him. She got out a makeup thing with a mirror."

"A compact?" the girl asked.

"Yeah, whatever. She opened it and started looking at herself and talking. He talked, too. Neither of them ever looked at each other. Then she closed it and put it back in her purse, and stood up and left. She left the envelope on the chair. He didn't even look at her. Didn't even look up. He just sat next to it. She walked toward me, so I went into the john. When I came out she was gone, and the guy was gone."

"Brandon, when was this?"

"Couple months ago. Before Christmas," he said, still crying. His girlfriend had sat up and curled against him, holding on for dear life. "What about my mom, Mr. Flood? Is she dead? Did somebody kill her because of the money?"

Flood finally caught his eyes in the rearview mirror. It was time to come straight out with it.

"Brandon, when I was driving down to Champaign I received

a phone call telling me your mom's car had been found. It was dumped in the water. She wasn't in it."

He watched for a reaction. Brandon kept stroking the girl's hair as she pulled away from his chest to look at him. She wanted to see his reaction, too, to see whether he comprehended what Flood was saying. It all still sounded so horribly baffling to her. Brandon did not return the look from either of them. His eyes were fixed blankly on the back of the driver's seat. After a moment he closed his eyes and laid his head against the car window. Flood would have liked to have left him alone for a while, but there was no time for that. This was a terribly unfair set of circumstances. Brandon had understood for weeks that something bad was happening at the center of his mother's life, that the envelope of hundred-dollar bills was not her money and it was not a good thing that she was carrying it around in her bag and then dropping it into the seat next to a distinguished-looking man in a gray suit at the university's student center. He knew that was all bad, that it was not the sort of string of events that signaled the repairing of the family. But it had all existed in the category of bizarre turns, priming the urge to know what odd thing would happen next. Now the odd thing had happened, and it was more than odd. It was death. It was gunshots, and blood on the wall, and cars pulled from the canal.

Flood let his eyes drift off the mirror and back to the road. He was ashamed to feel unmoved by Brandon Westlake's misery.

The girl was back in the land of the cognitive as Brandon drifted further away, into the cold reflections of the window and the black speeding night outside. She gingerly leaned forward from the other side of the back seat, giving Brandon his space. Her pretty, tear-stained face appeared over the seatback. She rested her chin on the gray cloth of the passenger seat. She looked like she might be a handful under normal circumstances—a smart, good-looking blonde on a college campus, her attitudes and personality stiffened by a steady stream of attention from the opposite sex. But at the moment she had been reduced to a little kid too scared to throw a tantrum.

"Who are you?" she said. It was so meek that Flood wanted to squeeze her hand.

"I'm who I said I was back at the house," Flood said. "My name is Augustine Flood. I'm a lawyer who was hired last week by Brandon's father to try to find Mrs. Westlake."

"How did you do that to those men?"

"I was an FBI agent until a few years ago. I was trained to do things like that."

"Did you ever kill anyone before?"

It was the question people weren't supposed to ask cops. But he was glad to have it spoken. It helped.

"No," he said. "I shot a man once, but he lived."

She was so delicate and faint, resting her small weight against the seat that she seemed to Flood like a little baby bird, undernourished and dying. She kept her eyes on him.

"Is that why you looked sick?"

"I guess."

"Who were those men?" she whispered.

"They were killers. They work for a mobster and do things for him—they collect money, run errands and hurt people, mostly. I don't know them, but I've known men like them. They're all alike. There's never anything very interesting about them other than their badness."

She did not care about all that, he realized. She interrupted.

"Is the one who got away going to kill us?"

"He's not," Flood said. "He's going to run and hide until either the FBI finds him or his boss finds him. He and the fat one were supposed to kill you and they failed. So his boss will probably have him killed as punishment and to keep him from telling the FBI what happened. I think he had a concussion. I hit his head against the wall pretty hard."

He realized that his actions—stealth and accurate shooting one moment, stumbling into walls the next, screaming threats into the phone and then sobbing in despair, probably left her feeling less than confident that the next death she witnessed would not be her own.

"I want to go home."

"I know," Flood said. "What's your name?"

"Katie."

"Katie, it's going to take a little while to sort this out. The FBI will want to talk to you and to protect you for a little while. This mess we've gotten into is part of a bigger mess that they're trying to clean up. It's a very large investigation. Did you understand what Brandon and I were saying about the casino?"

"Sort of."

"The FBI is trying to arrest everyone involved, including the guy who got away from me, Chucky. Until all those people are locked up, they may want to keep you close, just to be safe."

"Where will Chucky go if he can't go to his boss?"

They were all on a first-name basis with Chucky now.

"I don't know where Chucky is."

Brandon sat back up.

"I want to see my mom's car," he said, sounding impatient with the conversation between Katie and Flood.

Flood sat back and found Brandon in the rearview.

"The agents will have to show it to you."

"I want to go there right now and see it."

"Brandon, I don't know where it is, and they wouldn't let us in to see it if I did. It's probably in a police garage right now, with evidence technicians going through it."

Flood watched his face in the rearview mirror. Brandon was listening selectively. He was not accepting explanations or arguments, only screening what Flood said for the only response he would accept: *I'll take you there immediately.*

Flood thought about what it would mean to Brandon to see his mother's empty ruined car, dripping with filthy canal water and caked in mud. She would not be there. Perhaps he was feeling her slipping away, from the realm of the unexplained missing to the realm of the unaccounted dead. Perhaps Brandon needed to witness the car, to place it in the continuum of her passing. His expectations were long since shattered, Flood realized, and while he suspected Brandon would fear the worst, he was really just bracing for the inevitable, determined to experience it in a way that made sense to him. Flood would not argue against Brandon's need to see his mother's Lexus sedan. It was probably as close as he would ever get to seeing her coffin. It was the closest thing to her end that he might be able to touch. Flood would try to make it happen.

Chapter Twenty

Flood pulled over for gas at Bourbonnais and went inside the mini-mart to get away from Brandon for the moment. He was going to leave one more message for Daniel Westlake. He dialed and the phone rang over to voicemail.

"Dan, this is Augie Flood again. I know you're in town because I know you flew back from Grand Cayman this morning with Pam Sawyer. I know you went down to get your money and that she used your wife's passport to get it. I know everything you've done, including using me as cover while you pretended to be looking for your wife. I know that you really needed this money to keep your own casino investment alive and that now you are in more trouble than you could have dreamed of. I know plenty to go to the FBI right now and redirect their whole investigation to include you. If you want me to do that, don't return this call. If you want to make another arrangement, you'd better be sitting at the bar of the Grand Hyatt on Wacker at twelve-thirty tonight. Don't bother calling me back. Just be there."

Flood went back to his car, finished pumping the gas and took off again, heading north on the highway.

He drove, eyes on the road, but his mind vanished into himself, somewhere deep and timeless, coddled by the darkness of the howling highway. He tumbled back in time, examining the events that led him here, as if they were old letters tucked inside a yearbook. His first stop was the discovery of Pam

Sawyer's body, mangled and shot through the head. Next, it was an hour before when he had the impulse to talk to her again. Back again and Barry McManus was wiping the bar and giving him a look and then calling him with the memory of Westlake stalking Marcy with a piece of paper to sign and Bepps looking on with his cold, murderer stare. He passed over the dead body of Vincent Tortufi lying in a hole and went back again and got stuck—on Daniel Westlake. The sad sack of a cuckold who begged Flood into this mess, and then pulled his own little disappearing act, for what, four days now?

Flood picked up his phone again, scrolled through his numbers he'd dialed and waited.

Brandon leaned forward.

"What are you doing at one o'clock?" Brandon asked.

"I'm meeting somebody."

"Who?"

"You don't need to know."

"I'm going with you."

Flood smiled. Brandon had passed some kind of threshold and now wanted to be a part of everything. He felt that he owned this disaster and was entitled to it. Flood knew otherwise.

Jamie finally answered.

"Where are you?"

"In a bar. Where are you?"

"Driving back from Champaign. Jamie, I need you to leave the bar right now. I need your help for something that is very dangerous."

Jamie said he was on a date, but he was already accepting of Flood's commands. He could read Flood's voice, and he instantly knew that there was no question of what he had to do.

"I need you to go home right now and get your car. Then call me back."

"What's going on?"

Flood hesitated. His impulse was to say that the people who killed Marcy Westlake had kidnapped Jenny. But he did not want to say that in front of Brandon.

"I've gotten to the bottom of this, Jamie. It's the mob, and they've kidnapped Jenny."

There was no immediate response, and Flood feared he'd lost him to a bad cellular connection.

"Jamie?"

"Jesus, Flood. Don't say this."

"I need your help."

"I'll call you in twenty minutes."

He hung up.

"Who's Jamie?" Brandon asked.

"He works for me."

"What are you going to do with him?"

Flood kept his eyes on the road. On his right a big green road sign stood up from the ditch, noting that the Peotone exit was one mile ahead. Flood sped up.

"I'm going to kill the men who took your mother," he finally said, having no idea whether that was true.

Chapter Twenty-One

When Jamie called back, Flood told him to rent a room at the Grand Hyatt and to give the parking attendant fifty dollars to keep his car parked out front in the wide parking plaza that faced the river. An hour later Flood had his car parked in the same way and made his way to the room with Brandon and Katie.

As they entered the room and Flood made introductions, he saw that Jamie had been crying. He was scared out of his wits for Jenny. The redness in his eyes made Flood feel sick to his stomach as he thought again that this was completely his fault. Brandon went to the window and looked out on the twinkling city, which was given space to breathe by the river divide. To the left the Wrigley Building was washed in brilliant white light and its clock stood above Michigan Avenue facing off against its rival across the street, the Tribune Tower, more of a gothic monument than an office building. A strip of river-walk plazas ran eastward along the river under a large box of green and yellow light called the Gleacher Center, which was the University of Chicago's downtown facility. Directly across the river, the NBC Tower loomed like a backdrop. Katie sat nervously on the bed, her back to the city and Brandon, watching Jamie and Flood talk.

"I'll get her back," Flood said in a low voice, trying to calm his friend. "I don't care who I have to hurt to do it. I'll get her back."

Jamie was consumed with thoughts of where she was at that moment, what was happening to her and what terror she felt.

"There's nothing we can do about it right now," Flood said. "But it won't be long."

Jamie nodded but looked worse by the minute.

"Listen to me, Jamie," Flood said, whispering so Brandon and Katie would not hear what he said. "If this is going to turn out all right, I need you to be right with me. I need you to make sure these two stay here, and then I need you to be downstairs and watch Westlake after I've talked to him. There's no room for screwing up. Understand?"

Jamie nodded. He was beginning to think.

"Can you handle this?"

"I can handle it."

Flood slipped out and took the elevator down to the mezzanine level where the expansive, wide-open bar faced an enormous atrium of windows that looked north, across the river at a lower version of the view seen from the room. A sprawling inventory of liquor bottles was arrayed on rows of long glass shelves scaling the wall of windows, creating a glittering, partying-in-orbit feel for the bar. Flood made sure Westlake was not already there and then went down to the lobby, found a discarded newspaper and sat down in a remote lounge chair and pretended to read. If Westlake didn't show, Flood would face the Bepps crew alone. But he believed that in Daniel Westlake he had a potential wildcard to offset the mobsters' advantage.

At 12:25 the red Lincoln Navigator pulled in to the drive, and Westlake got out. He was dressed in his pressed khakis and another ugly sweater. He was wearing a large gray overcoat and insulated tan leather work boots. He looked around nervously and then entered the hotel, looked around again, and headed up the escalator to the bar. Flood put the newspaper down and followed.

He watched Westlake order a Chivas on the rocks and then walked into the bar, which had been very crowded most of the night but was now beginning to thin out. Flood sat down.

Westlake stared straight ahead into the glittering windows, seemingly unable to look at Flood. Shame, indignation, anger—it did not matter to him what Westlake felt. To Flood he was now a life not worth protecting. He was a piece on the chessboard of the night. In a couple of hours he would be able to look at Westlake as a man again, but not now.

"How much do you want?" Westlake said.

"I want a lot more than your money, Dan," he said. "I need your life."

Now Westlake had no choice but to look at him. His tired eyes were watery and lost.

"Either way, you've had it. I'm not taking any money to keep mum. It's too late for that. Bepps has taken a woman hostage, and he will kill her unless I give him your son and his girlfriend. He wants to kill your son because Pam Sawyer told them that Brandon saw your wife give Art Callahan a packet that contained a hundred thousand dollars in cash. They plan to kill Brandon so that he can never testify to what he saw."

He paused, "Did Brandon ask you about the money, Dan? I figure it scared him so much he resorted to asking you or telling you."

He hoped Westlake would say something, but he wasn't ready. He was still taking it in, redirecting himself to handle the shock. So Flood went on.

"Dan, I'm sorry to say that I don't really know whether you love your son or not. I hope you do, but even if you don't, I guarantee there is no place for you to go to enjoy the rest of your life if you bail out on him. I promise you that. I'm here to get the woman back. Not to protect you, and not really to protect Brandon. Your best bet is to help me because I'm likely to kill everyone I see in order to get her back. And that would help you and your son stay alive."

Westlake drank his Scotch but then looked like he might throw up. He was sweating. Flood guessed Westlake had been driving around all night in his Navigator, with a $350,000 deposit slip in his pocket and no clue what to do next. He had probably at least been past Pam Westlake's condo when she did not answer his phone calls. The yellow tape and police vans clogging the street would have given him a pretty good idea what had happened and that would have been enough to keep him away from his own house or business.

"What do you want me to do?" he finally asked.

"Outside there is a staircase in the middle of the sidewalk that takes you down to Lower Wacker. You're going to walk down those steps and meet with Bepps and beg for your kid's life."

"What are you talking about? Where is Brandon?"

"I've got him close by."

"Nicky Bepps is here? You want me to go see him? That's crazy."

"It's what's going to happen, Dan. I am sick of you and your family and I want my girlfriend back in one piece. I will gladly trade all of you for her."

"So what am I going to do about it?"

"You're going to go down there and offer yourself to them instead. Understand? You're going to tell them your kid gets to live because he doesn't know anything. He'll be in FBI protective custody within the hour. You'll tell them only you know the whole story.

"I've got news for you, Dan. Your life is over. Pam's dead, and the feds know exactly what you've been up to. They know you were working your way into Kajmar's casino bid and screwing over your wife so that Bepps would get caught rigging the deal. You are not going to get rich. You are going to go to prison and be ruined, halfway responsible for your wife's murder and, if you don't play this my way, responsible for your son's murder, too. How does that sound?"

Westlake stared straight ahead, his vision lost in the layers of glittering bottles and glass of the back bar.

"It won't work."

"What do you mean it won't work?" Flood said. "How the fuck do you know what *works?* All you've done is screw everything up and get a bunch of people killed. What did you think bringing me into this would accomplish? Did you think I wouldn't figure out you were full of shit? Did you think I wouldn't stick my foot in the middle of this muck? I've got both feet in now, Dan, and I am not getting stuck and Jenny is not getting murdered."

Westlake looked lost, like he wanted to curl up and cry but didn't know how. His eyes went blank.

"What do I do?"

"You sit here for twenty minutes, and then you walk out the door, turn left and walk down the steps to Lower Wacker. There will be a car there, probably a Lincoln, idling at the corner of Stetson. You walk up to it and put your hands up. When they get out, you tell them who you are and what you want."

"Then what? They're just going to give you the girl? I told you, this won't work."

"Dan, I'm not going to disappear. I'll be there. They'll know what they have to do."

Westlake shrugged.

"Can I see my son?"

Flood looked at his watch. It was 12:36.

"There isn't time."

"I won't do it unless you let me see Brandon."

Flood dialed his cell phone and got Jamie.

"He wants to see Brandon. It's OK."

Jamie put the phone down and told Brandon his father wanted to see him. Flood heard nothing in response. Jamie came back on the line.

"He doesn't want to see him. He said no."

Flood hung up.

"Brandon doesn't want to see you."

Westlake looked straight ahead again. He knew Flood was not lying.

"This has to happen right now, Dan."

Westlake nodded, and Flood turned and walked away from the bar and headed down the escalator. He called Jamie back.

"I'm moving. Get down here."

Jamie hung up and left the kids in the room. He headed for the bar to keep an eye on Westlake. In the driveway, Flood hopped into Jamie's Mini and pulled onto the street. He took a quick turn on Columbus, down the ramp to Lower Wacker and across the river, turned the car around and parked it illegally, ready to speed back across the river when he spotted what he was looking for. He took out binoculars he had told Jamie to bring and watched all the intersecting streets: Lower Wacker, Upper Wacker, Columbus, upper and lower. That little chunk of the city was like a piece of layer cake sliced by the river, vertical with its horizontal levels open to view from the north.

Five minutes passed, and then he saw the car pull into view. It was a black Lincoln Town Car coming up Columbus. It rolled slowly through the intersection of Lower Wacker and Columbus, and turned left. Behind it, Flood saw a van turn left before Wacker and head for Water Street. That was the second vehicle—the one he wanted. The Town Car continued on and then made a slow U-turn and sort of backed into a parallel spot facing the river on Stetson.

Flood got back in the Mini and raced across the bridge, crossed Wacker, made a right on Water Street, following the path of the van. It would need a place to idle. It could have gone down another level and idled outside the parking garages or up the ramp to the upper tendril of Columbus in front of the Fairmont Hotel and the fire station. Flood thought about it, and decided they would not want to park near the fire station. He drove down the ramp toward the underground garages for all the skyscrapers in the area. He came to a corner in the underground network of streets and saw the van sitting parked along the curb about a hundred feet off of Columbus.

Flood turned the other way and drove out of sight and parked the Mini. He called Jamie one last time and told him things were moving, and he'd be out of touch for a few minutes. Jamie said Daniel Westlake was still sitting at the bar. Flood got out and started walking toward the van. He put up the collar of his coat and started to weave as he walked down the pavement. The back of the vehicle came into sight fifty yards down the street, lit by weak, greenish fluorescent lights.

His head down, hands in his pockets, he pretended to be drunk.

The van was a pale blue Ford Econoline panel van with no windows in the back. It was the same van that had carried Vincent Tortufi away from the Napoli Tap to his death. He knew they had no intention of giving Jenny back to him in one piece, but they would have brought her just in case they needed her for bait or insurance. Flood guessed she would be inside this van. He hobbled along until he was about twenty feet behind the rear bumper. He did not look up to check if he was being watched in the side mirror. He knew they were watching him. He stopped and bent over with his hands on his knees, as if he was going to throw up, spitting for effect. After another moment he straightened up, looking unsure of himself, and hobbled forward. He took a few steps and then stumbled to his left, tripped over the curb and found himself directly behind the van. Flood turned around and sat down on the van's bumper and put his head in his hands. Almost immediately, he heard both doors open and the suspension lightened as two men got out, one of them cursing.

The street was deserted and the only sound was the thrush of passing cars on Columbus down the block. Suddenly two pairs of feet were in Flood's field of view as he looked down through his fingers.

"What the fuck, pal?" said the one who had come from the driver's side. He gave Flood a kick in the shin. "Get the fuck off my van, you drunk fuck."

Flood groaned and started to collapse more, as if in a delayed reaction to the kick. But he didn't move to get up, and he didn't look at them.

"Well," the driver went on. "I guess it's going to be a pleasure to kick your drunk fucking ass. Come on, Eddie, help me get this piece of shit off my bumper."

Both men reached for Flood's arms at the same time. As they started to take hold, Flood came to his feet, lunging at the driver, swiping his hand down and driving his left fist into the man's Adam's apple. The driver collapsed as Flood whirled into the other man, who was fumbling in his leather jacket, surely for a gun. Flood took him by the arm, spun him around and rammed him face-first into the van. As he went down, he turned slightly, and Flood kneed him in the face. The man keeled over on his back and his head hit hard on the concrete.

Flood took the duct tape from his coat and turned both of them over on their bellies and bound them, working feverishly to have them immobilized before the stun wore off on each of them. The man who had been in the passenger seat was lying on the sidewalk when he finished, but the driver was in the street so Flood dragged him to the curb. He held his breath and opened the back door of the van, wondering whether she would be alive and, if she was, if she would ever speak to him again.

The cargo area was empty. The emptiness just about knocked the wind out of him. The floor was covered in plywood and plastic sheeting. But no person. Flood had miscalculated. He had gotten it wrong. His phone rang; it was Jamie.

"Westlake just walked out the door. He's heading for the steps."

"I'm coming."

"What about Jenny?"

"I haven't seen her yet."

"Goddamn, Flood. How could this happen?" He had never heard anything close to that kind of anger from Jamie. He had been holding it together the last half hour, but now people were starting to move, the final stages of this mess were in play, and still no Jenny. Flood knew he was to blame for Jenny's kidnapping. If she were killed it would be his fault.

The keys were in the van's ignition. He got in and lurched off the curb, turning around and heading for Stetson, and then came squealing around the corner toward Wacker. He could see Daniel Westlake already there, standing in the headlights of the Town Car. Men got out of the Town Car, their backs to Flood as he approached.

Westlake took something out of his pocket. Flood heard a crack and the driver of the car fell backward. Westlake had a gun. He had his own plan, and somehow it made a lot more sense than Flood's plan to surrender, at least if you didn't care what happened to Jenny. Flood pulled the van over and got out. The surviving hoodlum didn't know which way to look. Westlake was looking at Flood, but the gun was still pointed at Bepps's surviving thug.

"I didn't like your plan, Flood," Westlake finally shouted.

Flood hadn't liked it, either, but it was the only thing he could think of to buy him a few minutes to find and rescue Jenny. That hadn't worked out. He had drawn his own gun but didn't know where exactly to point it. He decided to point it at the mob muscle who was still standing, whom he had never seen before. It wasn't Chucky, but he had been cut from the same cloth.

The other one lay in the street by the door of the car, rolling slowly over. He'd been shot in the chest and was probably dying. He said nothing, just slowly rolled, lost his strength and slipped back, and tried to roll again.

Westlake shouted, suddenly: "Get out of the car!" He was looking into the back seat now, and Flood could see two heads there, both older men.

"Out of the car," Westlake shouted again. "I will shoot him."

He jerked the gun at the man standing outside the passenger door. Slowly the back doors of the car finally opened. Two men got out. The one on the passenger side was Nicky Bepps, dressed in a long formal black overcoat and wearing tinted glasses the same color as his thinning rust-colored hair. Flood had never seen him in person before, but he had studied the photos for years. The other man was his brother, Aldo. Neither one of them said anything. Westlake looked confused.

"Flood," he shouted. "Which one?"

"Which one what?" Flood shouted back, assuming nothing. He now had his gun trained permanently on the henchman standing by the passenger side of the car. With more men on the street now, Westlake could get distracted and let his guard down.

"Which one's Bepps?" he shouted.

"Both of them. They're brothers," Flood yelled back. "But if you mean, Nicky, he's this one on the passenger side."

Nicky Bepps slowly turned around to see who was standing behind him giving him up to the crazy man with the gun. Then he looked past Flood and saw the van. It registered that his people were no longer in the van and would be no help to him. Flood nodded ever so slightly at him.

"Mr. Bepps, why don't you give me back my girlfriend and we'll calm down and put away our guns and all go home happy and safe."

Bepps said nothing, but just turned around and looked at Westlake again.

"I don't believe we've met, sir." It was not the voice from the cell phone. Flood figured that voice must have been Aldo's.

Westlake shook his head.

"Once. At a restaurant. My wife was there. Remember her?"

Bepps smiled slightly and nodded after a moment.

"Oh, yes. There was a scene. Something to do with money."

"Where is she?"

"Where is who?"

"My wife."

"I haven't the faintest idea, sir," Bepps said.

Flood wondered if he wanted to get shot. The man on the ground had stopped trying to roll over. He was lying still in a pool of blood now.

Westlake shouted at Bepps. "Come here. Over here."

Bepps hesitated, but then gingerly started to walk across the pavement and stood in front of Westlake. When he was a few feet from him, he stopped.

"Turn around," Westlake commanded. It seemed to Flood like Westlake's own plan had run out, and he didn't know what to do next unless he got up the nerve to kill Bepps himself. When Bepps turned around, Westlake took a step forward and seized him by the collar and put the gun to his head. He jerked, and they stepped back together.

"Dan, what are you doing?" He hesitated to ask the question because now, in the balance of things, Westlake was in Flood's camp, or vice versa. He did not want to undercut Daniel Westlake too far and give the Bepps crew an edge. But he also wanted to talk down the tension—to get Jenny and her survival, or at least her whereabouts, back into the discussion.

Westlake looked at Flood. Flood could only think of Jenny. His mind was preparing itself for the news of her death, and he was fighting it. Westlake kept him in the moment.

"Augie, he killed my wife," Westlake said, poking the barrel of the gun into Bepps's ear.

Bepps winced with the jab of cold steel against his frozen ear. It seemed a strange accusation coming from Westlake, after he had contributed to and then exploited his wife's demise. But something told Flood to ease Westlake along in the direction he wanted to go.

"I know he did, Dan. Everybody knows it. So it's time to let go. It's time to tell the FBI, Dan. They'll take care of it."

"No," Westlake shouted back, his voice breaking. He shook Bepps by the collar. "They'll let him off. They'll send me to prison, and this piece of shit will walk. I know how it works."

"I killed no one," Bepps barked before Westlake shut him up with a rap on the back of his head with the gun.

"Dan, listen," Flood continued. "If you shoot him, everybody's going to start shooting. That asshole with him will start, and I'll start shooting, and then it'll be a real mess and the whole truth will never come out.

Westlake was crying but held tight to Bepps.

"My poor Marcy," he wailed. He was crazy now, rewriting history and muddling the part where he double-crossed her. "I let her down. I didn't mean to. And he killed her."

"You didn't let her down, Dan," Flood said.

"Yes, I did. And he killed her."

"You wanted me to kill her," Bepps said, indignant. The wrong thing to say.

Westlake bashed him on the head again with the gun. He was crying hard, his chest heaving and a constant exhaust of grief seething from his vocal cords.

Bepps was right, sort of. If Westlake didn't want her dead, precisely, he did want bad things to happen to her, and given the company she was keeping, bad things easily could mean death. Flood tried to figure out what to do.

Just when he thought it couldn't get any more precarious, Aldo Bepps turned and walked to the trunk of the Lincoln. He reached into his coat and pulled out a very large revolver. It looked like a .357-magnum. He placed the barrel against the trunk of the car, and he looked at Westlake.

"Let my brother go, or I start filling this trunk with holes. Somebody's inside. Maybe it's your kid."

"You haven't got my kid," Westlake shouted, pointing at Flood for an instant with the gun. "He's got him."

Flood looked at the shiny black surface of the trunk lid. In an instant he knew she was in there.

"Fuck he does," Aldo Bepps screamed back. "Did he tell you that? He traded your kid for that broad. An hour ago. We got your kid in this trunk."

Flood didn't know whether to call his bluff or not. She was in there, and she might be alive. He needed calm. Not screaming and arguing. He instantly thought of Brandon refusing to come to the phone to speak to his father. Was Daniel Westlake thinking of that now, wondering if Brandon was even up there in the hotel room?

Westlake was almost hysterical.

"Flood has Brandon. Flood has Brandon," he screamed, shaking Nicky Bepps by the collar.

"Don't believe that, you stupid fuck." Aldo Bepps was taunting him.

"Open the trunk!" Westlake screamed. "Show me."

"Let go of my brother!" he shouted back.

"Show me!" Westlake was losing it, and so was Aldo. He was shouting right back at him and slamming the barrel of the gun against the trunk of the car with every syllable. Flood couldn't stand it. He wanted to blow Aldo Bepps's head off but he saw the hammer of the .357 was pulled. If he shot Aldo, the old man might still squeeze the trigger before the lights went out. The barrel was still pointed at the lid of the trunk.

Westlake was crying, his tear-stained face distorted and twisted, and he screamed. He couldn't take it another second. Flood couldn't breathe. He held his gun tight and aimed at Aldo Bepps's head, but his hands were shaking. He didn't know if Westlake was going to shoot Nicky Bepps in the head and then turn the gun on himself or try to shoot Aldo or just stand there until somebody else's gun went off.

It seemed for a moment it would have to go one way or the other. But just for an instant.

Westlake kept the gun trained on Bepps's head, but he stepped away from him, trying to find a new vantage point so that he could stay out in front of everybody and at the same time see the trunk of the car. It was the separation from Bepps that pulled the trigger.

In the distance, they heard a dim, thudding clap. Flood's ears pricked up in the same instant, registering the sound as well as recognizing that it was too late to react, that the bullet was already there. He began to anticipate the echo that would come on the heels of the whistle and thud. Daniel Westlake's body jolted forward a half-step, and then he crumpled backwards as his knees buckled and he slumped to the ground. Flood instinctively dropped to the pavement. Bepps stumbled in confusion, and his henchman turned his gun toward Flood. He got off one shot, which ricocheted off the concrete behind Flood. Flood shot back, hitting him twice in the belly.

Aldo Bepps pulled the trigger on his fat revolver, as if startled into doing so. The bullet cut into the metal of the trunk, but Flood could not see the trajectory. Flood rolled onto his side and fired again, hitting Aldo in the neck.

Blood spattered on the dark paint of the car and Flood could not see whether there was a hole in the trunk. He scrambled to the car and slid his hands through the slippery blood, searching for holes. There was a hole and a gouge in the steel at the far right edge of the trunk lid. Within seconds, Flood heard sirens and could see flashing blue lights coming their way across the Michigan Avenue Bridge and southward on Columbus from the direction of Northwestern Memorial.

Now it was just Nicky Bepps and Flood standing there—Flood frantically searching for signs of life in the locked car trunk and Bepps dazed and confused, suddenly having no one to care for him. He stood numbly for a moment while Flood shouted at the trunk, hoping to hear Jenny shout back. The sirens grew louder, and Flood couldn't hear anything. As Flood swung around the car to the open driver's-side door and stepped over the now-dead driver's body, Bepps seemed to regain his wits and started to run—like a weak old man in a heavy coat runs—toward the stairs that led back up to Wacker Drive in front of the Hyatt.

"Stop!" Flood screamed, pointing the gun at him. "I'll shoot, Nicky. I'll shoot you!"

Bepps came slowly to a stop and raised his hands a little, turning around and looking at Flood with disgust.

A police car with two uniforms came to a screeching halt, and the public address speaker on the roof of the car blasted at Flood: "Put the weapon down and raise your hands."

Neither cop had gotten out of the car yet, but both front doors were open, giving them cover as they drew their guns and crouched. Flood turned the gun in his hand so he was holding it by the barrel and laid it on the hood of the Town Car and then started to back away with his hands in the air. He wanted to beg that the trunk be opened, but he knew it was pointless, these cops wouldn't venture into anything heroic until they had the gun and both Flood and Bepps on the ground and cuffed. The horn on the car blasted again: "Lie face down on the ground. Both of you!"

As Flood did as he was told, he heard more sirens coming closer. The cops ordered Bepps to the ground again. He started to whine about his age, and they screamed through the amplifier until he managed to lie down. As Flood was watching the old mob kingpin slowly get on all fours, more shots rang out in the distance. They sounded like they came from across the river—short pops from a handgun, not the long concussion of the sniper's rifle that had killed Westlake. The officers, who had been walking slowly toward Flood pointing their guns at his back, erupted in shouts at each other, "Shots fired!" and then back at Flood and Bepps: "Don't move! Don't move!"

They scrambled forward at Flood, screaming more threats at him, as if he was responsible for pulling triggers on the other side of the river, while they barked futilely into their radio mics that shots had been fired close by. The radio spat back desperate news from other officers.

"Officer down! Officer down! Blue Cadillac DeVille late model northbound on Fairbanks. Repeat, officer down at Ohio and Fairbanks!"

Flood felt a knee sink into his back almost immediately. And in the next thirty seconds it seemed that the entire world was lit up by blue strobe lights. There were no more urgent, terrible words in the police vocabulary than the gasp of "officer down" over a crackling radio frequency. Sirens blared from all directions. Flood was kneed and kicked as the officers jammed his wrists into handcuffs. But he didn't feel the pain. He just started shouting back.

"There's a woman in the trunk. A hostage in the trunk."

Now there were dozens of Crown Victorias parked in the intersection, both blue-and-white squads and unmarked cars. But the four bodies on the pavement had created chaos. When the officer on his back told him to shut up about the woman in the trunk because they'd "get to her when we fucking get to her," Flood started shouting back at them to call Special Agent John Ridgeway of the FBI. "This is his case."

The officer softened a bit and said, "Just shut up a minute."

But one of them walked over to an unmarked Crown Vic and a gathering cluster of men in civilian clothes and overcoats. As Flood studied them, he realized that some of them he knew. They were police brass in the upper reaches of the command staff; being called in the middle of the night was to be expected if a cop got shot. They probably didn't even know yet that the old man pinned on the ground twenty feet from Flood was the boss of the Chicago Outfit. One of the men was in uniform—white shirt and gold star under his short blue insulated jacket—and he nodded as the officer spoke. Flood recognized him immediately as the Deputy Superintendent of Patrol, the man who ran just about every aspect of policing the streets. He was a good, smart cop who wanted to be superintendent, and Flood wasn't surprised to see him in uniform at one A.M. That was the new Chicago Police Department: constantly trying to convince the rank-in-file that they were with them, in the wee hours, and in the rough gang-banging neighborhoods. The boss of Patrol—Seabrook—had probably been in the gang war zones of the 10th and 11th Districts on the West Side when the officer down call came in. He would have been only five minutes away once he hit the Eisenhower at 90 mph.

Flood was still pinned to the ground, with a cop's knee in his back as he strained his neck to hold his head high enough to watch the conversation. Eventually Seabrook looked his way, and they made eye contact. The recognition in Seabrook's eyes was immediate, and he walked over in a hurry.

"Augie Flood."

"Mo."

"Tell me I can have them let you up, Augie."

Flood nodded, and Seabrook motioned to the officer with his knee in Flood's back. The pressure lifted and then Flood felt a sudden jerk and pull in his elbows. Flood winced but didn't say anything.

"Easy," Seabrook said. "He's a good guy . . . I think."

When Flood was on his feet, he nodded at the Town Car.

"Mo—the trunk. There's a hostage in there."

With another wave of Seabrook's hand, three plainclothes cops descended on the car and released the trunk lid.

She was pale and unconscious and bound in duct tape—hands, feet, mouth.

The scene exploded in a rush. Paramedics descended on the trunk and shoved Flood out of the way. Everybody barked into their radios at once. The cops holding Bepps quickly snapped shut the doors, took their seats and rushed off to sit on the mob boss in a holding cell instead of at the scene. Four cars roared out with them, running interference and providing security.

Jenny was put on a stretcher, and an EMT took an angled, dull-ended pair of scissors to her taped hands and feet. She was breathing, but barely and they could not wake her up immediately. They wheeled her into the back of an ambulance, covered her with blankets and peeled through the crowd and up Columbus toward Northwestern Memorial.

Chapter Twenty-Two

The scene was now swarming with people Flood knew. Seabrook stuck close to Flood until a contingent of feds, including Ridgeway, arrived. It seemed half the FBI's Chicago field office was on the scene. The superintendent of police pulled in behind the taped-off area. His chief of detectives, the commanders of Special Operations and the First District joined Seabrook. There were several tactical lieutenants and even the News Affairs flacks. Police had closed the bridge and Wacker Drive for three blocks in either direction. The television news trucks had arrived and were mustered on Columbus in front of the NBC Tower.

Flood stood stunned, backing away from the open car trunk until he bumped up against a concrete wall. Her still, expressionless face burned in his eyes. Her beautiful mouth erased by a thick square of silver tape, he felt a dreamy urge to touch her lips, to warm them from blue back to pink. He looked across to his car and saw Jamie with his back to him, looking north in the direction the ambulance had gone.

Flood wanted to go to the hospital, but Ridgeway would not let him.

"She's going to be OK," he said. "And, Flood, you really have to come with us."

They put him in a car and drove him back to Adams and Dearborn. In the interview room on the fifth floor of the Dirksen Building, Flood gave a full and complete accounting. His interviewers did not include Ridgeway or Feinberg, so he started from the beginning. It took an hour to get to the events of the previous afternoon and evening, including the discovery of Pam Sawyer's body and the events in Brandon Westlake's house in Champaign.

The interview then backtracked and went over the same ground three, four and sometimes five times. The sun came up, and they were not finished. Finally, Ridgeway came in. Flood supposed he'd been listening for the last half hour or so. He had softened considerably from his tone in the last interrogation. Flood wondered why. Had he gone so far that Ridgeway was no longer trying to save him from himself? Was he just filled with pity for Flood at this point?

Ridgeway sat down next to the two agents who had been questioning him. They all looked very tired, and Flood could only guess how bad he looked.

"Well," Flood said. "Have you called for an A.U.S.A. to come charge me with something?"

Ridgeway smiled.

"Let's see, obstruction would be the obvious one. A slam dunk. But there's also murder, but you killed two—wait, three—very bad men, all of them brutal killers, so we're inclined to let those go. I don't suppose you have a license for that gun, or a license to carry a handgun in the city of Chicago at all, do you? Hmm, what else? You tramped through the murder scene in Hinsdale and didn't report the scene until an hour later. I know that one for sure, and I'm guessing you were in Orland Park two nights ago. You've been leaving a lot of murder scenes lately, haven't you?"

He wasn't arguing. He could tell where this was going.

"We're not going to charge you with anything. But the ARDC may want to reconsider your law license. You should hire a lawyer to defend you on that. Know any?"

Flood nodded.

"Oh, one thing," Ridgeway said, looking at Flood's hands. "Whose blood is that?"

Flood looked at his hands and realized his palms were smeared with blood, and there was a pattern of drops on the back of his right hand.

"Well, Bepps's on the front, from the trunk of the car after I shot him. And on the back, the guy in Champaign, from when I hit his head."

"We'll need to swab that one on the back for DNA evidence," Ridgeway said, looking at one of the agents, who immediately stood up and walked out of the room.

Flood was barely following the discussion.

"How's Jenny?" he said.

Ridgeway gave him a nod, as though he'd been avoiding the topic and was waiting for Flood to remember.

"Alive. Hypothermia and a concussion. But she's awake and alert. They'll let her go home tomorrow, probably."

Flood closed his eyes.

"How is she emotionally," he asked, eyes still shut.

Ridgeway hesitated. He was not particularly good with these kinds of descriptions.

"Unstable," he finally said.

Flood opened his eyes. He shouldn't have been surprised by that, he knew, but he had felt such a sense of relief since they cleared the scene at Stetson and Wacker. With the exception of Westlake, everybody in his circle was alive. He didn't know how to reckon with this, either.

He imagined her in her hospital bed but could not bear to conjure her face. He feared the accusations in her eyes. Why had he allowed her to be terrorized? This was his fault. Any harm done to her was his fault. He did not know how he would face Jamie, either.

"What did they do?"

"What you'd expect. Convinced her she was going to die a very bad death. Beat her. Felt her up. Um, handled her . . . touched her in inappropriate ways."

He was trying to figure out ways to say it, then felt he needed to add, "She was not raped."

"I want to go see her."

Ridgeway was shaking his head even before Flood finished.

"You're still in a pickle as far as this whole investigation goes, and we're not done talking to her yet. Maybe in a couple days, but we need to keep our ducks in a row until we're finished interviewing her. She'll have to testify. Aggravated kidnapping wasn't what we had in mind for Bepps, but we may need it."

Flood felt sick. He was having a difficult time seeing how he would get through the next few minutes without seeing her, let alone days. He needed to be there in front of her to say he was sorry, that what happened to her was all his fault and that he understood his guilt and hated himself. He needed to have her hear that from him right now.

"Where's Jamie?"

"He's with her."

Flood nodded.

"What's the deal, Flood? She's your girlfriend or his? He's gay, right? But it seems like they're, you know. And he works for you?"

"They're good friends," Flood said. "Yes, he works for me."

He resented the question for all of its strange ignorance and insignificance. Who cared what the three-way dynamic was?

Ridgeway must have sensed it. He rubbed his face in fatigue in a way that made Flood feel they were on the same side for the moment. Ridgeway nodded.

They sat quietly until the agent came back with a small evidence kit and swabbed Flood's wrist to take the sample of

Chucky's blood. When he was finished, he went out again. Ridgeway nodded to the other agent, and he picked up his legal pad and walked out.

Still, they sat quietly for a little longer. Flood began to wonder how much of this either of them could take before falling asleep.

"What about Westlake?" Flood asked finally.

Ridgeway nodded.

"Bepps is down the hall. I've been in there most of the morning."

"Is he talking?"

"He's trying to lay as much as he can on Westlake and Tortufi. We sort of missed that whole end of things, I guess." Ridgeway said. "This all started as a scheme for Westlake and the Hinsdale woman to use his wife to derail Bepps so that George Kajmar's bid would end up with the casino permit?"

"Sort of far-fetched. But it's true," Flood said. "I think Westlake lost his grip a while ago. What's Bepps saying?"

"He says Marcy Westlake was a woman he did not know very well at all, other than she was dating Vincent Tortufi, who Bepps said was nothing more to him than his brother-in-law's business partner," Ridgeway said, taking on the weary tone of the cop who believes everyone is lying to him twenty-four hours a day. "He says he's shocked that Vincent Tortufi would try to manipulate the casino business, and he's saddened even further in his grief to learn that his brother Aldo may have had some knowledge of what was going on."

"He really said that?"

Ridgeway nodded his weary nod.

They were at a dead end, and Flood decided not to tweak Ridgeway over what the feds didn't know.

"What'd you find in her car?" Flood asked, satisfied with the futility of Westlake's actions and the inevitability of Nicky Bepps's new alibi.

Ridgeway shrugged.

"Not Marcy Westlake. Driver's side window was shattered."

"I'm pretty sure she's dead," Flood said.

Ridgeway nodded.

"For once they got rid of a fucking body. Everybody else—Tortufi, Pam Sawyer—was left for us to find. Those kids would have been a messy scene too, if you hadn't showed up and gone commando on them."

"I suppose they tried to bury Tortufi," Flood said, adding, "from what I read."

Ridgeway sighed.

"You going to help us out on that?"

"I'll see what I can find out."

Flood smiled, but Ridgeway did not. He knew Flood had witnessed the burial of Tortufi and had been the one to uncover him. Ridgeway was probably wondering how far he would have to take forensic analysis of the 911 call to the Orland Park police in order to prove the voice was Flood's.

"Where do you think Marcy Westlake's body is?" Ridgeway asked.

"Burned up, probably. I'm guessing the Outfit still has enough pull to get a few moments alone with a steel-mill furnace."

Ridgeway didn't respond other than to let his lower lip curl a little bit as he contemplated the image of a woman's body sliding into a pool of molten steel.

"Are there even any steel mills left around here?"

They both shrugged.

"Flood, who's your client?" Ridgeway asked. His eyes were pinched a bit in the struggle to understand motives he did not share. "Why are you still in this?"

"It was Daniel Westlake."

"But he didn't want you to find anybody, really. Did he?"

Flood shrugged.

But Ridgeway persisted.

"No, really. Why didn't you let this go?"

Flood waited a while. He did not really want to go into his reasons. They weren't very professional, and he knew Ridgeway never found him to be the most consummate professional.

"I figured out something was screwy. I was being played, and I didn't like it. And then it was too late to get out. I figured out they would kill the kid next."

Ridgeway frowned.

"I don't get that. Why'd they want to kill the kid?"

And now Flood had to peel away a little more of the mystery. It would cause Brandon Westlake trouble, but it also would help put a more decisive end to all of this.

"He saw his mother make the payoff. He saw the money, and he saw her take it and hand it to Art Callahan."

Ridgeway's face lit up. He had no idea. Flood just nodded and smiled.

And now Brandon Westlake would end up being the government's star witness, and the FBI didn't even know he was relevant until this moment because Flood told them.

"But he didn't know who Bepps was?" Ridgeway said, weakly. "Why kill him?"

This seemed a waste of time, Flood thought. He was too tired for rudimentary exercises in criminal logic, but he didn't see much choice but to indulge Ridgeway.

"It didn't matter that he only had a piece of the puzzle," Flood said. "It was a big piece, and you needed it to finish the puzzle. When it came down to it, you guys were going to have a hard time pinning this whole thing on Bepps. He was going to lose the casino license, but he was probably going to beat the racketeering and bribery rap, and the fifth floor was going to blame you. I'm sort of surprised this U.S. Attorney had the balls to get indictments."

Flood pointed his finger at the floor, toward the U.S. Attorney's office downstairs.

"We'd have got him," Ridgeway said, lamely.

"Maybe not." Flood smiled. "You should have nabbed Marcy Westlake months ago. You didn't because you didn't know about her until I called asking about Tortufi. And even then, you didn't understand her role. Bepps was smart to kill her first, and he was smart to kill Tortufi, and he would have been smart to kill Brandon."

"You're taking a lot of credit for our investigation," Ridgeway said, starting to get his pride up.

"I'm not taking credit for anything, John. By a ridiculous set of coincidences I got involved in this from a totally different angle, which very logically ended up leading me to Brandon Westlake."

"How'd you make the connection, between the wife and the casino?"

"Tortufi. The kid had calls on his cell phone bill from the motel where they were meeting to screw—Tortufi and Marcy Westlake."

"How'd you know they were the ones making the calls from the motel?"

"I developed information," Flood said, smiling as he used the FBI vocabulary of obfuscation. He thought of the sad, helpful middle-aged front desk manager whom he had lied to in order to get information.

"Good work." Ridgeway nodded, impressed and maybe a little jealous. "But how'd you put Tortufi in the middle of the casino thing?"

Flood shook his head, as if to say that he himself had no idea how the connection was made. He didn't answer. The same name was on both of their minds, however. Reece.

It was time to leave, whether Ridgeway was ready to let him go or not. Flood stood up.

"John, I'm really tired. I want to talk to Jamie and see how she's doing, and then I want to go to bed."

Ridgeway gestured to the door, dismissing him. The congenial moment was over. Flood was an outsider again.

CHAPTER TWENTY-THREE

When Flood tracked Jamie down, he had a scone in his mouth at a crowded chain café across the street from Northwestern Memorial. He was drinking a latte and looked like he had never tasted coffee and milk together before. In fact, he looked like he had never been in a coffee shop, or been to Chicago or eaten bread before. Jamie looked like a child lost in the cosmos. Maybe he was in shock. Maybe he had come out of shock and saw the world with fresh eyes.

Flood sat down.

"Do you want some coffee?" Jamie asked after taking a big gulp. He asked in a way that made Flood feel he was trying to explain to him that, if he did want coffee, this would be a good place to get it because they sold it in cups up at the counter.

Flood shook his head. "I don't. I feel kind of sick."

Jamie nodded and chewed.

"How is she?" Flood asked, a little annoyed that Jamie needed prompting.

"OK," he said, meaning neither good nor bad. "She's finally asleep."

He chewed some more, then put the rest of the scone in its little brown paper sleeve and finally looked at Flood with something approaching focus.

"She had a bump on her head. A mild concussion but not that serious, except she almost froze to death and has a horrible headache."

He stopped there for a minute and both of them thought about her headache, a kind of pain they could empathize with.

"She thought she was going to die," Jamie said. "I saw something in her eyes I've never seen in anybody before. Terror. It's like she . . ."

Jamie stopped for a bit, trying to figure out how to say it.

". . . like she had all her control taken away."

Flood thought about that for a bit. Imagining what that would look like in her eyes.

Jamie took the half-eaten scone out of the bag and had another bite. He peered down the drinking slit of the lid on his coffee to see just how much was left. He asked about the person who shot Westlake.

"I think he's a guy named Chucky. They haven't found him yet."

"Are you worried about him?"

"What do you mean?"

"Coming back."

Flood shrugged.

"If he's smart, he's running. He dumped that car and is halfway to Miami. Take a fishing boat to the Bahamas or something. Maybe Bepps'll have him killed. He's part of the mess now."

They sat and thought about warm weather for a bit. Flood thought about Chucky with a big bandage on his head, trying to keep it out of the sun. Jamie shifted in his seat, and Flood's thoughts came back to the moment.

"Ridgeway told me to stay away from her."

"That's probably best," Jamie said. "You know, she's emotionally a little fragile right now."

"She probably wants nothing more to do with me."

Jamie frowned.

"This isn't your fault, boss."

"I got you both into this," he said. "I saw them in the hotel bar two nights ago. They were watching us. I should have protected her."

"Listen," Jamie said, reaching out and laying his hand on Flood's arm. "I didn't mean any of that last night. I was scared and freaked out and, God, I thought she was dead. I was so afraid she was dead."

Flood withdrew his arm and put his face in his hands. His skin and hair were greasy, and he needed a shave. His neck ached with exhaustion. He was so tired. At the moment, he just wanted to walk away from everything for a while. Even Jenny, and he felt guilty about that immediately, but he still felt it.

Jamie saw a possibility in Flood's angst that he didn't like.

"What are you going to do about Jenny?"

"What do you mean? I want to see her."

Jamie waved his hand dismissively.

"No, Flood, really. Is this where you start to check out?" Jamie asked. "It's OK if you do. You've only been together a few days. And this is a lot of stress, and I know you'll be a pal about it. But I'm spending time with her and she's asking me how you are. I need to say something. I'm not going to tell her you can't wait to see her and get started again if that's not true. You don't owe anybody anything, but don't make me make a promise for you that you're not going to keep."

Flood wanted to fight back and defend his sincerity, but he could not. He just sat there and took it because he knew it was something to think about.

Jamie had made his point and now relented.

"I'll tell her you're very worried about her," he said. "Go home."

The guilt he felt over wanting to be free of all this seized him a little harder. Why wasn't his impulse to stay as close as possible to her, keeping vigil whether she could see him or not

Hadn't she earned that much devotion from him?

"Are you listening to me?" Jamie said. "Go home. Sleep."

"What about you?" Flood lifted his head out of his hands. "You've got to be a wreck."

Jamie shrugged. His little lost boy look had gone, and he seemed more himself.

"Her mom is flying in from Maryland. She'll be here around two, I think. I'll go home and crash after that," he said, looking at his watch and smiling. "Can I have tomorrow off, boss?"

Flood sat back and winced.

"Christ, Cronin and Marty. I haven't told them where I am. I'm afraid I'm not your boss much longer."

Jamie stood up.

"If you go, I go. I may be sleeping on your couch for a while. I don't think I can go back to Starbucks."

"You worked at Starbucks?"

"Two years."

"Jesus, if I'd known you were one of those people, I never would have hired you."

They walked out together. In the bright sunlight there was no wind, and it felt almost warm after a few seconds adjusting to the naked air.

Jamie stepped off the curb and looked sideways at Flood as he started across the street toward the hospital. He went diagonally across the pavement, practically walking down the middle of the street. Flood watched him walk, waiting for the traffic to come at him, but the lights were all red and the street was empty. Jamie called back to him one last time and then was gone. Flood stood there deciding whether a walk home would further wear him out or wake him up. He decided it would wake him up. As he looked around there was a white taxi idling t the curb. He raised his hand, and it eased forward, almost e it had been waiting for him.

Chapter Twenty-Four

"Wabash and Hubbard," he said to the young cabbie, who wore sunglasses and a stocking cap. "Take Wabash down."

The cabbie nodded without saying anything. As they crossed Michigan, Flood was in a mood to lay out the damning news about his involvement for his bosses and took out his phone. Better to get it over with. But as soon as he dialed Cronin's cell phone number, the low battery warning beeped and the call cut out. The phone was dead. He'd call from home. As the cab eased down Superior toward Wabash, Flood felt himself starting to nod off. He opened the window a crack to let the cold air hit his face.

At Wabash the light was green, and the driver slipped through the intersection without turning.

"Where are you going?" Flood said, leaning forward a bit.

"Sorry," the driver said, slurring his words a little. "I'll take State."

He turned south on State Street and Flood sat back. He thought about calls he should make before going to bed. He still wanted to call Cronin or Marty Drew. He had to, in fact. After all, it was a work day. He wasn't sure which—Wednesday or Thursday—but he was supposed to be in the office. And he wanted to call Reece, to fill him in, as well as to hear what he knew. The morning TV and radio news had reported that the intersection of Columbus and Wacker was closed part of the night for some kind of "police action" that included a shooting but there had been no details. Flood wondered whether Ridgeway would keep his name out of it or whether he'd sic the television reporters on him just to teach him a lesson.

Reece surely would be already in the throes of putting the story together. He'd probably pulled an all-nighter. During Flood's interview with the FBI that morning, his phone had been vibrating nearly constantly in his coat pocket, but he'd had to let it go. There were probably a half dozen calls from Reece. The constant vibrating likely was responsible for wearing out the battery.

He'd call Reece before he nodded off. If nothing else it would keep the reporter from knocking on his door. That was the only problem with living downtown, anybody could show up at your door any time of the day. Reece's office was a three-minute walk from the lobby of Flood's building. He thought about just dropping by the Tribune in person, but that seemed a bit much. He was just so tired. So, he would call Cronin, and he would call Reece, and then he would sleep. He no longer had Daniel and Marcy Westlake to worry about.

That meant, of course, that Brandon Westlake was now an orphan. It seemed such an outdated word, but it was real. He was twenty and his parents were both dead. He had no other immediate family. Poor Brandon. He did want to be free of their pettiness and fighting, but now he would crave having that much strife back in his life.

The cab skipped Hubbard Street, and Flood didn't notice. He was lost in his drowsy thoughts. They turned left on Kinzie, and the street descended underground, past a handful of loading docks and makeshift parking lots. Wait a minute, he finally thought, where are we going?

The driver turned his head slightly to take hold of something under his coat. His profile registered with Flood in degrees. Familiar, but he wasn't quite placing it. He wanted to reach over the seat and take the driver's shades and cap off. The driver leaned back and looked at Flood in the rearview mirror. Flood realized he was holding something in his left hand and stretching a bit to hold it to his right. Over the seat back, and through the plastic sliding window, the double barrels of a pistol-gripped sawed-off shotgun finally peeked over at him.

"Sit tight, motherfucker," the driver finally said, smiling but not too much. He wasn't that amused by himself.

Now it all fell coldly into place for Flood.

"Where do you get all these guns, Chucky?" Flood said, no longer drowsy.

"I got as many guns as it's gonna take to waste your ass."

"I count three. This one, which is a really nice one. Did you saw it off yourself? The rifle you killed Mr. Westlake with. Were you in the Army or something, Chucky? That was a really good shot," Flood said. "Oh, and the third one. The one you gave me that I used to blow that fat fuck's brains out. I just handed that one over to the feds a few hours ago."

Chucky didn't like Flood's tone, and he was taken aback by it. He expected to inspire terror and he had surely hoped for pathetic and futile pleas for mercy. That's the way he had imagined this last hit; not getting lip from the doomed.

"Sometimes I wish I was a cab driver," Flood said. "I think it would be sort of freeing, just driving people where they want to go. Is that why you like it, Chucky?"

"You know I'm gonna fucking waste you, you piece of shit? You know that?"

"I know, Chucky," Flood said in a soothing, fatherly tone. "Nobody's saying you're not going to waste my piece-of-shit ass."

Chucky was driving erratically. He turned right on red a nearly got sideswiped, then wove across the bridge, tryin keep a nervous eye on Flood. Now they were going we

Lower Wacker. Flood was getting tired of Lower Wacker.

"The thing that really sucks for me," Flood went on, "is that my cell phone's dead. Otherwise I would have called somebody right now, and they'd figure out what was going on. I'd give them signals, like saying we're going west and now south on Lower Wacker."

"Shut up, bitch," Chucky growled at him, jumping around a bit to try to see in the rearview mirror if Flood was holding his cell phone. "Give me that fucking phone."

Flood started to hand the phone over, bringing his hand close to the barrel of the shotgun.

"Sit the fuck back," Chucky shouted, changing his mind.

Chucky never turned around. It appeared he couldn't. He kept the stocking cap on. Flood was starting to build a little profile. Chucky had nobody left to go to, otherwise he would not have come alone. Driving and holding the shotgun on Flood at the same time was too unwieldy and precarious. There was something wrong with his neck, otherwise he would have turned around to look Flood in the eye when he told him he was going to kill him. Lastly, that stocking cap was disguising a head wound that had not received much treatment since Flood gave it to him last night, bouncing his forehead off a doorframe. It meant he wasn't quite thinking straight. If he had been thinking straight, he never would have said a word to Flood. He would have just stuck the gun over the back seat and fired it into his belly and then pulled over and walked away from the cab. But he had it in his head that he needed to take Flood somewhere special. Maybe he was thinking he would redeem himself by delivering his head on a platter to whoever would replace Bepps ow that he was headed to federal lockup. As if whoever that son was would want to see Flood's head. Chucky would be d for doing something stupid like that. The thing that ed and alarmed Flood the most was that shot last night that killed Westlake. Given all Chucky's current maladies, it was an amazing shot in that it killed Westlake and did not even graze Bepps—from two hundred yards. All this was valuable information for Flood to add up, but it did not yet balance with the black steel circles of the shotgun barrels aimed at his throat.

Chucky took an abrupt left up a ramp and onto Harrison Street, back into the cold hard light of day. When they turned down Wells, Flood realized the field trip was coming to an end. They were about to run out of street; in another two blocks they would dead-end at a large vacant lot of about five acres that butted up against train tracks and the Roosevelt Road bridge.

Flood kept talking.

"So, Chucky. I've never figured some of this whole deal out. Tell me what the lady in Hinsdale told you while you were breaking her fingers."

"I'm not telling you shit."

"She knew Marcy Westlake was fucking Vincent Tortufi, and she figured out that he was involved in the West Bank casino bid, right? My guess is that she figured out Marcy was playing some kind of role in bribing the Gaming Board."

"Aren't you smart," Chucky said, still slurring. "I'm gonna feel so guilty blowing your smart fucking brains out."

"Oh, it's fine, really," Flood said. "So, let's see. She and Westlake decide that if they can get a piece of George Kajmar's casino bid, then they can screw up your boss's lock on the license by tipping the feds to exactly what's going on with the bribes. So then, when the scandal blows over, eventually, they'll be in a perfect position to win the bid. It seems clever, but it was really quite stupid, wasn't it, Chucky?"

Chucky turned left and then turned right down a dirt lane of a vacant lot lined with parked cars. On his left, across vacar land, was Clark Street. On his right, sitting on the bank of t

South Branch of the river, was a big round apartment complex called River City. The building looked like something out of a science fiction movie in the 1970s—a big gray marshmallow of poured concrete, with rows and rows of round windows.

"But things really got ugly when Pam Sawyer—that's the situation you took care of in Hinsdale, Chuck. Anyway, when she and Westlake tipped the feds. They leave Marcy out of it but tell the story of Art Callahan getting bribed. The money, even the location in Champaign. It's enough to get the feds rolling, and they start piecing everything together. They don't know about Marcy, but your boss does, doesn't he?" Flood went on, full of rhetorical questions at this point. "He's awfully smart. And he knew immediately that George Kajmar would have the most to gain from his tragedy. But Kajmar didn't know anything about it. In fact, I think he got pissed off when Westlake laid it out for him last weekend. Kajmar knew the whole thing was bound to blow up in his face. He probably knew it wouldn't take long for your boss to link it back to him. Were you guys going to neutralize that situation, too?" he asked, getting no answer. Flood kept using euphemisms for murdering people. The non-threatening, non-judgmental language was an interrogator's trick, but Flood was using it to mock Chucky. He rambled on, studying Chucky's face as he talked. "Kajmar is connected to Westlake. Westlake, obviously, is connected to Marcy, and Marcy was connected to Vincent. Didn't take your boss long to connect those dots, I bet. So Pam and Westlake created a scenario in which Marcy became a problem, Chucky, didn't they?"

"Fuck you."

"Come on, Chucky. Tell me about Marcy Westlake. I know you took care of things. Tell me where and how."

At the end of the lane, Flood could see the cars dissipated and there was just one sitting there. It was another black Town

Car, facing out. Chucky had gotten rid of the purple Cadillac. Flood had about ten seconds left. If it had been him behind the wheel, he wouldn't get out of the car without pulling the trigger first.

"She ran out of road. Just like you're about to run out of road, dickhead."

Flood studied the door locks. They were childproofed, and he'd be locked in at the driver's mercy. He had removed his leather belt and held it in his hand out of sight of the rearview mirror, but he had not figured out what use it would be to him yet. The damned plastic safety window would shield Chucky from him. He needed to get his hands on the shotgun.

Chucky started to nod his head in short little bobs, as if he was keeping time to some rapid beat that got faster and faster. Flood could feel the momentum building in his abductor as he stoked his courage to pull the trigger, to kill again like he had been killing people for weeks. Chucky had killed from a distance last night, a cold shot in the middle of the cold night across a cold river. Now he needed to kill again, at a warm and sickly close reach, in a heated cab that already smelled too much of other people's bodies. It would be a kill made of deafening noise and splattered blood and the smell of a hole ripped in a live man's body.

Chucky nodded faster. The gravel ground and spat louder under the cab's tires as the end of the lane came at them and he slowed the car.

And then Flood's mind cleared. The world had never presented itself so clearly to him, with so little thought and so little doubt. He put the leather sole of his shoe against the har plastic of the car door and it felt firm and right. He push hard and launched himself to the left, toward the corner of back seat. Chucky's head jerked and the shotgun explode deafening blast, and sparks and smoke and most of the covered backseat disintegrated into a cloud of fluff seat filling. The shot had missed him. The decibels of the blast obliterated all other noise in an instant, and only the hum of his shocked ears followed in its wake. In the instant that the buckshot shattered the seat, he looked forward, through the smoke, at the shotgun. Chucky had not anticipated the kick. Holding the gun like that, with one hand across his body, made him a one-shot gunman. The gun had jerked wildly up and back, and it was all he could do to hang onto the stock, which had been chopped into a crude pistol grip. The barrel was waving at the ceiling of the car, and Chucky's finger wasn't even on the trigger. He would need to get a grip on the gun again and then use his thumb to switch the lever over to fire the other barrel. But Flood's hand was already through the safety window. He took hold of the blazing hot barrel and rammed it into Chucky's temple, into that tender wound covered by the stocking cap. Chucky howled and let go of the gun. But his foot jammed into the gas pedal and the cab lurched forward, colliding with the parked Town Car.

They piled forward, Flood plowed into the plastic window and the back of the driver's seat, Chucky into the steering wheel. The airbag popped and thrust Chucky back against the seat, whipping his head violently. The shotgun fell from Flood's hand and bounced into the corner of the floor in the front passenger side. He lunged forward but was stuck, unable to get even one shoulder through the window. He was trapped still by the window and the locked back door, and the gun was on the floor of the passenger side. Chucky regained his wits and lunged cross the seat toward the weapon. Flood had his right arm all e way through the window and caught him by the neck. cky grappled at Flood's hand, trying to get free. If he could e Flood's grasp, there would be little Flood could do but r him to aim the gun and fire. He held on and squeezed, trying to counter the strength of Chucky's hands with a crushing grip on his throat. Even if he could kick out the window, he wouldn't have time to crawl out before Chucky got hold of the shotgun, and then he would be even more vulnerable, half hanging out the window, presenting his side and spine to be blown away with 12-gauge shot. He held on and tried to locate a pressure point on Chucky's neck with his thumb. He found nothing. Chucky began to twist the rest of his body, trying to turn around in Flood's grasp and take away Flood's angle on his throat. It was working, and Flood was losing his grip. Chucky was turned around on the front seat and almost facing Flood. He looked Flood in the eye and gurgled something that was supposed to be a curse but was merely unintelligible spittle. He gurgled it again and began to reach back for the gun, still in Flood's grasp. He almost had his hand on the gun, but he reached too far and his left leg slipped off the seat. He lost his balance and lurched sideways. Flood let go of his throat and grabbed the collar of his sweater and pulled as hard as he could while his foe was still off balance. He spilled back, headlong toward the plastic window. Flood reached through the window with his left arm and hooked his belt under Chucky's chin and pulled harder. He thought he had him in a strangle hold, but Chucky had managed to get his hand under the belt, and they struggled as Flood pulled tighter and Chucky pushed with all his strength to loosen the noose.

As Flood pulled harder, Chucky started to make gurgling, gasping noises. But he wasn't quitting. Flood could see Chucky's feet flailing around together on the floor of the passenger side, where the shotgun had tumbled. He was trying to pick it up with his feet. As he maneuvered, the barrel finally slid over his right foot, and he clamped his left foot down on top and began to try to lift the gun to his hand.

Flood pulled even harder on the belt, but it seemed that th

pressure was not increasing any more and Chucky was still able to take small sips of air. All Flood could do was pull as hard as he could and wait for the barrel of the gun to swing toward him again. Sweat was pouring down his face and back, and he was having a hard time breathing himself, with the sickly swirl of seat fluff, cab stench, gunpowder smoke and Chucky's breath all coursing down his windpipe.

Suddenly, both front doors of the car opened. From the right a man with a gun lurched in and swiped the shotgun out of the grasp of Chucky's feet. From the left a bare hand holding a 9mm pistol appeared, backed by a voice.

"FBI! Put your hands on the dashboard. Now! Flood, let him go!"

Flood didn't let go just yet, but he bent and peered through the window. It was Feinberg. He released Chucky's neck and slumped back, exhausted. They dragged Chucky out and put him face down in the snowy gravel. Feinberg unlocked the back doors and helped Flood out.

Flood took a deep breath of the cold clean air, and his head swam. He felt like he might be sick for a moment, but then his senses began to clear and he leaned against the cab and put his hands on his knees.

"Who is he?" Feinberg asked, pointing his gun back at the man on the ground.

"He's my friend Chucky, Feinberg. Where the fuck have you been? You were clearly tailing me from the hospital if you're here at all."

"We thought you were having some kind of meeting when you rolled back here, and we were setting up a surveillance point. It took us a bit to figure out what was going on."

"The shotgun blast didn't give it away?" Flood asked, starting to brush the seat fluff from his coat.

"Couldn't hear it. So, again, who is this guy?"

"He's your sniper and cop shooter from last night, for starters. He's the guy in the purple Cadillac. He's the guy who killed Pam Sawyer, the guy who was torturing Brandon Westlake and his girlfriend, and he's probably the guy who killed Tortufi and Marcy Westlake," Flood said. "Great fucking guy."

Feinberg walked over to Chucky and peeled off the stocking cap and pulled his head up off the ground by his hair to see his face. The rough treatment pulled a moan of real pain out of Chucky, and then Feinberg's face brightened as he recognized him.

"Hey, hey," he said. "Carlo Spizek. I didn't recognize you with your bleeding head the size of a fucking watermelon. Looks like we're going to hook your ass up good and high, Carlo."

He dropped Carlo's head, which plopped back into the gravel, and walked back to Flood.

"Why'd you call him Chucky?"

"That's what the fat guy I killed last night called him."

"Huh." Feinberg shrugged. "Carlo's the new generation of mob hitman: from Hillside to Desert Storm and back to Hillside. Expert marksman, we hear."

Feinberg was almost giddy. He took a step back in Carlo Spizek's direction and shouted at him, "No more chocolate martinis and window tables at Jilly's for you, you douche-bag!"

"So gleeful, Feinberg," Flood said, still picking fluff out of his coat.

"I know, but I can't help it. He's been a slippery fucker."

They stood around for a moment soaking up the bizarre force of the accumulating mayhem. Never had either of them seen so much excitement and peril associated with a case. The typical case was months of sneaking around with wiretaps and surveillance, then subpoenaing records and then arresting somebody surrounded by about a hundred people in bulletproof riot gear and fully automatic M-4s that had never been fir anywhere but a practice range. In the last week Flood had nearly lost his life three times and had killed three men.

Ridgeway pulled up in a black Taurus and stumbled from the car in a rage.

"Here we go again," Flood whispered to Feinberg.

Ridgeway stormed past Carlo Spizek with barely a glance.

"Goddamnit, Flood!"

Chapter Twenty-Five

Reece was buying lunch at Shaw's this time, and they weren't in the bar. They were in the dining room, the dim, warmly lit, wood-paneled cavern, ordering off the full menu. The raw oysters, lobster bisque, grilled trout and bottle of fumé blanc were on the newspaper expense account. It looked like a business lunch, but it really wasn't. Flood didn't have any tips left to give, and Reece wasn't writing a story. He had already written them all.

Five days had passed since the "Shootout on Lower Wacker," as the tabloid paper had billed the murder of Daniel Westlake and demise of Aldo Beppo and two of Nicky Bepps's men. Flood had been in federal court that morning at a preliminary hearing, identifying Nicky Bepps as the man who showed up to claim Brandon Westlake after a spate of cell phone conversations with his henchman. At this stage, there was no point in a secretive grand jury to sort out all that was going on. The U.S. Attorney's office just hauled everybody in before a judge, and the press went crazy, and in the end perhaps there wouldn't even be a casino downtown, so miserable was this scandal for the mayor's office. Everybody would lose.

Bepps's lawyers were trying to get the judge to dismiss the charges that the mobster had attempted to kidnap Brandon Westlake and his girlfriend with the intention of murderin both of them. The lawyers accused Flood of being a secret age of the FBI, who attempted to entrap Bepps by luring hin

Columbus and Wacker. The lawyers argued that Bepps, who had first tried to set the meeting for remote Peotone, merely wanted to meet there to look at a piece of property he was interested in selling to Flood and that Flood was the one who had injected foul play into the situation when he set up the meeting downtown.

Bepps's lawyers also claimed that Jenny's kidnapping was not his doing—but perhaps had been part of his brother Aldo's poor decision-making. In any event, he claimed ignorance. The car was technically hired livery—not his property—even though Bepps controlled the company through the gambling debts of its official owner. But Jenny was able to identify Bepps in a photo lineup, so that was that.

Flood veered from amusement to high anxiety over the claims Bepps made. It was not a serious threat to him, he knew, but he wasn't sleeping much anyway. In fact he was lying awake nearly all night, trying to fall asleep for hours before giving up and just looking out his big bedroom windows at the tall buildings and the river below, waiting for gray light to begin to bleed into the picture.

He had offered his resignation to Cronin, Drew and Guzman as a courtesy, and they had not hesitated to accept it. So he was unemployed. Jamie had not been fired immediately, but Cronin had called him yesterday and told him there was no work for him. Just as Flood predicted.

Jenny had gone home from the hospital and now was back at her work at the museum. They had spoken twice on the phone, but she said she was not ready yet to—he was not sure what. To resume their relationship? To see him in person to put an end to their relationship? He knew nothing except that he was in no position to ask for clarification. He would just wait. He longed for her to be back with him, to sit with her and lay with her and feel her breathing the same air as him. He had been ready for her in his life, but then this.

Brandon was close by. He was staying with a college friend who had already graduated and was living a few blocks west of Flood in the Presidential Towers complex. Flood visited him a couple times, and they had dinner together once. Another time they went for a walk by the river and then stopped into Lizzie McNeil's for a pint and watched the end of an Illinois basketball game on TV. They didn't talk much. Brandon asked him for details about how investigators would go about finding his mother's body. Flood told him it was very likely that his mother's body would never be found. He wondered whether they would offer deals to some of Bepps's men for information about what happened to her. Flood thought they might offer something, but it could be hard. They probably wouldn't give anybody a pass on prosecution or prison time to find out because they already had multiple murders with a lot of evidence. His mother's body was on Brandon's mind most of the time. Flood could not tell exactly whether Brandon accepted the answers he gave him, but he did not argue anything. Brandon did not get emotional about it. He just wanted his mom's body, to put it in the ground so he would know where it was. He did not cry, and Flood did not counsel him to get in touch with his grief. They just sat and shared each other's company and sipped their beer.

Brandon had dropped out of school for the rest of the semester. He planned to go back over the summer to finish up and then look for a job. Flood looked at Daniel Westlake's finances and found that the $350,000 from the Cayman Island account had been deposited in the suburbs where the family had always banked. Most of Westlake's assets would be tied up by the courts for months, but Flood had found a little savings that Brandon could use to live on for a while.

★ ★ ★ ★ ★

Reece poured more wine.

"You need to be your own boss," Reece said. He actually was repeating it. Flood had not responded the first time he said it. Now he just grunted a little and picked up the fresh glass of wine.

"Once the dust clears, people will come to you," he said, grinning. "The word is you solved the case that the FBI bungled."

"I'm a pariah," Flood said.

"Only to a small group of people. You're really a hero, for the most part. And you took the attention away from the politicians and focused it on the mobsters, so City Hall will secretly like you. You're a better story than getting to the bottom of who corrupted the Gaming Board."

"I'm a pariah," he repeated.

"People will come to you," Reece repeated, too.

"The FBI didn't bungle it," he said. "They just moved quicker than usual, which is almost admirable in this case, and they didn't see the whole picture yet. In a sense what they did get is remarkable—in just a few months. And they actually acted on it, instead of putting it all in a file and then doing nothing."

"People will come to you," Reece said a third time.

"I don't want people to come to me, and I don't want to do their work. I don't want to be involved in other people's business." He thought he was being honest. "I want to be a cook."

"Here we go."

"I'm serious."

"OK. Open your own restaurant," Reece said, going with the flow of the idea so he could exhaust it quickly and get back to the point he was really trying to make: Flood as franchise.

"No," Flood corrected. "I don't want to open a restaurant. I don't want to open, or own, or operate. I just want to be. I want to be a cook. I want to cut vegetables and make stocks and cook rabbits and large pieces of pork."

"You'll take orders," Reece stretched to go along.

"I'll take orders. Only if they're written down and not spoken to me. No one may speak to me."

"A Howard Hughes figure in the kitchen."

"I will not be seen as eccentric. Only simple. A simple man who bothers no one and, in return, is bothered by no one."

Reece thought maybe he was drunk and had hidden it well up until right now. But Flood was not drunk. He was just out of his mind, temporarily insane, while he waited for the synapses to be reconnected. Then Flood's whole body seemed to exhale, his eyelids drooped, his chin dropped and his shoulders slumped.

His fantasy of reclusion had passed and now he would tell Reece his idea was a thought worth thinking, and he would credit Reece and not say that he was already thinking about his own office, and answering to no one but himself.

The subject died, and Reece decided it was time to change it. Back to the matters at hand and whether the FBI had done a good job.

"So the feds put together this whole investigation and never even knew they were supposed to be looking for your Mrs. Westlake?"

"They knew there was somebody like her out there, but they never figured out who she was. She would have been an important witness."

It had been three days since Reece introduced the readers of Chicago to the marital problems of the Westlake family, Marcy's scheme to make a new life for herself with a big payoff from the mob for playing courier and social hostess to a corrupt gaming official and how her best friend and her estranged husband had set her up so that they might get rich on casino dollars once the mobbed-up bid was exposed.

The details, of course, were scant. All of them were dead.

Reece raised his glass and looked into an imaginary distance, as if summoning the attention of all of the remaining Daniel and Marcy Westlakes and Pam Sawyers of the world.

"A word to the wise," he began, turning heads at nearby tables. "Just because *the Outfit* in Chicago seems like a cliché or an anachronism, doesn't mean that, if you mess with their money, they won't still shoot you in the back of the head."

Flood looked around at the puzzled and embarrassed glances of the other diners who heard that, smiled a *come on and join the fun* smile, and said, "To our health."

When the wine was gone Flood felt very tired. The waiter offered coffee, but he didn't want any. There was no pepping him up. He wanted to walk out of the restaurant and fall into his bed and sleep for the rest of the week. He might do it. He had not slept, and it was time he did. Other than sitting around silently with young, devastated Brandon and eating lunches with Reece, he had no one to talk to except Jamie, whom he kept promising to help find a new job. Jamie had said he did not want to work for anyone else. Cronin and Drew had given him a decent severance check, so he was not in a bind. But Jamie was serious. He did not want to work for anyone else.

"You can get a job anywhere," Flood had said the last time they'd seen each other. "You're good, and you weren't involved in any of this, really. You were just an unlucky employee drawn into my scandal by loyalty."

"Scandal? Listen to you, you big pussy." Jamie was listening carefully, as always. "I'm working for you, so you'd better get your fucking act together and open some kind of office or practice or whatever you want to call it."

The severance check they'd given Jamie surprised Flood, but he figured finally that they just wanted any connections to

Augustine Flood to vanish quietly and without resistance. There were other considerations. They had clients with business connections to Bepps. Those clients weren't necessarily mobsters. But they were friends of City Hall, which wasn't always the same thing, but sometimes it was. Friends of City Hall at least tended to know people who knew people who were connected to people like Bepps. Suffice to say the publicity of Flood's . . . heroics . . . was a liability and not an asset to the little law firm.

Reece paid the bill and said he might go to a movie. But Flood knew what he would do. He'd buy a giant cup of coffee at Starbucks and go back to his cubicle and sober up a little and then make phone calls to sources and talk to them for hours. And tomorrow in the courtroom, he would know what was going to happen before it happened.

Flood did just what he said he would do. He went back to his apartment and closed the shades and took off his clothes and got in bed and began to experience the peaceful weakness of sleep. He rolled off into darkness and slept for an entire day. As he went deeper into slumber, the darkness receded and took him into new caverns of experiences. It was the kind of sleep that took him on journeys that produced their own new exhaustions. The dream went on and on, interrupted by his occasional sleep-breaking snore and stumble to the toilet. Flood wandered in a land of half-remembered places he had almost been, through rooms that had nearly existed. The thing about such dreams was that there was no going back in them to ask questions or get a second look. He was just along for the ride, watching his errors unfold as a spectator, as if on a little train chugging through the amusement park of his deconstructed experience.

Nicky Bepps was not in his dream, but John Ridgeway was. Flood betrayed his trust and paid him no respect, and Ridgeway asked him why as he stood in the doorway to what might have been the locker room from Flood's high school football days. Ridgeway was wearing that heavy gray overcoat and maybe there was a little bit of somebody's blood smeared on it. It could have been from many bodies. Flood had no good answer for Ridgeway's question and just said that he was not a careful man. He did not always consider other people's needs in his decisions. It was not that he lacked respect for authority, but merely that he lacked consideration for other people, regardless of their station in life. Ridgeway said he was done with him, once and for all. He cut Flood's last tie to the organization. That last tendril of experience and shared sacrifice that kept him connected to the Bureau and its people was severed, and he drifted from it. As his view widened and receded, he saw Feinberg sitting with Willie Nelson at a little bar table, sharing a pitcher of sangria. Then they were gone, and Flood was looking forward and seeing nothing but his empty apartment—all its furniture removed—and the frigid river below.

Jenny was not in his dream, but Marcy Westlake was. He tried to make love to her and almost did—and this bent his body back and forth across the warm, gray sheets of his bed. They were somewhere elegant: a bedroom in Pam Sawyer's condo—almost but not quite. It was a different place somehow. More space and more fabric, and the carpet replaced with gleaming white marble and all color replaced with shades of blue. And it was on an angle, almost upside down, tilted against gravity, yet they moved through it naturally and comfortably. Marcy Westlake had stepped out of the photograph of her in a negligee that had been hidden among the things Daniel Westlake showed him. The intimate attempt at rekindling their romance that Flood was not supposed to see, he now took and made his own and inserted himself into her intentions. She was lovely and supple, mature flesh that radiated sensual experience and was not old—God, no—not for decades yet. She pulled herself gently off of him, every lick of friction between them agonizing to him, and she reminded him that no one knew whether she was dead or alive. Flood told her he believed she was dead, and she seemed saddened by that. He still pulsed with anticipation, but his suspicion of her demise was news to Marcy, and she had nothing to disprove it so she just looked at him. It doused the moment of passion between them—the little train kept going with Flood onboard and Marcy left behind—and he slipped through the rest of the dream—through public places and crowds—naked and hard and exposed, knowing he should feel embarrassment but only feeling anxiety that his lack of embarrassment kept him from covering himself.

When Flood finally woke up, he sat on the edge of the bed for five minutes, reconciling the real world from his dreams. He stood up finally and went to the kitchen and opened the freezer looking for something to cook. There was a package of chicken thighs and a small pot roast, but he did not like the idea of either one. He opened the refrigerator and took out a bag of apples. He had tried one before and it was too tart to eat. He heated the oven for a minute and then turned it off and set two sticks of butter on a plate on the rack to soften. Then he took a shower and shaved. He put on blue jeans, a long-sleeved t-shirt and a clean pair of wool socks. Flood went back to the kitchen and started a pot of coffee. He poured a glass of orange juice instead of a scotch and then started kneading flour into the soft butter. He peeled the tart apples, squeezed a lemon and measured out brown sugar and cinnamon. He made an apple pie and put it in the oven and then went into the living room with his coffee and sat down with *Outerbridge Reach.* But he did not open the book. He looked out the windows and wondered what time of day it was and thought about how many messages there were on his voicemail and how long it might be before he chose to listen to them. He wore a watch but did not look at it. Warm, pinkish sunlight was falling on the skyscrapers across the river. It came from the west, and the gray and glass sides facing the lake were dimmed in shadow. So it was sometime in late afternoon, Flood's favorite time of the day. He was glad he had woken up when he did and not earlier when the light was still harsh or later when it was dark. He did not look at his watch because he did not want to know exactly what time it was. He did not want to start counting the minutes of light left, feeling them slip away from him. He was content like this, not measuring anything but brown sugar and cinnamon.

Chapter Twenty-Six

The phone rang. He let it ring three times, feeling the way the sound jarred his ears and nerves, mastering his reaction to the sound. He picked up the phone and answered.

"Hello."

She said, all at once and serious, "Hello it's Jenny."

He repeated her name, "Jenny," as if he had been waiting for permission to say it and it finally had been granted. And then, without any hint of self-consciousness, he said, "It's so good to hear your voice."

She listened to the silence after he said it. She had needed to hear him say it just that way.

"We're OK, Augie," she said. "Aren't we? Are you OK?"

"I guess so," he said. "But I was reckless. And you got hurt."

There was a little more silence, which somehow comforted them both, and then she said, "I'm OK . . . I've missed you this past week."

The oven timer dinged, and it rang through the apartment. She heard it over the phone and asked what it was.

"I baked an apple pie. It's done." He sounded groggy, as if the bell had dragged him backwards for a moment and not forward toward more full alertness.

She laughed.

"A pie?"

"Yes," he said, embarrassed but sticking by the truth. "And it's a good one."

She laughed again.

"Well, you're in luck, Flood. I've got a sweet tooth."

ABOUT THE AUTHOR

David Heinzmann has covered crime for the *Chicago Tribune* for nearly a decade. He started his journalism career with the Associated Press in Baltimore and Atlanta and also worked at the *Daily Southtown* in Chicago's gritty south suburbs before joining the *Tribune*. He has appeared numerous times on national news outlets including CNN, National Public Radio, MSNBC, and NBC's Dateline. Heinzmann grew up in rural Metamora, Ill., earned degrees from George Washington University and the University of Illinois, and lives in Oak Park, Ill., with his wife and two sons.